Marion Harland

His great self

Marion Harland

His great self

ISBN/EAN: 9783743658011

Printed in Europe, USA, Canada, Australia, Japan

Cover: Foto ©Andreas Hilbeck / pixelio.de

More available books at **www.hansebooks.com**

HIS GREAT SELF.

BY

MARION HARLAND.

"My heart weeps to see him
So little of his great self."
KING HENRY VIII.—ACT III., SCENE 2.

PHILADELPHIA:
J. B. LIPPINCOTT COMPANY
1892.

PRINTED BY J. B. LIPPINCOTT COMPANY, PHILADELPHIA.

TO MY FRIENDS,

MAJOR AND MRS. DREWRY,

OF WESTOVER,

IN AFFECTIONATE MEMORY OF HAPPY DAYS SPENT UNDER THAT ANCIENT
ROOF, AND IN ACKNOWLEDGMENT OF VALUABLE ASSISTANCE
RECEIVED FROM HOST AND HOSTESS IN THE COLLEC-
TION OF MATERIAL FOR MY CHRONICLE,

THIS VOLUME IS

DEDICATED.

HIS GREAT SELF.

CHAPTER I.

"'TIS certainly a convenience, under certain circumstances, to have a husband, and for a plantation to have a master."

Madam Byrd said it musingly, as one who weighs a matter fairly. She stood in the front door of her home, watching a little fleet of three boats just parting from the pier at the foot of the lawn. Two were broad, clumsy punts, each carrying two horses saddled and bridled, with grooms at their heads. The third, which led the way across the river, was a large wherry, English-built—sharp of prow and keel. Her wet sides glistened in the sun; lines of foam swept to the right and left as she cut a straight trough in the water under the powerful strokes of three pairs of oars. The negro boatmen in all the boats wore white shirts, blue trousers, and wide scarlet belts. In the wherry-bows a stately figure arose to wave his hat to the wife in the doorway.

"Especially such a husband as yours!"

The laughing reply was made by Mrs. Carter, a pretty and youthful matron, as, from her easy-chair in the hall, she craned her neck for a view of the fleet.

"Somebody called him in my hearing, the other day, 'a trinity of perfections,'" she continued in the same strain,—"'a Sidney, a Raleigh, and a Bayard fused into one form, and that a model of domestic virtues and graces.' I quoted for reply what Governor Spotswood said to Colonel Byrd, when teased about his fondness for the wife he married late in life,—'Whoever brings a poor gentlewoman into so solitary a place, from all her friends and acquaintances would be ungrateful not to use her with all possible tenderness.'"

"He spoke of Germanna!" retorted the other, briskly. "The colonel says it is a very wilderness. The governor's is the only house worth naming in all the region. How Lady Spotswood and her sister can abide to live amid such desolateness passes me. And, within-doors, such strange doings! The colonel, on one of his visits, was carried into a room elegantly set off with pier-glasses and much fine furniture ; but would you believe it ? not only three dogs, but two tame deer were let to follow the ladies into this apartment where the table was ready laid for supper. One of the deer, spying himself in a mirror, leaped to get at the image, broke the glass to pieces and fell back upon the table, shattering much china. Had so unlucky an accident happened in my house and in a stranger's presence I should have died of mortification."

"But we must not forget, mamma, that papa said 'twas worth all the damage to show the moderation and good-humor with which Lady Spotswood bore the disaster," said a voice from the neighboring drawing-room.

"Tut, child ! 'twould be best on that head to have

in my lady as a witness rather than your father. I'll
warrant that deer was ready for the spit in twenty-four
hours' time. 'Tis easy prating philosophy and resignation over other people's mishaps. Should any ill
befall the mantel-glass your father and you are so vain
of, we should have Job's story over again. When he
was touched to the quick, he cursed the day he was
born."

" 'Tis a noble mirror," remarked Mrs. Carter. " I
doubt if there be one to match it in America."

" One of the colonel's extravagances !" said the wife,
in affected petulance. " Heaven knows the building
we've been at these six years has cost us enough without
paying five hundred pounds for a mirror to reflect his
charms of person—and his daughter's !" glancing slyly
toward the drawing-room and purposely raising her
voice.

A low, musical laugh acknowledged the hit, but no
one appeared.

Mrs. Carter—the wealthy mistress of Shirley, a lordly
estate higher up the river that had come to her husband
through her as an only child—lifted her eyebrows
slightly as the price of the glass was named. In mar-
rying Maria Taylor, a London heiress of suitable age,
Colonel William Evelyn Byrd, already the owner of
what a contemporary calls " a principality" in the New
World, doubled his fortune. The fair *châtelaine* of
Shirley, born and brought up in America, fancied
sometimes that she detected in Madam Byrd's bearing
and speech a flavor of purse-pride, a quality which only
age and habit can refine away. Still, madam was an
esteemed neighbor, and while her tongue was glib and

upon occasion, sharp she was sound-hearted and true and at her best when her friends were in trouble. Too well-bred to express surprise at the cost of the mirror, or at the mention of it by the purchaser's wife, Mrs. Carter diverted the conversation :

"You should be well content with the result of your years of pulling down and building up. If Westover were ever one of the solitary places whereof our uxorious ex-governor speaks, you have made it to rejoice and the wilderness to blossom as the rose."

Madam tried to look more indifferent than complacent, picking diligently at a knot in her netting-thread before replying,—

"Aye! 'tis well enough—for Virginia! Nothing can make it London or England. Though, to do him justice, the colonel has wrought long and well to content me in my exile. I have little to fret over,—except, of course, servants. And I chose mine own lot. As you say, there are not many men on either side of the sea comparable to the father of my children."

She had remained standing in the doorway all this while, thread and shuttle in hand, and now fluttered her handkerchief in adieu to the fast-dwindling wherry. The day was sultry, and she pulled a chair into the draught in the middle of the hall.

"There!" she sighed, establishing herself with due regard to the folds of her silken gown, "I shall see no more of him for a full month, I suppose. If I could put from me the imagination of the perils he may encounter,—the nights he will spend on the damp ground, the ill-savored victuals, the agues and swamps and tiresome marches and the chances of death at the hands of hostile Indians,—I could be quite easy now that he is gone. For, though, as I said awhile ago, 'tis convenient to have a husband and pleasant when he is an accomplished gentleman, a smack of liberty refreshes every woman now and then,—were she Griselda herself."

"Are you sure that you have not an unruly hankering after absolute sovereignty?"

It was the voice that had called her "mamma," and, in speaking, a young woman emerged from the drawing-room, with a sleeping child in her arms.

"Lady Bess has fallen asleep, Mrs. Carter;" dropping her tone of affectionate banter for a more cautious, "Shall I lay her here on the settle, or is it your will that I shall take her up to your room?"

"The naughty minx!" chided the mother, rising in haste. "I should have distrusted that somewhat was amiss when she was quiet for so long. Evelyn, dear girl, lay her here at once. Her weight is enough to bend you double."

By now she had arranged a shawl and pillows upon the roomy hall-settle, and the child was gently laid upon them. One of Miss Byrd's admirers had once, on seeing her pet fall asleep upon her shoulder, likened the twain to a rose and bud,—a compliment that moved her as little as did Mrs. Carter's more homely protest. As she stood erect, after parting with her burden, the richer carmine of her cheeks was the only token of unusual exertion.

"My bonnie maid!" she murmured, looking fondly at the sleeper. "She is every day more the 'little fairy' papa calls her. She crept into my arms like a tired kitten, and was in dream-land before I suspected her of drowsiness."

Lady Bess—so nick-named by her godfather, Colonel Byrd—was a spoiled darling from the first moon of her existence. She lay curled up among the folds of the rose-colored shawl like a fay asleep in a shell, the fairer for the proximity of a tall press of black oak, elaborately carved and surmounted by the Byrd coat-of-arms.

"I wish, sometimes," continued Evelyn, softly, "that I might read my beauty's future. If I might cast her horoscope, she would have many sunny days and no more cloudy than the dear Lord sees are for her soul's growth."

"Her lot will not be like to differ from other people's," said Madam Byrd, practically prompt. "Just what the Almighty appoints and does, without holding counsel with the stars or with us. Her mother and your father are agreed in fetching about a match between her and my Will. More, as I have told them over and over, because the plantations of Shirley and Westover march together than because the children were made for one another. 'Tis a sort of royal-alliance affair that jumps well with the pride of the heiress of Sir Edward Hill and the ambition of William the Second of Westover. As for the happiness of the poor puppets, that—God help them!—may go to the wall."

"Fie, fie!" cried the amiable neighbor. "As if my Bess could fail to make your boy the happiest of men, or William the Third grow up to be one whit the less charming than his father! We shall have you mad for the marriage in a dozen years or so. It will be *my* part, then, to hem and haw and doubt if the best man the Lord ever made can be good enough for my daughter."

While the good-humored badinage went on, Evelyn leaned against the oaken *armoire*, seeming, by her half-smile, to hearken, but silent, her eyes upon the slumbering child.

The day was unseasonably warm even for September in tide-water Virginia, and her gown was of white muslin, girt about the waist with a blue lutestring cincture. One arm was thrown a little way above her head, the hand supported by one of the carved pomegranates on the panels of the press-doors. The loose sleeve, slipping down to the elbow, showed a forearm of exquisite mould and fairness; her cheek rested against the umber wood that made a background for her profiled face and form. Her eyes were large and brown; her hair was a shade darker; her complexion was delicate and sensitive, the bloom flickering through the skin as she spoke or moved, as flame wavers in the wind. The fine oval of her face, the graceful turn of her neck, the slope of her shoulders, the pose of her head and her perfect hands were indices of old blood and gentle breeding. The lips were well cut and mobile, and the red fulness of the lower had in it a suggestion of passionate sweetness contradicted by the placid indifference which, thus far, she exhibited to lovers, gentle and simple. The modulations of her voice, although singularly refined and pure, were more varied than those of her English step-mother, and she spoke her father's tongue with a slight foreign intonation,—it was hardly an accent,—very bewitching to ears used to colonial carelessness of speech.

She had, in fact, been educated in Paris from her sixth to her twelfth year, at which time her father, in the third year of his widowerhood, wedded an English-woman, and leaving the two daughters of the first marriage in charge of a governess in London, sailed for America and settled upon his patrimonial estate.

His beautiful girls were the toast of Virginia cavaliers some years later, driving some unsuccessful wooers out of the colony, and, according to their witty parent, forcing so many to take holy orders as a solace for earthly disappointment that he congratulated the obdurate belles upon their success in the propagation of the gospel. Lucy Byrd married, at seventeen, Mr. Chamberlayne of Eastern Virginia, and went to live upon her husband's plantation, more than fifty miles away. Evelyn passed two years of her girlhood with friends in England, was presented at court, and honored by the admiration of royalty. Rumors of her belleship and social triumphs were rife in her distant home, when her father departed from America in one of his own fast-sailing vessels, arrived unexpectedly in London, and bore off his daughter with him on a continental tour, embarking at Genoa for his native land.

This was five years prior to the September morning when, in the chastened loveliness of perfected womanhood, she lent divided attention to the chat of her step-mother with her guest, and resting indolently against the oaken *armoire*, dreamed—was it only of Lady Bess's future?

The noble mirror of which Madam had feigned to speak lightly received through the open door of the drawing-room the faithful reflection of the musing figure defined in strong relief against the sombre panel by the sunlight flooding the hall.

In the small chamber opposite the state apartment, a man, looking up from his desk as the door swung ajar in a wandering breeze, caught sight of the picture, and sat moveless, pen suspended in air.

"My private secretary, Mr. Bass," was Colonel Byrd's usual formula of introduction of the demure scribe. His outspoken consort affirmed that " he made no more difference in the house than a tame sheep, and even less, for the sheep might bleat if you stumbled over him, whereas Colin Bass would not whimper though you trampled him to a jelly."

The secretary-sheep was not ill-looking. His powdered hair was combed away from a round forehead and tied with a black ribbon behind a round head. His eyes were deep-set and of an opaque gray; except that the upper lip projected beyond the lower and that both were thin, the mouth was not amiss; his chin was square, with a sunken scar on the left side, in which he had a trick of laying his forefinger when thoughtful. It went up now and rested there, his regards never stirring from the mirror. His brows met with the effect of depressing the round forehead and giving a sinister cast to the eyes; his chin was the squarer for the gradual clinching of the jaws that narrowed the lips to a thread. His fingers played nervously with the quill of his pen, but he neither glanced at them nor at the page he had been transcribing. It was the look of one who hungered with a mortal hunger— with the desperation of a forlorn hope—not despair.

The Westover library—described by the historian Stith as "the best and most copious collection of books in that part of America"—lined the walls of a spacious apartment adjoining the drawing-room. In the heat of the summer weather and the general free-and-easiness of a house so hospitable that inner and outer doors stood, like "the golden gates of gospel grace," open night and day, that joining the two rooms was seldom shut. It had been wide open while Evelyn permitted Lady Bess to doze off in her arms. By means of it, another pair of eyes, full and expressive, surveyed the goodly picture set between the masses of grapes, tendrils, and leaves, sculptured in Carrara marble, which formed the border of the glass,—a framing that accounted satisfactorily to connoisseurs for the sum paid by the affluent planter for his recent acquisition.

The occupant of the library was a man of thirty, with an olive-pale, clearly-chiselled face, replete with strength and intelligence, tempered by mildness that was indescribably winning, even to strangers. He was dressed in black, the sign at that date that the wearer was a clergyman, or in mourning for a near relative. The nominal residence of the Westover chaplain and rector of the parish church was in bachelor's quarters two miles away, upon a glebe-farm; but he was more at home in the Westover homestead than there. He had, on this morning, accompanied Colonel Byrd to the landing, seen him embarked, and returned to the house by a side-entrance. In the act of drawing a book from the shelf, he was arrested as by a vision. So nearly perfect was the reflection and so motionless, the figure seeming to float in the far, dusky depths of the mirror, that a sensation of dizzy unreality passed over him. It was as if his thoughts had taken visible shape. A second explained the illusion, but he did not move to take down the book.

Had Evelyn glanced toward the drawing-room door, she must have seen both gazers in the tell-tale glass, and, perhaps—for the brain behind the liquid eyes was quick—learned what would have put the woman within her on guard. When she did turn, it was to reply to her step-mother's incisive address:

"Bless me, child! while you stand mooning there the day is half-gone, and all those bushels of roses wasting for the lack of picking. There will likely be rain by to-morrow, and then, what waste! There's nothing so uncertain as September weather."

"I did not forget the roses, mamma; I only waited for the dew to dry off."

"Dew! You might have walked across the lawn in white satin slippers at sunrise and found not a drop! Another token of rain! Pray GOD the Colonel get not the rheumatism this night!"

As the girl passed from the field of the mirror, the unseen spectators changed each his position, involuntarily, to follow the flitting image and their eyes met in the glass. A dull glow suffused the secretary's face; the better-bred man returned the defiant look that was yet embarrassed, with one so calm and keen that Bass bent his head again over his manuscript.

The table was littered with loose sheets of varying sizes, closely written, but disfigured by erasures, interlineations, and marginal notes. Bass's task was to make a fair copy of them in a large volume bound in vellum.

These remarkable MSS.—still in excellent preservation—deserve more than the brief notice which the novelist may fitly give of an authentic and valuable relic. Some years previous to the date at which my reader is introduced to the *dramatis personæ* of my story, William Evelyn Byrd, Richard Fitz-William, and William Dandridge, Esqrs., members of His Majesty's Council in Virginia, were appointed to meet with four commissioners from North Carolina, "to determine the Controversy relating to the Bounds between the Governments of Virginia and North Carolina." In pursuance of this object, these gentlemen led a party of four surveyors and twenty-one assistants, with servants and Indian guides, through the heart of the Dismal Swamp. Never diverging by the hundredth part of a degree for morass, jungle, or creek, they carried out the work for sixteen weeks to a scientific and legal conclusion, deserving and receiving therefor high commendation from royal and colonial governments.

Colonel Byrd is delineated by an eloquent annalist of colonial life as "a man of brilliant wit, of high culture and the richest humor, a Virginian of Virginians, and the perfect flower of his time." Another says, "His extensive learning was improved by a keen observation, and refined by an acquaintance and correspondence with the wits and noblemen of his day in England." His epitaph informs us that "he was admitted in youth to the Bar in the Middle Temple, visited the Court of France, and was chosen Fellow of the Royal Society; that he was Receiver-General of His Majesty's revenues in Virginia, thrice appointed public agent to the Court and Ministry of England, and, being thirty-seven years a member, at last became President of the Council of the Colony."

With all these—and this is neither the season nor place for recounting how much more—he was more vain of the project which had recently occurred to him of preserving in permanent form the history of his various expeditions in the New World than of his manifold accomplishments and dignities. He collated his records under the caption of "History of the Dividing Line, and Other Tracts." These "Tracts" were compiled from the diary he never failed to keep when absent from home. His minutes were sometimes jotted down in cipher upon the pommel of his saddle, sometimes pencilled by the glare of the watch-fire while his comrades slept upon the bare ground about him, or scribbled in wayside hostelry and in the finest private mansions Virginia could boast. Every scrap was jealously treasured, and finally committed to his secretary, whose skill in deciphering the least legible of the discolored fragments was no mean recommendation to his patron's favor. That his position as scribe was not a sinecure is evident from the author's critical editing of the carefully-written pages.

In Colonel Byrd's absence, Colin Bass prosecuted the important undertaking with what looked to the bustling mistress like dull diligence.

"He ticks like a clock," she had complained that morning to her guest, taking no pains to lower her voice while she drew the door to the lock. " I'll e'en shut to the case and muffle the sound. It makes my flesh creep and my eyes snap."

The monotonous scratching was sharply audible after the chit-chat of the matrons ceased and their footsteps died away in different directions. The scribe wrote slowly in the neat chirography modelled upon his employer's, forming each letter with equal care, and not intermitting the labor except to turn the loose leaves or to substitute another for the scrap just copied. At the bottom of each page he stopped to re-read it, rounding a looped letter here, dropping a comma there, crossing a *t* or dotting an *i*, then setting below the last line the word with which the next page was to begin. He was not an imaginative man, nor was there the slightest sign of nervous expectation in eye or action, yet he was moved inwardly by a consciousness of an impending interruption, and a disagreeable one. For awhile his strained ears heard nothing but the pleasant murmur of women's voices far down the gravel walk leading away from the house, where Mrs. Carter was helping Evelyn gather fragrant petals for Madam's famous " rose-jars ;" the soft " hushings" of the breeze, rocking the trees to sleep upon the lawn ; the twitter and whir of a bird in the branches nearest his window ; and, loudest of all, the rhythmic amble of his pen from left to right of the broad page.

The man whose rebukeful gaze he had met had not left the library. Had he crossed the floor, or so much as fluttered the pages of a book, the secretary believed that he must have heard it in the late-summer silence of hall and chambers.

Yielding at length to an uncontrollable impulse, he

arose, slipped through the half-open door, without moving it on the hinges, crept, cat-like, across the hall and into the drawing-room to the library entrance.

A still figure sat at the round table in the middle of the room, his face buried in his hands.

Colin Bass had never seen the courtly rector succumb to selfish emotion. He knew him to be no weak dreamer. It might be that the flash in the dark eyes that had pierced his conscious soul was mere surprise. Yet, when he had stolen back to his lair and labor, he could not get away from the vision of that bowed form and hidden face or forbear to listen for the something he felt was coming.

"Ah-h-h!" The pen slipped upon the curve of a capital C at a movement in the library,—the grating of a chair upon the oaken boards, followed by a pause, during which he knew that the rector was on his feet. Bass rectified the crooked curve before a footfall vibrated upon his tense tympanum. His jaw squared, his lips straightened as the door was pushed back, but his eyes were cold and lustreless.

"Good-day, Mr. Fontaine," he said, in dryest civility. "I had not known you were in the house till I chanced to see you in the mirror over there, awhile ago."

His accents were habitually suave to his superiors,— "like the run of warm treacle," Madam had declared. His self-control was phenomenal, and the intruder, aware of these things, could not have been unobservant of the latent insolence in his remark. He spoke as if he had not noticed it.

"Good-morrow, Mr. Bass. Colonel Byrd requested

me to look in upon you occasionally during his absence——"

"For what purpose, may I inquire?" without waiting for the end of the sentence.

Something in the little episode of the mirror seemed to have brought him nearer the level of one he was wont to treat as of higher rank than himself. In his heart uprose malicious exultation such as greeted the fallen Lucifer. The polished scholar, the reverend overlooker of three aristocratic parishes, for all the strained purity of his Huguenot blood and the guards of his holy office, was become like unto him,—the abject slave of a woman!

Mr. Fontaine regarded him in tranquil dignity.

"To a certainty, *not* because he is not fully assured of your ability and industry," gravely courteous. "But since I had the honor of bearing my little part in the toils of the expedition whose history you are recording, he did me the further honor, this morning, of asking me to review such pages as you have copied, and make minutes of any errata that may have crept into them, in spite of his care and yours."

"I am duly grateful for the condescension that links my poor name and endeavors with those of our patron," said Bass, rising, with an overshow of deference. "Nevertheless, had I aught to conceal from him or from you, gratitude would not blind me to the indignity of espial. Let that pass, since my conscience is clear. May it please you to note Colonel Byrd's pencilled private mark at the foot of this page, showing that *he* had inspected my manuscript up to this point? I have transcribed to-day four pages—no more. If you will likewise examine these,"—taking up a handful of creased and soiled scraps, apparently torn from a note-book, and covered with hieroglyphics, —"you will see that the task was not easy. With these remarks, which I pray you to forgive, I resign my chair and table to you."

The ostentatious servility of the pretended apology brought to the listener's eye the spark his rudeness had not kindled.

"'Patron' and 'espial' are words that hardly belong to a land and generation where and when all gentlemen of birth and breeding are equals," returned Mr. Fontaine, with no other show of temper. "Colonel Byrd is my friend and parishioner, whom I respect too much not to seek some more auspicious season for complying with his request."

A sneer went over the secretary's smug visage, belying the travesty of obsequiousness he chose to maintain.

"I beg you to believe, sir, that one season with me is as another. In the words of the Book most familiar to you, I am as one who watches for his lord. I can, however, comprehend the impatience of a member of the favored order for whom sunshine and roses are created, and who recollects that neither lasts forever."

A meaning glance out of the window pointed the innuendo. The dark cheek of the clergyman burned. He had reached the door, but wheeled abruptly and took a step toward the speaker. Bass faced him as quickly, and the two stood at bay, looking into each other's eyes, and through these, for the instant, unguarded gates, into one another's souls.

Fontaine was the first to speak. Tone and smile were totally unlike anything Bass had ever beheld before in the master of himself and men :

"I am your debtor in that you have reminded me of my devoir and my privilege," he uttered in ironical distinctness. "The wise man is he who sees Providence in Opportunity."

He bowed, closed the door with intention after him, and went out with agile step and head erect into the sunshine.

"He also shuts the case !" soliloquized the secretary, a white, wrung smile upon the countenance just now so stolid. "When the clock strikes, they will hear it all over the house, whether they will or no !"

Each entry of the journal kept during the survey of the Dividing Line was dated. "*March 24, 1728,*" was the last written by the copyist before the entrance of the unwelcome visitor. He finished the section mechanically :

"The Truth was they now knew the worst of it, and cou'd guess pretty near at the Time when they might hope to return to Land again."

Automatic as was the action of one-quarter of the scribe's brain, the words awoke him to a sense of their odd parity with the operation of the rapt other three-fourths of him. The pallid glimmer revisited his face.

"I know the worst," he said, aloud. "But do I care to return to the Land I have left ?"

It was fully ten minutes before he began to decipher the next loose leaf :

"The Air was chilled this Morning with a Smart Northwest Wind which favour'd the Dismalites in their

Dirty March. They returned by the Path they had made in coming out, and, with great Industry, arriv'd in the Evening at the Spot where the Line had been discontinued.

"After so long and laborious a Journey they were glad to repose themselves upon their couches of Cypress-bark where their sleep was as sweet as it wou'd have been on a Bed of Finland Down."

Over against this record the secretary, his eyes fiercely vacant with pain, and his fingers clammily glued to the quill, inscribed "*1729, March 25.*" It was the date on which he, a gawky country lad, lowly-born and lowly-bred, had taken service with the master of Westover. In reviewing the page, the blunder caused by his moody abstraction was unperceived, and, still wrapped in his own thoughts, he began the next record with the same date, carrying it forward to the close of the "Tract." Strangely enough, the anachronism escaped the eye of the august author, and stands thus to the present hour.

CHAPTER II.

THE first Byrd who emigrated to America—yclept William the First in family papers and talk—bought in 1674, from Theodorick Bland or his heirs, the finest building-site upon James River. The plantation of Westover is mentioned in colonial annals half a century earlier, but it came into prominence under the *régime* of the first Byrd, and into eminence among colonial houses under the administration of the second and greatest of the name,—Colonel William Evelyn Byrd.

After his father's death and the beginning of his own permanent residence in Virginia, he enlarged the house erected by his predecessor, and made mansion and grounds worthy of his taste and wealth. The central building of English brick was joined to the wings by corridors, and underrun by cellars that were models of stolidity and spaciousness. The sloping lawn was defended against the current and periodical freshets by a river-wall of massive masonry. At regular intervals buttresses, capped with stone, supported life-sized statues of mythological deities, fauns, and dryads. Gardens, fences, out-houses, and conservatories, fashioned after European designs, were the marvel of the colony, and won the admiration of travellers from older lands.

The sward rolling gently from house to river was smooth and luxuriant, dotted with grand trees standing singly or in clumps. At the right and the left of the broad flight of squared stone steps a tulip-poplar flung out, on this early autumn day, danger-signals of approaching frost to the double line of trees bordering the sweep of gravelled walk connecting the iron gates on each side of the lawn. The river—singularly clear for the tawny James, by reason of infrequent up-country rains—danced and shimmered in the sunshine; grasshoppers sang in the turf regardless of the beacon-fires burning here and there upon maple and poplar; butterflies and humming-birds swam and swooped above the roses. The air was bland, languorous, and laden almost to excess with rose-scent,—the September blossoming that often exceeds in abundance and beauty that of June.

As Pierre Fontaine emerged from the hall-door and halted upon the stone platform, the sweet waves brought ecstasy to his senses, enticing fancies to his imagination. He was man as well as priest; he was young, and youth will have its day. Without tracing the feeling to the origin Madam Byrd had frankly given, he, too, was conscious of a sense of larger liberty in the absence of the masterful lord of the manor. The will and energy that had created and kept up the paradise that lay about the beholder, an Eden the fairer for encompassing wilds, impressed the owner's personality upon all whom he encountered. His rule of household and community might be wise, and, when not opposed, benignant; but it was despotism, clear and simple, the more absolute because of his acknowledged superiority in talent, learning, and accomplishments to his associates. His regard for his chaplain was sincere; his fondness for his society undisguised, and to a vainer man would have been flattering. Nothing could have been further removed from sycophancy or slavish constraint than the clergyman's bearing towards the seignior of Westover. He said and he felt that companionship with such a mind was a continual education, a boon for which he could not be too grateful; that conversation with him, whom he had proudly called " friend and parishioner," brought out what was worthiest from his own mental store.

Still, in strolling between the rose-hedges towards

the white-robed figures he descried at the end of the vista, he took in deep draughts of intoxicating incense warmed and spiced by the sun, and felt more light of heart, more eager of desire, than he had for many a long day. He put from him the thought of the interview which had strangely ruffled his spirit as easily as he brushed away a bumblebee that droned too near his ear. This was not a day in which to heed the buzz of insects. The world was wide and life was beautiful.

The result of Mrs. Carter's and Evelyn's work verified Madam Byrd's boast of "bushels of rose-leaves." The baskets into which the ladies gathered them had been emptied, as they were filled, into a hamper set in the middle of the walk, and at Mr. Fontaine's approach Evelyn was stooping over this, pressing down the contents to make room for other relays. Her shepherdess-hat had fallen back, and hung from the ribbon caught under her chin; her cheeks glowed with the reflected blush of the damask petals in which her arms were sunk to the elbow; her eyes danced with fun.

"You are just in time to take this to the still-room!" she called, gayly. "Now, Mrs. Carter, pour the rest in, and let him have all!"

For answer, her friend turned both baskets upside-down over the girl's head, veiling her with the rosy rain.

"Danäe—with a difference!" said Fontaine, as she issued from the flood, laughing and shaking her head to free her curls from clinging petals. "Let me do that!" stepping forward when she would have collected with her scooped hands a heap from the gravel.

Restoring the roses by double-handfuls to the hamper, he stayed Evelyn as she was tossing in more. " Wait! I am sure I espied the glitter of gold!" he said, dipping his fingers gingerly into the scented mass and burrowing watchfully.

"Danäe—without much difference after all?" queried Mrs. Carter, roguishly.

Both women eyed him in lively curiosity as he poured the petals back into a smaller basket, and finally abruptly reversed the hamper upon the short turf.

" Let us hope that you will always choose to do the right thing," bantered Evelyn, seeing him separate petal from petal. " You will never swerve——Oh !"

With the stifled scream she snatched a chainlet of gold hanging from his finger. Her hand went hurriedly up to her throat, and fumbled among the muslin folds covering her bosom.

"Look further !" she panted, pale as a ghost. " I have lost something else !"

She went down upon her knees on one side of the pile, Mrs. Carter, wondering and sympathetic, upon the other, and, assisted by Mr. Fontaine, they sifted the roses with anxious assiduity, until all were back in the hamper.

"It is not there!" breathed Evelyn in a frightened whisper. "I have dropped it ! I do not know when or where ! What shall I do?"

" What is it, dear ? Something of value ?" asked her friend.

A rush of crimson throbbed into the blanched cheeks, the fingers clutched the chain more tightly.

" I have had it this great while. It is a locket—a

little one—with my mother's hair and——Hush! pray not a word!"

She hid the chain in her bosom, as down the walk sailed Madam Byrd, her trim waist begirt with a voluminous white apron, her sleeves pinned back to her shoulders,—in short, in housewifely battle-array. As soon as she was within speaking distance, she opened fire.

"Had I guessed that the church was pressed into service, I might have waited more contentedly for my harvest. I hope your reverence has blessed it with bell and with book, to warrant the leaves against shrinking or running to water? If the ceremony be over, I will begin the work that has hung upon my hands these three hours or more."

Evelyn laughed nervously.

"Dear mamma! it is not yet quite an hour since we talked with you in the hall, and see what we have! An accident befell the roses, too. The hamper was overset, and we have but just gathered up the spoils with Mr. Fontaine's help. He will bear them in for you."

"*That* will he not!" protested the dame. "No ordained minister of the Word shall be beast of burden upon my premises while a score of lazy servants eat my bread and drink my cider."

She blew into a silver whistle that had dangled from a chain of the same material at her girdle, together with a pair of silver-handled scissors and a silver nutmeg-grater. A mulatto lad in the Byrd livery appeared with alacrity that bespoke strict training, hoisted the light weight to his head and bore it through a side-gate into the house.

Mrs. Carter gave Evelyn an expressive look behind her mother's shoulder.

"You will suffer me to see how you make your incomparable *pot-pourri*, won't you?" she said, coaxingly. "Either the Shirley roses are not so sweet as yours, or I fall far short of your skill. By the time my rose-jars have been stocked for a month they might as well be filled with dried currants. Colonel Carter will have it that they smell like mince-pie. And, while we are in the still-room, perhaps you will let me copy your receipt——"

The rest was lost in the distance as the matrons walked amicably together to the small gate, through it, and around the corner of the house.

Evelyn heaved a hysterical sigh.

"I seem but a foolish creature to you, Mr. Fontaine," the slight foreign accent giving pathetic precision to her speech. "But I am sore bestead. If I should not find my locket; if some one has picked it up——" a gesture of intensest uneasiness said the rest.

"We will look for it at once, and so diligently that nobody can forestall us," said Fontaine, confident and cheery. "It may have been wrenched from the chain by a rose-tree. If you will take one side of the alley and I the other, there is no fear lest it should not come to light. Will the hamper return? Must *all* the roses be harvested to-day?"

She could not but smile at his whimsical alarm.

"Only those that are in fullest bloom. Even the *pot-pourri* maker has compassion upon the buds and half-blown. But, by to-morrow——" shaking her head in mournful significance.

3*

Her habit of supplementing words by action was among the "French tricks" reprobated by her step-mother and admired by the men, in whose sight they were another and a maddening grace.

"Your study-door is bewitched, colonel," his wife had said yesterday. "The blacksmith swears there is nought amiss with the lock. Yet, close it when I may on some days, it clicks open at its will without the aid of hands. Again, and oftentimes, it must be wrought upon and wrenched before it will yield."

"Then, my dear Lady Maria, you must work a countercharm and shame locksmith and devil by your wiser witchery," the gallant spouse had made reply.

Afterward, and not in her hearing, he had bidden Colin Bass, "see that the latch is righted, or have a new one made."

Reminded of the commission by the mysterious click, which for the third time that forenoon undid the door of the "clock-case," the secretary got up, with an ejaculation of profane disgust, and began the examination of the offending bolt. While working it up and down, he became carelessly conscious that Lady Bess, having had her nap out, was chattering to herself, still lying on the settle. Upon his appearance, she accosted him affably. Although not four years old, the "little fairy" had many and individual opinions, and was fluent in expressing them.

"Does 'oo want to loo*l* at mine p'itty bo*ts*?" she said to him, as the only auditor in sight. And, at the churlish silence of a bachelor to whom all minors were cubs, she persisted, in a louder key, "Say, *t*um an' 'ook

at mine p'itty bo*ts*, dis *minnit.* If 'oo don't, I'll *holler*
—*youd* !"

Bass shot a glance at her in time to see the bauble
slip from her grasp to the floor and the sparkle of
jewels as it fell. He picked it up without other purpose than to rescue a valuable from the infant bar-
barian who had probably stolen it from her mother's
jewel-chest.

"Isn't it boo'ful?" said Lady Bess, gratified by his
practical interest in her prize.

Bass turned it over in his hand. It was an oval
medallion, less than two inches long, of wrought gold,
encrusted with diamonds and hinged at the back. His
deft fingers quickly detected the hidden spring, and the
opening case revealed a miniature, painted upon ivory,
of a young man in the uniform of the Royal Guards.
In the chased gold band encircling the portrait and
below the face was enamelled the legend, "*J'attends.*"
Opposite the miniature, under glass, were intertwined
a lock of golden hair and one of dark brown, almost
black.

Without other suspicion of the ownership of the
trinket than that it probably belonged in the Carter
family, Bass looked again, and closely, at the pictured
face. It was comely, he decided, and patrician. Because it was both, he considered it coxcombical ; but as
a painting it was exquisitely executed, although so
minute.

"Dive it to me, p'ease!" importuned Bess. "It is
Yady Bess's p'itty sing !"

"It is none of yours," retorted Bass, roughly. "And
I shall keep it !"

Lady Bess was angelic when with angels. If her wings were rubbed the wrong way, she shed them with diabolical celerity. Bass, who knew little, and cared less for children, was unprepared for her next movement, which was to spring to her feet upon the settle, and launch herself upon him like a shrieking catapult. Instinctively casting the hand containing the miniature behind him, he reeled and staggered several paces. At the shock of the cherub's onslaught, the locket flew from his hold. He heard it strike the floor and skim along the polished boards to the front door.

Bess had fastened upon his lappels and ruffled shirt-front. In shaking her loose, an action performed with the vigor and despatch he would have used in ridding his person of a wild cat, he left long strings of cambric in her claws. The noise brought her maid from the upper story. In common with the Westover negroes, and her class generally, Sally despised the hireling whose one advantage above herself lay in the lack of coloring-matter in his skin. Her outcry and rush toward her afflicted nurseling were dramatic and insolent:

"For de love o' heaven, what you bin do to her, *now?*"

He had never, to his knowledge, touched the dreadful infant before, but disdained to repel the insinuation. Bess rolled over on the floor, eluding the nurse's arms, and grabbed his ankle when he would have retired in dignified reserve to his study.

"*Dimme* mine *bots!* Tate it f'om him, mammy! He too*t* mine boo'ful sing!"

Bass shook his leg impatiently, and the negress caught up the writhing child.

"Fo' de Lawd, ef you had 'a' dared to *kick* 'er, I'd 'a' tored you' low-lived eyes out, ef I had 'a' swung for hit!" she snapped at him, and carried her screaming charge off, answering her kicks and her wails for her "bots" with adjurations "not to have nuthin' ter do wid nobody but *reel* gen'man 'n' ladies! Mammy would give her a sugar-cake, so she 'ould!"

Yells and soothings were deadened by the flooring of the upper chambers, and the secretary, smiling evilly, looked about him for the lost bauble. He was not interested in restoring it to Mrs. Carter, but knowledge of the value of the gems moved him to search in corners, on the steps and gravel-walks without, whither a smart *ricochet* might have carried it. It had vanished as utterly as if Lady Bess had swallowed it at her first howl. The circumstance was odd, but not disquieting. Should inquiry be instituted for the locket, he had the choice of telling the truth,—or, what he would prefer, holding his tongue. The gibberish of the baby-purloiner could not convict him as a receiver of stolen goods.

Nobody was in sight from the front-door. The rose-pickers whom he expected to see were not at work or visible; but a monstrous gobbler, the Anak of his race, reared and domesticated by Evelyn Byrd from a wild chick trapped with the mother in the forest, strutted along the walk, picking tentatively at pebbles. He stiffened his drooping red cockade at Bass's approach, ruffled every feather, put up a vast semicircle of tail, and emitted a hoarse "gobble—gobble—gobble!"

c

Bass laughed outright.

"*You* may have got it!   Then it's safe enough until Christmas.   I'll keep my eye on you, my fine fellow."

The conceit of the possible lodgement of miniature and diamonds in the turkey's craw or gizzard, or in whatever other cranny of his anatomical apparatus he stored gravel-stones and the like, appealed so forcibly to his peculiar sense of humor that he stayed his pen more than once that day to chuckle over it.   Whatever had become of the ornament, the affair did not concern him personally, and it was not in his line to disquiet himself in vain over other people's business.

Evelyn's tedious and futile quest for her lost treasure was interrupted by the second appearance of the mulatto in livery.   Her step-mother required her attendance in the still-room.

Fontaine's heart beat fast and warm at her mute, dismayed appeal to himself.

"I shall seek until it is found," he answered her. "Unless the earth has opened her mouth and swallowed it up, you shall have it within the hour.   Trust me."

"I do trust you—*always!*" coloring vividly in the pause severing the emphatic phrase.

The solid earth quaked under the lover's feet as she flitted away.   Rose-scent, bird-song, the wind's wooing whisper to the trees; mellowed sunshine and flashing river—the knowledge of all these made harmonious ripples in a great tide that lifted his soul and swept his senses into a sea of rapture.

"I do—*always!*"   Faithful echoes rang melodious changes upon the words.   Had she lingered one instant longer, the hidden stream of love must have burst bounds in passionate speech. He murmured delirious phrases of endearment, of hope, of longing to himself as he walked, ungratefully forgetful of the mission he had undertaken, until brought rudely back to earth by the angry scream of a child.

It proceeded from the open front-door up to which he had strayed. Glancing that way, he espied the blaze of what looked like a live coal upon the sunny steps. With one bound he secured it, and, without look or thought for the animated tableau in the hall, hurried in the direction of the still-room.

CHAPTER III.

MADAM BYRD'S still-room was as famous in the mouths of her sister-housewives as were her lord's gardens, stables, and fields among his fellow-planters. It was a long, low-ceiled apartment in the left wing of the house. Two windows overlooked the river; a wide-mouthed fireplace at one end was fitted up with cranes and pot-hooks, for here pickling, preserving, and potting were done under Madam's supervision. The products of her skill crowded cupboards that reached from floor to ceiling on one side of the room, and were protected by locked glass doors. The front wall was lined with open shelves filled with empty jars and gallipots of delf and china awaiting their contents. At that early epoch of Virginia housewifery the mistress appreciated the necessity of keeping delicacies, particularly sweets, under lock and key. Madam's key-basket was never two feet away from her, day or night. When she went abroad or to church, she locked it up in her wardrobe and carried the key of the wardrobe in her pocket.

A table ten feet long and three in width was in the middle of the floor. The deal top, white from assiduous scourings, was half-concealed by a fair linen cloth, on which the harvest of rose-leaves was piled. Madam, enveloped in a snowy apron, the ruffled bib touching her rounded chin, was taking these up singly and dropping them into a big jar beside her, the mouth being on a level with the table-top.

Mrs. Carter, at her ease in a rocking-chair, surveyed the process in amused admiration.

"*I* heave mine in by the peck," she confessed.

"What is worth doing at all is worthy of well-doing," rejoined the hostess, pithily superior.

"But there are *millions* of them, dear Madam Byrd. It must require an eternity to take them up one by one."

"Eternity, as well as time, is most wisely spent in the right performance of duty," rebuked the flippant criticism. "Evelyn, child!" as her step-daughter entered, "I sent for you half an hour ago. 'Tis said to be the nature of young blood to be hot and hasty. I'm sure 'tis the nature of young limbs to move slow. But one might suppose you had run a mile from the way you pant and your color comes and goes. The heat should not affect you who were born here so much more than me who have lived in Virginia scarce ten years."

" You sent for me, mamma ?"

Evelyn, resting the finger-tips of one hand lightly on the table, and raising the other involuntarily to her throat as if to steady her respiration, waited for commands. She knew her step-mother, and the necessity laid upon the exemplary matron to " have her talk out" when talk seethed within her.

" *Of* a certainty I sent for you, or you had not come. I marvel you will waste the life of an immortal being in asking needless questions. Here's Mrs. Carter who has asked, at the least, twenty times to have two or three trifles copied for her from the Westover receipt-book, and she still goes a-begging. Sit you down over there at the table, out of the way of the roses. Caliban ! will you stand grinning all the day and never set a chair for your Mistress Evelyn !"

Evelyn took the seat the lad hastened to bring, drew to her the standish, paper, and pen ready for her use, and opened a book bound in worn sheep-skin. The leaves were dog-eared and spotted in sundry places, and the ragged ones had been mended by pasting a margin of stout paper along the edges.

" I shall be most happy to oblige Mrs. Carter," said the young lady, politely. " Where am I to begin ?"

" What a flurry you are in ! One might fancy Hercules's tasks were appointed unto you, and all to be done in a day."

Madam's mood was not sweetened by her occupation.

" Mrs. Carter would like to know how the Westover wine is made ; and it wouldn't be amiss to add to that Mrs. Otway's receipts for clary and sherry wine, and Mrs. Shut's receipt for birch wine,—though that she will not need till March, and we may all be in our graves by then. Life in a new country is ever uncertain. But there's Mrs. Blackiston's receipt for elder wine, and the berries are black as sloes this very hour. Or, stay," as Evelyn dipped her pen in ink, "Bass can copy those in plainer hand than yours. It passes me that you've never rubbed the French accent off your pen any more than off your tongue. I'll get Colin at those receipts before he's a day older. What he can't do, and what you can,—the Lord knows there're not many things,—is to write down in *English*, mind you, the first Mrs. Byrd's receipt for making portable soup."

Evelyn turned the battered leaves without change of expression from the pale abstraction that nettled her step-mother into a harangue which made the visitor uncomfortable. The girl was as used to the sleety patter of the tongue, under—if not *in*—which was the law of kindness, as to the tapping of the pigeons' feet upon the slated roof of the still-room. Their cote was hard by, and they courted and quarrelled incessantly upon the sun-warmed area during summer days.

"'*Duchesse of Lorreign's Receipt for Making Soupe*,'" she read aloud, impassively docile. "Is it that you wish me to copy?"

"Surely, girl! Have I not said it six times within the past ten minutes? I wonder what you dream of that you never hear a word I say! Did not I instruct you in the plainest language to copy that receipt, I having no faith in Bass's knowledge of French? Though there's your father, who will have it that Solomon was but a babe in long clothes compared with his secretary's wisdom. You may have heard, Mrs. Carter,—for idle talk travels far,—that Colonel Byrd was named 'The Black Swan' by certain lively fellows among the younger nobility in London because of his prodigious learning and polite accomplishments, so far exceeding—they were pleased to say—those of other native-born Americans who visited the Mother Country. I rally the colonel upon the saying, now and then, telling him he should pass on the title to the cygnet he has discovered among the ducks of the lower James. 'Tis amazing the trust he puts in one who, to my way of thinking, has little sprightliness and less wit."

Mrs. Carter was spared the necessity of passing judgment upon the comparative justice of husband's and wife's views as to the secretary's endowments by the housewife's digressive orders to Caliban to go on with his task of crushing with a rolling-pin upon a board the salt for the *pot-pourri*. The guest was more interested in the taciturn step-daughter than in the matron's dissertations. Evelyn wrote fitfully,—now fast, now lingeringly, glancing toward the front windows at the end of each line. There was a plait of care or anxiety between her brows, a heaviness about the broad-lidded eyes, an air of expectation in form and feature, assumed by the neighbor to be certain indices that the locket containing her mother's hair had not been found. Why the loss was not to be named to the sensible second wife, who spoke openly and without jealous disrespect of the "first Mrs. Byrd," and had set Evelyn to translate a recipe from the original in her own mother's hand, was more of a puzzle.

Madam's talk subsided presently, perhaps under

the monotony of her employment, or the lullaby of the muffled crunching of the rock-salt before the roller, and the coo and tiptoeing of the pigeons overhead. A long term of silence was interrupted by the whistling whir of wings as the startled birds forsook their promenade. Hasty steps grated upon the gravel and struck the flat stone at the back-door.

"Pardon me, Madam Byrd," said Mr. Fontaine from the door-way, "but Colonel Byrd instructed me to report myself for orders before going home. Is there anything I can do in his absence to serve you?"

"Going home, when dinner will be on the table in an hour! Not a foot do you stir, fasting"—began the hostess.

The bright blood had flown into Evelyn's cheeks at the intruder's voice; her eyes met his eagerly, and the smile exchanged was seen by both matrons. Evelyn arose hastily.

"That missing volume of Froissart, Mr. Fontaine!" she exclaimed, a sort of happy break in her tone, also noted and misconstrued,—"I found it yesterday. I will get it for you before I forget it again."

She had joined him and they disappeared together ere Madam Byrd found her tongue and Mrs. Carter's imagination could fairly receive the new and astounding impression made by the swift scene.

"Go to the kitchen, Caliban, and tell Isis to hurry dinner, and yourself see there is a place set for Mr. Fontaine," ordered the mistress, discreetly. Then to her friend,—

"Did you see that?"

Mrs. Carter nodded in emulative discretion.

"You don't suppose it can be possible——"

Her crony smiled dubiously.

"It looks a good deal like it," she committed herself so far as to admit.

"Great heavens! what *would* the colonel say?"

The bared arms and plump hands dropped prone upon the yielding heap of petals, and were buried out of sight. The confidante forbore reply by look or word, awaiting clue and cue.

"Mr. Fontaine is a gentleman, to be sure," resumed Madam, thoughtfully, but as one seeks for consolation and finds none,—"of excellent family and education. The colonel likes and admires him. I have never heard a syllable from him disrespectful of Mr. Fontaine. But sure am I that he has never dreamed of him as Evelyn's suitor. His ambitions for his daughter are past finding out; but, after all the distinguished offers she has had, *this* would be a bitter pill. I dare not think of what may lie before us!"

She looked really frightened; her sanguine complexion was sallow, her chin trembled like a baby's. The gentler and meeker woman was amazed at these tokens of timidity in one whom she had regarded as too stout of heart and will to fear the frown of man.

"Both of us may be mistaken,"—essaying comfort. "There is nothing so deceitful as a girl's blushes, unless it be her smiles. And Mr. Fontaine being her rector, and so much at home here——"

"No! no! no! There's *something* between them! I never saw him look so before—nor her. Not that I wonder at *him.* Most men who know her come to that, soon or late; but I had set it down as a truth past altering that she would live and die Evelyn Byrd !" cried the step-parent in odd vexation. "And here it is all to be gone over with again, and me between father and daughter like cloth caught in the shears ! If *Colin Bass* had begun to sigh and ogle, and she to blush at him, I could hardly have been more upset."

"Now you *are* going too far," demurred Mrs. Carter, laughingly. "Mr. Fontaine's birth, breeding, and character are above reproach. He is handsome and good, and richer than most clergymen. Colonel Byrd is the most reasonable man I know. When he sees that Evelyn's heart is set upon her lover her father cannot hold out against his favorite child."

"You don't know William Evelyn Byrd, Esq., of Westover, Virginia," enunciated his spouse in slow portentousness. "His is the iron hand in the velvet glove. And when the velvet is stripped off, the iron is *red-hot !* Ah-h !" her fine eyes enlarging with mounting tears, "I was too light-hearted this morning. I shall never tempt Providence again by casting off care so entirely. The smell of rose-leaves will always make me *sick !* You must have marked their dalliance over the hamper before they espied me—poor, prating, purblind fool that I was !"

"Nay !" remonstrated Mrs. Carter, seeing the salt drops trickle upon the petals with which the plump hands were again mechanically engaged, "in *that* you err. There was no love-making over baskets or hamper. And"—awkwardly to redeem the lapse she had so nearly made—"there is really not an atom of proof that these two will ever be other than friends."

Madam reached out an arm to draw toward her the

sheet on which Evelyn had been writing. The kindling fire in her eyes scorched up the moisture.

"Look at *that!*" in accents trembling with sorrow and wrath, yet dashed with triumph. "Did not you hear me bid her, times without number, to write down that receipt in honest *English?* 'Tis plain to be seen her wits were running upon her French-born suitor. His tongue could wile a bird off a bush. I mind me, now, of coming out upon the front steps, a week ago Sunday night, where she, with my Jane, Mary, and Willy,—the dears never mistrusting they were but a cat's-paw,—sat still as mice, hearkening to his Reverence's tale of how his father—also a clergyman of the Reformed faith—was persecuted out of his native land, obliged to shift for his safety in forests and deserts, was stuck into a noisome dungeon and laden with chains, and a deal more piteous stuff, in hearing which my little lambs cried outright and the fair Evelyn was fain to mop her eyes, while as for me, soft-hearted mole! I couldn't count the stars for the tears!"

Silenced and confounded, Mrs. Carter followed the freshly-written lines traced by the dreaming amanuensis :

"*Bouillon Sec ou portatif, très Commode et Utile furmer à L'Armée, et en Voyage.*

"*Prenez deux vieux Chapons ou Coqs, Concassés en les Os sans endommager la Chair ; huit livres de Bœuf maigre et L'Eschine, ou d'un autre bon endroit, avec un Os de Moëlle, et un demy pied de veau, mettez-le tout ensemble dans un pot de terre bien vernisse ; mettez de L'Eau suffissamment, faites-le cuire auprès du feu ; écumez-le bien, ajoutez-y une pièce de Gingembre, vingt grains de poivre, Fruit Cloux de Giroflé; trois grandes pièces de fleur de muscade, deux feuilles de Laurier; continuez à le cuire à petit feu, sans flamme———"*

"'*Petit feu, sans flamme!*'" ejaculated the step-mother, with an angry sob. "'*Grand feu, avec flamme!*' she had better have written. She has her lover to console her—unless, indeed, her father judges fit to risk the chances of carrying her over to the other side to part her from *this* one. The Lord only knows how 'twill end! But one thing is sure. I, who am least to blame, will get the brunt of it all. How many million times have I charged you not to burst into a room in that fashion?" to Caliban, whose bounce over the threshold merited the reproof. "Go back and scratch upon the panel, as you have been taught. *Now*,"—the prescribed form having been observed,—"you come to say that dinner is served?"

"Naw, mistis," drawled the servitor. "But de Buckley kerridge drivin' down de road."

"The Berkeley carriage! Where is your Mistress Evelyn?"

"Waitin' at de gate, wid Mr. Fountaine, for de kerridge. 'Twas her sont me fur to tell you dere was comp'ny a-comin'."

The mistress of Westover collected her dignity.

"Be at the gate in time to let down the carriage-steps. 'Tis not Mr. Fontaine's business. When you have seen how many persons are there, go bid Osiris lay that number of covers the more at table. Get you gone!"

It was characteristic of Evelyn and her unconfessed lover that she did not ask if he had opened the locket he had found, and that he did not offer to explain that he had not.

"It lay on the front steps, twinkling like a star," he said, in restoring it. "The marvel is that I passed it on my way out without espying it."

He felt himself color slightly in the recollection of the haste and heat produced by the dialogue in the study, that had made him unobservant. Evelyn, heedless of his confusion, in her joyful relief from anxiety, holding her recovered treasure close until it seemed to give back the warm pulsing of her palm, poured out thanks and blessings as upon a benefactor.

"I am right glad nobody else discovered it! that I owe the pleasure of having it back to you, *mon ami!*" falling into and going on in his native tongue, as she often did when no listeners were by. "I hope the good GOD will put it into my power one day to give you a great pleasure in return. For it is a great service you have done me, M. Fontaine. I have many jewels, but I value none others as I value this. It never leaves my neck, whether I sleep or whether I awake. I recollect now that Lady Bess toyed with the chain while she was in my arms. The clasp must have been loosened thus, and the locket have fallen from my gown upon the steps. I shudder to think if I had lost it forever!" kissing it before putting it into her pocket. "It is my amulet,—a charm; not against pain or sorrow,—oh, no! I think only death can secure us against *them!* but against heart-break and despair!"

"Heart-break and despair!" echoed Fontaine, incredulously. "The words do not become your lips."

He was not given to gallant formula, and she answered in grave simplicity,—

"Because I am the petted daughter of a rich man, and seem to want for nothing? For all that, sorrow and I have been close acquaintances for many a day. We joined hands when I was a child. I was but nine when my mother died. Of small-pox, too!" shudderingly. "*She,* fair as the angels ever are, and delicately nurtured.

"My sister and I were at school in Paris. Our mother had left us but a fortnight before. I remember how unwilling she was to go. But there was a great court-ball in London, and my father would have her attend it with him. He was very fond and proud of her, but she lent him obedience in all things—as everybody does.

"She came into the nursery early on the morning of their departure and knelt down by our bed to say 'good-by.' As she kissed me, a tear dropped on my face, and I began to cry. I held her fast by the neck and prayed her not to go. I said I was afraid I should never see her again. My father laughed and frowned at me, and bade me 'behave less like a baby. He would bring her back in a week,' he said. 'Didn't I want the king to see the prettiest woman in his dominions?' She was feverish on the night of the ball, but sooner than disappoint my father she would not complain. She was never handsomer than she looked that evening—my poor, beautiful mother! I have her court-dress, the last she ever wore, and her jewels. The fever heightened her color and brightened her eyes. The king danced with her, and, in returning her to my father when the dance was over, kissed her hand, and asked my father 'if there were many other *birds* in America as beautiful as she.' That was much for His Majesty to say."

"The talent for fine speeches does not run in the House of Hanover," observed Fontaine, smiling. Deeply interested as he was in the story, so näively recited, a compassionate impulse warned him to change the theme. "You were, yourself, presented at the court of our present king, were you not?"

"Yes; how long—how very long ago it was!"

They had sauntered away from the house into the garden, passing between two immense box-trees cut into the shape of peacocks, with tails broadly unfurled. A gate in the garden-wall opened upon a level green, over which a gravel walk led to the little parish church. Other clumps of box flanked the gateway, and were clipped into the semblance of gigantic urns, in obedience to a fantasy of harmonious approach to the burial-ground surrounding the chapel. In the shade of one of these lugubrious ornaments, Evelyn leaned on the wall, her eyes fixed upon the ivy-mantled church, close to which slept two generations of her kindred.

"It is like a dream now," she went on, softly. "I was very young. I seem to have lived a century since."

The bees hummed in shrill, sweet legato about the hives on the sheltered side of the wall; the September sunshine was a pale amber tissue upon land and water. Even here they could discern the smell of the roses, like the memory of a love-dream.

"You loved the Old World very dearly, did you

not?" said Fontaine, sinking his voice to the pitch of hers. "If you had had your will, you would never have recrossed the ocean?"

He had put her on her guard. Whatever scene was conjured up in that brief reverie, stealing seductively between her and the ivied walls, it fled more fleetly than it had come.

"Nay,"—the exquisite courtesy learned from her father informing smile and tone,—"that would have been ingratitude, you know. Westover is my birth-place. I have too many dear friends here and else-where in America to think or speak lightly of exile. So far as I can read the page lettered with my name in the book of Destiny, I shall live on quietly here and thus, until I am borne by this gate to my home over *there*. I have thought, sometimes, that my sleep would be more peaceful if the shadow of the church fell likewise on my mother's grave. But that may not be. Forgive me!" with a deprecatory smile, as she saw the unfeigned pain in the dark eyes turned upon her; "this is sorry, foolish talk for summer weather. You are ever such an indulgent hearer that I prate my thoughts, be they wise or simple, grave or gay, quite as if I were talking to myself—— Surely that is the Berkeley chariot at the far gate! I was hoping, not an hour ago, that Anne Harrison would be over to-day."

If her companion did not sympathize in the pleasure that lent wings to her feet, he was not ill-content in following her down the long alley towards the house. The blessedness bound up in her ingenuous confession that converse with him was almost like self-communion gave strength sufficient for many days of fasting from other assurances as sweet. The hope he had never, until to-day, permitted himself to recognize in its true form and fulness, much less to foster, had feathered itself bravely in the last few hours.

"She knows me; she likes me; she trusts me!" was his rapid summing-up. "Let me be assured that love may follow, and no mortal force can bar my way. Least of all——"

He set his well-cut lips in unclerical indignation, as over the paling dividing front and back lawns flew what Evelyn playfully called her "*coq des Indes*," alighting with screech and flutter at his mistress's feet. On the thither side of the fence, peering through the lilac hedge, Fontaine caught sight of the pale, sardonic smile of the secretary. The teasing gobble of the turkey, uneasy from indigestion or other cause, had worn the scribe's patience to threads.

"What fluttered my Hassan?" cried Evelyn, stooping to offer her hand for the harmless peck that meant a caress from the odd favorite.

Fontaine answered distinctly, and with meaning lost upon her, but comprehended upon the other side of the hedge:

"Some evil thing, doubtless. The instinct of bird and beast oftentimes perceives and is affrighted by what human reason overlooks."

CHAPTER IV.

THE Manor-House of Berkeley was less than a mile
from Westover, and visible from the roof-windows.
Harrisons and Byrds had been close intimates for ninety
years, but between no two representatives of the respec-
tive families had ever existed fonder friendship than
the wife of the present proprietor of Berkeley and
Evelyn Byrd felt the one for the other.

The gentlewoman who now stepped from her chariot
into her friend's embrace had done far more than her
nominal mother to fill the place left in the girl's heart
by the early death of the beautiful woman who had
given her birth.

"Robert Carter, Esq., of Corotoman, Lancaster
County, of His Majesty's Province of Virginia," is
better known in colonial history by the sobriquet of
" King Carter,"—bestowed upon him on account of his
immense possessions and the regal sway he exercised
over them.   He was the father of twelve living children.
The love-match of his fairest daughter, Anne, with
Benjamin Harrison, of Berkeley, brought about the
marriage of his son John to the only child of Edward
Hill, Esq., of Shirley, knighted baronet for services
done the Crown.   The princely estate of Shirley was
a fortified plantation as far back as the days of Sir
Thomas Dale, and that a young man whose twelfth
part of even such a realm as King Carter's did not

rank him as a householder with other of Miss Hill's suitors, should have secured the heiress, was ascribed by many, besides the chagrined non-suited, to his sister's diplomatic talents. True or unjust, the suspicion did not mar the satisfaction in existing relations of those most nearly concerned. The sisters-in-law remained upon affectionate terms ; John Carter left his estate in the management of an overseer, and passed months at a time with his wife and children at Corotoman, consulted by and co-operating with his father in the government and transfer of patrimonial acres, his heiress-spouse expressing herself as well-pleased with the arrangement. One and all, baffled lovers and disappointed fortune-hunters, in due time forgave Mrs. Harrison, each cheerfully contributing his quota of attractions to win for Berkeley the reputation of being the most popular house on the river.

Having married early, Mrs. Harrison was, in the teeth of the rebutting evidence of half-a-dozen children, still so youthful in appearance, so pretty and so vivacious as to make her confidential intercourse with the belle of the tide-water region altogether congruous.

Like most of the James River mansion houses, Westover had two fronts,—one commanding the water view, the other towards carriage-road, fields, and back country. The gate within which the friends paused for a whispered word supplementary of their greetings, hung between two square pillars. A stone ball surmounted each ; on these globes were perched two leaden eagles (mistaken by some natives of the soil for turkey-buzzards), wings half-spread and beaks pointed upward. From pillar to pillar was an arch, filled with iron scroll-work wrought in and about the monogram, "*W. E. B.*"

For many years afterward Pierre Fontaine never passed beneath this lintel without recalling the indefinable thrill that shot through him as the two graceful heads leaned together for a hasty second, and light sparkled from face to face. He drew aside in intuitive forbearance not to hear the mutual "aside." Had it reached him, it would not have made him uneasy or serious.

"Contrive to see me apart for ten minutes," said Mrs. Harrison.

And Evelyn: "I have had such a fright! I must tell you of it."

Madam Byrd advanced to the edge of the stone platform outside of the rear door of the hall to receive the visitor. Ceremony she owed Benjamin Harrison's wife. Courtesy was a matter of *noblesse oblige.* Cordiality, or a show of it, went with the *entrée* of her house. Her bitterest enemy would have had under her roof-tree civility and lordly cheer. She would not affect, beyond these, complaisance she did not feel. And she had reason for not feeling over-complaisant. Once, when nobody except her husband and step-daughter was by, she had flung a caustic gibe at her fairest and nearest neighbor. Evelyn repelled it with spirit, and her father supported her by a smiling defence of "a charming woman, who would ever find detractors among her own sex, especially among those who had erst been slim and fair themselves."

Madam had never exactly loved this particular charming woman. From that hour she would have

disliked her as heartily as one good Christian can dislike another had she not been "Ben" Harrison's faithful wife. But nobody heard another overt criticism
from her.

"You are just in time to take pot-luck with us," she
said by the time she had shaken hands with her new
guest. "Caliban, call Canute to take Mrs. Harrison's
horses around to the stable. I wish you had brought
Mr. Harrison with you, and your girls to see mine.
I hope they are in fair health? Here is Willy come
to ask why Ben has not been over to play with him for
a month of Sundays," stroking the head of her pretty
little son. "No, Evelyn! do not drag Mrs. Harrison
to your room, when she must come right down again.
She can lay aside her hat in the hall."

There is an excess of hospitable attention that ap-
proximates rudeness, and Madam Byrd's behavior
escaped this so narrowly that Evelyn became nervously
apprehensive. The excellent matron was, as she would
have phrased it, "in a *swivet*." Whatever degree of
general upsetativeness the word may define, her sensa-
tions were unenviable. Her lord had been gone less
than four hours, and she found herself confronted by
a complication beyond her management. Already it
began to dawn upon her humbled soul that the true
word spoken in jest was when she averred a husband
to be a convenience. Liberty was one thing, and responsibility another. And Evelyn, usually a sensible,
dutiful girl, of whom she was very fond, had behaved
badly in coquetting with, or encouraging Mr. Fontaine,
whichever it might be. Her temporary guardian was
impatient to have the house clear of visitors, that she

might "have it out" with the young woman and be confirmed in or disabused of her misgivings.

Dinner was not served for a trying hour, despite Madam's message to the cook and assurances to her guests. When served, it befitted the wealth of the Byrd's and their reputation for high living. After the fish, which was set before Madam Byrd, and the mast-fed ham (salted under the eye of the mistress, then smoked with seasoned hickory-chips), that stood at the far end of the board, were removed, a pair of boiled chickens, stuffed with York River oysters, took the place of the first-mentioned dish, and a mighty haunch of venison superseded the ham. Besides these bul-warks of the feast, there were veal collops garnished with olives, larded sweetbreads, a chine of mutton, stewed terrapin, roast guinea fowl, a *purée* of pease; potatoes, Irish and sweet, green corn, artichokes; a tongue done in jelly balancing a young turkey simi-larly embedded on the other side of the table, and a salad of lettuce.*

Of sweets there were no less than twenty different kinds, including East India sweetmeats, and persim-mons, gathered last Christmas and preserved in lucent syrup, according to an original recipe of that notable housewife, Madam Maria Byrd.

Two colored footmen, assisted by two sable hand-maidens, their heads done up in starched muslin tur-bans, waited under the captious superintendence of Osiris, butler-in-chief and second in command upon the plantation in the absence of the master. Even

------

* *A bona fide* bill of fare.

Madam Byrd deferred to him once in many whiles, and addressed him habitually in accents several semitones removed from the imperiousness which, according to her creed, was absolutely essential to the preservation of discipline among what she chose to consider half-barbarous vassals. Caliban's office combined the functions of call-boy, bearer of despatches between kitchen and table, whipper-in, and flying-artilleryman, but he stood, when allowed to stand, behind the chair of his young mistress.

Charley Carter sat with madam's four children at a side-table, the sable damosels aforesaid having this in especial charge. Lady Bess's high chair was between her mother and Evelyn Byrd. Of the six bairns, she was the only one who spoke unless when spoken to during the hour given to the meal. The rule that children, although of necessity visible to the naked eye, need not be audible, obtained in force in those primitive times. Even the spoiled elf conversed in whispers with her neighbors to the right and left, and issued orders to Sally who waited on her by twisting her head half around, or throwing it back until those opposite had only a ludicrously fore-shortened jumble of dimpled chin, cherry mouth, tip-tilted nose, and yellow curls. That she should be at the "grown folks' table" at all was a violation of Westover law and precedent. The juvenile Byrds looked on in wonder, mixed with indignation, only to be appeased by a message privately conveyed through Caliban that their half-sister had become security for her pet's good behaviour.

The minx, put upon her honor, disturbed nobody

except the two nearest her until she preferred a whispered petition for " more cream-pudding."

Her mother replied aloud,—

" Say, ' Mr. Bass! I will take a little more pudding, if you please.' "

" Yady Bess 'ont *not* say ' p'ease' to dat bad man," piped the infant, ruffling up like a game pullet.

" Bess!" from her horrified parent.

" My darling!" in a whisper from Evelyn.

" Hoity-toity! these be fine airs!" from Madam Byrd, temporarily forgetful of hostesshood in dread lest the example should be contagious.

The secretary sat at the foot of the table when Colonel Byrd was away. His hands were thick, with short, blunt fingers, but they were white and smooth, and exceptionally deft and strong. He had not spoken all dinner-time except to utter the formulas inseparable from his office as carver. Both tables were served with ham, venison, mutton, fowls, and pudding from platters set before him. He carved skilfully and rapidly, and contrived to get in an abundant repast for himself consistently with his duty to others.

" He is one witted (wicked) man," continued Bess in treble crescendo, accentuating the iteration with a chubby index finger. " Yady Bess 'ont not say ' t'ankye' or ' p'ease' to dat ole *tat!*"   •

A titter from the side-table and a strangled snicker from Sally applauded the figure, and both mothers arose to the occasion.

" Right sorry am I to hear child of mine giggle at such language, albeit from a baby," said Madam, sitting an inch higher in her chair.

"Leave the room, Sally!" ordered Mrs. Carter. "Bess! look at me. Now, say, 'Mr. Bass, I beg your pardon!'"

Instead of submitting, Bess glared upon the secretary, who was eating his own share of pudding with every symptom of unconcern.

"He knot*ted* me down an' too*t* mine p'itty bo*ts* 'way f'om me. I s'all tell Turnel Byrd and mine fader fen dey tum home. I *fink*"—meditatively-murderous—'dey 'ill bof of 'em *till* him dead. Wif a *dun*! An' *buckshet* int' it!"

The climax in the baby-patois, joined to the complacent enmity of the cherubic visage as she gloated over the anticipated vengeance, was irresistible. Discipline went to pieces in the general struggle for a decent measure of gravity, only the secretary remaining uninfected by the prevailing disorder. Charley Carter and Willy Byrd made a simultaneous rush for the door, and were overheard going into convulsions on the lawn. Madam was obliged to cough behind her handkerchief, and Mr. Fontaine forgot clerical decorum. With it all, nobody thought of analyzing the child's jabber to ascertain whether or not there were an admixture of fact in her sweeping arraignment. The stolid composure of the accused had much to do with the omission. Plebeian phlegm, if stanch, is not a bad substitute for patrician self-command when no better material is at hand.

Mrs. Harrison saved the day for the nonplussed mother with whom articulation was an impossibility.

"Did you see the Jaquelines' sloop go by this morning?" she inquired of Madam Byrd, her voice treacherous from inward laughter. "It brought me a barrel of peaches, besides oysters and yams, and two crates of grapes. I must not forget to ask for your receipt for making claret. These are red and purple grapes. I should beg you to accept one crate, but you are so lucky with everything you raise and make as to leave your friends little opportunity to do anything neighborly for you."

Mr. Fontaine's eyes at this instant met Evelyn's across the table in a mirthful gleam that irritated the step-dame into resentful recollection of the unfinished receipt left on the still-room table.

"You flatter me," she said, dryly. "As to the receipt, you are welcome to it. That is, if *Mr. Bass* will copy it from my household book."

The secretary bowed assent, comprehending as little of the animus of request and tone as Evelyn, who colored sensitively.

"I will copy it for Anne, mamma. I have still to complete what I was doing for Mrs. Carter——"

"Enough!" Her step-mother stayed her with a majestic wave of the hand. "Mr. Bass will transcribe the receipt for Mrs. Harrison *in English*. I hope the Jamestown folk are well?" to Mrs. Harrison, with the air of dismissing an unsafe subject. "Mistress Martha will be shaming the rest of us with her Paris gowns and furbelows. Does she speak of coming up the river to let us have a peep at her finery?"

"I had a letter from her." To Mr. Fontaine, if to no one else, occurred the idea that Mrs. Harrison avoided looking at Evelyn while she said it, directing her gaze full at the hostess. "She says naught of her Paris gear, but we are like to have a chance of judging of it for ourselves, since she promises to make me a visit next week."

Evelyn cried out with delight.

"And me also, I hope! I love no girl better than Martha Jaqueline, and we have not met,—it is now a good twelvemonth!"

"Is it also recorded in your calendar that ten of the twelve were spent by Mistress Martha on the other side of the ocean?" Madam's temper strained upon the curb. "She was ever more French than English, though, like yourself, Mistress Evelyn, born in America under an English king. Without doubt she will have quite forgotten her mother-tongue, having, as I hear, given much time while abroad to her father's kinspeople in France."

"It is not a Frenchman whom she has brought home in her train." Mrs. Harrison's sparkling face did not reflect the uneasiness beginning to appear in that of her sister-in-law at the subacid suavity of the lady of the manor. "But an English cavalier. So she writes to me in asking consent to bring him up the river with herself."

The turn was cleverly conceived, and successful in smoothing Madam's ruffled plumage.

"An English gentleman! The sight will be welcome to one pair of aching eyes! Did she name him? Does he belong to the gentry? or, perchance, to the nobility?"

"She writes him down simply as 'a Mr. Francis,' and adds little by way of description."

"Nor that she means to wed him?" with the provincial scent for gossip of courtship and matrimony.

"Nay—*that* she did not hint," rejoined the other, laughing. "Only that he was her fellow-voyager from Havre; that he is a gentleman by birth and breeding, not deficient in learning and the fine arts, and a traveller in many lands. Furthermore, that he had letters to her mother."

"*That* brings all right!" in judicial satisfaction. "The widow of Edward Jaqueline receives as honored guests none who cannot produce good reasons for presenting themselves at her door. You will not fail to allow Westover a share in the pleasure of making Mr. Francis welcome to our rude provinces? Being learned and a traveller, he will the more readily excuse our deficiencies than some who are not used to see better things. Mr. Fontaine, if I cannot prevail upon our friends further to honor my humble fare, will you return thanks?"

The day was wearing toward evening when Mr. Fontaine's studies in the library were interrupted by a light, hasty step. The four ladies had spent the afternoon in the breezy hall, the hum of their voices sometimes unheeded by the reader, sometimes distracting his senses so completely that for several minutes he did not turn a leaf. He needed not the evidence of sight to tell him that Evelyn had left the party three or four times, once remaining absent for half an hour. At the touch of her foot on the threshold his frame was electrically alert, but he arose with his usual calm courtesy.

She came up to him swiftly.

"Mrs. Harrison is going," she said in French, low and breathlessly. "I have had no opportunity for a minute's private speech with her, though both of us have essayed it once and again. Will you propose that we shall all walk with her part of the way home, and will you escort Mrs. Carter—and mamma, should she go?"

"Evelyn! Where has the girl gone *now?*" cried Madam from the hall, and the daughter fled soundlessly by way of the drawing-room door.

Mr. Fontaine, hat in hand, waited at the eagle gate to hand Mrs. Harrison into her chariot, adieux having been spoken, and according to rural custom the whole family attending the departing guest to the carriage. Her foot was on the step, but she turned to heed a proposal that was evidently an after-thought.

"The sunset from the top of the hill will be fine this evening," said Mr. Fontaine, naturally and persuasively. "Am I bold in suggesting that you send your chariot forward to wait for you at the trysting-tree while these ladies"—indicating the group she was quitting—"walk with you that far? I know"—with his pleasant smile—"that I am selfish in offering myself as escort for the party."

Madam Byrd would have been at a loss with the lights then at her call to state why she had of intention hindered Evelyn's coveted *tête-à-tête* with her friend. She would have been more perplexed if asked to account for the heat that coursed through her veins and heightened the fresh color in her comely cheeks at the prompt acquiescence in Mr. Fontaine's suggestion that put it out of her power to negative it. Mrs. Harrison had stepped back to the ground, declaring that nothing could be more charming. Mrs. Carter and

Evelyn had chimed in with exclamations of like effect.
Madam could, and did, decline to join the party, and
she called after the quartette a warning, voiced like
a threat, of the danger of the river-air at sunset.   A
Londoner by birth and life, she was an authority upon
fogs.   Mrs. Harrison answered merrily over her shoulder; Mr. Fontaine looked back to lift his hat in acknowledgment of her kindly concern in their behalf,
then walked on to offer his arm to Mrs. Carter.

Re-entering her own hall frowningly, Madam faced
the secretary. A brass-bound cedar pail of water stood
on a shelf just within the door. He was in the act
of dipping into it the white gourd that hung, when
not in use, upon a nail beside the pail. The action
was common, the man's air commonplace, yet she
divined that he had witnessed the scene at the gate
and liked it even less than she. The consciousness
hurried her into indiscretion unusual in such presence.

"I wish Colonel Byrd would stay at home to look
after his daughter, instead of racketing off to the mines,
and Lord knows where else!" she ejaculated, pettishly.

The smile that replied was the pallid, joyless gleam
that had provoked Fontaine to sarcasm at noon, but
the thin lips were not parted, and as she swept up-
stairs she heard the click of the study-door that shut
him in. The remembrance of her peevish outbreak
did not annoy her. Colin was a good scribe, and a
convenient man to have about the house, but laggard
in wit—poor wretch!

The trysting-tree marked the boundary line of the
Westover estate. Beyond lay the Berkeley Plantation,
—the "Berkeley Hundred" of earlier days. From

time immemorial the pretty custom of Harrisons and Byrds was to take their evening meal together many times each summer, under this wide-branched oak. Servants from each manor-house brought thither hampers of provisions, napery and table plenishings, and young and old, members of the two families and guests, supped jovially in good fellowship.

Beneath this tree, and on such an evening as this, Benjamin Harrison first beheld and instantly fell in love with blithe Anne Carter. Rumor said she had the incident in mind when she brought together, under like circumstances, her brother John and the heiress of Sir Edward Hill. Certain it is that she liked the spot passing well, and dwelt fondly and often upon trysts and love-scenes that had made it memorable for much besides such natural beauty as greeted the eyes of the pedestrians on this afternoon.

The two friends had walked briskly up the slight ascent, but, while Mrs. Harrison was flushed by the exercise, Evelyn was pale and agitated when they halted amid the green shadows.

"Martha met him many times, you say, and they talked of me?" she faltered. "That would mean——"

"That he is true—and resolute! Why do you tremble, dear? Martha will tell you all when you meet next week,—in six days more. She is a brave and loyal friend; oh, so brave! Think over what I have said, for it is but to prepare you for more and surprising things she has to tell,—may be to propose. I have kept until now a letter enclosed in mine for you. Here it is. Nay, you must not open it yet; for hear what she directs of it in mine," drawing it from her pocket. "'Tell Evelyn not to break the seal of that which I enclose unless she feels in her heart warrant to trust herself to a love that believes all things, hopes all things, and dares all things. I counsel her to wait until she is safely shut within her chamber, and the door double-locked, and Madam asleep (if she ever closes more than one eye at a time!). Then and there, having said her prayers to the Defender of the right, let her, still kneeling, open and read and ponder the pacquet I herewith send to her. Unless she promise these things, I charge you to fling the said pacquet into flood or fire, as may be more convenient. Return reply from yourself and Evelyn by sloop which drops down the river with the tide to-morrow morning.'"

Mrs. Harrison returned the letter to its hiding-place and continued, hurriedly:

"The others will soon be here, dear child. They would have overtaken us ere now were not Mr. Fontaine an angel in a black coat. Should your answer to Martha be 'Aye,' send me this"—plucking a knot of blue ribbon from her sleeve—"as soon after sunrise as may be possible on the morrow. I do not ask you to write, for that may not be easy when you have read your letter. And keep it until you are in your own room to-night, as Martha says. Good-by, my darling! GOD bless you and make you strong!"

To cover the agitation her companion could not at once master, she moved in front of her to meet the forms just appearing among the bushy growth below, hailing them scoffingly,—

"'Go to, now, ye sluggards! consider *our* ways, and be wise!"

CHAPTER V.

THE demon of perversity, Lady Bess's preferred familiar, instigated her that evening to refuse to be put to sleep elsewhere than in the gentle arms that had cradled her for her morning nap. Having carried this point, she moved, furthermore, that she would sleep all night in Evelyn's room and bed—or nowhere.

Mrs. Carter almost wept over her recalcitrant offspring, and opined, as millions of other mothers have since that "all so long ago," that "children always seize upon the occasions of being abroad or in company to behave their worst." Madam Byrd, her lips tightly plaited, watched grimly the contest which took place in the hall soon after supper, and Mr. Fontaine, booted and spurred for his homeward ride, looked on in silence as compassionate as hers was severe.

For the girl over whom the unequal contest went on was the sad shadow of her whom he had seen in the mirror-depths ten hours ago. Her eyes were dark and large with wistfulness; her cheek was as colorless as a magnolia-petal; her very figure looked slighter and her hands thinner. Madam Byrd had remarked upon Evelyn's lack of appetite at supper-time, and attributed her lassitude to the depressing effect of riverside walks after sundown.

"One might think that people who had lived in an unhealthy region all their born days would learn not to expose themselves recklessly."

Fontaine winced at this, but not for himself. It was plain that Evelyn was weary from some occult cause, and in need of rest, and he did his best towards gaining it for her by an early leave-taking.

She forestalled his intention by a sudden movement.

"Let me have her," she said, stooping to lift the sobbing child from her mother's knee. "She will make herself ill. Bess! do you hear what I say? Leave off crying and we will go up-stairs, and you shall sleep in my room. Yes, I know that you love me!" a smile like wan sunlight flitting over her countenance at the fervor of the spoiled imp's embraces, and the shower of wet kisses rained upon her brow and cheeks. "But you must kiss poor mamma, too, and promise to be a better girl another night before I can say that *I* love you."

At the outcry from mother and nurse at the sight of the slight form swaying under the weight of the baby, Mr. Fontaine interposed:

"Lady Bess will let me carry her up-stairs, I am sure."

With a gurgle of innocent pleasure, the beauteous load nodded approval. She even locked her fat arms behind his neck on the way up and cooed, "I yove 'oo!" In the same breath she spat out virulently, "Bass is a ugly *nigger!*"

"Poor Mr. Bass is in her black books to-day for some unknown reason," said Evelyn, waiting in the open door of her room for him to transfer his charge to her. "She hates as she loves, with her whole heart. Thank you for bringing her up, and for all else you have done for me this day."

He bowed reverently. The maiden-bower, the interior of which he now saw for the first time, was a shrine. He could not have told the position of a single article of furniture, or what it was ; but he carried away a dream of purity and fragrance, of cool, gray dusks and reaches of silvery moon-rays, and in the foreground a figure and face like an angel's, that looked gratefully up at him.

His way home lay through the heart of woods where owls, startled by the beat of his horse's hoofs, hooted dismally ; rabbits ran across the road in front of him, whippoorwills cried to one another, and frogs bellowed hollowly in the bayou swamps. Letting his rein hang loose upon the horse's neck, he rode onward with dreamful eyes that saw only the vision he bore with him, and ears that heard but the silver ring of a woman's voice, thanking him " for all else he had done for her that day."

Lady Bess took her own time—and plenty of it—for getting to sleep. Endued in her night-gown and cap, her curls escaping, like rings of floss-silk, from the lace edge, she lay against Evelyn's shoulder, harmless and fond as a turtle-dove, cooing and lisping that her guardian was the " boo'flest *yady* in 'ee worl'," and that she " *yoved* her a whole heartful, an' ten million barnfuls," —her artless head the while crushing the muslin folds above Martha Jaqueline's unread letter.

Colin Bass, strolling down the moonlit, rose-bordered walks curving from the east to the west gates, heard a faint voice singing a lullaby, and looked up at the unlighted windows from which the music floated down to his greedy ears. Half an hour later, while on the same beat, he saw the gleam of a lamp, and the singing had ceased.

"The little she-devil has let her off at last!" he muttered to the discreet moon.

Literally obedient to the behest of her imperious friend, Evelyn said her prayers before unsealing the packet she longed, yet almost feared, to read. She prayed silently, her face hidden in the drapery of the bed whereon Lady Bess slept the sleep of the conscienceless unjust. Now and then a shiver ran through the body and limbs of the kneeling figure, and once an audible moan shook the white stillness of the chamber. Not until her petitions were ended did she light the lamp upon the stand at the bed-head, and then she did not rise from her knees. There was a vein of superstition in her nature to which Martha Jaqueline's adjuration appealed with force. While breaking the seal of the letter, she said aloud, "GOD help me!" and "GOD forgive me if I am doing wrong!" before unfolding the sheet.

She read fast and excitedly after passing the first lines, eyes dilated and quivering lips apart with eagerness. At the very foot of the last page, below the signature, a line had been added by another hand than that which had written the rest:

"*Eva! J'attends encore! j'attends toujours!*"

She raised the sheet to her lips, kissing these last words over and over, between sobs and inarticulate cries, laughing and weeping together.

Madam Byrd's prejudice against early and late rambles was apparently not shared by her lord's secretary. The sunrise of the day succeeding Mrs. Harrison's visit saw him in the broad lane dividing the Westover and Berkeley plantations, and opposite the gate of the latter, on his return from a walk of three miles into the back country. He wore knee-breeches, black stockings and stout shoes, and a jerkin of buff leather buttoned to his chin; a silk skull-cap, that would not be in the way in his tramp in the low-boughed forest, was upon his head. His complexion was freshened by the damp air, and he forged ahead in the middle of the road, swinging a big stick, with the gait and mien of a well-made, healthy, and unfatigued man.

Right at the Berkeley gate lay something white and small. Bass crossed over and picked it up. It was a dainty parcel, soft to the touch, done up in silver paper. Opening it, he beheld a knot of ribbon which he had remarked yesterday upon Mrs. Harrison's sleeve. His forefinger went up to the scar upon his chin; with his head tilted a little to one side, he studied the bit of finery with a vague, irrational idea that it portended something. How came it here, and thus enveloped? The wearer had not gone home by this route. From his lookout in the shadowy hall, he had certainly seen that both sleeves were adorned with blue satin bows, as she took Evelyn Byrd's arm and walked on in advance of Mrs. Carter and Mr. Fontaine. He plumed himself, and with reason, upon the eyesight which was as quick and vigilant of every detail as that of an Indian scout.

Light came soon, and from an unexpected source. In the avenue, more than half a mile long, leading straight to the Berkeley manor-house, he saw a moving form tacking from side to side of the way,

and stooping occasionally to examine a clump of grass
or weeds. As it approached, Bass saw that it was
Caliban. He was a handsome fifteen-year-old half-
breed, the son of a negress and of an Indian father, who
had bequeathed to him stature, litheness, and cunning.
The secretary knew himself to be the object of contemptuous dislike with Colonel Byrd's unsalaried de-
pendents, and liked none of them, while affecting not
to notice sly impertinence and overt disrespect. Between himself and Caliban there was war as open as
was safe for the slave to wage against a white man
protected by his master and mistress. As it was, the
manœuvres by which the scribe had contrived, on
divers occasions, to bring certain elfish tricks practised
upon himself to the mistress's knowledge without actually playing the tell-tale, had drawn down condign
retribution upon the perpetrator.

In a twinkling, the secretary had the key to the present enigma. Mrs. Harrison had lost the ribbon-knot
on the path to the trysting-tree; it was found by the
returning party. Evelyn had sent her page over with
it to the owner; he had dropped it, and not discovered
the loss until he reached Berkeley house. He was now
searching for it.

Without further hesitation, Bass pocketed the trifle
and walked right on to meet the delinquent. Caliban's
black eyes were rolling perturbedly; his skin was the
hue of a dusty copper-kettle; his violent start on perceiving the secretary was palpable evidence of guilt.
In the shock of the meeting, he lowered his guard so
far as to pull off his cap to Bass, who would have
passed without speaking, and to accost the last man to

whom he would in ordinary circumstances have applied for information or help.

"Mornin', Mr. Bass, suh! You ain' happen fur to see a little teeny bundle lyin' roun' nowhar on de groun', is you, suh?"

Bass looked him over from head to foot in cold disdain, and moved onward without halting or speaking. It was his hour, and he improved it. Beau Brummell could not have achieved more superb nonchalance if addressed on the Mall by a shabby creditor.

Caliban stood still in the middle of the road, glowering after his enemy. He clenched his fists, and his lips curled back from gnashing teeth. The savagery in his veins leaped past the merry, devil-may-care guise under which most people knew him.

"The low-live' limb o' Satan!" he hissed. "I'd give my hade ter know ef he done foun' it. I'd ruther take nine-'n-thirty on my bar' back 'n' have to tell Mis' Evelyn I los' dat bundle, else I 'ouldn' 'a' let myself down so fur ez to ax him 'bout it,—de low-down houn'!"

Nobody was astir at Berkeley except the servants; but Bass took the precaution to ask for Mrs. Harrison's own maid, and to deliver the parcel into her keeping, without condescending to explanations, and doubled upon his track, serene in the consciousness of having done the woman he loved a good turn, and a foe he despised an ill.

Shrewd and cool-headed as he was, he, like every other creature of mortal mould, had his pet superstition.

"I have picked up two valuables within twenty-four

hours," he said, smiling sourly in thinking of Lady
Bess and the voracious gobbler. "The third will be
along soon, and be most precious of all."

The morning was less bright than at dawn, overcast
by clouds, and not fogs. He recollected Madam Byrd's
prognostications of falling weather, based upon the
dewless sward. The sun had arisen luridly before he
reached Berkeley, dyeing the river blood-red. The
smoke from the chimneys of the Westover "quarters"
fell and spread broadly at the level of the tree-tops;
the boding cry of the rain-crow sounded from the
church-yard as he neared it. His scheming brain was
usually allowed a rest before breakfast. His matuti-
nal tramp was conscientious recreation. He was sys-
tematically as kind to himself as he knew how to be,
and he had made self-benevolence a study. He had
walked his body into a capital appetite, and his diges-
tive apparatus into tone that would justify him in in-
dulging his palate. What he had observed as he went
along was considered as superficially as was consistent
with his principle of letting nothing escape notice or
memory. He caught a glimpse of the rusty-brown
bird of ill-omen flitting from one branch to another
and uttering his discordant cry, and having scraped
together a smattering of natural history, with a little
of everything else from his erudite chief, he wondered
why even colonial ignoramuses should refer the creature
to the genus *corvus*.

Down the central alley of the garden, over the intervening paddock and past the chapel, flitting between
the tombstones, and so, straight to where he had paused,
wonder-stricken at the apparition, Evelyn Byrd sped

up to him. Her hat was in her hand, having evidently been caught up as she ran out of the house; there was not a tinge of color in her face; her eyes were wild with fear.

"Mr. Bass," she began, when within speaking distance, "did you find—I have lost—that is, Caliban dropped—I thought, perhaps——" Here breath and voice failed her.

Bass plucked off his cap and bowed respectfully.

"I think I found what your messenger lost, Miss Byrd. I carried it over to Berkeley, and sent it up to Mrs. Harrison. I hope I acted wisely?"

Every one of his measured words appeared to convey exquisite relief. She clasped her hands, and looked up at him as to a deliverer.

"Wisely! Oh, *mon dieu!* How can I thank you? I was in terror lest——"

She leaned against a tree and burst into tears, weeping so violently that she scarcely knew who led her gently into the church-porch and seated her on a bench. Calming herself the sooner for the quiet and seclusion of the place, she smiled presently, still with suffused eyes, at seeing Bass fanning her with the hat she had let fall.

"Pardon me. I was very silly," she was beginning to say, when he interrupted with,—

"You ran too rapidly, and the morning is close. Such an attack of faintness and breathlessness is quite natural in the circumstances. Allow me to explain that, finding the parcel, and recognizing to whom the ribbon belonged, I guessed that she had lost it and you found it. I took the further liberty of restoring it to the owner. The whole affair is perfectly simple,—such a trifle as not to deserve your thanks."

Evelyn put out her hand impulsively. He took it in his and held it for one supreme, intoxicating second. He had never touched it before. The distance between him and the daughter of the house was an established fact,—a fixed gulf. His breath clogged his throat; the blood beat upon his brain; he staggered a step, and rested against the post of the open door.

Unobservant of his agitation, Evelyn ran on, not yet coherently,—

"You have done me a signal kindness—and Mrs. Harrison a favor. I was so terrified when Caliban told me of his carelessness—and the time was so short—that I fear me I behaved strangely enough. Forgive my folly. I slept ill last night,—if, indeed, I slept at all."

"On account of that wretched child," escaped Bass's lips before he could catch himself up.

Evelyn blushed painfully while trying to speak gayly.

"Do not cast the blame upon poor little Bess. She slept soundly enough. I was but trying to show you that there are excuses for my weakness. You will not betray it to others—or think of it again, I am sure?" with a look that ravished his wits.

"Never while I live!" he protested, earnestly and absurdly.

"Nay! a less vehement oath would suffice!" She looked and spoke like her usual self, and arose with maidenly dignity. "It was a kind thought to bring me hither. There are strength and comfort in the very air of a church," glancing into the cool shadows of the interior. "The winter we spent in Rome, I used to go with only my maid to St. Peter's, and sit there a long time, thinking out perplexing things. The place and the spirit pervading it helped me. I could not tell why."

"Yet you are not a Catholic?"

He had put his hand under her elbow, as any man, even a footman, might, as she descended the two steps of the porch, and still dizzy with the renewed throb and thrill of the contact, spoke at random.

She turned suddenly upon him, lips ready for speech as impetuous as the movement, then checked the impulse, and walked beside him for a silent minute, her face toward the river and averted from him.

"Not a *Roman* Catholic!" came at length, in a tone that was all gentleness. "But I believe in the Holy Catholic Church, and in the communion of saints. We are too prone to forget who said, 'Other sheep I have that are not of this fold.'"

"She got that from her ghostly director," meditated Bass. And still inly, " —— him !"

Instead of following the walk leading to the garden, Evelyn had taken one skirting the river-bank, then bending towards a tall iron gate capped by the Byrd coat-of-arms, that gave upon rose-walk and lawn. She moved languidly, and neither offered further remark until they were at the squared stone steps before the front door of the mansion.

The day could not breathe under the blue-black pall rolling up all around the horizon; the water was like slow molten lead; the leaves of the poplars lay back flat against the stems, the whitish under side upward.

"It will rain of a certainty," Evelyn aroused herself to say, pausing upon the platform.

"The Jamestown sloop is lucky in that she goes down with the tide," answered Bass.

He had no small-talk at his command, but feeling for the first time on a level with her, unconsciously imitated the tone and ways of those other men he had hated for enjoying the right to lounge beside her in her walks, sit by her when she sat, and chatter society banalities. In another moment she would be gone. He would detain her while he could.

"*Mon dieu!*" broke from her a second time. She leaned forward eagerly to look out upon the river to where a small vessel, with but half her rigging un-furled, wallowed sluggishly down the channel.

As if fascinated, the girl continued to watch her until she was on a line with the dock. Irresolution, doubt, fear, and vivid gleams of a light the observer could not define, appeared and were gone, like shadows upon water. In the delusive atmosphere presaging storm, the craft seemed so near one might have hailed her with hope of a reply.

"I suppose it would be quite possible to stay her even now, if one wished," said Evelyn, in forced levity. "My voice is not strong, but if I should make a speaking-trumpet of my hands, thus, and halloo, the sailors would hear me, would they not? If I were to bethink myself of something to be sent to my friend, Mistress Martha Jaqueline, the captain could heave to, have the helm turned inland, and come into the West-over dock, could he not? I would fain try."

"Oberon would mistake it for Titania's call!" ven-

tured the enchanted secretary in clumsy compliment;
"or a troop of obedient fairies, headed by Puck, would
troop up the lawn."

He thought the turn neat, and was somewhat dashed
in spirits that she paid no attention to it. She was so
distractingly lovely in her capricious changes of mood
and countenance, that he could have stayed to watch her
all day, had she given him never another word or look,
only leaned forward in that attitude of eager, almost
expectant grace, hardly seeming to breathe while following the vessel with her beautiful eyes.

He knew so little of women's witcheries and weakness, that when the sloop had slipped down a bow-shot
below the wharf, and, throwing out another sail, tacked
boldly for the other shore, and Evelyn, with a low cry,
"*She has gone!*" sank, a breathless heap, at his feet, he
was wholly unprepared for a revulsion so entire and
alarming.

CHAPTER VI.

A MESSENGER on a bare-backed mule trotted over
from Berkeley through the pouring rain that afternoon.
Mr. Harrison had been taken seriously ill during the
night, and grown so much worse by noon that the
neighborhood physician had been sent for. At four
o'clock he had not arrived. The errand of the drip-
ping Mercury was to beg of Madam Byrd one of the
simples for the preservation and use of which she had
a reputation, and that she would look in upon the
patient as soon as the weather would permit.

She ordered her chariot forthwith, and stocked it with the desired remedy in abundance, eight or ten bundles of herbs, and as many gallipots and phials, with a supply of jelly, broth, and gruel that would have nourished the ward of a city hospital. The county held not a better or a more willing nurse, and that she knew her worth in this regard did not make her otherwise than gentle and efficient in the hour of need.

Instead of returning home that night, she sent back for a change of clothing, and held the fort against surprise and siege by death for four days. Evelyn, still pallid from the indisposition that had overtaken her on the morning succeeding the riverside ramble, spent part of each day with her afflicted friend, but was regularly ordered home before sunset by the commander-in-chief, whom even the surgeon durst not gainsay.

"*She* will be coming down next," complained Madam on the fifth day, which was Sunday, to Mrs. Carter, who had prolonged her visit to Westover at the earnest petition of the hostess and her step-daughter. "She looks like a puff of air would lift her now. I have ever insisted that September is the sickliest month of the year in the low country, and mayhap, when I and my poor children are food for worms, Colonel Byrd may come around to my way of thinking. That girl has wasted to a shadow in less than a week. I have put her upon port and bark to-day, and would be obliged if you will see that she takes it thrice a day. Also, bid Osiris prepare a bottle one-quarter full of well-rusted nails and filled up with hard cider, of

which she should take a glassful at rising and another
at bed-time. Were it not that Mr. Fontaine and she
appear to be on such excellent terms, I should suspect
a lover's quarrel. The Lord forgive me for naming
him or any other man as her lover, and her father
away from home!

"I'm reckoning high upon Martha Jaqueline's
coming to cheer Evelyn up, and the English gallant
will doubtless divert her from the dumps. And this
is what I wanted to see you about. I've fairly worried Anne Harrison into agreeing that they shall be
put off at our wharf, instead of at Berkeley. It stands
to reason that her husband will be driven fair beside
himself to have such junkettings and curvettings in
the house as go with Martha Jaqueline everywhere, to
say naught of his wife's place being at his side. Stay
you, then, at Westover and play duenna to the young
folk until I can come back, which, please GOD, will
be soon, if Ben grow no worse. I have a soft spot in
my heart for him, now he's in so sore a case."

"She has a soft spot for everybody who is in trouble,
I think," said Mrs. Carter, in repeating the talk over
the dinner-table to Evelyn and Mr. Fontaine, the taciturn carver at the foot of the board counting for nothing. "She has a marvellous head, too, as you would
know had you heard the messages sent by me to the
servants. I prayed leave to write them down. My
brain would not carry them. Yet she forgot naught
from guest-chamber to cellar. She even named the
men who are to man the boat to be sent off from the
wharf to stay the sloop on her way to Berkeley. She
will herself write the note to Martha conveying the

invitation and giving reason for the change of plan, which is to be sent in the boat. It would best come from her, she says, and not from you, Evelyn."

Mr. Fontaine lent the narrator courteous but divided attention; for Evelyn's fork had fallen from her hand and the glass of water she lifted to her lips shook. She caught his eye before he could look away. Her glance was that of a hunted thing ready to fly, yet entangled beyond the possibility of moving. She drank hastily, set down the tumbler and laughed, strainedly; her voice was almost sharp,—

"Fate is fate!" she cried. "Martha had no right to promise Anne Harrison a visit that should have been mine. I shall tell her so, and show how destiny is on the side of equity. And, then, we will do our bravest to reconcile her to the exchange of residence and— mamma's absence."

The others laughed at the demure addenda. Madam Byrd's wordy encounters with Mistress Martha were historical. Colonel Byrd likened them to the English and French forces, and took huge delight in pitting them against one another.

"Mistress Martha is proficient with the rapier," he said. "Madam will have no weapon but the broad-sword. Both are fair marksmen; but one has skill in pistol-practice, while the other brings the blunderbuss up to her shoulder and draws a fine bead upon her man, in honest British fashion."

Mrs. Carter's reply was not, then, so irrelevant as it sounded.

"Madam Byrd deserves all the more praise, these things being so. Her orders are that all hospitable honors shall be done your friend and 'Edward Jaqueline's daughter.' Her respect for his memory is great."

"Colony and church had an incurable loss in his death," rejoined Mr. Fontaine, and led the talk to reminiscences of one of the noblest, as he was one of the wealthiest, men of his day and region.

Evelyn's friendliness towards the rector was marked for the rest of the day. Encouraged by it, he drew a chair to her side as she sat awhile before sunset in the middle of the hall, Lady Bess on her knee, and the big Dutch Bible, clamped at the corners with massive ornaments of wrought brass, upon the table before them.

Bess was in a Sabbath mood, oddly dissimilar to that in which she had menaced her brother and the Byrd children with clenched fist and flashing eyes from too near approach to what she had pre-empted as her preserves,—Evelyn's lap, and Evelyn's talk of the curious engravings embellishing the mighty volume. Her golden poll rested against her guardian's shoulder; her chubby hands were pressed together like thoughts adjusting themselves for prayer; her eyes were clear and rapt; even her smile was serenely slow. Her chastened beauty would have made her fond mother tremble for the continued life of her darling, had she been there to see, instead of having gone again to Berkeley for the latest news of the beloved patient.

The great book lay open at a picture which teacher and pupil were contemplating seriously as Mr. Fontaine joined them. It was a fearfully realistic representation of the scourging in Pilate's hall. The hands of the victim were tied at the wrists to an iron ring made fast

f

in a pillar ; behind the executioner was a Roman soldier, holding a bundle of fresh rods ; a lean, wicked-eyed dog crept up to lick the bloody pedestal.

Evelyn looked up mutely at the rector's approach, then, again, as silently to the awful object-lesson.   Lady Bess said with sugared imperiousness,—

"'Oo *wead* 'e hard words, Misser Fonten."

"Papa read the Latin to her one day, and the sound pleased her ear," added Evelyn.   "One might almost believe that she comprehended their meaning."

The reverent voice of the scholar rendered the inscription,—" *Vulneratus est propter iniquitates nostras ; attritus est propter scelera nostra : disciplina pacis nostræ super eum, et livore eius sanati sumus.*"

" P'itty ! p'itty !" sighed Bess, satisfiedly.

Evelyn's eyes brimmed with warm, sweet tears.   She raised her hand furtively to brush them away before she spoke,—

"A strange impulse came to me this morning in church," without looking up.   "Something tempted me to wait on my knees until the others had departed ; then to ask you to listen to my confession, and to absolve me.   Are you displeased?   Have I shocked you ?"

He was serious, but not stern, to her arch pleading. Beyond the seriousness was the steady glow of a pure fire that illumined the fine face.   He laid a finger impressively upon the bowed Figure in the picture :

" *There* is the only Confessor ! ' *Disciplina pacis nostræ super eum !'*   Unto Him is the cry of the human heart : ' O Lamb of God, who takest away the sins of the world, have mercy upon us !' "

" He is afar off, Mr. Fontaine."   Her mouth trembled ; more tears were ready to fall.

"Dear Miss Byrd, no earthly friend is so near. Surely you know this !"

She shook her head, setting her teeth upon her lower lip to control the quiver.

"Once,—perhaps ! Of late, my prayers rise no higher than my head."

Fontaine's theology would not second the plea put in by his heart for the belovéd sinner, that the symptoms of physical malaise were often confounded with those of spiritual disorder.   He was a priest, and a conscientious one.

" That would seem to show that something had come between your soul and GOD," he said, fearlessly.

She winced and blenched as at a needle-prick.   Her eyes returned to the stricken Form, the cruel scourges, the creeping cur.

" Yet you will not confess me?   Will not appoint me a penance?   Will not absolve me?"

Each whispered word was a tempter to the man within him.   Had his Protestantism been of a more ductile type, he would have crossed himself and said a mental exorcism.

"GOD forbid !" he said, fervently.   " He knows, too, how every thought of you is a prayer that His peace may possess your soul——"

She interrupted him.   "That is a *pax vobiscum !* Thank you !   Whether you meant it or not, it does my soul good like a medicine."

" Yady Bess don' yike nossy med'cin' !" commented the cherub, in pensive dissent.

Fontaine answered as if Evelyn had said it: "Old Samuel Rutherford writes to an afflicted friend, 'Be sure the Lord must love you very much, or He would not give you so much and so bitter medicine.' The saying has helped me, oft and again."

"'So much and so bitter medicine!'" repeated Evelyn, musingly. "Suppose one had lived upon that—and little else—for years and years; had it mingled with his bread and drink; found each morning at rising the bitter draught set at his bedside; in every scene of pleasure felt the acrid drops upon his lip,—would that soul be sickly or healthy, think you, Sir Priest?"

"The Great Physician makes no mistakes. The cup given to each man to drink is for himself, and no other. Health and sickness depend upon the spirit in which the draught is swallowed."

"Is *nothing* sweet wholesome?"

She asked it abruptly. His soothing voice atoned for the didacticism of the reply: "With God's blessing, the bitter is sweet!"

Lady Bess twisted herself around to cast her arms about her friend's neck.

"Mine Eva is sweet!" kissing her fast and hard. "Mine Eva! Her is nobody's Eva but jus' on'y mine!"

A crimson rush suffused the girl's face,—a blush that burned and hurt by the impetuosity of the tide. Without a sound, she snatched up the child and carried her off up the stairs.

Fontaine had arisen with her, and stood gazing at the landing where she had disappeared, a flush like the reflection of her blush upon his olive cheek. A chuckle from the door of the study aroused him from his stupefaction. Bass was coming out of the room, hat in hand, bound upon his evening walk. He might have seen and heard all that had passed in the hall. He might be ignorant of everything except Evelyn's flight and his surprise.

The secretary sneered openly in glancing at the open tome;—"So endeth the second lesson!"

It was dignified and characteristic that Fontaine feigned not to catch the purport of the sentence, imperfectly smothered behind the scoffer's teeth, as he walked leisurely past him to the door. The rector resumed his seat and seemed to study the ancient print.

Twenty years later, on another summer afternoon sitting with his little son upon his knee, he happened to turn the leaves to the same picture, and blinding mists of memory drove between it and his eyes; resurgent waves of emotion beat him faint for an instant; his temples throbbed, and his heart ached again under the weight of anger and love striving together for mastery in a soul that would not stoop to use weapons he began to perceive were directed against him by his inferior and rival.

CHAPTER VII.

THE wind blew straight from the sea next morning, dissipating the fog that had lain like soft wool upon the lawn all night. It left the glitter of diamonds upon every blade of grass and freshened the late roses into the richness of early summer. The Westover household was astir as early as if the mistress were to preside in person over the preparations for the guests. As soon as it was light enough to discern the close seams in the oaken flooring, the rub and squeak of waxed brushes were resonant in halls and lower rooms. The kitchen-hearth, never cold from Christmas to Christmas, prevented the dawn with its glow; an army of retainers, under the direction of an upper servant in each department, wrought with diligence, and what was for negroes and half-breeds, despatch, until by the time the Jamestown sloop, flying the English and French colors, appeared at the lower bend of the river, bustle was exchanged for the calm of conscious readiness.

The great lawn was swept clean of withered leaves; the gravel walks were rolled; the crisp folds of fresh curtains swayed in the open windows; tall jars of roses, bergamot, lilies, and southern-wood were upon mantels and stands; and, as the lookout set upon the house-top ran down with the news that the sails were in sight, a hospitable party left the front door for the pier.

As was fit in the absence of her parents, Evelyn came

first. Mr. Fontaine was at her side, and Lady Bess hung upon her other hand. Mrs. Carter was escorted by Master Willy Byrd, a handsome urchin of eight; but the secretary walked beside her, and behind them were Charley Carter, Jane and Mary Byrd, demure and best-frocked, under the surveillance of Mammy Teena, the head-nurse. Sally, Bess's custodian, off duty for the time, brought up the rear with Caliban. No matter who came or who went, the smart servitor was to the fore,—partly because of native audacity and the favor of master and mistress, partly because he was clever and handy. His ostensible business on the present occasion was to bring up from the wharf such light luggage as the owners might not care to commit to the handling of the liveried boatmen waiting upon the bank for the arrival of the vessel.

The wind was with her, and she had flung out every stitch of canvas; the spray broke whitely over her prow.

"There is positively a Cleopatra-barge-ish look about her!" said Evelyn to her companions. "It would sound like profanation to tell how she came up last week with potatoes and oysters in her hold."

"One might know that Martha Jaqueline is on board," rejoined Mrs. Carter in like mirthful vein. "Nothing ever goes fast enough for her, be it a horse, a vessel, or a human being. She will not live out half her days."

Evelyn flung back a laughing retort, and walked more swiftly down the incline. A marvellous transformation had come over her in twelve hours. At bed-time last night, as Mrs. Carter silently reflected, she

looked—although nothing could make her unbeautiful
—fully thirty years of age. To-day, but for the perfection of her figure and the easy elegance of carriage
that bespoke familiarity with the fashionable world, she
might have been eighteen. Over her shoulders she had
cast a blue crêpe shawl,—an Indian fabric, as was the
white embroidered muslin of her gown. The sea-wind,
or the joyful anticipation of meeting her friend, had
brought soft, yet brilliant bloom to her cheeks; there
was a happy flutter in her laugh, her eyes were wells
of changeful light. The kindly neighbor considered,
furthermore, that the visit of an intimate friend whom
she had not seen for a twelvemonth, was no trivial event
in the life of one who had known little of gay life of
late, and yet had had so much of it in her girlish prime.
After all her reasoning and indulgent allowance for
circumstance, she was forced to appreciate the existence
of an underlying force the nature of which was a secret.
The girl had drunk of the elixir of life between sunset
and sunrise.

Neither of the men, whose observation of the belle
of the county was, to say the least, as close as that of
her nominal duenna, detected anything equivocal in the
restored bloom and animation that gave lustre to her
loveliness. Fontaine, standing at her side, Bass, a little
behind her, as the sloop headed for the pier, saw the
delicate hands seek and clasp each other until the flesh
was bloodless, and her whole form shaken by irregular
respiration, and both thought the agitation altogether
natural and becoming.

The gangway had scarcely touched shore when a lithe
figure, in a costume which Mrs. Carter at once discovered

was Parisian and ravishing, darted down the tilted plank to throw herself into Evelyn's arms, with a shower of French ejaculations, mostly diminutives,—the more remarkable that the new-comer was half a head shorter than she who was thus saluted. At a prudent distance, picking her steps gingerly, followed a woman with wasp-like waist and stature like a grenadier's. She was attired in a stuff gown of rusty black; a voluminous calash, like the top of a Conestoga wagon, protected a mob-cab, and within the fluted borders of this were the smallest head and face that could, by any elasticity of imagination, be supposed to belong to the grenadier's height.

This was Miss Lotsie Johnson, companion, housekeeper, *ci-devant* nursery-governess,—a little of everything and a good deal of most good things to the Jaqueline household. She was led by the captain of the sloop, who held the tips of her mittened fingers as if afraid they might break forth into talons.

Lastly,—having waited, courteously, until both ladies were safely landed,—a man ran down the steep gangway. In touching the pier, he bared a head covered with close blonde curls, undisfigured by the powder which most men of fashion wore in abundance.

"Mistress Evelyn Byrd," said Miss Jaqueline's clear soprano, French in pitch and accent, "I have the very great pleasure of presenting to you my friend, Mr. Francis, of London. He was my fellow-voyager over the ocean, and has been for some days the honored guest of my mother at Jamestown."

"I am glad Madam is not here to note that introduction," thought Mrs. Carter. "Mistress Martha has assuredly picked up a fine art or two at Court."

8*

Miss Byrd curtesied low, her eyes on the ground, her color wavering enchantingly, then going out, so that a very pale face met the gaze of respectful admiration bent upon her, as the stranger recovered himself from a bow as profound as her curtesy.

Mistress Martha, considering apparently that the claims of etiquette were satisfied by the length and ceremony of her presentation-speech, now absorbed within herself general attention by voluble embraces distributed among Mrs. Carter, the little girls, Willy and Charley, and shaking hands with everybody else, beginning with Mr. Fontaine and ending with Caliban. She was popular with people of all grades, but particularly and immensely with children and the lower classes. Caliban adored her as second of created things, his young mistress rating as first; the boys, deserting all others, clave to her forthwith. She shed upon Mr. Fontaine the sunniest of her smiles in giving him a reticule of gilded leather to carry, telling him that it contained "*beaucoup de trésor*," and handed a small casket to the secretary.

"I know of old whose discretion to trust," coquettishly. "Nobody but Mr. Bass shall handle Pandora's box. Mr. Fontaine! I am going to beg the support of your arm up the terraces. I saw from the sloop that Mr. Bass had the honor of escorting Mrs. Carter. Evelyn, here is Mr. Francis a-dying to ask for the pleasure of your company. Now, boys and girls, I have something in my portmanteau for the one who has grown fastest in the past year, and I can't see who is to have it unless you all walk in a line like soldiers ahead of us. March! forward! heads up and toes out!"

There was one exception to the omnipotence of her fascination. Lady Bess, at Miss Jaqueline's approach, promptly wrapped her head in Evelyn's muslin skirt, and shrugged a mutinous shoulder when her mother implored her to reply to the young lady's blandishments. When curiosity, and pique at being taken at her word drew her from her covert, she carried her nose high in air and affected utter unconsciousness of the interloper's presence, holding fast all the while to Evelyn's hand.

Miss Jaqueline laughed, well content and amused.

"True to her first love! No blame to you, monkey! She is ever and ever so much better worth the loving than I. And people who love her once, love her ever, I find. I like you the better for the excellent taste you display."

The procession, headed by the children in line of march, as directed by their divinity, and ending with Mam' Teena and Miss Lotsie, hobnobbing in friendly familiarity, was followed at a gradually-widening distance by Evelyn and Mr. Francis. The sea-breeze tempered the heat of approaching noon, but could not make the day cool, and Lady Bess's short legs flagged in ascending the hill. The path ran parallel with the river-wall for a hundred yards or so, then arose by stone steps laid in the bank, and zigzagging easily up to the brow of the hill. A low wall of masonry overrun with vines defended the wall from the wash and drift of heavy rains. None of the party in front looked back until the last terrace was gained. Martha Jaqueline talked incessantly, her voice ringing above the children's prattle, Mam' Teena's gutturals and Miss

Lotsie's harsh, chopping tones, that, according to Martha, " would not be unmusical if her vocal organs could be taken apart, cleaned and oiled."

"There is a balm for every bane," said that vivacious young woman, pausing at the lower gate of the lawn to take breath and face her audience. " We, whose lot is cast in a region where the rise of land in every mile is less than an inch, ought to live longer than you who waste lungs and limbs in riotous climbing. Yet Westover is beautiful for situation, the joy of the whole river."

" I am afraid Bess may be troublesome," Mrs. Carter was saying anxiously, apart to Mr. Fontaine. " My mind misgave me in leaving her so far behind. I should have insisted upon releasing Evelyn from the care of her, especially as she is in company with a stranger."

" I will go back and fetch her to you," was the response, so promptly given and acted upon that he was beyond the nearest turn in the crooked path before remonstrance could be offered.

A flush darkened Martha Jaqueline's mobile face; she compressed her lips ; her black eyes opened and closed fast and repeatedly,—a trick of her impatient moods, which were not a few. Colin Bass looked from her to Mrs. Carter's embarrassed countenance, and queried inly why both should be averse to breaking the virtual *tête-à-tête* between Miss Jaqueline's admirer and a more beautiful woman than she.

Fontaine caught sight of the loiterers from the second terrace. Lady Bess had been lifted to the top of the wall and sat there at her ease, swinging her dumpy legs. Evelyn's back was towards the unseen spectator, but something in the droop of her head and slight but eloquent inclination of the graceful figure made his heart sink in unreasonable pain. Thus might a flower bend towards the sun, a willow lean to the water that fed its roots. Dismissing the unwelcome similes as absurd, he yet paused in momentary incertitude whether to go on or to retreat unnoticed. The group was picturesque. A rock-maple, one bough of which, tipped with scarlet and gold, almost touched Evelyn's head, shielded them from the vertical sun; Bess's hat lay on her lap, and she was sticking wild asters in the ribbon band. Mr. Francis had uncovered his head, and from the step below Miss Byrd looked up steadfastly into her half-averted face.

"As goodly of countenance as a Saxon god!" thought the observer.

Goodliness that was not all in finely-chiselled features, in the clear skin and the glow of youth and health, the deep, blue eyes, the fair curls crowning the noble head, and the athletic symmetry of the figure. The light of smile and eye had a glory of its own, the curve of lips that could be haughty was now playful,—and—it could *not* be tender!

Fontaine's second thought and impulse were of vehement indignation. How dared this foreign fop, this courtly coxcomb, the suitor—perchance the betrothed of that other girl awaiting the recreant at the top of the hill—thus stare and smile at one he had known scarce ten minutes? Well might a modest maiden shrink beneath his bold regards!

He strode forward resolutely to protect her from further insolence.

Lady Bess was the first to hear his step upon the stones.

"Misser Fonten!" she shouted, clapping her hands, "'Ook at mine p'itty hat!" holding aloft the triumph of sylvan millinery. The instinct of self-indulgence potent in the shrewd angel moved her to add, her mouth drooping plaintively,—"Yady Bess mighty tired! P'ease *tarry* me up 'ee hill!"

She relieved the embarrassment of a surprise that was evidently an interruption.

"I came back for her," said Mr. Fontaine, with grave directness. "Mrs. Carter is uneasy lest she may hinder you in mounting the hill."

Mr. Francis interposed himself between the speaker and Evelyn, who without turning was hurriedly gathering up the scattered asters from the wall. The back of her neck and the one small ear that was visible were of a vivid pink. She had, then, resented the stranger's audacity.

He spoke courteously enough, and his ready laugh had in it nothing of bravado or bashfulness.

"I offered my poor services as porter to her ladyship, but she would none of me, even insisting that Miss Byrd should lift her upon the wall. Once there, she would go no farther. We were conspiring to dislodge her by strategy. I had in mind an ambush of Indians in the thicket over there, but Miss Byrd assures me that red savages are no longer a terror to American babies. Nor would her tender heart consent to a scare from bogie or ghost. We are your grateful debtors, Mr. Fontaine."

He spoke in fluent French, and the frankness of the

laughing eyes and the indulgent smile that rested for an instant upon the spoiled child, reversed instantly the current of criticism. The explanation was too plausible not to be true. Fontaine's responsive laugh was the heartier for the relief from disagreeable suspicions. The blue and black eyes met in mutual good-will.

"Come, Lady Bess! Mamma is wondering if her bird has flown away!" said the rector, gayly. "What! I must shoulder you! Be it so, then."

He sprang lightly up the steps, unhindered by his burden, leaving the others to follow at their pleasure.

"I have been unjust to an innocent man," he was schooling himself by saying when the precocious infant spoke out one of the many pieces of her mind.

"Yady Bess finks she doesn't yike dat gempleman. Not *vewy* much, I don't fink!"

"It is not kind to dislike a pleasant gentleman who has done nothing to vex you," replied her porter, in gentle reproof.

"Yady Bess 'ould yike him if he didn' say 'Mine Eva!' She is *mine* Eva! Nobody else s'all call her so but mine own self."

"He said nothing like that!" retorted Fontaine, emphatically. "Bess is only a foolish little girl who does not understand all that grown people may say. Mamma would be grieved to hear her sweet daughter tell such a silly thing."

To his sensible inner self he subjoined : "What a fallacy is contained in the adage, 'Children and fools speak the truth!' They are the most unsafe, because the most ignorant of eaves-droppers."

CHAPTER VIII.

THE fortnight succeeding the arrival of Mistress Martha Jaqueline at Westover was monumental for half a century thereafter in the social annals of tidewater Virginia. With the speedful certainty of the message of the crosslet stained by fire and blood to Highland height and loch, the news flashed up and down the river that high carnival would be held in the Byrd mansion, where there were room and welcome for all. All day long chariots and horses were halting at the tall gate surmounted by the monogram of the princely proprietor. Lighted windows from ground-floor to steep roof, blinked to passing vessels like fiery eyes until midnight was far sped. Strains, jocund and sweet, from players upon instruments, and wildly-plaintive as the song of the Lorelei, from daughters of music whose fame is not yet forgotten, mingled with the river-breeze and kept the whippoorwill silent.

Madam Byrd had never been happier in her prosperous life. Mr. Harrison's rapid recovery was a brave feather in her cap, and the publicity given by the influx of guests to the talk of his danger, and the share she had in his cure, was a continual triumph. She was able to return to her own house with a good conscience on the fourth day of the visitors' sojourn there, and fell in love out of hand (in matronly, virtuous fashion) with Martha Jaqueline's " friend."

That he was all the word implies when it flies quotation-marks was palpable, or assumed by everybody to be obvious. Had doubt lurked in the worldly-wise mind of the *châtelaine*, it could not have survived a confidential chat held in the still-room a few days after her home-coming, with Martha's chaperone.

Miss Lotsic Johnson had brought up Martha Jaqueline "by hand," and estimated her proprietorship in that lively damsel, as compared with the nominal mother's vested rights, as ten to one. The smaller number represented the title Nature grants to her who, willingly or of necessity, brings an unconsenting infant into the world for the Lotsies to take care of. The two housewives, seated side by side at the long table in the still-room, were flavoring loaf-sugar for cake-making by rubbing the hard white lumps with lemons and fresh peach-leaves until they were yellow and green, then pulverizing them in a small marble mortar, after which the powder was sifted through coarse muslin. The process, insufferably tedious in the telling to a modern cook, was necessary in the absence of flavoring extracts for culinary purposes; so common that nobody thought of complaining of it, yet too delicate to be intrusted to menials. Miss Lotsic had charge of the lemon-flavoring; Madam's capable fingers bruised the peach-leaves against the granulated surfaces without abrading her knuckles or breaking her nails. The sugar came to colonial store-rooms in conical loaves a foot high, enveloped first in white, then in purple paper, as thick and stiff as a board. To prepare it for use, it was broken into lumps with a hammer and stout knife; afterward cut into small cubes with "a clipper," a wrought-steel implement with keen nippers and a powerful spring.

The blended fragrance of lemon-peel and prussic acid scented the air; each worker had a low, ample chair, cushioned on seat and back, and used a footstool to make a lap commodious enough to accommodate the big bowl into which the green and yellow lumps were dropped. At a smaller table at the far end of the room, Caliban, enveloped in a checked apron from chin to instep, was cleaning tankards, pitchers, urns, and other silver vessels, with scraped rotten-stone, oil, and vinegar. Occasionally his mistress raised her voice to admonish him to diligence or caution. The house was unusually quiet. Martha Jaqueline's riding-horse had been sent up from Jamestown for her use the day before, with an imported English mare for Mr. Francis, and a large equestrian party had set out for Shirley two hours ago. Mrs. Carter had gone home with her children as soon as Madam Byrd was fairly settled again upon her nest.

"I shall be easier when the young folks are safe home," Madame said, in the course of more desultory talk. "Mr. Francis is, I suppose, a skilful horseman. All the English gentry are. But 'tis a tempting of Providence to back a creature with such a temper. I was in nowise surprised when she reared so soon as he touched the saddle. And did you note that his thought was all for the terror he had put me in? What Virginian cavalier would have bowed to the saddle-bow, doffing his hat and begging my pardon for having affrighted me? 'Twas weak, doubtless, to scream on seeing his peril, but my nerves have scarce recovered the trial of

Ben Harrison's sickness. I could but compliment Martha Jaqueline on her composure, and own that I and Evelyn showed like faint hearts beside her."

"She knows the mare—and Mr. Francis," said Miss Lotsie, gratingly.

"True enough. And, judging from the signs of the times, she is like to become better acquainted with one of them. Ah, well! so wags the world, and young people's fancies will run where they will. It must be a comfort to you and the young lady's mother that Mistress Martha's affections would seem to be so well bestowed. Was Madam Jaqueline in health to see Mr. Francis while he was at Jamestown?"

"Yes. She enjoyed his company."

"As well she might! I would not say it to Martha's self, since to praise her lover would be to flatter her, but a goodlier man and a more charming mine eyes have seldom lighted upon. And I surmise from his deportment and acquaintances in dear old London town that he is of excellent family?"

"I have heard as much," returned Miss Lotsie, rubbing a lump upon a fresh lemon with the regularity of a machine.

"Madam Jaqueline would make sure of that, of course. The young couple have my best wishes for their happiness. As you know, Martha and I have had some passages at arms in the past; but she is her father's daughter, and has a warm, true heart, as her friendship for Evelyn testifies. I only wish that Providence had deigned to send the twin-brother of this same young traveller over the seas to fall in love with my step-daughter, who is like to fill a spinster's grave."

"She does not lack for admirers."

"Admirers, forsooth!" in lofty contempt. "Such as they be! Caliban, when next you pick peach-leaves for me, look to it that there are no slugs among them! Faugh! Bring me hither water and napkin for my fingers!" As the lad vanished, she continued, more at her ease: "When one has tasted old wine of prime quality, she will, belike, make a wry face at that which is new and sour. And what blame to her? I can only hope she may not have heard what my English letters brought me,—it is now over six months since,—that *he* has come into his grandfather's estate and title. I took Mistress Martha aside the day of her arrival, when she drove over to Berkeley to inquire after Ben Harrison, and catechised her sharply as to what she knew of the matter. She had heard, while in England, of the old lord's death, and even seen him who was Charles Mordaunt several times at court and elsewhere. She manifested more discretion than I thought was in her in agreeing with me that it would be best not to name him to Evelyn. He is still unmarried, she says, but there was talk of a match between him and a certain Mistress Mary Cox, a young woman of fortune. The name speaks nothing for her lineage. The right judgment displayed by Mistress Martha in telling me thus much (which I know to be true, inasmuch as my London letters had already advised me of it) wrought well towards altering my opinion of her whom I used to upbraid for light speech and romantic fancies. Beside yourselves, there is nobody this side of the Atlantic to whom I dare speak of this matter. Certain it is, that I could confess to no one but you, Lotsie, what I would not whisper to the walls were Colonel Byrd within fifty miles of me, to wit, that my mind misgives me grievously, at times, as to the wisdom of his action in a certain affair."

"In refusing to let his daughter wed a Papist?"

"Papist! Fudge! you've caught the Huguenot Jaqueline cant! Some of the best blood in England is Roman Catholic, and the young gentleman,—whom I never clapped eyes upon,—from what I can learn, was well enough, even had he not a title in prospect. And, having fallen in love with the American beauty who was quite the fashion at court that year, he might, under proper management, have been brought to view Protestantism in a reasonable light. Moreover, and above all,"—sinking her voice mysteriously,—"were it not that I know of old how safe is the secret confided to you, Lotsie, I would be racked to death before I would lisp it,—there was somewhat behind this show of churchly zeal. Colonel Byrd was a roistering young blade in his day, and had his fling even while he was a widower. Not that I esteem him the less for it. He was ever a man of honor, and if he had—which all popular young men have—a woman's secrets to keep, he was as close as wax. This young nobleman's father, Mr. Mordaunt, was shockingly gay, so I've heard, and the two men were rivals in some affair, and quarrelled.

"That is all I know, except that the Colonel hated his very name. I chanced to let it fall one day in Paris, whither we had gone on our honeymoon, and I had to listen to some biting things, I can assure you, such as tied my tongue on *that* subject forever after.

9*

Well, this poor Mordaunt died years ago,—before I
ever knew there was such a man as William Evelyn
Byrd, or such a place as Virginia, for that matter, and
the tomb should swallow up enmities of all kinds.
But the Byrds have long memories, and—you know the
rest. It served the Colonel's turn, being stout for his
religion and church, to swear that his daughter should
never marry with a Catholic; and he got no small
credit with some for his behavior. Here 'tis never
spoken of, and I shall wish, when I've said my prayers
to-night, that my tongue had been blistered before I
wagged it over all this story; but you do wheedle
things out of one."

"Perhaps Colonel Byrd would change his mind if he
knew Mr. Charles Mordaunt had come to the title."

"If he knew! I'll wager my best diamond bracelet
against that lemon in your hand that he knows all about
it, what with the piles of letters every mail brings
him, and his correspondence with the nobility, and all
that. He must have had tidings of the old Earl's
decease soon after it happened, but never a word has he
let slip to me of it. As to changing his mind, a title
or two more or less would not avail one tittle with him.
He lived hand-and-glove with dukes and earls and
viscounts too long to be awed by them. Charles Mordaunt, to whom he refused his daughter's hand, would
get no other answer were he to present himself to-morrow at Westover as Fourth Earl of Peterborough and
Second Earl of Monmouth. Those are his titles."

The mournful intonation was not to be mistaken. Her
husband's familiarity with peers might have bred in him
republican contempt, or patrician indifference to rank.

Madam Byrd, formerly Mistress Maria Taylor, the great London heiress, loved a title with British loyalty.

Engrossed in the subject, she had sat, her wrists crossed and palms uppermost, awaiting Caliban's return with basin and napkin,—an event which she foresaw would be tardy. Perceiving him now at her elbow, she dealt him a perfunctory cuff for hindering her task so long, washed and dried her hands, and took up a stainless lump of sugar and a bunch of tender leaves with another section of her discourse. Caliban was, practically, no drawback to conversation, yet Colonel Byrd's helpmeet bore in mind, when she did not forget it, that diplomacy takes no needless risks. She mentioned no more names.

"The Lord above only knows how any young woman of quality is to mate herself properly hereabouts. But His will be done! My heart sinks with the thinking what a certain distinguished parent would say should he discern how the land lies between a nameless belle and a certain divine. I shall not open his eyes, but I cannot shut mine. Nor, I dare say, can you——

"Caliban, you feckless rascal! pick up the lemon Mistress Johnson has dropped! Wash it, dirty fellow! Do you think her as foul as yourself, that you give it to her right from the floor, and with your bare hand? One would think there was ne'er a tray in the house!"

"Yet he is a proper gentleman," remarked Miss Lotsie, with her usual economy of words.

"I don't deny it. And of gentle blood. But when a man who has lived in courts, and has a great fortune, has but one marriageable daughter, and she a celebrated beauty at an age when most women in this country show signs of fading, he is not like to be content with a country parson for a son-in-law. When the tug comes, you will see the Huguenot fare no better than the Papist."

"Will not she make choice for herself?"

"That will not she! Time was when *I* would have 'scaped down a rope-ladder from a turret-window to run away with the man I loved. She stands too much in awe of the powers that be. It must be owned she loves him too dearly besides. She will not let me so much as hint that he has a fault—which every sensible, right-minded wife must do, now and then—men being what they are."

Miss Lotsie's qualifications for the post of confidante-general would have seemed scant to a passing acquaintance. She looked grim; she was ungainly, and shy and taciturn to a proverb. Yet people of all grades and tastes dropped secrets into her ears as naturally as letters into a post-box. She might say little, but she had a genius for listening, and her mind was ever bent upon promoting the interests of others rather than her own. The meanest of mortals was esteemed better worth the serving than herself; so far as in her lay, she effaced her own individuality and magnified the personality of her neighbor.

Martha Jaqueline brought to her once, when a child, the question put by the Jewish lawyer.

"You are all the time talking about your duty to your neighbors, Aunt Lotsie. Who are they all?"

"Anybody I can help, child!"

It was the key-note of her life.

Her dormitory at Westover was in the very top of

the house, but she never repaired to it at night, however late the hour, until she had seen Evelyn and Martha, who roomed together, in bed, and, seated at the foot of their couch, chafing the feet and ankles of her nurseling, had heard the tale of the day's pleasures and perplexities. Martha likened her, in one of their conferences, to a miser's treasure-chest.

"Her ear is the hole in the lid. Her mouth is hasp and staple, and always padlocked. The coffer must be full to bursting by this time. If the lid *should* fly off, we would be in a pretty pickle—eh, Evelyn?"

"I'm not afraid!"

She lay high upon the pillow, one arm cast over her head; her eyes beamed softly; her cheeks had the flush of an oleander petal; countenance and mien were expressive of blissful content.

Martha raised herself upon her elbow to kiss her.

"*Mon ange!*" she said, fondly. "How any one can look at you without guessing what has made you a young girl again, and the loveliest thing out of Paradise, passes me! Where do people keep their eyes and their wits?—What is it, Aunt Lotsie?"

To Evelyn, the duenna had given no sign of interrupting the other's speech. Martha felt the sinewy, gentle hand pause in the slow passage up and down her foot. It went on as Miss Lotsie said:

"Mr. Fontaine has both!"

Martha laughed, carelessly. "*N'importe!* What his eyes see, his wits will construe into flattering evidences of *his* influence over her. A man in a black coat is not less nor more than a man!"

Evelyn looked pained.

"If you would imply that Mr. Fontaine cares for me except as a friend, you err grievously. You need not smile incredulously! He thinks of me but as a parishioner—a mere child—a foolish, weak girl who looks to him for counsel and guidance. Ah! he is good! so good that your suspicion dishonors him."

"As if to love you were not equal to a patent of nobility to any man!" cried Martha, warmly. "As if all men must not adore you, from Monsieur L'Inconnu to the sleek, sly, sober, silent secretary!"

Evelyn's gesture of fine disdain did not check the gay rattle.

"I caught him watching you this evening through a crack of the study-door, where he sits all day, pretending to copy the Colonel's manuscript, like a cockchafer nibbling a morsel of cheese. The wind blew the crack wider, and showed me his face. You were at the harpsichord, singing, and somebody else was watching you, leaning on the instrument. Colin had a view of you both, and I saw a fire light up his eyes that made them red and ugly, and his crest lowered and flattened like a snake's, and up went that diabolic forefinger to consult the scar on his chin, and I thought of a wizard in his cave, and a toad in his hole, and all manner of creeping, eerie, slimy things. Then it was that I sidled up to Bayard,—as being his betrothed I had a right to do,—and, the song over, fastened upon his sleeve and walked him out into the hall, and so up and down, hanging upon his arm and looking lovingly sidewise up at him, while I berated him soundly for his imprudence, and told him to whom he had nearly betrayed himself."

"I saw you!" smiled Evelyn. "Would I could play my part as well!"

"You improve!" Martha conceded. "And Monseigneur is not bad, except that his eyes are now and then derelict. Eyes are the loop-holes of the heart, and Cupid shows his face at them oftener than is safe if he would not be recognized and aimed at. But to our secretary! While we loitered in the hall, he feigned to pore over his blotted scraps of dirty paper, although you were still in full sight, talking to Major Mumford. And what does my squire do at our tenth round but clap the study-door to in passing! 'This door is ever ajar, letting pass all sorts of pestilent draughts!' quoth he, coolly. I'll warrant you, Colin owes him no good will!"

"The poor man means no harm," interceded Evelyn, still smiling. "'Twas cruel to shut him up on a warm night because he dared look across the hall,—doubtless because the music disturbed his calculations of pounds, shillings, and pence. He keeps the plantation-books, and I know not what other tiresome volumes, and never thinks of a woman, gentle or simple, unless he stumbles over her in the corridors.

"But, Mr. Fontaine! I cannot suffer you, or Miss Lotsie, to nurse ridiculous fancies concerning a noble gentleman whose thoughts are set upon higher things than love and courtship,—especially when both would be vain. I would not scruple to confide everything to him to-morrow, were I in a sore strait for a friend and helper. He would judge mercifully, and lend me a brother's aid.   Heaven send I may never be driven to cast myself upon his compassion ! but it would not fail me.   I could rest upon his friendship as upon my mother's love."

CHAPTER IX.

THE master of Berkeley was restored to sound health, and his lady-wife summoned the country-side to rejoice with her, and do honor to Miss Jaqueline and her English gallant.

It was now October; the evenings were long, and cool enough to justify the pleasure-loving dame in calling the rout for which she issued invitations, a ball. For fifty miles up and down the river, and twenty back of the noble stream, little was talked of for a fortnight by the women but dancing and toilettes, while the men looked forward with interest as eager to the run of the Berkeley race-course set for the morrow of the ball.

The important night was fair, and glorious with moonlight. Williamsburg magnates of College and Court,—grave, gallant, and gay,—in powdered wigs, in uniform, and more sober-hued coats, laced upon collar and cuffs,—jostled burly planters who depended upon wives and daughters to show that "the river" was not ignorant of the elegant mysteries of gala-raiment. From Turkey Island, Brandon, Wyanoke, Wakefield, Shirley, Curles, Presque Isle, Tuckahoe, Bermuda Hundred,—as far up the James as Henrico, and as far down as Jamestown and Hog Island, and from Rosewell and

Weroweomoko on the York,—the current of revelry ran in the direction of the hospitable homestead set high on the river-bank.

Madam Byrd, handsome and imposing in purple satin, brocaded with silver thread, a turban of white crêpe and silver heightening her stature, entered the ball-room upon the arm of the English stranger. He was conspicuous by his height, comeliness, and the fact that, although richly attired in the prevailing mode, he wore neither wig nor powder. His blonde curls were gathered into a loose knot at the back of his neck and tied with black ribbon. They grew close to the rest of the head in natural waves, instead of being combed away from the forehead and temples, and strained smoothly toward the queue upon the nape of the neck,— a fashion which with young men was superseding the full-bottomed wig, formerly *en régle* for all ceremonious occasions, social or public.

Madam Byrd had, as we know, given her matronly favor to him at sight, and each day strengthened his hold upon her liking and admiration. To-night, her pleasure at being singled out from the brilliant crowd as the object of his especial devotion was imperfectly concealed. Uppermost in her mind was the intention to have what the American of over a century later would call "a royally good time." Her husband's return from his distant possessions and surveys had been postponed from week to week, until the novelty of freedom had somewhat abated, but not the enjoyment of it. Association with her courtly guest and talk of her old home had revived her taste for polite society. Unconsciously, her manner took on something of gracious stateliness with which her Virginia congeners were unfamiliar. Ornate phrases tripped from her tongue, and she surprised herself by the facility with which she rounded repartees which she would have despised a month ago.

"I am a poor dependent upon your bounty, to-night," Mr. Francis was saying, as she suffered him to withdraw her from the surging crowd into the embrasure of a window near the principal entrance. "But for you, I should be 'remote, unfriended, melancholy, slow,' in this gay throng. You will allow me to linger beside you for a little while—will you not? Recollect that I am a stranger in a strange land, and take me into the secure retreat of your sympathy."

"Fie upon you!" cried the flattered lady, "when all the beauties present will be pulling caps presently for the honor of your hand in the dance! There! I came near doing it again! I actually was on the point of saying, 'your lordship's hand!' And the like has happened sundry times before. It is, maybe, the force of old habit, for 'my lord' and 'your lordship' were used to be as pat upon my tongue as plain 'mister' and 'sir,' and much converse with you provokes me to recollections and tricks of the dear olden times. If you can put up with the chatter of an old gentlewoman, when younger belles are languishing for your notice, I shall be only too happy to tell you who are somebodies, and who next-to-nobodies,—though Mistress Harrison has few besides notables here to-night. East Virginia can boast no braver array of her best people than you see now."

"I can easily believe it," said the gallant, his glance

sweeping the room to return to his companion's face, as having found nothing to excuse distraction from his devoir. "Grant me the honor!" taking her fan and beginning to fan her with the same air of absolute devotion.

"If you will engage to use it heedfully! It is a holy relic, being nothing less precious than the fan I bore when presented to our late gracious sovereign, King George the First of blessed memory. He condescended to salute me, and as he stooped to my lips, my fan brushed his sacred shoulder. Until to-night I have never borne it since. There are not many men to whose keeping I would commit it for an instant."

Mr. Francis bowed, hand on heart. His eyes said that his sense of obligation was unspeakable.

"It is a superb relic," he observed, handling it circumspectly. "It could have been purchased nowhere but in Paris."

"You guess aright. At my special request, my step-daughter likewise sports to-night the fan she bore to the drawing-room of our present sovereign. She was foolishly reluctant to bring it forth from the silver paper in which she is used to keep it wrapped, but our dear Mistress Martha added her petitions to mine. Not that the workmanship of Evelyn's fan can compare with mine, but she is disposed to sentimentality,—and there were circumstances connected with that occasion that she cannot easily away with."

Mr. Francis turned the fan to examine the reverse. He was, apparently, less interested in Miss Byrd's presentation than in her step-mother's. Perceiving this, the matron waxed generous:

"Mistress Martha is looking passing well. That yellow taffeta and amber ornaments become her rarely. My Evelyn looks but a colorless chit beside her."

Her companion's eyes followed hers to where the girls stood together, surrounded by a bevy of beaux. Evelyn's gown of white taffeta draped her in large, soft folds; it was belted by a rope of pearls; a pearl collar banded her beautiful throat; the one touch of color in her attire was the painted fan she waved slowly to and fro. Mr. Francis passed his hand over his eyes,—a swift, unstudied motion. A sentence from an old book he had read aloud to his mother went through his mind :

"The Interpreter looked upon her and said unto her, ' Fair as the moon !' "

Then the courtly smile returned to his lip, the light ring to his tone :

"Laburnum and lily ! Virginia is a gracious soil, bringing forth none but brave men and beauteous women. May I ask the name of the young lady in blue satin talking to that gallant warrior? For warrior he looks to be in lineament and carriage."

"What eyes and what judgment ! That is Mistress Hannah Harrison of Wakefield. Her father, Nathaniel Harrison, is the Admiral of James River, and his daughters are prodigiously admired by our provincial beaux. The ' warrior,' as you call him, is Lieutenant Maynard, of whose prowess you may have heard in far-off England. But what am I saying? You must have been in the nursery when he headed an expedition to Pamlico Bay against the pirate John Teach, otherwise known as Blackbeard. Lieutenant Maynard boarded his vessel, killed the monster in a hand-to-hand fight, and sailed back up James River to Williamsburg, with Blackbeard's head dangling from the bowsprit.

"This happened before my marriage, but I have heard the tale so often I seem to have been in the provinces when the awful scenes were enacted. Thirteen of Blackbeard's men were hanged at Williamsburg. His skull was mounted in silver as a drinking-vessel and presented to Lieutenant Maynard by admiring friends. I have oft seen and handled it; but so squeamish am I, meseems I could never drink from it, though it were filled with nectar."

Mr. Francis looked curiously at the hero of the ghastly adventure. Beyond his martial deportment there was nothing to indicate his sanguinary trade, much less the ferocity with which it had been plied. He was hard upon forty years of age, frank of face, jovial in eye and laugh, and assiduous in ballroom gallantries to his pretty companion.

"It is rumored that they are betrothed, or like to be," resumed Madam Byrd in a confidential key. "I shall be glad if this be so,—very glad,—and thankful, as his friend and well-wisher."

The listener was the impersonation of interrogatory attention, as she meant he should be. She took her fan from his idle hand, held it before her mouth, and talked through lips that hardly moved:

"The phrase escaped me unawares. But your relations to the Jaquelines—my tried friends of years—justify the confidence. Lieutenant Maynard was once a suitor of Mistress Martha. He is a man of stubborn disposition, and his persevering pursuit of her begot in me fears I perceive now were groundless. I appeal to you, Mr. Francis, as one versed in the more refined sensibilities of the female heart, if it be natural for a tender, delicate woman to contemplate with complacence the vision of a husband who chopped off a pirate's head with his own cutlass, and who has the bleached skull filled, each Christmas, with eggnog in which to drink the king's health and confusion to the king's enemies!"

"Do I understand that Miss Jaqueline shares your womanly sensibilities anent the buccaneer-butcher-hero?" asked the auditor with labored gravity. "Or had the gory head fascination and the silver-lipped cranium charms for the girlish imagination?"

"Martha has ever showed true maidenly reserve touching the affair. She is brave-hearted, and not easily daunted by the details of war; but it was not from her that I learned of the Lieutenant's obstinate suit, you may be sure. She mentions him with profound respect as a brave gentleman and her father's friend. I entreat you to forget the unwarrantable indiscretion that has given you a glimpse of what you'd better have heard from another tongue than mine."

"Do not, I pray you, dear lady, apologize for that which honors me and invests you with a new charm in my eyes," returned the young man, impressively. "It is not unlikely that I may erelong beseech you to hearken to confidences of mine own that will tax your patience and good-will. Then I shall venture to remind you that I was emboldened to thrust my poor matters upon your indulgence by the noble candor you have displayed here and now."

" I do protest that your lordship flatters me beyond my deserts !" cried Madam, fluttered out of her wits by the subtle compliment of word and manner.

Unaware that the slip of the tongue, so often imminent, was an accomplished act, she was hurrying on with further disclaimers when she was struck by the ashen terror in one face, the ill-concealed astonishment in another, and felt that the broken sentence had been overheard.

The crowd was in general motion, the dancers *en route* for places in the first cotillon. Evelyn Byrd, on her partner's arm, was so near her step-mother in passing, that the white silk and the purple satin met in whispering folds. Colin Bass, who never danced, had fallen back to the outer wall to make room for those who did. Both were within hearing of Madam's seldom-subdued speech, now shrilled by excitement.

Evelyn's fan slid from her fingers, and was caught by Francis before it touched the floor. The silver cord-and-tassel attached to it was entangled in her skirt. Francis dropped on one knee to disengage it, and the secretary caught a rapid murmuring of French as he restored the toy to the owner. So quickly did all this pass that Madam Byrd had not time to exclaim upon her step-daughter's pallor before her complexion was normal, even rosier than usual.

" May I conduct you to a seat ?" prayed the Englishman, with proffered arm. " I am afraid that I must leave you to look for Mrs. Harrison, who deigned to promise me her hand for this set. Dare I hope that you will reserve the next cotillon for me ?"

She entered fully into his implied regret that duty to

his hostess had prevented him from asking her to take the floor with him now, and dismissed him beamingly.

"I release you!" waving him away. "Do not linger one instant on my account. Mr. Bass will find me a chair or a place on a bench"—turning upon the secretary with a total change of voice and expression.

He drew back to designate the cushioned window-seat behind him, and, without waiting for further demands, brought a footstool and a cushion for her back, settling her luxuriously. The window was raised, admitting delicious sluices of night-air fragrant with sweetbrier and honeysuckle. She had the whole ballroom and the hall beyond in view. Not another woman there was arrayed more richly, or was a personage of greater consequence than her buxom self. She carried more weight upon her shapely feet than in her spinster-days, and was not ill-pleased to sit still for awhile before the next set. She knew herself to be a good dancer, and that Mr. Francis would have no cause to regret the exchange from Mrs. Harrison, who was leading the frolicksome troop down the floor in singleness and gladness of heart, feeling as young as the most youthful of her guests, simply and unfeignedly happy because others were. The Englishman chatted politely with her in the pauses of the dance, but his devotion was less pronounced than when the older woman was his interlocutor. What subjects in common could he have with Anne Harrison? A worthy creature in her way, but lacking the polish which only life in the old world could impart.

Madam Byrd, overlooking the vari-colored waves of revelry, her ears filled with the lively music of the fiddlers ordered up from Williamsburg, was in a frame of most Christianly resignation to the providence that had cast her lot exactly there, and just then, and un-dutifully reconciled to the dispensation of her lord's absence. He was never so well-content as when fording ice-cold creeks up to his saddle-cloth, or trudging through canebrakes, with five chances out of ten of a moccasin-bite, or the thrust of a wild boar's tusk. He would rather, at this instant, be lying in the middle of an open field, a blanket between him and the earth, and his head pillowed upon his saddle, exchanging broad jokes with his companions, or, while they snored about him like so many swine, gazing up at the stars he knew so well by sight and name,—than to be the cynosure of this bril-liant assembly ; to warm himself in beauty's smile, and presently, to help make away with the supper prepared by the famous Berkeley cooks. Far be it from the exemplary consort of the many-sided man to controvert destiny, or run counter to her spouse's will !

The pious submissiveness of temper and desire lasted throughout the cotillon graced by her presence and action. She wasted less thought upon the hireling she had left leaning against the wall than if he had been a caryatide. She recked as little of the trivial trip of the tongue that had blanched her step-daughter's face, and drew upon her the secretary's stare, as the tourist of the pebble his foot displaces which may yet set an avalanche in motion.

A minuet succeeded the second cotillon. Between the two the young people had strayed out upon the lawn and porches, and the room was the fresher for comparative emptiness. Sconces, holding branching candlesticks, lined four sides of the ballroom ; between them swung festoons of running cedar. Feathery asparagus-boughs, speckled with red berries, filled the fireplaces and wreathed the frames of mirrors and pictures. The oaken floor was waxed and rubbed until it shone like glass. Portraits of Carters and Harrisons looked down upon their multiplied descendants and the friends of a later generation. Wall-benches were packed with dowagers and matrons who had given over dancing ; elderly men stood about in halls and doorways.

Colin Bass had pressed himself into the recessed window deserted by Madam Byrd. Lieutenant Maynard had sued in good and set ballroom phrase for the honor of her hand in the stately dance, and in her gracious assent there was no trace of the recoil she had defined as inseparable from refined sensibilities.

Mr. Francis smiled as the " buccaneer-butcher " led the willing dame down the long apartment to their allotted places. Bending nearer his partner's ear, he spoke low and laughingly. The secretary's furtive glance had not left the pair since he saw that Evelyn Byrd was to dance with her friend's lover. He noted this motion as more familiar than the comparative strangerhood of the parties authorized, then, the answering flash of meeting eyes bespeaking cordial mutual understanding. As Francis raised his head, the light from neighboring candelabra struck athwart his face, and Bass saw what made his steady brain totter.

The opportunity of inspecting the miniature in the locket he had taken from Lady Bess had been brief, but his habits of minute observation, and the tenacity of memory he cultivated as part of his business capital, had fixed every line of it in his mind. Upon more than one occasion he had been puzzled by a flitting fancy that he had seen this man before; by an elusive resemblance to person or picture that was gone ere he could seize it. He recalled, now, how strong and perplexing had been this impression one evening as he watched Evelyn singing at the harpsichord, with Francis hovering near her,—the same night on which the insolent patrician had stayed his promenade with Miss Jaqueline to close the study-door with a mocking allusion to "pestilent draughts."

He knew now the meaning of suspicions and the vague boding that had ever attended them. His shrewd wits forged, link by link, a chain of probabilities that sickened his soul.

The child had fallen asleep in Evelyn's arms. The locket may have been lent to her as a plaything, and forgotten by the owner. It was more likely that it was abstracted by the thievish little fingers without Evelyn's knowledge. It had, assuredly, not belonged to Mrs. Carter, and this accounted for the circumstance that no inquiry succeeded the loss. The opaque sallowness of the reasoner's skin was cadaverous as he admitted the almost certainty that the handsome face he now scanned was identical with the original of the picture he had seen surrounded by diamonds, and bearing the French legend,—and that Evelyn Byrd had worn the miniature above her heart.

Colonel William Evelyn Byrd was puissant in his colonial principality, but he could not muzzle the tattlers who had bruited through the region the rumor

of his beautiful daughter's ill-omened betrothal. It
was merely a rumor,—a faint sketch of a story, and
outline and detail were as varied as the mediums that
transmitted the romance. The secretary, who heard
everything and forgot nothing, had constructed a tale for
himself of harmonious excerpts. Miss Byrd—according to this—had been sought in marriage while in England, by a person of quality : her father had raised
objections to the union, and brought her home out of
the reach of danger. All this was six years ago. To
one who knew Colonel Byrd, it might as well have
been sixty. Having once decreed the dissolution of
the contract—if contract there were—no arguments
framed by man, and no tears wept by woman, could
stir his resolution.

Yet here was his daughter's lover—still hers—the
favorite of the Byrd household, in the master's absence
and under an assumed name making the most of the
privileges accorded him by the step-mother's partiality
for him above all other visitors, and the daughter's
complicity in the conspiracy devised by Martha Jaqueline and her fellow-voyager ! Divers names and titles
had been fitted to the mysterious suitor for whose sake
some prophesied that the fair Evelyn would die un-
wedded,—but " Francis" and plain " Mr." were not
among them. The one joint in the evidence which
Colin had difficulty in adjusting was Madam Byrd's
connivance in the deception. Her awe of her husband
and dread of angering him would be potent dissuasives
from any course of conduct that opposed his will, and
joined to these was her notorious impatience with
Evelyn's affairs of the heart. She probably wished to

see her step-daughter settled in life before her own girls came upon the carpet, but Colin had detected too many tokens of intolerance with the adoration of Miss Byrd's numerous admirers to credit her active co-operation in a scheme so perilous as this. Under the show of deference paid by Mr. Francis to his hostess, there probably lurked the design of securing her as an ally against the day of battle which was inevitable, but Madam was not the woman to serve wittingly as a stepping-stone or blind for sentimental amours.

Still, his own ears had heard her call him, "Your Lordship!"

It is within bounds to say that never, since the outset of his ambitious career, had the rising man of his tribe been more befogged, more utterly distraught, dubious as to fact, and undecided as to action, than while he continued to play caryatide against the wreathed walls of the drawing-room to which he knew he was admitted upon sufferance as the humble *protégé* of one who set and defied laws at his audacious pleasure.

"M. Tartuffe appears to-night in a new part,—as the Knight of the Rueful Countenance," remarked Evelyn's partner, in the practised subtone that enables one to say the most confidential things without exciting suspicion of secret-service work in the minds of lookers-on. "And sustains it passably well."

Evelyn's soft laughter was irrepressible. It was easy to move her to merriment this evening, and a glance at the dourness of a visage in ludicrous contrast to the universal hilarity about him overcame the im-

pulse to pity the lonely man. She recovered herself
in an instant, to say, remorsefully,—

"Why will you name him 'Tartuffe'? He is no
hypocrite, nor yet especially religious. He lays no
schemes for working harm to others and profit to himself. He is a commonplace, respectable, faithful re-
tainer of our family. But for him a token you wot of
would have miscarried the other day, and you would
not have been here to-night. I am ashamed to have
laughed. You ought to repent that you made me
laugh."

"I repent of nothing that blesses my eyes with the
music of lang syne. As to yonder knight, while I
must say of him, always, what came to my mind the
first moment my eyes beheld him,—

> 'Non amo te, Zabidi, nec possum dicere quare ;
> Hoc tantum possum dicere, non amo te,'—

I could be grateful to him for winning that laugh for
me. You look, this evening, as you looked in the
first months of our acquaintanceship, as on the day of
your first drawing-room, when you honored a trembling
adorer by accepting the fan won in a wager. Fairer—
if that could be ! Not a day older, nor a degree more
sedate. Something has beguiled you out of partial
shadow into full sunshine,—my lily among thorns !"

She raised a look to him it was lucky no one else
saw. Martha Jaqueline's simile of the unguarded
loop-holes was just.

"That is because I am strangely happy ! I cannot
tell you—or myself—why. Only that the burden and
the clouds have been rolled away—after so long a

time,—oh, how long! They may return to-morrow; but to-night"—with pretty defiance of Fate—"I am happy! I will say it!"

"And hopeful—at last?"

She suffered the passionate gaze to read her soul; repeated the words with a smile like clear shining after rain,—

"And hopeful—at last!"

The majestic measures of the minuet permitted the by-play of earnest talk, but neither spoke again until the foot of the room was reached. The admiring regards of one and another were attracted to them as they passed along, hand-in-hand, until all were gazers, and a babble of exclamations underran the rhythmic beat of feet, the wail of the violins. The high-bred air and striking beauty of the pair would have distinguished them in any assembly, but to the dullest imagination they seemed to carry with them an atmosphere of their own. The world had fallen away from them; they were two freed, rejoicing spirits, guarded by grave-eyed loves, each with finger on lip to warn back trespassers from the hallowed ground trodden by maid and man.

At the bottom of the room they turned in the order prescribed by the dance, and stood, still silent, still hand-in-hand, the same mystic glory of exaltation in face and attitude.

A bustle about the door diverted the wondering attention of the company. There had been arrivals since the minuet began. A magnificent figure appeared at the entrance of the drawing-room, bowing to his companion to precede him.

Mr. and Mrs. Harrison, who were not dancing, hastened to receive distinguished and belated guests. An eager buzz went down the double ranks of the dancers, arousing the two rapt dreamers to the very present and actual:

"Colonel Byrd and Governor Spotswood!"

CHAPTER X.

DECIDEDLY Madam Maria Byrd's fine spirits and glib tongue were in league against her common sense that night, and Mr. Francis was a circumspect confidant.

Martha Jaqueline would have shrieked in wicked glee, Hannah Harrison been lost in mild astonishment, and Lieutenant Maynard would have sworn in his beard, had they known the purport of the voluble dame's divulgations to the stranger within her ornate gates. The listener, while he had a tolerably correct idea of the facts in the alleged betrothal case, did not consider himself called upon to betray familiarity with the "warrior's" antecedents, or that he had divined his identity at sight.

Martha Jaqueline met Lieutenant Maynard to-night for the first time in a year and more,—a meeting that quieted whatever gossip connecting their names had outlived the twelvemonth. It was not his place to tell that ever since her return he had been cruising the Carolina coast in quest of smugglers and pirates in smugglers' clothing, and in the intervals of duty, cursing the luck that had sent him out of the James and the Chesapeake when he most ardently longed to be within hail of the big, square homestead, swathed in ivy, flanked by "orchards fruited deep," and overlooking, as far as eye could reach, acres of low grounds fat with alluvial deposit. He was, as has been intimated, past the earlier prime of manhood, his hair was grizzled upon the temples, and his close-cropped beard streaked with like mementos of years past and passing. Martha Jaqueline, his junior by over a dozen years, had a lively sense of the ridiculous that made her the terror of, stupidity and incompetency. Hannah Harrison was little older by calendar-rendering, ten years the elder in staid propriety of demeanor. People had laughed until they were tired of the jest, at the gallant officer's open devotion to the madcap girl in her teens, and frowned at the naughty encouragement it suited her humor to give him. Everybody winked approvingly when he seemed to come to his senses, after throwing away more time than a man of his age could spare, and transferred his allegiance to Admiral Harrison's well-endowed daughter. Hannah was his firm friend, and in no danger of taking offence if, while dancing with her, he looked at and talked of the black-eyed girl in gold-colored taffeta selected in Paris to match the amber ornaments he had given to her at their parting, a year ago.

Nothing of which entered into Madam Byrd's complacent imaginings. Her eyes saw far, but only along the surface of the field,—a not uncommon peculiarity in people who pride themselves upon penetrative acuteness, and are diffuse in advertising the property. Foam does not belong to deep-sea soundings, as the noted pirate-hunter could have told her.

Martha was then, and ever afterward, grateful for his chance proximity when, glancing toward the door at the confused hum of announcement, she beheld the last man upon earth she cared to see at that moment. Instinctively raising her fan to the level of the mouth she felt was working uncontrollably, and not daring to look toward Evelyn, she said in incoherent haste,—

"Say something, or do something—*quick!* No matter what!—only make people look at *you!* Don't look to see who is at the door! For heaven's sake— *now!*"

Accustomed to quarter-deck discipline, and ever readier to act than to think, the sailor, thus adjured, hung his left heel in Madam Byrd's satin train,—in the effort to extricate it, slid hopelessly with the right foot upon the glassy boards, and measured six feet of robust humanity directly across the dancers' track, with a concussion that shook the solid beams. In a paroxysm of thankfulness, Martha Jaqueline sprang forward and offered both hands to assist him in rising.

"Well done! well done!" she said, in accents strangling between laughter and crying. "But can you do *nothing* in moderation? Half the fall would have served my purpose and bruised you less!"

The music stopped; everybody crowded around to inquire—to sympathize—and, when it was evident that no harm was done, to join in the laugh led by the unterrified warrior and Miss Jaqueline.

Her face was glowing, her voice shook hysterically, as after quiet was restored she conducted Mr. Francis up to the two most distinguished men in His Majesty's Colony of Virginia.

"Will your Excellency allow me to present Mr. Francis, my particular friend and Mrs. Byrd's guest,—who is visiting Virginia from England?

"Colonel Byrd! the only drawback to our sojourn under your roof has been your absence. Your return leaves nothing for us to ask of Fate."

The lie was dashingly enunciated. It was not a time for consultation with conscience. She might commend half-way measures in the matter of the Lieutenant's bones, but nothing stopped or stayed her when a leap was to be taken.

The rugged features of the Colony's greatest Governor relaxed; the deep-set eyes twinkled at sight of the dark, arch visage upraised to him with the confiding fearlessness of a petted child who expects indulgent notice. He bestowed a cordial handshake upon her "friend," spoke a few words of welcome to Virginia, and laid his brawny hand lightly upon the girl's smooth brown arm.

"My dear young lady! if I were not fearful of arousing the envy of every other man present, I would claim a salute from your lips in token of the friendship I bore your father, whose face I see repeated in your own."

"Is it quite fair in your Excellency to let the dread of angering a few dozen *men*"—disdainfully emphatic—"outweigh the honor such recognition would confer upon *me?*" retorted the witch, with a tempting pout of the ripe mouth.

The soldier-ruler, the Tubal Cain of Virginia, the lately-appointed Postmaster-General of the American Colonies—stooped his grand head and kissed the fair pleader in heartiness of good-will that called forth a chorus of applause.

"What can the man do that cometh after the king?" said the rich, sonorous voice of the Master of West-over.

He bowed so low in pressing Martha's hand to his lips that the reverence was almost a genuflexion. "I beg you to believe, sir,"—to Mr. Francis,—"that, if the Englishman and stranger needed other commendation to my regard than these circumstances, he has it in the friendship of this fair lady."

The two men looked squarely into one another's eyes during the little speech, and while the stranger replied:

"I am proud to owe to her the consideration with which you distinguish me!"

They took the time and pains to say such things in that All-So-Long-Ago, and would have reckoned as boorishly curt the address that disdained gracious ceremony. For all that, blood and passion were no gentler than in our realistic times. One heart, at least, quailed at a certain settling of the urbane muscles about the mouth, as Evelyn saw her father bestow a more searching look upon the face of his new acquaintance, as if something in voice or feature impressed him—and not agreeably.

By tacit consent, Mr. Francis came near her no more that evening, and supplied the gossips with no more spice by apparent wavering from his fealty to his reputed betrothed. He was Martha Jaqueline's shadow, sparing never a look in the direction of the lily others thought sweet and fair. The one other woman singled out for his particular attention was the hostess whose partner he was in the Virginia reel that wound up the festivities.

"Come to us to-morrow!" she said, under a conventional smile. "The risk is too great to be taken needlessly,"—continuing, after he had "turned" her in the figure,—"my heart failed me for fear when I saw him. His last letter home said he would be away a fortnight longer."

"Since it must come, let it come!" Francis uttered with lips whose curves told no more than hers. "The masquerade is 'an excellent piece of work, Madam Lady!—would it were done!'"

"Yet you come of a race of diplomatists!"

"Aye!" They were at the top of the set, and no other two were, to all appearance, chatting more lightly. "Since my ancestor, Henry Mordaunt, was proxy for his liege, King James the Second, then Duke of York, and brought home to England the beauteous Mary of Modena, who afterward followed his broken fortunes into exile. But the part suits me ill. I favor *finesse* less than fair fight. I am sorely tempted to risk all upon one bold throw."

"You would lose all!"

"Not if I have read aright twin-stars that were never brighter than to-night!"

"Sweet stars!" Mrs. Harrison's own eyes glistened. "I marked them—and so did many who read their meaning less truly. But"—returning to the charge— "come to us on the morrow! Martha will, I am positive, agree with me. The carriage will call for you at noon."

"You could propose nothing, in the circumstances,

i

that would better suit my humor. It is hardly honorable to play sapper and miner to the house in which I eat bread and salt. But Colonel Byrd has already, in my hearing, invited Mr. Harrison and sundry other gentlemen to meet Governor Spotswood and my humble self at his table to-morrow, and I fear that I could hardly refuse to remain until evening without seeming uncivil. After dinner, I shall be gratefully at your service, and Mistress Martha's. When I have withdrawn to longer range I shall conduct the siege vigorously. Within two days I drop mask and domino, and claim mine own—in other things as well as name and title."

The great hall-clock struck twelve as the Westover party entered the arched doorway on their return,—a deep-throated chime, mellowed and measured as a cathedral-bell.

"Another day is dead!" said the Master. "To nest! to nest! my bonny birds! if you would hop and chirp at dawn! Here comes the mother of the maids to drive you up with her!" as Miss Lotsie rustled her stiff black gown down the staircase. "And you, my lady-wife,—albeit your roses are of a hardier sort than those that faded in the lassies' cheeks an hour agone,—must get rest, that you may shame them in the Governor's eyes at dinner. Mistress Martha! grant the humblest of your votaries place in the background of your dreams. Evelyn, child! it is well I came home to save you from the consequences of too much junketing. And so, good-night, and GOD be with us all!"

He said it airily, giving none opportunity for dissent or other reply; with hat under his arm, handed Madam Byrd up the first flight; kissed his daughter's cheek

and Martha's hand, and ran lightly down to the group
of men left standing below.

A pull upon the bell-rope brought a sleepy footman
from the dining-room, and Caliban, agile as a cat, and
wide-awake as a night-hawk, from the direction of the
kitchen.

"Lights in the drawing-room!" ordered the Master.
"Decanters, glasses, and pipes!"

In an amazingly short time the gleam of six wax
candles was thrown back from the mantel-mirror and
struck out keener glints from cut-glass and silver set
in array upon the central table. A chandelier depended
from the ceiling, and to this Colonel Byrd pointed,
without speaking. Caliban produced from behind the
green branches filling the chimney a slender wand of
pitch-pine, ignited the tip, and reached up at the length
of his arm, to kindle the dozen wax candles overhead.
A wave of the Master's hand dismissed the elder servant; Caliban took his station behind his owner's
chair, ready to fill glasses, and light the capacious bowls
soon filled with tobacco.

Colonel Byrd and his companion, ex-Governor Spotswood, had ridden forty miles that day over a rough
country, arriving at Westover half an hour after the
chariot had driven from the door bearing the revellers
to Berkeley. The two men had supped together,
dressed, and repaired to the gay scene, to ruffle it there
with the bravest for two hours. It was significant of
the social customs of the age that neither servants nor
guests saw anything strange in the preparations for
"making a night of it." The courtier-planter was
indefatigable alike in business and in pleasure, and

complimented associates by assuming their physical
forces to be equal to his own.   There was meaning in
the selection of the drawing-room as the theatre of
what could not be vulgar orgies while he presided, and
Mr. Fontaine made one at the board.   It was such fes-
tivity as became the rich toilettes of the merry-makers.
Had they come in, spurred, booted, and muddy, from
chase or journey, pipes and liquors would have been
served in study or library.

Madam had her whisper to Miss Lotsie in the hall
above-stairs.   Her sanguine complexion had paled;
her eyes were startled; her double chin was flabby.

"My holiday is over!   And—it may be only the
vapors, after so much routing and racketing—but I
feel as if there were thunder in the air, and the lightning
were going to strike not far from me!"

"You are out of sorts, now!   To-morrow you'll feel
better!" grated the friend of her neighbor.

Then she shut herself into the room where Evelyn
had sunk upon the floor, her silken robes crushed about
her, her head in Martha Jaqueline's lap.

———

CHAPTER XI.

"Pray be seated, gentlemen!" entreated the Master
of the house of Governor Spotswood, Mr. Fontaine,
Lieutenant Maynard, and Mr. Francis,—and, affably,
to the sixth personage present,—"sit down, Bass, and
have a glass with us!"

Too well-bred to patronize one who, by his invitation,

was to put his feet under the same table with himself, he yet contrived a subtle difference between his manner of bidding him and that directed to the rest,—a difference flattering or humiliating, as one chose to construe it into favor or good-humored toleration. The secretary sat down a marked man to the apprehension of his companions. It could not be surmised from the smug stolidity of his visage whether or not he appreciated the fact.

"I abhor semi-obscurity!" continued the Colonel, drawing a full breath through the stem of his gold-mounted pipe. "When once a man's courting days are done, he considers twilight a blunder. It, with the moon and stars, would seem to have been continued for the especial illumination of Fools' Paradise. Saving our good chaplain's presence, I might, reverently, suggest a doubt if the game be worth so many candles. I mistrust that my excellent friend, Colonel Spotswood, will challenge me on this head. Less, it may be, out of jealousy for the honor of the Creator, who presumably apportions means to ends, than for fear my Lady Spotswood might hear of my heresy. You, Maynard, who must have a sufficiently lively recollection of the railing accusations he was wont to bring against matrimony in the days of his unregenerate bachelorhood, would be edified and confounded could you see what an uxorious Benedick he has become. In practice and in precept, he is the exemplar to all husbands within a dozen miles of Germanna. But, having the honor to be tolerably well acquainted with her who has wrought the revolution, I can testify that seldom has a man had fairer cause for a change of creed and behavior."

The Governor's visage was crimson—in the seamed cheeks, purple—with a queer sort of shamefaced satisfaction, very comical to the beholders. Never adroit at jovial repartee, he twisted uneasily upon his seat and diverted the conversation at a right angle.

"Is this Varina tobacco, Byrd?" he asked, in the strident tones his enemies—and they were many—were used to hear in philippic and mandate.

"It is a worthier brand than Varina. (By the way, we say 'Henrico,' now!) It was grown and cured, then ripened at Westover, and has a finer flavor than ever belonged to the once famous Varina tobacco. *That* lived upon its reputation for half a century, until it—the repute, I mean—fell to pieces from sheer rottenness.

"Varina, you will understand, Mr. Francis, is a plantation near the head of navigation on James River, and was once owned by Master John Rolfe, who wedded Pocahontas, the daughter of King Powhatan. The whey-faced son-in-law was a thrifty man and a cunning. I do not affirm that he set on foot the idle tale of certain valuable secrets connected with the culture and curing of the bewitching vegetable, tobacco, which had been confided to him by his royal relative. But his crops brought larger prices for the tradition."

"Aspersion of John Rolfe would not come with a good grace from you, Colonel," observed Fontaine, to spare the stranger the trouble of reply upon a subject of which he was probably ignorant. "*He* was brave enough to put into successful operation your favorite scheme of Christianizing the savages,—to wit, intermarriage with the English settlers."

Francis laughed.

"We believe what we like of that, Mr. Fontaine! The fame of Colonel Byrd's nice taste in such matters is too well established to be easily shaken."

The Colonel fixed his brilliant dark eyes—so like his daughter's—upon the Englishman's face, which he seemed to study while he went on to vindicate his position. His manner—courteous, yet seldom free from the dash of cynicism or banter one traces in his diary and correspondence—was, or so Fontaine and Bass fancied, slightly abstracted during the harangue, as if he sought for some forgotten clue.

"At the risk of endangering my reputation for fastidiousness with you, Mr. Francis, conscience urges me to full confession of my sentiments upon what you and other Englishmen of fashion may consider as an unsavory subject. It is my deliberate and unalterable belief that, had the first English settlers in America intended either to civilize or convert the savages, they should have encouraged intermarriage with them upon every conceivable occasion. The natives could by no means persuade themselves that the pale-faces were heartily their friends so long as the meanest of them disdained to take an Indian maiden to wife. The French have not been so squeamish in Canada, where, upon trial, they find abundance of attraction in the Indians. Their late Grand Monarch thought it not below even the dignity of a Frenchman to become one flesh with this people, and therefore ordered that a bounty of one hundred livres be bestowed upon any of his subjects, man or woman, that would intermarry with a native.

"By this piece of policy we find the French interest much strengthened among the savages, and their religion—*such as it is*"—unable, as a zealous Church of England man, to withhold the fling—"propagated just as far as their love. And I heartily hope that this well-concerted scheme may not hereafter give the French an advantage over His Majesty's good subjects on the Northern Continent of America."

"The thought of amalgamation is odious and vile to my way of thinking!" Maynard struck in, bluntly. "With Mr. Francis, I decline to credit your sincerity. Zounds, man! fancy yourself the husband of a copper-colored wench, shining with fish-oil, and with no clothes on to speak of except a blanket strapped about the waist by a thong of deer's hide! Think of the filth and vermin of her wigwam, as you and I have seen it! Ugh!"

Colonel Byrd put down his pipe, and produced his snuff-box from the pocket of his embroidered waistcoat, without change in the half-smile of friendly *camaraderie* he had worn all along; tapped the lid, opened it, offered it to Francis, and took a pinch with dainty thumb and finger. On the lid, laid right under his eyes, Francis read, "*In memoriam Johannes Cary & Jacobi Dryden. January prim. 1679.*"

"Your imagination should go into the buck-basket, Maynard, to be bleached and lavendered," resumed the mellow accents. "*I* was not an early settler! Had I made up my mind to other trials contingent upon my duty to King and New Country, I would have brought my stomach to embrace an alliance manifestly so prudent as this. The Indians would have had less reason

to complain that the English took away their land
if the white men had received it by way of portion
with their daughters. Had such affinities been contracted in the beginning, how much bloodshed had been
prevented, and how populous would the country have
been,—consequently, how considerable! Nor would
the shade of the skin have been any reproach at this
day. If a Moor may be washed white in three gener-
rations, surely an Indian might be blanched in two."

He passed the snuff-box over to Maynard, who shook
his head impatiently.

"Gloze it over as you will, the idea is filthy, immoral,
and unchristian! By your own showing, you put blackamoor and Indian upon the same footing. Let them
practise voudoo and pow-wow together and mingle
bloods. Don't degrade the finer race to which you
belong by such horrible unnaturalness of doctrine."

"It is rappee—ripe and royal!" The Colonel continued to hold out the snuff-box, insinuatingly, his
smile full of arch enjoyment. "No? You would feel
better if you took it! To proceed with our argument.
The aboriginal Indian is many degrees higher in the
scale of being than the African negro. Our savages
are usually tall and well-proportioned, a circumstance
which ought to make amends for the darkness of their
complexions. Add to this, that they are healthy and
strong, with constitutions untainted by evil practices
and not enfeebled by luxury. Besides, morals and all
considered, I cannot think the Indians were much
greater heathens than the first settlers at Jamestown,
who built a church that cost fifty pounds, and a hostelry
that cost five hundred. Had they been truly pious and

wise in their generation, they would have had the charity to take the only method of converting the red-skins to Christianity."

The stalwart ex-Governor had hearkened up to this point in silence that was plainly not acquiescent. Knowing himself to be no match for his polished friend in word-fencing, and looking, perhaps, for aid to the clergyman whose reticence began to look ominous, he had held in as with bit and bridle the energetic protest that now burst forth by its own weight.

"*I* call such talk idle and ribald! Were it not that I believe you to be carrying out a jest which is in anything but good taste, I would not sit at the same table with you. The Indian's soul is as white as yours or mine, and must be saved by the same means. In our school mission at Fort Christanna we taught them to pray out of our Book of Common Prayer, to read their Bibles and to live decent Christian lives. I am glad to be able to state, as the result of these teachings, that the women—who were straight and well-limbed, of good shape and extraordinary good features—were very modest and faithful to their husbands, and mighty shy of Englishmen. They would not let one of us so much as touch them!"

It was not in the man-nature of that liberal day to refrain from a shout of laughter at the climax, especially as the resentful intonation of the early portion of the defence of his *protégés* swelled out with odd effect in what he designed as a "clinching" fact.

The Westover magnate lay back in his arm-chair, his eyes shining with mischievous delight, and struck his palms together.

"Bravo! bravo! Or would you rather we gave you a vote of sympathy? We need only lend Maynard rope enough to see him hang himself as cleverly. Even now he dare not wag his tongue in denial of my dogma that, after all that can be said, a sprightly lover is the most prevailing missionary that can be sent among the Indians at large, or any other infidels—unless we except, by courtesy"—laughing musically—"Governor Spotswood's Christanna lambkins!"

Mr. Fontaine interposed with characteristic tact and delicacy.

"Our wise politicians settled the question for us in Virginia, once and for all, at the beginning of our settlement here. When they heard that Rolfe had married Pocahontas, it was deliberated in Council whether or not he had committed high treason in that he had taken to wife an Indian princess, and had not some troubles intervened which put a stop to the inquiry, the luckless lover might have been hanged for doing what other statesmen beside Colonel Byrd reckoned the most just, natural, generous, and politic action that was ever done on this side of the water. The action of the Home government put an effectual stop to all intermarriages of this sort—that is, between whites and Indians."

Caliban had moved out of the shadow of the tall back of his master's chair to replenish Lieutenant Maynard's glass, compounding the beverage with noiseless dexterity, and gliding back to his ambush as Mr. Fontaine paused before the last section of his remark,— a pause that pointed his meaning.

"Pass the tobacco, my boy!" said the Colonel, kindly,

and as the light streamed upon the lad's supple limbs and golden-russet complexion, he added—"*Intermarriages!* yes! When there is a choice of evils, the wise man takes the lesser. We would not use a moral method to convert the savage. The cross of races is effected all the same. The Puritan fathers, the Baptists, and other New England dissenters, were of like mind with the first adventurers to Virginia, anent Indian alliances, false delicacy that created in the natives a jealousy that the English were ill-affected toward them. Many of the poor wretches paid for their scruples with their lives, so we will not add our censure to their miseries. The Quaker favorite of a Popish prince—William Penn—managed to carry his dish straighter. He purchased lands of the Indians, and paid for them—only a trifle, to be sure ; but that they paid anything gained them the credit of being more righteous than their neighbors. They had, likewise, the prudence to treat them kindly, which saved them from many of the wars and massacres wherein the other colonies were indiscreetly involved. A people whose principles forbid them to draw the carnal sword have no right to give provocation. They vaunt somewhat overmuch the harmlessness of their sect, and having, like their founder, no vices but such as are private, they have made Pennsylvania into a very fine country."

It was at this stage of the discussion that Francis chanced to look up at a portrait upon the wall directly opposite his chair, and experienced a faint shock, as of one who is covertly watched. The blaze of the wax-lights met upon the face and figure of a man superb in the costume of Queen Anne's court. His right hand rested upon his hip; on a table at his side glittered a heap of medals and chains. Conspicuous among his personal adornments was a medallion-miniature of his royal mistress, surrounded by brilliants, on the right breast. His cravat and wrist-ruffles were of priceless lace; a flowing perruque framed a haughty, handsome face. There was a lurking, sardonic devil in the eyes that seemed, to the young man, to survey him mockingly.

He had heard the story of the picture from Madam Byrd. The original, General Daniel Parke, a Virginian by birth, was the father of the first Mrs. Byrd. He had served under Marlborough at Blenheim, and by his splendid valor earned the right to bear news of the victory to the Queen. The immediate reward of Marlborough's messenger was the miniature so proudly displayed. The more valuable gift was the governor-ship of the Leeward Islands, where, after four years of a cruel and arrogant administration, he was killed in an uprising of the people. Madam had, in Evelyn's absence from the drawing-room, supplied graphic details of the public and private misdoings of the girl's maternal grandfather. Francis had mentally discounted the tales to his own satisfaction, but the sinister regard he felt upon him now recalled the most unpleasant of them. As a puff of wandering air swayed the candle-flames, he could have fancied a sneer upon the full lips.

He had known that he could not remain under Colonel Byrd's roof after the master's return, and respect himself. He had not expected discomfort and self-contempt to begin so soon, or that they would be engendered by the steadfast gaze of a living man and intensified by the furtive scrutiny of a portrait's eyes. There was something uncanny in the chill that crept upward to his heart while the talk, which seemed impersonal, proceeded, as if, once in a while, the coil of an anaconda were cast about him.

Spotswood was speaking when he again lent an ear to outward things.

"No other colony has thriven more steadily than Pennsylvania. Had Penn lived until our times, he might have said with Jacob, 'With my staff' passed I over this Jordan, and I am now become five bands!'"

"Six! my dear Governor! six! His original grant was for a slip of land lying between the Jerseys and Maryland, containing three counties. He pushed his interest still further with His Pope-loving Highness, and obtained a fresh grant of New Castle, Kent, and Sussex, which still remained within the New York patent, and had been luckily left out of the grant of New Jersey. All were incorporated, and dignified with the name of Pennsylvania,—a pretty pastoral title befitting the broad-brimmed hat that promised protection to shoals of his peaceable sect. Verily, Friend William had a long head for this world, if not for the next,— and doubtless he has had his reward."

"Don't sneer at a better Christian than yourself, Byrd, because he belonged to a sect instead of to the Church. 'By their fruits ye shall know them.' Penn and his followers abide the divine test."

"By *what* fruits shall we know them?" The Colonel lounged indolently in his roomy chair, and with a silver tobacco-stopper pressed down the contents of the pipe

Caliban had filled and lighted. "By the public record, known and read of all men, or the secret history of which few on this side of the Atlantic have heard?"

"I am not advised of such a chapter," returned the Governor, coldly.

"Nor I!" said Maynard, stoutly. "And when the character of a dead man is involved, I dispute the story in advance, unless it be supported by indubitable authority."

Byrd's laugh and lounge were undisturbed by the unflattering tone of the doughty couple.

"The tale was well known in England, where I first heard it, long after the parties most nearly concerned were in the dumb grave. It was surprising to Penn's contemporaries who were not behind the scenes, how a Quaker should be so much in the graces of a Popish prince, but it was pretty well accounted for by those versed in back-stair politics. This ingenious gentleman was not born a Quaker, but in his earlier days had been a man of pleasure about the town. He had a beautiful form and very taking address which made him successful with the ladies, and purchased for him the reversionary right to a favorite of the Duke of Monmouth. She presented sweet William with a daughter who had beauty enough to raise her to be a Duchess and continued to be a toast full thirty years.

"Don't be afraid of that brandy, Mr. Francis!" seeing him put his hand over his glass as Caliban would have filled it. "It was made from peaches grown on the plantation in 1715, the year my daughter, Mrs. Chamberlayne, was born, and has been twice to the West Indies and back. That your right-hand

neighbor is a water-bibber signifies nothing in the way
of example. It is our excellent chaplain's one weakness, to refuse the noblest form in which the kindly
fruits of the earth are offered to sinful man."

"I am no water-bibber," rejoined Francis, smiling.
"But British brains must be seasoned gradually to
American potations. Suffer me to commend the
brandy with no stint of word, however grudging you
may esteem my deeds. I have tasted nothing so fine
in any country. It has the gleam of the topaz, the
sweetness of honey, and the smoothness of oil."

The bland seignior bowed profoundly.

"Which right eloquent tribute to a princely drink
shall go on record in the archives of the Westover
Cellar. Mr. Bass will forget not one whit of it and
transcribe it in clerkly wise to-morrow. Our brace of
scandal-mongers are chafing with impatience at the
interruption in our *chronicle scandaleuse*,"—feigning
to frown at Spotswood and Maynard. "Life in the
provinces begets a taste for gossip as all dead things
fester into life. I grieve, gentlemen, that the most
corrupt part of the story has already been told. I
have but to add that the aforesaid amour had like to
have brought our fine gentleman in danger of a duel,
whereupon he discreetly sheltered himself under the
peaceable persuasion of Master George Fox. His
father had been a flag-officer in the navy while the
Duke of York was Lord High Admiral, and may have
recommended the son to his favor. I trust this piece
of secret history may wipe from the minds of my wor-
shipful listeners any suspicions that our thrifty Penn
was popishly inclined."

"If half you hint be true,* he would better have been a clean Papist," rejoined Spotswood, severely. "A shaven monk who wrote the Ten Commandments upon his bare back with a scourge were a better citizen. Not that I believe the tale to be worth contradicting. It is truly what you have named it,—a chronicle of the back-stairs. Thank GOD we have none such in our newer and cleaner land!"

"We have among us monuments in abundance of the rule of this same papistical influence," Byrd retorted, in unmoved calmness. "Virginia is scarred from head to heel, behind and before, by the knife forged and sharpened three thousand miles away. Witness the excision of her goodliest arm, the Maryland deeded one hundred years ago by King Charles the First—the Martyr, as we name him—to his favorite (or the Queen's), George Calvert. It begat much speculation, even then, how it came about that a good Protestant King should bestow so bountiful a grant upon a zealous Roman Catholic. 'Tis probable it was one fatal instance among many others of His Majesty's complaisance to the Queen. When to the influence of lovely woman at home is joined that of the Scarlet Woman at Rome, you have a devil no man—or nation —can lay."

His eyes, straying from the Englishman's non-committal face to the hand resting upon the table, saw the fingers contract spasmodically. The planter removed

---

* The author does not hold herself responsible for the "piece of secret history" related in this chapter. It is taken—for the most part *verbatim et literatim*—from Colonel Byrd's own MSS., and is therefore curious, if not valuable.

his pipe from his mouth and leaned slightly forward. His tone was gravely polite, with a sub-accent of apology :

"I crave pardon on my own behalf, as on that of my companions, if we are trenching upon debatable ground, Mr. Francis. In our slip-shod talk over cups and pipes we are losing sight of the possibility that the rough gabble may displease you. I have, perchance, taken too much for granted in supposing that the favored guest of the Huguenot Jaquelines must, perforce, be of their communion."

Francis looked up at the portrait opposite. Something in the malicious scrutiny of the dark eyes compelled an answering glance. The anaconda coil was tight upon his heart and lungs. He touched his dried lips with his tongue before speaking, but his voice was firm.

"If I hesitate to answer you directly, Colonel Byrd, it is out of fear lest you should reproach yourself overmuch for what was, at most, pardonable inadvertence. To Madame Jaqueline's household I have made no secret—I wish to make none here—of the truth that my faith is that of my fathers. Ours is an old Catholic family. I may suffer in the esteem of those with whom I would fain stand well"—a swift glance and almost imperceptible inclination of the head including all present—"by the confession, but to withhold it would be cowardly and traitorous."

Simultaneously, Spotswood, from one side, and Fontaine from the other, stretched out a hand of cordial sympathy.

The Governor added to his vice-like grip :

"That's brave and right, sir! Show your colors, young gentleman, let what will follow! This is a land of liberty and toleration. You are more welcome to it than before you spoke!"

The son of the Huguenot refugee said never a word, but the mute pressure and expressive eyes left no need for speech.

"Upon my soul!" blurted out Maynard, "one would suppose that the possibility of this sort of thing might have come into some of our numskulls. For myself, Mr. Francis, I can only beg a thousand pardons, and congratulate myself upon the lucky fact that you are more of a gentleman than I, or you would have cut our talk in two an hour ago."

In the excitement of the moment, the humorous side of the abject apology from one who had not opened his lips upon the Roman Catholic question, was seen by no one unless it were the self-possessed host. He arose, and bowed regretfully to his foreign guest.

"'Twould be but wasting words for me to reiterate my friends' apologies and assurances of deepest respect for one who is not ashamed to avow his true character and sentiments, whatever may be the consequences. '*Fiat justitia, ruat cœlum!*' The sky-fall in this instance should overwhelm us, not you, with confusion."

The young man had grown very pale.

"Let it pass, I implore you!" he said, huskily. "I do not merit all—or aught—of the gracious things that have been said. I am humbled by the hearing of them." He reached out for a pipe of tobacco. "If you will allow me, I will smoke the pipe of peace with all of you, and rejoice in so good an excuse to indulge myself in another bowlful of what Colonel Byrd calls 'the bewitching vegetable.' Westover tobacco is as seductive, after a modest sort, as Westover brandy. I never guessed until lately"—his voice regaining firmness and lightness—" what we owe to Sir Walter Raleigh for introducing it into Christendom. If I have been rightly informed, it was he who first brought it to England ?"

The Colonel lifted his glass to his lips in a gesture of indescribable grace. Amity, gratitude, renewed goodfellowship, and oblivion—all were pledged in the action.

" It is a privilege to meet one who is correctly advised upon a matter so interesting to Parent Country and Colonies. I have heard learned Englishmen—aye! and not unlearned colonists—discourse seriously of the probability that Christopher Columbus imported tobacco into Spain. Had this been, is it likely that so accomplished a gentleman as Walter Raleigh, and one who had travelled so much and so far, should not have known of the delightful narcotic, and adopted the use thereof ?"

Spotswood demurred :

" Yet the tobacco of Varina, Spain, was of so high repute in 1622, that Rolfe's plantation was named therefor. It was fancied that the tobacco raised there had somewhat of the same flavor."

" So worthy a thing would have made good a claim upon the consideration of mankind in forty years or thereabouts. I have looked narrowly into the question, and discovered no cause for doubt that Sir Walter's first expedition to these shores took back the first tobacco that ever touched European soil. I have heard my father relate how the gallant Baronet, having fallen in love with his new treasure, thought he could do no less than make a present of some of the brightest of it to his royal mistress for her own smoking.

"The Queen graciously accepted of it, but finding her stomach sicken after two or three whiffs, it was presently whispered by the Earl of Leicester's faction that Sir Walter had certainly poisoned her. Her Majesty soon recovering her disorder, obliged the Countess of Nottingham and all her maids to smoke a whole pipe out amongst them. There is no climate that produces everything since the deluge wrenched the poles of the earth out of place, nor is it fit that it should be so, because it is the mutual supply one country receives from another which creates a mutual traffic and intercourse among men. But I dare affirm that this same colony of Virginia brings forth as many, as various, and as valuable products as are to be found in any quarter of the globe. I doubt me if the Land of Eden were more prolific of the necessaries and the luxuries of life."

" Peach brandy standing for one, and tobacco for the other ?" queried the Englishman, again quite at his ease.

The planter smiled genially.

" If you like. Or you may reverse the order. Maynard! you are nodding! Don't perjure yourself by denying it! The energy with which you prostrated yourself at Mistress Martha's feet this evening has wrought upon your strength,—gamesome young buck

though you are.   And there are the races to-morrow !
We'll finish our pipes and toss off our heel-taps, and so
to bed."

A three-cornered note, with a few strands of hair
passed about it and caught together under the seal, was
stuck in the frame of the mirror above the toilette-table
in the room occupied by Francis that night.   It was
without address or signature, but the hand was Martha
Jaqueline's.   Francis looked closely at the hair, detached
it from the wax, smiled, and winding the stray threads
into a coil upon his palm, kissed it before reading the
billet of a line-and-a-half :

" *I shall go through the garden at eight o'clock to-
morrow morning to the church-yard.*"

CHAPTER XII.

The Berkeley race-course was laid out in an exact
circle upon the level stretch between the mansion-house
and the high-road beyond which lay the Westover
estate.

The perfect autumn day succeeding the ball brought
out the countryside in strength.   Chariots, from which
the horses had been removed, surrounded, in close ranks,
the outer sweep of the course, and were filled with gay
parties of both sexes.   The ladies and guests from the
two contiguous plantations had seats among the judges
on the grand stand, elevated by eight or ten easy steps
from the ground.

"Like—and yet more unlike unto Jacob's ladder !"

observed Martha Jaqueline, watching the ceaseless passage up and down of neighborhood beaux.

It was Colonel Byrd who replied:

"Like—because both lead to heaven. We need not search long for the ' unlike.' The angels came up hither in one troop—and remained. The wandering spirits who ascend only to descend, should have your pity— not scorn—if only because they *are* wanderers!"

"Oh!" sighed the girl, gazing up at him in genuine admiration. "Why does no bachelor understand me as readily and answer me as fitly as you? Yet there are those stupid enough to marvel that I am still Martha Jaqueline! Why was not Evelyn your son, instead of your daughter?"

The courtier stooped lower to her ear.

"In that event, I should to-day have the misery of seeing my son broken-hearted and his rival triumphant!"

"*Colonel Byrd!*" Reproachful look and accent were inimitable. "Could *your son* have a successful rival? You forget that other things would be altered by the transformation of my dear Evelyn into her dearer brother."

"Well done!" clapping his hands. "It is fortunate that our English cavalier has tolerable skill in wordy play, or he might look forward to many a defeat in the combat-matrimonial. He has told you, I take it, of the grievous *faux-pas* I executed last night and his magnanimous treatment of the same?"

"Told *me?* I have hardly set eyes upon him since you drove us poor women off to bed last night, like so many hens at roosting-time."

"You did not look at him then before breakfast? Even your fearless eyes drooped under the ardor of as eloquent a pair of blue ones as ever I beheld? Aha! that pretty air of bewilderment is admirably feigned! You left out of account when you appointed a meeting under the droppings of the sanctuary at bird-matins, that one of my few virtues is early rising. The black silk domino befitted a church-yard tryst, but could not disguise a figure and carriage that have not their like in America—if in the world. I was not near enough to be an eavesdropper, but I saw, with respectful admiration, that you had taken my daughter along to play dragon. She sat in the church-porch—poor thing! wrapped in a blue domino and despairing meditations upon the injustice of Providence in not sending a duplicate lover and a promenade upon the other side of the sacred building to herself."

There was no mistaking the sincerity of her concern as he began his raillery, or the relief she did not attempt to hide as he went on. Her black eyes sparkled with appreciation of the cleverness that had outwitted hers.

"You are ubiquitous! You wear fern-seed in your shoes! I shall never feel safe again within a thousand leagues of you! Fortunately, there is, in the present case, little to conceal—from *you*. One day, and before long, I hope, you will know all. Be assured that nobody else shall know sooner, or more. Until then, and even more afterward, may I ask your indulgence with whatever may seem irregular or unjustifiable in the—*affaire du cœur?* I could never do anything like other girls, you know. Promise me not to be so angry with me that you will strike me out of your books."

He pressed the little hand offered by the earnest pleader, and dropped the tone of badinage in which he habitually accosted her.

"Your father's daughter can ask me nothing in vain, my dear young lady!   Some time—before or after the promised confession—I would, as his deputy, question you somewhat closely anent this good-looking gallant. He comes of a Roman Catholic family, he tells me. It is good—if not noble?"

"Good and old!   I will give you the pedigree when I tell the rest.   But my friend needs no backing up of dead and decayed ancestors to commend him to the confidence of true men and women.   I ask for him but a fair field and no favor—or *disfavor*!   May I depend upon your impartial judgment?"

A keen look, sustained by her without flinching, prefaced the answer.

"You may,—unless it be that your preference must, of itself, bias me.   The Queen's seal carries weight."

"Thank you!   It is a bargain, then, that my signet buys honest and fair consideration for the bearer?"

He promised with cordiality that surprised him in the retrospect.   The girl's known openness of speech and deed, the high sense of honor he had seen her exhibit times without number since her childhood—and, perhaps more than the veteran courtier admitted to himself, her fascination of glance and language, her beauty and vivacity—wrought upon his confidence. They effected more.   They allayed the undefined sensation of discomfort to which he had been subject at intervals since the moment of his introduction to the stranger. The resemblance in person and voice that had at first puzzled, then annoyed him, was clearly accidental and should not influence the behavior of a rational man in association with an unoffending gentleman who was to wed his old friend's daughter. He brushed aside the cobweb of misgiving, and entered zestfully into the business of the hour.

The scene was brilliant and imposing. The space enclosed by the track had, some weeks in advance of race-day, been seeded down with wheat, which, springing up under favoring rains, now showed a carpet of living green. The course, beaten and rolled into the smoothness of a floor, was dotted with stray riders, usually youths in light- or gayly-colored raiment, trotting or galloping from point to point to show off the speed of their horses and their equestrian skill, while paying court to the fair ones in barouche and chariot. From the grand stand streamed the English flag; fluttering pennons were tied to half- and quarter-mile stakes; the solid forest-line closed the view upon one side; upon the other rolled and glittered the river. Beyond it were other plantations as fertile as the two divided by the highway. The air, bland with October mellowness, yet had a flavor of the sea.

The first race was to be run by negro jockeys, each upon his master's horse. Caliban, in scarlet cap and jacket, pipe-clayed breeches, and blue cockade, was conspicuous in the group gathered at the starting-post.

"A cross between centaur and monkey!" declared Martha Jaqueline, whose spirits were at flood-tide after the interlude above recorded. "It makes my heart ache to think how many scoldings and cuffs will be needed to bring him down to work-a-day life after this."

The boy was mounted upon Matoax, a blood-bay mare, and the finest racer of the Westover stud. Her coverings had been drawn off so carefully that not a hair of her burnished coat was roughened; her slender legs, shapely hoofs, small, nervous ears, and arched neck bespoke distinguished sires and dams. Her competitors were of the best stock in the Colonies. From Turkey Island, a Randolph had brought Lightning, a white stallion renowned all over Virginia for speed and symmetry. Rosewell, the ancestral seat of the Pages and the grandest mansion in the New World, contributed a dappled gray,—Hebe,—backed by her owner for a sum that made prudent men raise their eyebrows even in that day and age of racing and gaming. Mad Molly, notorious for having thrown most of her riders, broken the arm of one, and kicked another to death, was entered by John Dunbar, a neighboring squire. His son of the same name, in the next generation, married a Byrd, and, obeying the trend of hereditary tastes, divided his time so unequally between horse-racing and the pulpit, that he was deposed from the ministry, and subsequently fought a duel over a betting-book in sight of Westover church, at the altar of which he had once officiated.

From the Brandon stables came Clover-Top, a sorrel, perfect in shape and gait, with mane and tail like white silk. Far-off Corotoman, in Lancaster County, had sent Ajax, the pride of King Carter's heart,—black as midnight, sixteen hands high, with a stride phenomenal and traditional, a tail that brushed the ground, a neck clothed with thunder, and the disposition of a lamb. This prodigy of the celebrated Corotoman stock-raising plantation had arrived by easy stages at Shirley, several days before the races, and, perfectly recovered from the fatigue of the journey, was led past the stand by his jockey, a dwarfish negro, as black as the horse, and dressed in white.

Caliban smiled superior down upon him from his seat upon Matoax.

"How you gwine git up?" he jeered in an undertone. "You orter fotched er lardder 'long wid you!"

Those occupants of the stand who were observant of the episode guessed at the purport of the sneer from the grin of one and the fell glance of the other, as reaching a long arm up to the pommel, the dwarf vaulted into the saddle like a tiger-cat, and snarled dumbly at his tormentor.

"There isn't a jockey there who doesn't hate every other rider with all his mind, soul, and strength," said the Jamestown belle to her nearest companion. "Should either of those two chance to win the race, the other should be locked up, or there will be bloodshed."

The person addressed stepped forward to look over the railing, and, attracted by the movement, Colonel Byrd, and his secretary—who sat at a small table to record bets, and the results of the races—looked at him. The Englishman's remarkable comeliness was developed to fullest advantage by his costume, which was that of a gentleman-jockey of his country,—a jerkin and breeches of buckskin with high-topped boots. The simple attire was made elegant by an elaborate pattern embroidered in black silk upon sleeves and breast. His cap was of black silk, worked with gold thread, and a black silk scarf crossing the chest from right to left to be knotted upon the thigh, and there kept in place by a gold belt of chain-work, bore the legend, " *J'attends.*"

As Bass spelled out the letters, the pen slipped from his fingers to the floor. The confirmation of his gravest suspicions was like the death-sentence to his presumptuous aspirations. Martha Jaqueline's chatter of hatred and probable bloodshed would have taken on deeper meaning to one who had happened to espy the red flame smouldering in the deep-set eyes. By an inexplicable impulse, Colonel Byrd's glance passed from the striking figure leaning against the rail to the scribe, and before either could raise guard, each saw what surprised him with an intuition of intelligent sympathy. Bass recovered his pen and returned to his book, revengeful exultation beating along his veins in the premonition of a coming crisis. Beyond the startled flash intercepted by the man who knew him best—and at his worst—the Colonel gave no sign of emotion. His voice, as he stooped again, in confidential wise, toward Martha Jaqueline, was gay, sympathetic, even caressing :

" The scarf is, I suppose, a *gage d'amour?*

> ' Wrought by nae hands as ye may guess
> Save those of fairlie fair.'

The day of chivalry is not over. Or—is it the ancestral motto ?"

" He is to ride my Pixie, you know," said Martha, ingenuously. " It was but fair that I should supply the colors. Dear Fairy ! you are trampling my toes all out of shape !"

The welcome trespasser was Lady Bess, who pushed her way from her mother's side to Evelyn's knee.

"Ta*te* me yup!" demanded the tyrant of her thrall; "so's I *tan* see all the horses!"

As Francis lifted her to Miss Byrd's lap, she seized his scarf.

"Mine Eva did that!" she announced in her piercing treble. "I saw her ma*ting* it one day—an' she hided it. An' I *twied*, tause she 'ouldn't yet me have it! *'Oo'll* dive it to me, 'ont 'oo?" enticingly to the wearer.

Before the flooding scarlet burned to the roots of Evelyn's hair, Martha's laugh pealed out like a mocking-bird's call.

"I never will tell another lie as long as I live!" she cried in counterfeited confusion. "I wanted to pass it off as my own handiwork—every stitch of it. The fact being that I should never have finished it in time or eternity—I am so prodigiously lazy—had not this angel of mercy and diligence come to my help. You don't prize it the less now that you know the truth, the whole truth, and nothing but the truth—do you?"

For reply, Francis kissed her hand, and bowed gratefully to her co-laborer.

"On the contrary, the pretty confession enhances the value of the gift. I am this young lady's debtor, also, Mrs. Carter, and congratulate her mother for having trained her tongue to utter the words of wisdom and of truth."

As the buzz of talk about them recommenced, he muttered to Evelyn and her friend,—

"O for one hour of Herod! Thank Heaven, this will end soon!"

"Amen!" responded both girls, fervently, Martha adding, "I am aweary of Pyrrhian victories! Even a weasel has the right to sleep by day after waking all night. Hair-breadth escapes are strewing gray hairs among my raven tresses. But for the last thought of exchanging cloaks this morning, not one of us three would be alive upon the earth at this moment."

"I tant hear 'hat 'oo say!" whined Lady Bess, whose best efforts to take in the rapid murmur were impeded by Evelyn's dalliance with the curls hanging about the sharp ears.

"Cannot you, my astute cherub? It is a burning shame for anybody to so much as think of anything you do not know! Hark! there is the drum-tap! and there go the horses!" cried Martha, forgetting all else.

The foremost was at the first quarter-mile stake when Francis called over half-a-dozen heads to Maynard,—

"A hundred to fifty upon Matoax!"

The pirate-killer nodded, and the Englishman signed to Bass to write it down.

"An embroidered scarf against six pairs of French gloves!" cried Martha Jaqueline, excitedly, as the bay mare gained upon the leader, the Lancaster black. "Mr. Harrison! will you back Ajax on that wager? He is your father-in-law's horse, you know!"

Maynard moved nearer, raising his voice above the storm of cheers that marked the increasing interest of the race.

"Two dozen pairs against your scarf! provided you work it yourself!"

The brunette reddened darkly under the laugh raised by the innuendo. A dozen voices contended for the right to take up the wager; Bass's stolid face looked at the fair gamester for directions.

"Oh, put them all down!" she said, dauntlessly. "I shall not be obliged to call in help to finish one of the scarves, or to buy new gloves for ten years to come!"

Matoax came in two lengths ahead of her gigantic competitor amid cheers that rent the sky. As Caliban looked up, panting and exultant, cap in hand, to the grand stand, he beheld a purse dangling from Francis's forefinger; a gesture bade him hold up his cap, and the prize fell into it, a glitter of gold and silver showing between the meshes.

"By George!" quoth the ex-Governor, "the rueful visage of the beaten negro wins more upon my sympathy!" and he dropped a half-crown into the skinny hand upheld at his signal.

"I, surely, can afford to be like-minded!" rejoined Colonel Byrd, tossing a gold piece to the discomfited dwarf.

All three actions were so quick that few beyond the nearest bystanders saw what passed. Martha Jaqueline noted the scowl of the half-breed as he rode the victorious mare to the rear.

"The Colonel has hurt the centaur's feelings or pride," she said, aside to Evelyn. "He thinks that his services are ill-repaid by what he construes into public preference for his antagonist,—and, upon my word, I agree with the boy!"

"I will see to it that he comprehends how and why the money was flung to the other," answered Miss Byrd, and the incident slipped from both minds, speedily supplied with more interesting matter.

For the second and most important race of the day was now to begin. By the time the track was cleared, six gentlemen—a Carter, a Page, a Randolph, a Harrison, a Burwell, and the Englishman, Francis—rode from different points toward the grand stand. Three were arrayed in huntsman's "pink" (scarlet to the uninitiated), one in blue with a profusion of gold lace and brass buttons, one in sober gray. Buckskin of the finer quality had found slight favor as gentleman's wear with those who got the fashions once a year from England, and liked something brave in field and drawing-room "toggery,"—until Francis appeared in the arena. The pliable material allowed every line of a faultless figure to be seen, yet had not a wrinkle or crease. The black embroidery brought out the rich tawniness of the leather, and his fair hair shone golden by contrast. After saluting the grand stand, he waved his cap and bent to the saddle-bow in palpable homage to the beauties collected there. His blue eyes brimmed with happy light, his teeth gleamed in the smile of sanguine youth; he sat his curveting steed the impersonation of strength and health, refined by a patrician grace that made the sprucest provincial gallant seem burly of build and crude in polish.

"*Mon Dieu! qu'il est beau!*" uttered Martha Jaqueline, under her breath.

She had cast her arm about Evelyn's waist, as the two leaned over the rude balustrade, and pressed her more closely for the tumultuous throbbing she felt under her hand. She was hardly prepared for the impulsive movement with which her friend plucked a rose she wore in her bodice, and flung it to the waiting riders. Francis arose in his stirrups to catch it, pressed it boldly to his lips, with a look that turned Martha cold with apprehension, fastened it in his cap, and backed his mare into position.

"Pixie" had been selected by Miss Jaqueline in England, and was, she confidently affirmed, the choicest bit of horse-flesh that ever crossed the seas. In color a bright chestnut, with reddish reflections where the sun played on her satin sides, stepping on tiptoe with dainty hoofs that disdained the soil; steely muscles springing into relief under the thin skin, and the veins showing red in the translucent ears as the rider's pat upon her neck advised her that the waiting-time was nearly over,—her extreme beauty and spirited action elicited a murmur of admiration from spectators who were not sufficiently versed in turf-lore to recognize signs of racing blood in the firm barrel, broad chest, clean limbs, and perfect joints. So radiant an apparition as Pixie and her rider had never before brightened a Virginia race-course, and would have been notable upon any.

Silence settled upon the field for twenty seconds preceding the drum-tap. The former race had been clear sailing, the result depending upon the speed of the horses and address of the riders over a level stretch of field. Before the second began, four hurdles of varying heights had been set at irregular distances in the track; bagatelles to the fox-hunting gentry of the neighborhood, yet imparting an element of incertitude to the run in the estimation of timid beholders.

The six horses took the first hurdle comfortably,

Pixie coming third, rising to the leap like a swallow, and alighting on her toes in a skimming flight. The second was a foot higher, and the third, still taller, was but two hundred yards away. The foremost rider drove his heel into his horse's side, and lifted him at the first higher rail; another dealt the flanks of his a stinging lash, but all were over, and the hindmost was fifty yards beyond the barrier when the leader arose to the third hurdle. He was a big iron-gray, with a strong strain of the racer in him, and went at the stiff timber with a rush. It was said afterward, although denied by his owner, that he just grazed a hind hoof in clearing the top rail, and that the skittish animal immediately behind was startled by the click of the iron against a screw that struck out a spark. It was certain that the creature refused the leap, wheeling aside at so sharp an angle that he crowded himself and master broadside against the hurdle. Pixie, still third, was upon his heels; the rider of the refractory beast instinctively lay flat upon the neck of his steed, and the chestnut, without lessening her stride, arose in the air in a mighty bound that cleared horse, rider, and fence, landing her, still a-tiptoe, upon the further side.

A deafening roar went up from generous Virginian hearts, renewed as the flying mare, now on her mettle, sailed over the fourth hurdle, and made the finish a dozen yards ahead of the big iron-gray, jockeyed by his master, Page of Rosewell, the winner of a score of harder races.

CHAPTER XIII.

The victor of the most exciting race of the day was the hero of the dinner-table. The only ladies at the feast were Madam Byrd, her step-daughter, and Miss Jaqueline, and at their gracious request, their presence imposed no restraint upon the natural tendency of conversation to flow into sporting channels. Young Randolph of Curles, to whom Evelyn was assigned by the lady of the house when she herself went into the dining-room upon Governor Spotswood's arm, and her lord handed in the sparkling Jamestown belle, was, however proud of the distinction that had fallen in his way, extremely and unsentimentally hungry, and Evelyn had abundant scraps of time in which to hearken to the talk of others than her squire.

By accident, Francis sat directly opposite to her, and to whatever cause others might ascribe the growing brilliancy of her complexion and the kindling eyes that seldom met his directly, he noted and prized these tokens of her exultation in the honors paid to the now distinguished guest. Compliments upon his dexterity, his presence of mind, his riding,—were lavished upon him; everybody would take wine with him; military men consulted him upon army affairs; civic officials held grave discourse with him of home and colonial politics,—all presently drifting back to " horse talk." He won upon the liking of all, although—perhaps, partly because—he told no field-stories of his own and hearkened attentively to those of others, while affably ready to give intelligent and interesting information of English stables and the English turf.

Madam Byrd made the signal for retiring from the festal board at an unusually early hour. Her husband —magnificent in powdered curls, scarlet coat and lace ruffles, every lineament, from wide brow to cleft chin, bespeaking blandest hospitality—found occasion to telegraph to her beneath drooped lids that made the fine eyes almond-shaped and languishing when he willed to have them thus, and she was prompt to obey. The day had been stimulating, and the best liquors of the best cellar in the Old Dominion were in full gush. The smiling host had seen lips close abruptly to hold in a round oath or two, and anecdotes, unwisely commenced, come to fatuous naught, with a furtive glance at one or all of the ladies. The latter would be more comfortable above-stairs; the most gallant of their admirers the happier for their absence.

Madam insisted upon bringing both girls to her chamber, and summoning thither Miss Lotsie Johnson, " talked over the day."

It was a tedious, and to the young women, a worrying process. Every detail of the elaborate repast, concerning which Madam had endured untold mental anguish pending the races she was persuaded to attend by Miss Lotsie's promise to conduct, personally, every operation; the costumes of the women on the race-ground; two new chariots and one new livery; the behavior of her guests, the praises of the banquet and of the hostess,—each had place and dutiful note, high station being awarded to the lion of the occasion.

"I protest, Martha Jaqueline, that, were I fifteen years younger, I would break a lance with you for this same Englishman, whom I am continually on the point of calling 'my lord.' There's a certain air of distinction about him that means but one thing, and that is noble birth. I said to him last week that I'd like to have a peep at his pedigree, and he said 'twas 'as old as Adam, and not unreasonably honest,' and that, some day, he 'would take pleasure in going over the family-tree with me, if I would join him in a flight through the dusty branches.' He has a mighty pretty way of putting things. I had a lively argument with him before he would consent to stay at Westover until to-night. He seemed positively uneasy lest the Harrisons might take it amiss that he does not go to them, now that Ben is well. I assured him that we rude Virginians were not such sticklers for etiquette as court-people, and that though he was invited there first, the hand of Providence had, so to speak, turned him over to us. He made reply that though, like a good Christian, he had kissed the rod and might even be inclined to hug his chains, he must break away this evening. We shall see much of him still, I hope, Martha, my dear. It is my desire that the households shall be as one while you are at Berkeley;——

"Which reminds me that Anne Harrison and I have arranged for an out-door tea at the usual place to-morrow afternoon. She has a large party of people with her just now. I shall miss you, Lotsie, when I set about making cake and pastry in the morning."

"You will not be strong enough for that, or the tea-party, unless you rest now!" Miss Lotsie unpinned the lace turban from the still-abundant hair. "I shall send these girls away. They chatter too much. You must lie down!"

She opened the door, motioned the worried pair to be gone with her grimmest air, and shut them out with an impatient "slam."

"*Her* seat will be in the seventh heaven!" sighed Martha, when they were safe in Evelyn's chamber. "One sentence more, and I should have torn out my hair by handfuls, or gnawed the flesh from my arms, or done some other of the pleasant tricks maniacs are credited with. My child! you were never so beautiful before in your life as when the Colonel pledged the health of 'our brave and honored guest, Mr. Francis.' What a grand old fellow the Colonel is! If Heaven had made me such a man, I should have died for joy on the wedding-day!"

"Never—so long as you could live to play guardian angel to another woman!" said Evelyn, affectionately. "How could I have lived through last night without you? *Can* I live through the next week, even when you are by to stand with me in the forefront of the battle? I have sucked the sweetness out of each minute of this day—thirstily! I would not look backward. I dared not look forward. Against my will, I kept saying to myself—or heard a whisper that said—"This may be your last day of perfect happiness on earth!"

"It was a lying imp—and an impertinent! And you are a goose to heed it. The skies are bright and brightening. I could have married Dick Randolph on the spot—I'm not sure I shall not do it, anyhow—for affording our knight-errant the opportunity of vaulting into the Colonel's favor. Backing Matoax was clever play—a palpable hit—and the largess to Caliban. But the hurdle-scene bowled him clean over. Nor have I been idle. I have Monseigneur's word that he will listen heedfully to whatsoever petitioner may present my seal as his warrant. And when was a Byrd ever known to retract his pledge?"

"Provided it were given intelligently!" demurred Evelyn. "If I could only see with your eyes!"

"You must, and shall! Courage, *ma mie!* He who has waited so long is as brave as patient. As he told you this morning in the church-yard, he removes himself from this house that he may meet your father, as man meets man, unembarrassed by obligation of host and guest. To-morrow night—not one day or one hour later—he will shed the disguise he detests, and demand by word of mouth that which he asked by letter—five —almost six years ago.

"So long, long time ago, dear heart!" taking the yielding form into her strong young arms, and kissing the wet eyes and trembling mouth. "And not a shadow of change in that faithful soul! Whenever opportunity of eluding the vigilance that never sleeps, offered itself, came the same message from beyond seas—'I am waiting!' Ah, *mon Dieu!* what constancy in the teeth of temptation, of time, of cruel opposition and crueller silence! Evelyn Byrd!"—tender cooing exchanged for energy that was fierce,—"if you let that man go home without *his wife!*—yes! the word is spoken! (I would as lief as not shriek it in the ears of the wine-bibbers down-stairs!)—without the wife he has served for, as

Jacob for Rachel—I am afraid I shall hate you! I know I shall despise you!"

She put Evelyn away from her, and walked up and down the room fast—like one pursued. Her face was begloomed, her eyes flashed fire; she bit her lips angrily.

"When I think"—she spat out, vehemently, to herself—not to the listener—"of women who would sell their souls—everything except honor and loyalty—for what I have to beg this girl to take when it is thrust upon her, I ask myself why I do it—even for her"—and, inarticulately—"for *him?*"

Evelyn ran toward her and put both hands over the changed face.

"Hush! hush! I cannot endure that you should look like that! You are not my Martha—my precious, only friend! And"—lifting her finger, waves of lovely color breaking over a face that had been pallid under the strange, wild upbraiding—"you will be overheard! That is *his* voice!"

Martha drew her with her to the window and peeped over the sill.

Through the drawing-room windows and hall-door and front steps arose the babble of voices. The revellers were cooling heads and heels in the sunset air. Two men had strayed from the rest along the rose-alley and halted where the main building jutted beyond the right wing. A rustic chair was in the nook thus formed, and into this Governor Spotswood let himself stiffly down as the girls looked out through the screen of Virginia creeper curtaining the window recessed by the chimney. His companion took an easy stand against a tree near by.　With one arm thrown behind him, the right leg lightly crossing the left, the sunbeams weaving a crown of his hair, he stood in an attitude of unconscious and negligent grace, never suspecting what worshipping eyes were scanning him from above.

"The wear and tear of years and labors many, begin to tell upon me!" said the raucous tones of the older man.　"And the bullet I got at Blenheim reminds me somewhat more sharply of its presence than it was wont to do a score of years back.　You youngsters are not like to have such souvenirs pressed upon your attention."

"The less like because the men of an earlier generation had so many," returned Francis, deferentially. "We reap the harvest of your sowing, and, I trust, not ungratefully.　Men rail at war, but peace is the fruit thereof."

"That man drew in diplomacy with his mother's milk!" whispered Martha, in an agony of admiration.

The ex-Governor rapped his cane upon the gravel, smartly and repeatedly.

"A just observation, sir, and fitly spoken!　It is much the fashion, nowadays, to decry former times as rude and violent.　Your curled and laced jack-a-dandy talks mincingly of 'needless and foolish bloodshed,' wiping away the ugly word from his mouth with his scented cambric, and holding his nose at stories of battle-fields, never reflecting,—shallow-pate as he is!— that, but for the carrion of those fields, he would be a hind under the whip of a foreign master."

"Posterity will be more grateful.　We are too near the scene to paint it fairly.　When the smoke of battle shall have lifted, and such landmarks in the world's history as Blenheim be set aright, their true prominence will be seen to the eternal honor of those to whom our national freedom and national glory are due."

" Hear! hear!" motioned Martha's lips.

The cane scattered the gravel right and left.

" I would to heaven, sir, that a few of our young fools could be put to school to you!   Why, sir, there's not an acre of the tens of thousands that now blossom like the rose in this new land of ours that was not paid for with human lives,—with heart's blood, sir!   The very ground on which we now stand"—tapping it— " was strewn with corpses in 1622.   At Berkeley Hundred, seventeen men, women, and children were killed in the Indian massacre of that date.   At Westover, *thirty-three!*   Up and down the James River, *three hundred and forty-seven* innocent victims to savage cruelty perished at one fell swoop.   And of this—the price of lands, peace, and liberty—our coxcomb quibbles and prates!   A pest upon his tribe! say I.   I cannot contain my tongue in thinking upon it!"

" I was told, some days ago, of a curious subterranean chamber, connected with this house, which, tradition says, was constructed as a hiding-place from the Indians, shortly after the massacre of which you speak. Is it your belief that the tale is true?"

" True as Matthew, Mark, Luke, and John, sir! Had you descended the ladder into what is now the Westover meat-cellar, you would have found the opening to be a dry well, funnel-shaped and lined with mortar. Fifteen feet below the surface, this branches into two square chambers, also of brick, with smoothly-plastered sides. A round stone table is in the middle of each, spread to-day, I dare say, with cold baked meats left from the race-dinner,—a rare good one, by the way, even for Madam Byrd's kitchen.

"That cellar, sir, meant PERIL by day and by night ! Peril of rapine and murder, and torture worse than death ; and babies' brains dashed out before mothers' eyes, and fair virgins carried into captivity and loathsome concubinage, and young men roasted at the stake, and the Lord, who made mankind of one blood, alone knows what other horrors of these then dark places of earth ! To guard against these, the early settlers burrowed in the earth like moles, and plastered caves like beavers, sir. From the Westover secret chamber was laid a passage to the river by which the hunted ones might escape to the boats. The mouth of that gallery was bricked up long ago in the chamber wall and covered with mortar. The river outlet has probably caved in. In fact, I think nobody has troubled himself to look up the precise locality of it."

"In subduing and settling a country, little attention is paid to the preservation of historical relics," remarked Francis. "In another hundred years, the very site of Old Jamestown will be uncertain. As soon as a thing becomes unprofitable, it would seem to be abandoned without let or scruple."

The ex-Governor bored the ferrule of his cane slowly into the ground, his chin sunk upon his breast. The listeners above exchanged regretful glances Without verbal consultation, they were one in the desire that the young stranger should secure himself in the great man's good graces. Spotswood's influence with Colonel Byrd was more considerable than that of any other associate, and in the coming struggle they reckoned upon every possible ally. Francis had made his first false step. Germanna, the town founded by the Virginian Tubal Cain in the immediate vicinity of his own home, had been already treated of in Colonel Byrd's diary, after one of his visits, in the following airy fashion:

"This famous town consists of Colo. Spotswood's Enchanted Castle on one side of the street, and a baker's dozen of ruinous tenements on the other, where as many German families had dwelt some years ago, but are now removed, ten miles higher in the Fork of Rappahannock, to land of their own. There had also been a chapel about a bow-shot from the Colonel's house, at the end of an avenue of cherry-trees, but some pious people had lately burned it down, with intent to get another built nearer to their own homes."

The flippant lash at the man whom the people he had served never rightly esteemed when his popularity was greatest, tells more forcibly than animadversion, of the wane of influence and fortune. "The people of Virginia," says a Scottish historian, " ought to have erected a statue to the memory of a ruler who gave them the manufacture of iron, and showed them by his active example that it is diligence and attention which can alone make a people great. . . . Had he attended more to the courtly maxim of Charles the Second, ' to quarrel with no man, however great might be the provocation, since he knew not how soon he should be obliged to act with him,' that able officer might be recommended as the model of a provincial governor."

Although few except his beautiful English wife knew

it, he was even now revolving ways and means of retreat with least loss and mortification from a position that had become untenable. Exile from the beloved land of his adoption was faced as courageously as the foe upon the battle-field, but in genuine sadness.

One hand stole up to the jewelled horseshoe hung upon his breast, the only ornament of apparel that was studiously simple, as became his sturdy republicanism.

"Pardon me!"—Francis ended the painful reverie by saying in gentlest respect,—"but having heard the wondrous history of that badge, I have, naturally, the wish to be allowed the privilege of inspecting it more closely."

The facial barometers in the window overhead, had he seen them, would have relieved his painful misgivings. The misstep was retrieved. The veteran reared his head proudly erect, as, detaching the trinket from his vest, he placed it in the other's hands.

"You perceive that it bears the words, ' *Sic juvat transcendere montes,*' and, as you have probably been informed, only the brave men who with me planted the standard of King George the First upon the summit of the Appalachian Mountains, have the right to bear it. No man who cannot prove that he drank His Majesty's health upon Mount George dare claim membership in the Tramontane Order."

"A mountain that will be your memorial rather than that of His Majesty!" rejoined Francis, handling the badge in sincere reverence.

"Run to earth!" cried jocund tones, and the Master of Westover appeared around the projecting corner, with half a dozen men at his heels. "Alexander

Spotswood! have you no bowels of compassion, that you drag this innocent stranger 'thorough bush and thorough brier' to the top of the Blue Ridge, cram him with the constitution and by-laws of the Knights of the Golden Shoe, and—I dare swear, lest he should have forgot the memorable battles of the Duke of Marlborough,—have fought them over again for the nine-and-fortieth time within the month."

The roar of vinous laughter from his followers drowned Francis's eager protest. Spotswood, scorning all attempt at self-vindication, purpled furiously, put out an imperative hand for the precious memento, and was stalking away in wrathful silence when a fresh interruption occurred.

Beyond that wing of the house in which were the kitchen and other offices, the front and back yards were separated by a fence, a wicket-gate giving entrance from one to the other. The hubbub of voices in hot dispute preceded the bursting open of the wicket, and two figures, locked in deadly embrace, rolled across a strip of turf upon the gravel-walk, wrestling, scratching, and biting like wolves, too mad to see where they were, or in what presence, until the gentlemen hurried up in a body to separate them. Torn violently apart, each glanced at the other, panting and bloody, shaking with rage, not terror.

The combatants were Caliban, in the smart livery in which he had won the race and afterward waited at table, and Selim, the dwarfish jockey who had brought in the Corotoman horse second at the finish. The elfish blackamoor looked the uglier for the disorder of his white raiment, and the fiendish malignity contorting his features. His clawlike hands opened and shut convulsively, clutching the empty air as they might his adversary's throat. Colin Bass pinioned Caliban's arms with his powerful hands. Colonel Carter, to whose father Selim belonged, seized the dwarf, but could not manage him until Mr. Harrison, his brother-in-law, came to his help.

Colonel Byrd advanced a step in front of his guests, and surveyed the pair in cool disgust that shortly wrought upon them like a *douche* of icy water.

"A gentleman's door-yard is not the place for dog-fights," he observed when he had looked the trespassers over for a minute of dreadful silence. "When the dogs are mad—as these would seem to be—they are shot or hanged. If there is any doubt as to their madness, they are tied up for nine days, or until they foam at the mouth."

All this with judicial deliberation, open snuff-box in hand, thumb and finger delicately poised for a pinch, which he now partook of leisurely, holding the culprits with the glitter of his almond-shaped eyes.

"Harrison! Colonel Carter! I turn the Lancaster varlet over to you. As for the other, I wish the black-a-vised devil had strangled him outright for having disgraced his bringing-up by fighting another gentleman's servant upon my premises. Mr. Bass! take him off and give him nine-and-thirty, well laid on. If he resists, send for me!"

Caliban broke from his captor with a quick wrench and writhe of his supple body, and flung himself at the judge's feet.

"Marster! my dear marster! *you* may beat me to

death ef you like, an' I won' say a word! But don' let *him* tech me, for de Lord's sake. You may cut de heart out o' me! Any o' you gem'men may tromple on me! My marster may shoot me dade, or string me up ter er tree, dis minnit, an' I won' min' it! But, my marster—my good, sweet marster! you *won'* 'low no po' white folks ter lay er han' 'pon one o' you' servants!"

He begged like one at the door of death, tears, washing the blood and dirt from his face, showed the ghastly yellow of the skin beneath. He would have embraced his master's feet and kissed them, had not the Colonel drawn back as from a wet dog. The other side of the paling was lined with negroes, great and small, cowering with dread and terrified into dumbness, but the language of the rolling eyeballs was unmistakable. The secretary was the object of universal contempt that had suddenly heated into enmity.

The master readjusted the lid of his snuff-box, and filliped a few grains of the " Byrd mixture" from his lace ruffles.

"Where is Mr. Booker, Osiris?" he asked of the butler, who had come out of the front door and taken a stand in the rear of the group of gentlemen. The Colonel's manner was unmoved from the nonchalance with which he had pronounced sentence upon the evil-doer. "Ah! here he is!" as the dusky ranks opened to let the overseer pass through. "Mr. Booker! this boy is to be flogged, and by Mr. Bass,—if he will be so good as to do me the favor. Will you see that all goes well ?"

It did not sound merciful, but Evelyn, leaning in

m

strained solicitude from the open window, thoughtless of possible observation in her anxiety for the petted page, clasped her hands, and fell to weeping so violently that Martha pulled her back into the room.

"Thank God!" she cried. "Mr. Booker is never cruel! I could not have borne to have my poor boy misused! Did you see that man's look when Caliban was praying Papa that *he* should not touch him? It was but a flash, but it scared me like a glimpse of hell! I never dreamed he could be like that!"

"He is a snake!" Martha pronounced, composedly. "A cold, deadly, subtle, creeping snake that even the bottomless pit could not warm. I saw all that—and more!"

CHAPTER XIV.

WESTOVER was dark and still at an early hour that evening. Most of the guests had dispersed to their several homes before dark. The chariot containing Miss Jaqueline, her duenna, her maid and luggage, was escorted to Berkeley by Messrs. Francis and Harrison, Colonel Carter and Lieutenant Maynard. The ball of the previous night, the race and the race-dinner sufficiently excused Madam and Miss Byrd for non-appearance in the drawing-room after supper. The ex-Governor and his host had smoked an amicable pipe together at bedtime. The lord of Germanna was irascible, but never sulky, and the raillery that had touched him upon two tender points was soon forgiven. Since he must resume his journey upon the morrow, he sought his couch betimes.

A dreary, reactionary lull settled down upon the premises, as the autumn fog upon the river. Frogs bellowed at the foot of the lawn; tree-toads droned their high, teasing notes in the tulip-poplars by the front door, and a whippoorwill cried to the blind night from the burying-ground.

Caliban had waited at table, as usual, although his mistress—kind of heart if quick of reproof—would fain have spared him the ordeal. Colonel Byrd was not a harsh ruler, yet a martinet in the matter of plantation discipline. The lad's absence would have been construed into sullenness, and sharp account be demanded therefor. He was at his post behind Evelyn's chair, in neat livery. Complexion and eyes were dull, but he was not otherwise changed from his wonted aspect. Only, the kitchen junta knew what the least pickaninny there would not have revealed to a white under the cowhide. When the house-work was done, and the servants ready to partake of their nocturnal meal, and Isis, the priestess of the high rites, called the boy's attention to the liberal mess of delicacies Madam Byrd had sent out for his use by the hand of Osiris, he snatched it from the table, and tossed it through the door to the dogs waiting without for their pickings of the feast.

The general grunt that followed the act was succeeded by a united groan, as the humbled favorite dashed out into the darkness, and did not return.

"Marster done been gone too fur wid dat po' chile!" was the verdict of fat Isis, her turban nodding ominously. "He got Injun blood in 'im, an' tain' never safe ter fool 'long Injun blood. We ain' been see de las' o' dis day's wuk, man!"

The bad mixture of savagery in the boy's soul and body was in boiling ferment; heart and brain were on fire, as he plunged down the garden-walk, leaped the wall of the church-yard, and took his way up the river.

The bank was, for the most part, a jungle of brush-wood and interlooping vines,—grape, poison-oak, and bamboo,—but he threaded the labyrinth as if the time were mid-day, and the way a beaten path. There were black-snakes and moccasins in the thickets; he believed in ghosts and bogies more firmly than in the white man's God; now and then a thorny branch tore his ankle or shoulder. He tramped on until clean out of sight of lighted windows and the sound of human voices,—threw himself down on the brow of a cliff, cleft by a wooded ravine, and tried to put his trooping, maddening ideas in order.

His arms under his head, his face to the sky, where, between rising fogs, a pale star winked at him, now and then, he let the turbid flood of thought and feeling rack itself into clearness of sight and purpose.

The wrong done him was irreparable, the insult deadly. He had been exalted unto a heaven of favor to be thrust down to a hell of infamy. He could never again carry his head high and saucily in the sight of friend and foe. He recollected the Caliban of yester-day,—swaggering across the yard, admired and copied by the pickaninnies, strutting past Osiris in the still-room behind his mistress's back and sticking his tongue

into his cheek, his head on one side, to the holy horror
of the dignitary who durst not resent the insult in his
lady's presence. He recalled the harum-scarum as if
it were some one who had died and been buried since
then.

The whipping was nothing in itself. He had tasted
the overseer's lash more than once, and been no more
disgraced by it than by the thump of Isis's wooden
spoon upon his pate, or his mistress's box upon his ear.
It was a part of education and every-day experience in
his class. He despised poor whites upon caste and race
principles. If the flogging had been delegated to the
meanest field-hand, he would have been surprised, but
not degraded. The secretary sat at his employer's table;
slept under his employer's roof, and mingled upon
terms of apparent equality with the most distinguished
guests who came to the house. None of these advantages raised him the fraction of a degree in the respect
of the born serfs whom he reckoned as less than the
dust he shook from his well-shod feet. They were
cognizant of his ignoble parentage; they could have
named over to a man or woman all the "no 'count
kinfolks" he tried to forget, who lived "'way back in
New Kent County." That he had their master's confidence; that he was a capital accountant, a skilful
penman, and a man of tolerable erudition in many
branches of learning, weighed naught with them, and
less than naught. Any show of attainment and refine-
ment was "puttin' on a'rs."

Over and beyond all this, Caliban, as we have seen,
bore a personal dislike to the smug official, and knew
it to be reciprocated. Every stripe from Bass's hand

laid open his pride to the quickest core. He had not struck hard. The surveillance of the overseer—pledged to his conscience to see that his employer's property was never injured—prevented absolute cruelty. His master's cane would have drawn blood, and left bruises for days, whereas, he was no worse an hour after the punishment, for a single blow. What had added to the ignominy of the sentence was Bass's smile, as he brandished the whip before the victim's eyes and the taunt with which he laid it by, the flagellation being over:

"I don't soil my hands with this sort of work, generally, Booker. But the Colonel made a point of it, and I couldn't refuse him a favor. Not but what I rather enjoy cutting the comb of an impudent young rooster when I get a chance."

The boy rolled over the biting words in his memory until his fingers dug into the soil and tore up grass and herbs by the roots. One thing, and one only, could ever extract the shameful sting, or wash out the stain from his honor;—he would have that man's life, sooner or later. Upon his smarting soul he stamped a black cross against Bass's name.

When he left the house in which he was born, he meant to return no more. There were runaways in the depths of Virginia forests who had been "out" for years. In the Dismal Swamp—if the stories he had heard on winter's nights by the kitchen fire were true—was a colony of this most pitiable class of outlaws, who were free until caught by the militia patrol, and always dangerous. In a hut, not much better than a Westover dog-kennel, upon the edge of White Oak

Swamp, between the James and the Chickahominy, lived the only known relative he had on his father's side,—the Indian grandmother whose reputation as a witch made her to be both respected and feared by the negroes. Caliban's visits to her had not been many. When he was a little fellow, Miss Evelyn had prevailed upon her step-mother to send him by the hand of an older servant the ten miles and more that lay between his home and that of the squaw, that his father's mother might see into what a "likely" lad he was growing. Within the past year he had twice helped himself to a horse from the stables, and visited the crone by night, spending some hours in her cabin, partaking of the hot supper she hastened to cook for him, and returning before dawn with the "love-powder" the head-hostler had commissioned him to procure as the bribe for the liberal wink he would deal out next morning to the travel-worn condition of the steed.

Caliban's hastily-formed design had been to make her house a temporary asylum until he could open communication with the runaways. He had in his pocket the purse flung to him by the English gentleman that morning. He was counting the contents at the back of the kitchen when Selim prowled around the corner and made a grab for the coins, beginning the quarrel that ended so miserably. There was enough money to make him a great personage in the outlaw settlement.

But to go and leave unpunished the man who had robbed him of a good name, good clothes, good friends, a good home—was this consistent, upon second thoughts, with what he had been taught was his forefathers' highest law—never to forgive, or to forget an injury?

When he went, he ought to leave something behind him for people to talk about, a warning to evil-doers for the future. His "granny" had charged him to come to her if he ever got into trouble. She had said something else, her black eyes snapping, and skinny neck out-stretched like a snake's:

"If white man, or black 'oman git in you' way, knife an' bullet no good. Too much blood. Blood tell tales. I show you better way. Come to me."

He was less shocked than if tales of poisoning and "tricking" had not been rife among the negroes. He knew what she meant. He would go back to the house; bribe the head-hostler with a coin from his hoard, and consult the wise woman that very night.

The evil seed flowered and fruited fast. Others beside the secretary must be reckoned with. He could never forget how his master looked and spoke when he begged him not to let Bass touch him. And after he had won the race for him, he had given Selim money and had never a word for Caliban. He could fancy, too, how Colonel Byrd would hunt for him when his flight was discovered. Even "the Dismal" would not deter him, for he had headed the party that had laid the dividing-line through it, when Caliban was a little boy. Nothing else was talked of for weeks but that Dividing-Line, and the horrors of the mighty morass. Caliban had a fixed impression of how the mysterious Line looked, and of catching his foot in it as he ran, and being overtaken by his master before he could free himself.

It would be best to put the poison into the coffee some morning. The Colonel and his secretary took two cups apiece,—his mistress one, sometimes, generally preferring tea. She must take her chance, he decided. He owed her no good-will in his present humor. She had been tart with him, after supper, for dropping butter upon her gown, and had, in times past, made life miserable to him in many ways.

"Thank GOD," thought the murderous little heathen, "Mis' Evelyn allers take choc'lat!"

She had eyed him kindly as he passed the bread to her to-night, and the gentle, "No, thank you, Caliban!" when there was no need to do more than shake her head, sounded in his ear now like music. Nobody in the kitchen had dared speak to him directly of his humiliation, but Isis had managed to have him overhear her say to a scullion that "Viney says as how po' Mis' Evelyn done mos' cry her sweet eyes out, sence she see de carr'in'ons in de yard, dat ebenin'!"

Thought of the one sweet drop in the nauseous cup held to his lips at the close of the day he hoped to reckon as the proudest of his life, broke the boy's heart into a passionate rain of tears. He rolled on the ground in the violence of his voiceless sobs. He was hardly more than a child, and a petted child at that, and, although he would have flouted the charge as derogatory to his manhood, as soft-hearted as a baby where the affections came into play.

The plash of oars approaching the shore, and the soft "swish" of water on the land checked the paroxysm. He raised his head to listen. The bank on which he lay overhung the narrow beach, and the fog was so dense that his keen sight could discern nothing, although the boat was already beached with a muffled, crushing sound.

"Mighty funny dey should take all dat pains to come in easy," reflected the boy, on the *qui vive* in an instant. "Dem rowlocks done been wropped wid rags, else I'd 'a' heern 'em sooner!"

He dragged himself by his elbows to the brink and reached over, straining his eyes for other sign of the intruders than the crunching footfalls upon the sandy shingle, and an occasional whisper. There were two men, he soon concluded, and they were bringing ashore a heavy burden. He could hear their hard breathing, once in a while a grunt, and that they staggered in the yielding gravel. The load, whatever it was, was laid down; there was the rattling of dried sticks or twigs, and the rustle of green boughs, then the sound of letting a heavy stone down cautiously upon the earth, and the men went back for what they had brought to land. Then ensued the clatter of shoes upon a pavement, and all noises became oddly subdued.

The boy's hair stiffened and stirred upon his head. Stories of hobgoblins and spectres, of murders and abductions, and devils carrying lost souls into the side of a hill that closed behind them after they entered this one of the many ways to hell,—rushed in upon his memory. The cold sweat dripped from his face upon the crumbling verge that, every moment, threatened to cave in and precipitate him into the clutches of the ghostly visitants,—yet he durst not budge an inch lest the fall of a pebble, or the crackle of a stick should betray him.

They were coming out! He could detect the rub of clothing against the sides of the aperture, and that they straightened themselves in the open air with long breaths, as after stooping in a low chamber.

A rough voice spoke:

" 'Tis a —— sultry night, an' dark 's a wolf's mouth, with this —— fog!"

" All the better!" was the answer in a more cautious key. " Here's the crowbar! Up with her!"

Caliban fumbled wildly for the projecting roots fringing the bank, and clung to them desperately. His brain toppled, and his breath almost stopped. For the last speaker was the man whose death he was plotting, the being in all creation whom he had most occasion to dread and detest.

His wits cleared abruptly. Now that his superstitious fears were allayed, he was no craven. Imagination leaped eagerly to the belief that, by dogging the midnight prowler, he might taste a more exquisite revenge, than by robbing him of existence without letting him know by whose hand he met his fate. Still hearkening as for his soul's salvation, he heard the stone heaved back into position, the rustling foliage, the heaping up of what he now knew to be river-drift; then, the men seemed to kneel, and smooth the shingle with their hands,—no doubt to efface footprints.

Bass spoke again, so close beneath Caliban's head that he feared that his breathing must be audible:

" You'll be off, then, Monday night? Do you touch below this?"

" That's accordin'! I've a promise o' summat at Maycox, an' Wyanoake, an' th' Brandon overseer 's cut his eye-teeth, an' 's apt to take advantage of a good captain goin' down. Th' other places is mos'ly nigger-work, an' don' count fer much. 'Tain' every white man who's got your long hade, let 'lone niggers."

"Why do you fool with them, at all? You get enough to do without them."

"Every little counts! An' a man doesn' like to lose any chance o' turnin' a hones' penny!"

Nothing more was said. The men pushed the boat off, clambered into her, and the muffled strokes were lost in the distance.

Caliban worked himself back into his former position, and lay still, his hands clasped behind his head, staring up at the whitening sky.

"De moon risin'!" he muttered. "Soon 's she f'arly ober de top o' de trees, I gwine see what dis yere mean, my *gentleman!* I ain' been come out yere fur nuthin'!"

Having changed his purpose of running away, and postponed his visit to his granddam, he was patient in waiting. The silvery shimmer of the motionless mists showed him how to descend from his perch to the water's level. The shelving space below the cliff was nearly filled with drift and dead branches that seemed to have fallen from the trees overhead. He cleared these away, breaking them as little as possible, patiently and deftly scraping aside leaves and sticks, and holding back living branches growing low on the bank, until he touched a rough flat stone set perpendicularly in the earth. Foreseeing the need of it, he had cut a stout hickory stick in the wood above and sharpened one end. The improvised "jimmy" worked well. After some preliminary probing about the edges of the stone, he drove the sharp end of the stick into a crevice, bore heavily downward, and then outward, and felt the obstruction yield.

Stooping to the aperture yawning like a black mouth in the bank, he was met by a rush of cooler air, freighted with an odor that let the truth in upon him in a flash.

Tobacco at that date was subject to a duty of a penny per pound in English ports, and there was hardly an inlet or bay or river on the Atlantic coast that was not infested by smuggling-craft, hovering, like prey-seeking birds, along the edge of the richest plantations. The Westover overseer, Booker, bore an excellent reputation for honesty, but to him had never been entrusted the duty of making up the tale of bales and hogsheads of tobacco for shipment. Mr. Bass, as major-domo and confidential agent, inspected barn and warehouse, and kept account of the contents of each. If the Colonel's frequent and prolonged absences rendered peculation easy, despite his astuteness, his brother-planters congratulated him upon the incorruptible integrity of the manager that secured him against such losses. Bass's opportunities were many and tempting, but the most envious of his critics had never breathed upon his honesty in business dealings.

Caliban would as soon have been without his trusty clasp-knife as without tinder-box and steel. In the box was, also, a bit of wax candle. Feeling his way into the mouth of the cave, he struck a light. He was in an arched tunnel of brick masonry, paved with flagstones, in which he could not stand upright. Bales, boxes, and casks were piled against the sides. All, he was certain, contained tobacco, until he shook a barrel, and heard the wabble of liquid within. He brought the candle nearer to examine the head.

"Some nigger gwine ter be skin' when dat brandy is miss' !" he grinned.

The humor of the situation touched him, serious as he felt it to be. Just inside of the opening lay a cask, the make of which he knew full well. The Byrd coat-of-arms was branded deep in the head of every hogshead, barrel, keg, and box that left the plantation. This one had evidently been brought ashore that night by Bass and his confederate.

Caliban's tough muscles wrought toilfully at the prostrate stone before he could refit it into place. The rest was more easily done ; but the moon was in the zenith when he regained his perch. He was tired almost to death, yet too excited to seek rest in sleep, sat, elbows on knees and head in hands, doing the severest thinking that had ever vexed his busy brains.

The triumphant impulse to denounce his enemy to the master who trusted him died down under a withering breeze of common sense.

The goods would be saved to their various owners, for he at once connected the hidden store with complaints of mysterious thefts up and down the river he had heard of in house and kitchen. But who would believe his story of the midnight adventure and identification of one of the criminals? He had not seen Bass's face, and against the inevitable denial of the latter what weight would the word of a slave have, especially when his reasons for desiring to injure the secretary were taken into account? He must wait for more conclusive evidence ; must dog and pry and skulk with the patient ferocity of his forebears, until the night named as the time for removing the plunder. Even then, Bass might not be among those caught in the act by Colonel Byrd and such associates as he might summon to his aid. The fellow had the cunning of the devil.

The problem was still unsolved when the red sun pierced the river-fog to his head frosted with rime, bowed upon the knees where it had lain for four hours in the dead sleep of utter exhaustion.

CHAPTER XV.

THE great event of the month came to Westover on the morrow,—the arrival of the foreign mail. There was a package of books for Evelyn; for Madam Byrd, four or five gossipy missives from English correspondents, and two or three notes from tradespeople; and for the Colonel, a bulky parcel of letters and papers.

He undid the seals in his study, seated in an arm-chair beside the escritoire in the chimney recess. The light fell clearly over his left shoulder; his snuff-box was open near his right hand; his epistles were voluminous, and, in the main, interesting; replete with incidents of court and political and literary life, and seasoned —some of them—with racy items and équivoques. The reader of to-day would peruse these last with less gusto than was apparent in the handsome visage that lent diligent heed to every line. He laughed now and then, low and musically, over some particularly highly-flavored passage, or murmured inaudible comments.

The secretary had hitched his chair to the other side of the table as his superior established himself in his corner.   It was not respectful to sit with his back to his employer, and Colin never abated one jot or one tittle of the obsequiousness due to the potentate.   Should the examination of the mail leave the Colonel in a fair humor, he would give a digest to his subordinate of whatsoever it suited him to impart to other ears.   It was by such advantages that the man's education was carried on in whatever pertained to Old World affairs, social or public.   The Colonel was a *raconteur* of rare ability, and the auditor considered, with reason, mail-day a genuine treat in his sober-hued life.   After the entertaining abstract of the world's news, the plantation ledgers, of which a pile lay on the secretary's table, would be overhauled, every entry of expenditure and receipt inspected, account of stock taken, and balances compared by one whom his tombstone avers to have been "the splendid economist."

The book-keeper had nothing to dread from the rehearsal of his stewardship during the month of the master's absence.   Not one figure would give the lie to another; conscious rectitude, from her throne within his bosom, courted inquiry and snapped clean fingers at audits.   Meanwhile he occupied himself with the Colonel's pet volume of MSS.   The chronicle had grown apace since the author's last review of it.   The heap of disorderly notes—creased, blurred, and discolored—was diminished by the number of those impaled upon a file at the back of the table, and many pages of vellum were covered with the clerkly characters that, over a century and a half later, command our admiration.

By and by, when time and proof were ripe, and his
master's mood propitious, the scribe might have somewhat of his own composition and collocation to submit
to the august judge. The anticipation was uppermost
in his mind as, having trimmed and nibbed a fresh
pen, he stole a glance at the seignior's complacent face,
and bethought himself, for the thousandth and first
time, of the iniquity of a so-called divine government
that dealt out to one man every advantage of person,
wealth, station, and intellect that the most extravagant
eighteenth century Alnaschar could covet, and left
millions of the same race to work for daily bread. As
mechanically as a modern calligraph, he wrote the next
paragraph :

"Thus, in what part of the Woods soever anything
mischievous or troublesome is found, kind Providence
is sure to provide a Remedy. And 'tis probably one
great reason why God was pleas'd to create these, and
many other vexatious Animals, that Men should exercise their Arts and Industry to guard themselves——"

The obedient pen gave a little astonished jump, and
hung above the page.

From the lips that were, just now, set in the smile
of sunniest content, flew forth an oath so gross in its
profanity, so sounding, so deep, and so fiery, that the
hearer doubted his own faithful ears. Colonel Byrd
swore upon occasion, devout churchman as he was.
The Father of his country sinned along the same line
forty-five years thereafter. But the companion of his
least guarded moments had never, until now, heard
from him fulmination like this that set a tray of glasses
upon the table to ringing, and made the moteful stream

of October sunshine flowing through the windows vibrate. True to his phlegmatic custom, Bass neither started nor looked up. After that one little leap, the pen resumed its steady amble:

"——against them.

"Bears' Oyl is used by the Indians as a General Defence against every Species of Vermin. Among the rest, they say it keeps both Bugs and Musquetas from assaulting their Persons which would otherwise devour Such uncleanly People."

Between two sentences, the writer's eyes skirmished under his scant eyelashes.

The Colonel sat as still as a stone, one palm pressed flat upon the open sheet spread upon the desk, the other hand a tight fist upon his knee, his eyes blazing into vacancy. His lips were white, and the contracting muscles about them had the singular effect of shallowing the cleft that lent a voluptuous cast to the lower part of his face.

"Yet Bears' Grease has no Strong Smell, as that plant had which the Egyptians formerly used against musquetas, resembling our palma Christi, the juice of which smelled so disagreeably that the Remedy was worse than the Disease."

"Mr. Bass!"

The summons was in the Colonel's gentlest voice,—

"May I trouble you to order Pluto to be saddled and brought around?"

Pluto, the wickedest thing in the Westover stables, was made ready by three grooms with celerity inconceivable by one familiar with his playful manœuvres of kicking, biting, and rearing. The plantation quaked to a man when the Master expressed his intention of taking the air upon the vicious black, and all who could bear a hand in hurrying horse and rider off the place, sprang frantically to the task.

Madam Byrd, up to her eyes in cake-making, espying through the still-room window, her lord, booted and spurred, striding down to the monogram gate, and the caparisoned steed plunging until he lifted two hostlers off their feet by the short hold they had of his mouth,—was of one mind with Isis and her attendants, pressing to the kitchen-door to peep at the same actors :

"Lord-a-mussy! Dar's de mischief to pay when Marster fling he laig ober dat Plutto! I hope ter gracious de pa'r on 'em 'll shake de debbil offen de crooper 'fo' dey show dey faces hyur agin !"

The secretary sat between the open vellum leaves, when Madam sailed in, her fair face clouded, her key-basket jingling with trepidation.

"Had Colonel Byrd bad news in his letters? Or, is there somewhat wrong with the accounts, that he is so upset !"

"Madam?" The secretary had arisen; his face was an innocent blank. "Colonel Byrd said naught to me of information received, whether good or ill."

"How excessively annoying! I shall be in a tremble until he gets back. If he ever does! I never see him mount that imp of darkness—whose very name makes a Christian shudder—that I don't look to see him brought home with his brains knocked out. I protest I shall have no nerves left if this sort of thing goes on from day to day. After such a peace-

ful four weeks as we have enjoyed, these scurries and
hurries and worries wear me clean out. Where is the
Colonel's mail?"

" I presume that he put it away, Madam, before going
out. It was not to be seen when I returned from ordering his horse."

"And locked it up, I declare!" trying the desk-
lid. " I must own that looks suspicious when the only
persons likely to come in here are his wife and his
secretary! Had I but a key that would open this desk, I
should esteem it my duty, as a wife, to discover what has
put him in such disorder. A woman cannot sympathize
intelligently with her husband unless she has a clue to
his perplexities. But that is not what I am here to
discourse upon. We are to meet the Berkeley folk at
tea on the hill this afternoon. Will you give orders to
the carpenters to take up boards and trestles for a new
table? The old one is rickety, as I observed when we
last supped there, and 'tis but natural I should be
wishful to have things conformable for such a company
as we are to sup with to-day. Heigho! this house is
dull as Friday in Lent with all of them gone out
of it!"

Colin went as he was bidden, and willingly. Madam's
longing for intelligent sympathy in her lord's worries
did not exceed that of his faithful major-domo, but he
was the better content to wait for satisfaction of the
affectionate craving, since a key in his waistcoat pocket
exactly fitted the escritoire-lock, and he would have
ample opportunity for research while the *al fresco*
entertainment went forward under the trysting-tree.

The Colonel had not returned at dinner-time, and his

wife's appetite was but indifferent in consequence. The hall-clock was on the stroke of four when he drew rein at the iron gate, and flung the bridle to a triad of grooms who ran from the stable-yard at the sound of hoofs. Pluto was drenched with sweat, his sooty sides crisscrossed by welts; his mien was as meek as that of a twenty-year-old hack. The Master stayed to give explicit directions as to the mash to be administered when the animal was cool; ordered that he should be well rubbed down and covered without delay, and sauntered up the walk, snapping his whip playfully at a collie-pup that gambolled awkwardly about his feet. Meeting his wife in the hall, ready dressed for the sylvan gathering, he kissed her, held her at arms' length to survey the bravery of her apparel; vowed that she would eclipse the girls and bring a dozen duels with raging admirers upon his hands,—and ran up-stairs with the step of a boy, humming a popular ballad in a round, resonant voice a young man might envy.

Evidently he and Pluto, between them, had dislodged Satan from the crupper. The one had suffered loss in the achievement, the other came out better than new.

At half-past four o'clock, when the rural fête was in full progress, the Master of Westover, arrayed with the elegant precision for which he was distinguished, walked up the long slope capped by the trysting-grove, and halted in the covert of a clump of bushes to survey the scene.

The table, draped in spotless damask, was encompassed by a bevy of white-aproned servitors, Caliban, in the dual rôle of Mercury and Ganymede, flying between the board and the hampers collected under a branchy oak.   Fifteen yards away, upon the hill-brow overlooking the river, the company for whom the feast was preparing sat upon rustic benches and lounged on carpets laid over the sun-warmed turf. The spectator quickly singled out a group, withdrawn a little from the larger assembly, consisting of Lieutenant Maynard, Martha Jaqueline, Mrs. Carter, with Lady Bess playing at her feet, Evelyn, and Mr. Francis.

"Madam Carter plays propriety prettily for a young woman with charms of her own!" meditated the unseen looker-on, drawing out his inseparable confidante, and helping himself to a bountiful pinch. "Is she in the plot, I wonder? The easier question to answer would be, 'who is *not*—except myself.' 'Lover and friend hast thou put far from me, and my acquaintance into darkness!'" he repeated aloud, with a cynical laugh.

He had an eye for scenic effects, and tarried a deliberate minute to possess himself of the best points.

The weather was delicious : the pure October sky was flecked with a few pearly cloudlets sailing westward to curtain the day-god's couch. The grove, dashed plentifully with autumnal gold, purple, and scarlet, was merry with the voices of children playing hide-and-seek in the outlying thickets ; about Mr. and Mrs. Harrison was collected a body of guests, mostly young people ; Hannah Harrison and Mr. Fontaine talked together, seated upon a fallen tree ; the fair raiment of the women and the more gayly-colored garb of their beaux lent animation to the pastoral beauty of the picture.

"I longed, in despair, for Watteau's pencil and a blank fan!" Colonel Byrd declared to Mrs. Harrison after bowing his greetings to the company at large. "I stood behind my leafy screen half an hour, lost in admiration of the tableau. It was a human orrery, with yourself as central orb, planets and satellites ringed about you, and the children enacting comets and asteroids."

He was never in blither mood; never more impartial in the distribution of attentions that were subtlest flattery, but not until supper was handed by the servants and the younger gentlemen to the sitting groups, did he approach that of which Martha Jaqueline and his daughter formed a part. The Berkeley host had joined himself to them, also, and as the Colonel took a tall stool before Mrs. Carter, a position in which he faced the party, Mr. Harrison was anathematizing a grumbling tooth that had kept him awake the night before, and regretting that there was no dentist nearer than Williamsburg.

"There should be one upon each plantation, as we keep our carpenter and blacksmith and shoemaker," he said. "He would be kept in practice if the teeth of the white family and the negroes were properly looked after."

"Allow me to show you a more excellent way," said the Colonel, gravely, "and one which can be carried out with infinitely less thought and expense. Upon one of my journeys inland, I was greatly afflicted with an impertinent tooth in my upper jaw that made me chew with great caution. We had little else but biscuits to eat for days at a time, and I could not grind a biscuit in these circumstances but with much deliberation and presence of mind. I got rid of this troublesome companion by cutting a caper.   Fastening a twine, about a fathom in length, to the root of my tooth, I tied the other end to the snag of a log that lay upon the ground in such a manner that I could just stand upright. Having adjusted my string, I bent my knees enough to enable me to spring vigorously off the ground as perpendicularly as I could.   The force of the leap drew out the tooth with so much ease that I felt nothing of it."

"But mine is in the lower jaw!" Mr. Harrison objected, laughing.

"In that case, you should stand on your head and execute a somersault," said Martha Jaqueline.

"Not at all!" the Colonel answered, with immovable seriousness.   "An under-tooth may be fetched out by standing off the ground and fastening your string at due distance above you.   And, having so fixed your gear, jump off your standing, and the weight of your body, added to the force of the spring, will pry out your tooth with less pain than any operator upon earth could draw it."

He broke off upon perceiving that Lady Bess, leaning against her mother's knee, open-eyed and open-mouthed, had inserted a thumb and forefinger between her jaws and was working at one of her seed-pearls of teeth.   He stooped to take her on his knee.

"Don't borrow trouble, Fairy!   Never shake a tooth to see if it be loose.   Be sure you will find it out when it is!"

"A good practical saw!" conceded Martha.   "The principle which is at the root of it is a tenet in my religion."

"When mankind shall carry it into daily practice, the millennium will be on the dawn," said Francis's pleasant voice.

The gnarled root of a tree, cushioned with moss, was his seat. Evelyn's chair was close by, and their low-voiced chat was carried on under cover of the general conversation until Colonel Byrd's approach.

"He who dreads death, dies twice," the Englishman continued in the same easy, moralizing strain. "It may be decreed that a man is to die by lightning, 'though he knows it not. If he blench and cower at every flash, he perishes not once, but a thousand times, —nine hundred and ninety-nine times by his own appointment, once by God's."

Mr. Harrison's shiver was real, while he still laughed.

"If you knew me better, Mr. Francis, I should suspect that remark to be aimed at me. As my good friends here know, the fear of lightning is a confirmed weakness with me. I query, ofttimes, if the cowardice be not premonition."*

"There is no such thing as human premonition," Colonel Byrd replied, stroking the silken head resting confidingly against his shoulder. "Auguries were the lies of the pagans; presentiment is the sentimental fancy of the Christian whose vanity predisposes him to imagine that the Almighty will do naught without taking him into, at least, partial confidence. On the contrary, the Deity would seem, generally, to treat us

---

* He, with two of his daughters, was killed by lightning at Berkeley twenty years afterward.

as do false friends and secret foes,—beguile us with fairest hopes when the judgment is closest at hand.

"*À propos* to lightning," addressing himself to the listening circle, "the most amazing instance that ever I heard of happened at York, a little while ago. The story came to my knowledge only last week. A ship-surgeon had come ashore to visit a patient, and was walking about the sick-room when there came a dreadful flash of lightning that struck him dead, but hurt not the patient nor any other person, though several were near him. At the same time it made a large hole in the trunk of a pine-tree which grew about ten feet from the window. But what was most surprising in this disaster was, that on the breast of the unfortunate man that was killed was the figure of a pine-tree, as exactly delineated as any limner in the world could draw it. Nay, the resemblance went so far as to represent the color of the pine as well as the figure. The lightning must probably have passed through the tree first before it struck the man, and by that means have printed the Icon of it on his breast."

Profound silence reigned in the group and among others who were near enough to hear the anecdote. Evelyn grew terribly pale, and her eyes, turning appealingly to her lover, saw him make the sign of the cross. The hope that the rapid motion had escaped the notice of any other than herself was dashed by hearing her father say, in bland seriousness :

"You cross yourself, Mr. Francis, and I, from my Protestant soul, respond, 'Amen !' 'From battle, murder, and sudden death,'—which I take to mean a violent taking off,—'Good Lord, deliver us,' one and all !

"Which brings to my mind that my distinguished friend Colonel Spotswood and you held some converse last evening relative to the Indian massacre of 1622. He gave me to understand afterward that the dialogue broken in upon by my irreverent jest pertained to that bloody episode in the history of these colonies, and not to the battle of Blenheim,"—laughing lightly. "I only judged the present by the past in assuming that I was your benefactor,—not an interloper,—and I crave your pardon, as I entreated his."

"We had passed Blenheim and the massacre," replied Francis, catching the gayety of his tone. "I had just made bold to ask the particulars of the romantic expedition of the Knights of the Golden Horseshoe."

"I withdraw my apology on the spot, and reclaim the meed of gratitude!" rising, amid the shout that greeted the sally. "In the certainty that Blenheim and Mount George left no time in which to do justice to the massacre, I shall take pleasure, if these fair despots will parole us, of walking with you to a spot whence I can designate to you the route taken by the savages on that occasion. Mistress Martha! I depute you to recall us and come to the rescue of the captive knight, should the sanguinary recital threaten to equal in length the storied battles of the Duke of Marlborough!"

Francis arose with alacrity and moved away with him after a word to Evelyn, a bow and smile for the others. All heard the beginning of the narrative as the two strolled toward the river :

"Westover, at that time, was the property of Master

George Thorpe, the friend of Opechancanough, who was the uncle of the Lady Pocahontas. I might add that Thorpe was the friend of all Indians. He was explicitly warned of his danger by an Indian squaw employed in his family, but refused to credit her story or distrust his Indian allies,——

"No, Fairy!" to the child who escaped from her mother and chased him with the petition that she might go along,—"we are talking of ugly things that would frighten little ladies out of their small wits. Go! tell Caliban that Colonel Byrd sent you for a piece of plum-cake as big as your two fists, and make the fists as great as you can!

"You do not take snuff, Mr. Francis?" producing the box inscribed to the memory of John Cary and Jacob Dryden. "But you will excuse the petty vice in one who cannot tell a story aright without this stimulus to memory and imagination."

"'Twould argue monstrous arrogance in me to call it a vice of any dimensions whatsoever, sir!"

The young man, accommodating his bounding step to his companion's stately gait, looked happy and spoke brightly. He felt that he gained ground hourly in the esteem of the man whom he wished above all others to win.

"I thank you for a graceful and a gracious consent!" He regaled a nose classic in outline with the aromatic dust, while they sauntered forward. "We waste pity, after all, upon those who met a speedy fate from the tomahawk. The prisoners taken alive merited more compassion. They were put to death—nay! they *are* put to death at this day with all the tortures that ingenious malice and cruelty can invent. And (what shows the baseness of the Indian temper in perfection) they never fail to treat those with the greatest inhumanity that have distinguished themselves most by their bravery. If he be a war-captain, they do him the honor to roast him alive, and distribute a collop or two to all that had a share in stealing the victory."

"Yet the parent government would legislate for the protection of these fiends!" ejaculated Francis. "They should the rather be extirpated like wolves and serpents!"

"There spake the intolerance of youth!" punctuating the phrases by application to his "stimulus." "Dare classical scholars reproach the poor Indians for this when Homer makes Achilles drag the body of Hector at the tail of his chariot for having fought gallantly in defence of his country? Was Alexander the Great, with all his famed generosity, less inhuman to the brave Tyrians, two thousand of whom he ordered to be crucified in cold blood, for no other fault but for having defended their city most courageously against him during a siege of seven months? And I should add that the braves on both sides perfectly comprehend what seems to us monstrous cruelty. If the victim belong to a hostile tribe, he makes it a point of honor all the time to look as pleased as if he were in the actual enjoyment of some delight, and if he never sang before in his life he is sure to be melodious on this sad and dismal occasion.

"We are now"—halting unexpectedly and wheeling full upon his companion, but with unaltered face and accent—"beyond the boundary-line of Westover, and

standing within the limits of Berkeley. Upon Mr.
Harrison's ground, I may demand of my Lord Peterborough the motive and end of this scoundrelly masquerade!"

CHAPTER XVI.

THE one ill-advised word in the sentence that fell, a
blinding blow, upon the auditor, was the penultimate.
It stung like the whip of hail across the face, and
aroused all the patrician within him. The hurried
breath of utter astonishment had not passed his lips
when he was outwardly as self-possessed as his interlocutor.

"We will not quarrel as to words, Colonel Byrd,
when so much weightier matters claim attention. Else
I should resent the epithet you have chosen to apply to
my presence here and thus. You have asked a question for which I had not intended to wait. It was my
declared purpose to seek you in your own house to-
night, and to state boldly why I have crossed the
Atlantic, and why visited Virginia——"

"Under an assumed name! Excuse the interruption,
but I must, perforce, remind you that between gentlemen certain irregularities are difficult of explanation.
Sailing under false colors is one of these."

"The name is mine!" imperturbable as stone.
Native courage, race-tradition, the tenets and customs
of courts panoplied him in triple mail. He even
smiled faintly with a fine, cool disregard of the conse-

quences of action and word that compelled the other to a degree of respect. "My godfathers and godmothers in baptism called me 'Charles Francis.' The second name, coming from my mother's family, was dropped from daily use. The first was borne by my grandfather, my father, and myself. I am an honest man, Colonel Byrd, who wrote to you six years ago, expressing an honest love for your daughter——"

"If you please, we will leave her out of a discussion that may grow warmer than should such debates as men of honor and delicacy are willing to hold concerning their wives and daughters. I may be willing to accept the tale told by Lord Peterborough of the voyage to, and travels incognito in a barbarous country. Young men of quality and fortune have a right to their vagaries. I, as a humble householder and a parent, have a right to defend home and child from the possible consequences of these vagaries."

A light flush wavered to the young nobleman's forehead, but he evinced emotion in no other way.

"Yourself must know, Colonel Byrd—no man better —how preposterous is the suspicion that aught I could do or say could react unfavorably upon her whom I honor most of created things. You forbade me to see or write to her again in the letter which was the only sign you vouchsafed that my passionate appeals had reached you. You told me that you would not give your daughter in marriage to a Catholic——"

"Unless you object, I prefer, as more just, the term *Roman* Catholic!" interjected the Colonel, in punctilious parenthesis.

"As you like! When I returned from the Continent

in haste on hearing that you were in London, I found that you had taken your daughter and departed, none knew whither. I had said to her at our last interview that naught in the power of man or fate should separate us for aye. My grandfather admired Miss Byrd, as did all who had the honor to meet and know her. Yet he opposed my suit as strenuously as yourself, being bent upon my union with an English lady of his selection. I had but one answer for him and for you. I was not my own master, but dependent upon my grandfather for the bread I ate. I determined to carve out my fortune with my sword, and declared my purpose to him. Had Miss Byrd been willing to brave your displeasure, to fly in the face of your prohibition, I had never let her return to America.

"You know the rest. I have, in all my life, loved but one woman. Even after my grandfather's death made me the possessor of his title and nominal heir to his fortune, there were vexatious delays in the matter of legal adjustments that seemed endless to me. I never swerved, for one minute, from my intention to cross the sea and throw myself at her feet, so soon as I was free to do so. I have waited almost seven years for her. I shall wait for her while we both live."

"And her reply to the paladin who chose postern and pass-key instead of trumpet and drawbridge?"

The cutting sarcasm fell blunted against the mailed breast of the younger man.

"You have been, in your time, courtier and soldier, Colonel Byrd. It should be needless to represent to you the expediency of extraordinary measures when Necessity holds the whip—measures that would seem unjustifiable in ordinary circumstances. Had I presented myself at your door under my new title, I should have been coldly received; probably been denied speech of Miss Byrd,—or I should have owed more agreeable treatment to the fact that Lord Peterborough, and not Charles Mordaunt, sued for hospitality. I am still young and romantic enough to wish to make my way to your good graces and to those of Madam, your admirable wife, as a man, a commoner,—yet a gentleman, —who claimed no advantage from extraneous circumstance. I acknowledge that such design was not in my mind when I left England. My one thought was to seek, to win, and to wed the bride to whom I had remained so long constant. That which commended itself to me as the worthier scheme was conceived upon the voyage. I said, ‘I will not court favor for rank and wealth, or risk disfavor on account of the past.’”

“A scheme so clever betrays a shrewd wit and a delicate,” observed the listener. “I should be at no loss to detect the workmanship, even had I not known who was your fellow-passenger. ‘The woman tempted me!’ Your excuse is as old as Eden. One instant, if you please!” as a gesture threatened interruption. “Had I been conversant with none of these evidences of feminine complicity, my ingenious friend, Mistress Martha, has put a clue into my hands by a winsome special plea entered yesterday for the suitor who should present himself to me, bearing her signet. She stipulated that he should be heard for his suit’s sake, and not be prejudged by favor or disfavor,—the very phrase you have just employed. I engaged to give her hypothetical wooer candid audience. Albeit not so nominated in

the bond in the present showing, I do not withhold it.
To a rude colonist who has tried to bring up his family
to fear GOD, to honor the king and to speak the truth,
that section of your romance that has to do with the
imposition upon a confiding household of another
woman's lover as her very own will require even more
than feminine casuistry to justify it."

The blue eyes kindled under the sneer; reply trode
hastily upon charge, yet mien and language were temperate.

"You leave out of sight the circumstance that my
original intention was to become the guest of Mr. and
Mrs. Harrison. That, not until we were abreast of
the Westover wharf on our way to Berkeley, were we
aware of the change in our plans consequent upon Mr.
Harrison's sudden seizure. As Mr. Francis, Mrs.
Jaqueline's guest and the invited guest of Berkeley, I
had been announced. As such I must accept the
generous hospitality tendered by Mrs. Byrd as the
representative of her afflicted friends,—or return churlishly to Jamestown, foiled of my purpose. Miss Byrd
was upon the wharf when the sloop touched at Westover. I could not go back!"

The brief last sentence escaped against his will.
Having uttered it, he turned half-away, looking, by
chance, toward Westover and the trysting-grove. Above
intervening trees towered the windowed roof and the
tall chimneys of the homestead; between clumps of
shrubs he had glimpses of fluttering robes and lounging
figures. The children had been sent home after supper,
and only the low pulse of cheerful talk, and now and
then a happy laugh, stirred the sunset stillness.

In this fateful moment, by a caprice of mental action, recurred to him the tale of the Icon painted by the death-flash upon the victim's breast. Would he carry the fair picture he gazed upon always upon the inner chamber of his imagery?

For he knew already what was before him; that not one plea of his defence had availed against the determinate will of the man who feigned to balance the scales of rightful judgment in untrembling hands; the inexorable will that had never wavered in six years' observation of his daughter's patient pain; that had brought to this interview a purpose as calm as the October heavens, as resistless as the roll of the mighty river to the ocean.

Colonel Byrd filliped from his finger-tips a half-pinch of snuff with the smile of one self-remindful of a matter overlooked in more important counsels:

"We are forgetting the probability that your charming Portia, who has honored my daughter by standing proxy for her comparatively-insignificant self, may use the authority vested in her to end our talk should the time of your absence—I dare not say *mine*—appear tedious.

"Your fence is passably good, my lord. Had Providence called you to the bar, you would have established a reputation as special pleader. To save time—precious by reason of the probability I have hinted at—we will break the buttons from our foils and make a sharp end of the bout. Your grandfather, the late Lord Peterborough"—lifting his hat in grave respect—"was the Adonis, the Crichton, the Rabelais of his day, which was, by the ordinance of inscrutable

Heaven, a long one. My personal relations with his lordship were cordial. He was a man of the world, and we understood one another.

"Your father"—this time he did not raise his hat—" was—your father! This circumstance, albeit one over which you had no control, would seal my lips had the plea that replied to your former suit of Miss Byrd availed to abate your pretensions. I spoke truly in alleging my insurmountable objection to the union of any member of my family with one belonging to your communion. A distaste and a dread of Popery runs with my blood through my veins. I am frank with you in this, my lord, as I purpose to be in what is to follow. Had my daughter trampled upon the prohibition based on this ground, she would never have seen my face again, and thus I assured her in so many words. A Protestant young woman who has been properly nurtured, thinks—not twice, but twice two hundred times—before she braves the paternal curse."

"If causeless? Surely in this day of general toleration of religious opinion and faith, one may come to view such differences as of less importance than when the safety of a nation was believed to depend upon the precise shade of a sovereign's belief."

"You would add, in court parlance, ' *Nous avons changé tout cela !*' I take leave to differ from you there; but concert or variance of sentiment on this point happens to be of slight moment in the present instance. Your father, the Honorable Charles Mordaunt—recollect that I am driven to say it, Lord Peterborough !— was my mortal enemy, and I, his! I bear in my sword-arm the scar of a thrust dealt in the desperation of what his second and mine believed to be his death-agony. He recovered, and the duel was kept from public knowledge. We never met again, but I know that to his death he remained my implacable foe. I am confident of this, if for no better reason, because I would sooner slay my fair and well-beloved daughter with my own hands than give her into the arms of his son. You resemble him so strongly in person that I might earlier have penetrated the secret of your incognito but for the dust cast into my eyes by ingenious Mistress Martha Jaqueline. You may be as unlike him in heart and soul as Ithuriel to Satan, but his blood, his name, and his face are yours. This is my answer. I can have none other to give in six years more, or in six-and-twenty, should my disembodied spirit be then invoked. Shall we rejoin our friends?"

"One moment!" said Lord Peterborough, his voice no longer firm and full. "Your disclosure has shocked me unspeakably. My father, as you know, died when I was but a child, but I find it difficult to credit that he carried to the grave the resentful memory of a youthful quarrel——"

"And—your hesitation would signify—greater difficulty in comprehending how I, at my age, can hate a dead man in his tomb"—never a symptom of anger in accent or visage. "Mutual comprehension upon this topic being manifestly impracticable, we will receive facts as they are and close the argument. Your preference would be, I presume, that the unfortunate affair be brought to a termination without more tittle-tattle than is absolutely indispensable to the happiness of the divine creatures who compound gossip for the polite world.

"If, as I choose to take for granted in consideration of the amicable relations that have long existed between Berkeley and Westover, your present hosts are as profoundly ignorant of the lineage and title of the stranger under their roof as were Mrs. Byrd and myself when you were at Westover,—the rest will follow easily. I would, likewise, believe that the widow of my revered friend, Edward Jaqueline, is not a conspirator with her volatile daughter. The knowledge of the facts in the case being thus confined to four people, your exit from a neighborhood where, I regret to say, you can no longer be comfortable—*or welcome*"—dwelling blandly upon the emphatic words—"can be easily effected. You may rely upon me to use my best endeavors to accomplish an end so eminently desirable for all concerned."

He had taken a dozen steps toward the trysting-ground when he was overtaken by hastier feet. The resemblance to the man he had tried to kill more than a quarter-century before, was so marked in the son's face that the Virginian grasped his cane with a darting thrill of the old murderous desire.

"No degree of insult, overt or covert, can hurry me into forgetting that you are by many years my senior, and the father of the woman I love and intend to marry—aye! though she were hedged about by a thousand devils!" said the young man, arresting him authoritatively.

"Plagiaristic of Martin Luther!" commented the Colonel, regretfully. "But somewhat must be allowed to youthful excitement!"

"I have had your ultimatum"—continued the English-man, mastering his choler with a strong effort. "Now, hear mine! I do not consider myself bound by so much as the strength of a hair by your refusal to sanction my honorable addresses to your daughter. Refusal based upon rancorous revenge that dishonors humanity. If I can win her who is, already, in heart my wife, by fair means, it shall be done. If not—let foul means be met by desperate measures!"

The Master of Westover stopped a foot short of the line dividing the two plantations, and again had recourse to the heir-loom snuff-box.

"I know the Mordaunt blood, when hot, to be a most pestilent fluid," he uttered, composedly. "Since etiquette and expediency—twin tyrants to whom all Christendom does homage—require that we return to the revellers together and in seeming amity, we will e'en hoist a flag of truce figuratively, and declare an armistice until good-nights are said. After that, the black flag!"

"You stayed away for an eternity!" pouted Martha Jaqueline, tripping forward to meet them. "I could not half enjoy the sunset without you, Colonel, and here is Madam Byrd descanting upon the danger of river-fogs and night-damps, and all sorts of auguries of speedy separation. You've been long enough to kill, capture, and torture every colonist who ever set foot in Virginia. Marlborough's battles were nothing by comparison."

"So Mr. Francis is thinking, although too civil to repeat the words you put into his mouth!" retorted the Colonel. "Strike, but hear!—of the surprise I have prepared for you, one that might buy forgiveness from a sterner judge than your adorable self. Caliban! run down the hill to the persimmon-bushes yonder, and bid the fiddlers who should be in hiding there, come up. What say you to that, my dear Lady Disdain? Will not a dance upon the sward atone for our joint *lèse majesté?* What, ho! young sirs and merry lasses! 'Foot it featly here and there!'"

To the secretary had been committed the duty of stationing the fiddlers three in ambush, there to await the master's orders. Not until this was done did he consider it altogether safe to acquaint himself with the details he must master if he would sympathize intelligently with his chief's annoyances. He locked the study-door, unlocked the escritoire, and ran his eye over every paper that had come in the morning mail, until it alighted upon this paragraph in the letter of a titled correspondent:

"The new Earl of Peterborough has at last succeeded in possessing himself of all the property his grandfather could not spend, or take away with him. He would seem to be an improvement upon his father, whose only exhibition of discretion and propriety was in declining to outlive *his* father, the late lord. Take him all in all, we shall ne'er see Peterborough's like again. He was as gallant as Amadis, and as brave, albeit more expeditious in his journeyings. He had seen more kings and more postilions than any other man in Europe. It was the popular saying that he would neither live nor die like any other mortal. But die he did, and, as we may be sure, not of his free will. Otherwise, it was in him to cheat his grandson, as he cheated his son, out of a peerage. 'Tis said the young fellow—now rising thirty years of age—has much of his grandsire's wit and liking for adventures. If this be so, you will, belike, hear of him, for he sailed t'other day for America."

CHAPTER XVII.

"THERE is no such thing as human premonition!" the Westover oracle had pronounced.

Mr. Fontaine smiled, in recalling the dictum on his way to the Byrd homestead the morning after the sylvan fête. Notwithstanding Madam's prognostications, the fog had fallen late overnight. It had, also, been late in rising on the morrow. At ten o'clock the rime yet sparkled, like hoar-frost upon brake and grass, and silvered the webs spread over the stubble-fields. Evelyn had called them once, in his hearing, "the fairies' bleaching-grounds." At thought of the graceful conceit, the half-smile was more tender.

She was singularly gentle, even for her, to him, nowadays. Last evening, during the absence of her father and the English guest, her talk with him was confidential. She had doubts and scruples on divers points on which she would consult him. She desired to be upright and truthful, always, if she could. But if a great and long-coveted good could be obtained only by what strict moralists would account questionable measures—what was one to do? Was not the maxim,

"Of two evils choose the less," sound and safe in such a case?

"If one is absolutely shut up to the choice of an evil," Fontaine answered. "The deceitfulness of human nature often inclines us to the belief that there is no alternative, because we have already decided to do one of these two things, and we will see none other. There is seldom—scarce once in a thousand times—a direct conflict of duties. The fault is in our distorted views of right and wrong."

"But where the welfare of more than one person is concerned?"—Evelyn went on, her lovely eyes full of vague trouble. "Where it is not *possible* to do what two people—or three—or four would advise, and the claims of both parties seem equally good,—how can one decide what is really and simply and altogether right to do?"

It was very sweet to be deferred to, and to be allowed the privilege of ministering to the guileless soul in its perplexity. He did not venture another glance at her, lest she might divine how sweet he found it. He picked up a rose that had fallen from her hair before trusting himself to answer. She seemed not to recognize the flower in his fingers, and, by and by, he put it into his pocket.

When, full of years and honors, he returned a blameless life to Him who gave it, the embrowned petals were found in a sealed packet in a secret drawer, were speculated over idly and wonderingly, and cast aside with other rubbish.

They were rich in color and scent, and quivered with the warm pulses of the hidden heart while the rector made reply,—

"A good rule for general adoption is, 'the greatest good to the greatest number,'—*cæteris paribus.* But general rules are frequently a misfit in special cases. An enlightened conscience is a pretty safe counsellor."

"Ah!" with what her step-mother reprobated as her "Frenchy manner,"—"if one is satisfied that her conscience *is* enlightened! Suppose we, Mr. Fontaine, that you, as my spiritual guide, admonish me to do one thing, and my father, my natural guardian, command me to do another, and a diverse—what course am I to take?"

"'Who shall decide when doctors disagree'—if not the patient?" returned Fontaine, playfully. And more seriously: "There arise occasions in every human life when the soul feels itself to be solitary save for the Presence that ever attends it. It must act of, and in, and for itself. The nearest and dearest of earthly friends may not, then, intermeddle with its joy, or enter into its bitterness. Do not ask why this is so. It is GOD's will; therefore, in some way for our good."

At that others had broken in upon the dialogue. But for the interruption, he felt sure that she would have spoken more frankly and specifically of that which vexed and tried her. Whatever it might be, and whensoever she might confide it unto him, the confidence must strengthen their cordial mutual understanding, and lessen the distance between them.

Thus musing, and feeling the beauty of the day rather as in sympathy with his tranquil happiness than as an accessory, he rode through wood and plantation until he met Colonel Byrd, again mounted upon Pluto, at the outermost gate of his domain.

"*A la bonne heure*, Monsieur Fontaine!" cried the genial seignior, checking his restive steed. "You are bound for Westover, I hope? My Lady was wishing for you but now. A nasty happening has troubled her soul to the depths, and naught but the consolations of the clergy can calm it. I commit what slight share I have had in creating the commotion to your friendship and sterling judgment. Meanwhile, I choose the wiser part of valor. You are under the ægis of the cloth, and therefore safe. The blessing of the fugitive be with you!"

The chaplain was not alarmed. He knew too well the bland autocracy of the ruler of the realm and his spouse's wholesome awe of her polished lord to apprehend trouble for himself in deciding between them. Madam took life—with her, almost a synonyme for domestic worries—hard. The worst the umpire had to fear was some fresh act of contumacy on the part of William the Third, whose instructor in Latin and Greek Mr. Fontaine was in the interregnum separating the *régime* of one English tutor from another, or she suspected Caliban of pilfering, or Isis, Osiris and neophytes had failed in some cardinal culinary process.

Caliban flew out to the gate to hold his stirrup as he alighted, a marvellous condescension in so distinguished a member of the household staff.

"Mis' Evelyn say 's how she mus' see you, suh, arter Mistis done wid you!" said the lad, hurriedly, dropping upon one knee to brush the rector's shoes. "She say, 'don' go 'way, please, suh, 'tell she see you, ef 'tain' 'till plump night!'"

The message was as unique as urgent, and rendered

more peculiar by the sight of Madam's august self approaching the door through the hall.

"You are as welcome as an angel from heaven!" she cried, offering both hands, and pulling, rather than drawing him into the library.

When they were within, she shut both doors, and waved him to a seat beside her on the sofa.

"Welcome as an angel of mercy to this afflicted household!" she pursued, with real feeling that robbed word and action of melodramatic effect. "Such a terrible night and morning as we have had! Evelyn could escape after the awful scene with her father upon our return from the tea-ground last night. She has been locked in her room ever since, and only answers me through the door that she wants for nothing save to be left to herself."

"Yet she sent a message that she wished to see me!" thought the listener, grieved to learn that she suffered, yet inexpressibly moved that she turned to him for comfort, when others were excluded.

"But *I* must keep up and about, and smother my feelings, and pour out coffee and make talk at break-fast-table, on account of Colin Bass and the servants (not that *he* would ever discover anything that wasn't right under his nose!), and smile at the Colonel's jokes. It is his way—one of them—to seem in extravagant spirits when he is most dangerous. Heaven forgive me for the word! but I am sore bestead, Mr. Fontaine! For 'tis I who am blamed for the whole mischance. ' Had *I* been blessed with ordinary prudence, the man would never have been let into the house!' 'Tis I who am ' so crazy after English gentry that I must, forsooth, snap at this sprig of nobility and make him and myself the talk of the county by toadying him and giving the lovers all manner of opportunities of billing and cooing,' when if *he* 'had been at home, the trick would have been exposed in forty-eight hours after he and that arch-traitor Martha Jaqueline landed at the Westover wharf.'

"And this, though I plucked up spirit to tell him last night in Evelyn's presence that, by his own showing, 'twas not until the letter from my Lord Orrery arrived yester-morning saying that Lord Peterborough had sailed for America, that *he* suspected anything! How, after reading that letter, he could disport himself all the afternoon as if naught had happened; telling his funny and sad stories, and saying the gallantest things to Martha Jaqueline, who is, sooth to say, more to blame than the poor young lord, for, says not the poet that 'all's fair in love and war'?—passes even my understanding, and I've known William Evelyn Byrd for a dozen years. I'm sure I went into hysterics forthwith, when he marshalled me and Evelyn—who looked fit to faint at his first word—into the study when we got home from what I'd been saying was a mighty pleasant tea-drinking and dance,—and says, without a lisp of preface,—

"'My Lord of Peterborough and I had a right merry crack anent massacre and masquerade, this afternoon. I was minded'—so he ran on, smiling all the while—'to quote to him Samson's pleasantry about ploughing with an honest man's heifer, but conceived the figure, however apt, to be hardly respectful to you, my Lady Byrd,' he says. 'At any rate, until

I had assured myself how much, or how little you know !'

"I must say that Evelyn proved herself her father's child so soon as she gat back color and voice.

"'My mother knew naught of the matter you speak of,' she declared, never flinching one whit. 'Blame me, if you like, for I knew all. 'Twas I sent the token to Jamestown that lured him hither,' said she, head up and eyes a-light. 'But spare her. She is innocent !'

"Upon hearing which, as I said, I fell into hysterics that might well have lasted 'till now had not his dealings with Evelyn diverted my attention. She is not my own daughter, Mr. Fontaine, but my heart bled for her while hearing the cutting sneers and caustic reproaches she had to endure, and she moving no more than one of those stone posts out there, never trembling, nor letting fall a tear—only when he asked, sarcastically, of the next act in the farce, saying, as a statue might open its mouth and speak: 'I have given my word to marry Charles Mordaunt, papa, whether you will or no, and I cannot go back !'"

The narrator was crying so heartily that she was forced to muffle her face in her handkerchief and lose volubility in sobs.

Fontaine sat like the statue to which she had likened her step-daughter. From the wet tangle of the tale, he drew one thread that seemed to wind about and cut into his heart.

This Francis was Evelyn Byrd's early lover. She loved him still. She had always loved him. She would marry him. The beautiful dream that had glorified his own life—the dream that, of late, he had believed was shaping itself into reality that was divine—was more tenuous than the morning vapors, and left arid blackness after it.

Madam Byrd's suspicions—freely expressed to Mrs. Carter and Miss Lotsie, of the rector's passion for her step-child—were swept away and forgotten in the whirlwind of the new revelation. Perhaps the knowledge that the girl was adored by a nobleman put the idea of an untitled suitor with a moderate income so far out of mind that she would not have admitted to herself having indulged it.

For full five minutes her sobs were the only sound in the room. It was hard for her to stop crying. Her nerves had been racked, and the relief of pouring out the story to the only person to whom she had a right to speak of it brought a copious shower of natural tears. In the absorption in her own emotions, she was deaf, dumb, and blind to all else.

From where he sat, Fontaine looked through the window at the iron gate with the interlaced initials and curved tracery of the arch above; the clumsy eagles balancing themselves upon the globes surmounting the posts. He actually found himself dully numbering the stone balls and pineapples alternating upon the iron railing running to the right and left of the gate. Since he had entered the house, the gossamer-nets robing the stubble had dried into invisibility. The line of parti-colored forest defining the horizon cut keenly into the sky; he heard, in the same partial stupor, the whistle of a partridge above the confused clamor of the poultry-yard beyond the stables. Still further away, and heard as in a swoon, a band of negroes was "shucking" corn, and chanting a mournful plantation-melody. His world was under a spell. His life had sunk down dead at his feet; in the horrible suffocation of heart-constriction, he could not lift a hand or stir a limb. Presently, when the woman beside him ceased to sob, he must speak. He would rather die.

The door behind him, opening into the drawing-room, was softly unclosed. He divined by whose hand before Evelyn Byrd glided around to the front of the sofa.

"Mamma!" she said, quietly, "I knew that Mr. Fontaine was here, and I have come down to speak with him."

"Thank you!" as he set a chair forward for her, himself remaining standing, his eyes riveted upon the floor. "Do not stir, dear mother! I want you to hear what I have to say to this good friend of us all. Mr. Fontaine! you gave me yesterday as a safe rule, 'The greatest good to the greatest number.' Shall I deceive the trust reposed in me by him who has kept faith with me through years of temptation and absence? Shall I displease his friends and mine, violate my plighted word, and break my own heart—or obey my father's unreasonable command? This is the question I have been asking myself all night long. You are a good man—upright, humane, and wise. Were my case that of your sister,—if the man to whom her heart had been true for six years, offered her clean hands, a pure life, and steadfast love; if her father had found no fault in him other than his kinship to one who was his enemy a generation agone—how would you counsel her to act?"

The appeal was made with studied composure to the

last question let like a red-hot arrow into Fontaine's heart. This was not the docile, sensitive woman whose character he thought he had read from fly-leaf to "Finis." In the throes of the past night she had entered upon a new being. She was as remote from him at every point of this as if the width of the globe had divided them. In every tone and look he read that her mind was definitively made up. The manner of her reference to him was warning, not irresolution.

"Thus and thus stands the case!" it said. "GOD and I have decided it in the awful solitude of soul of which you spoke to me last night. As man and priest, dare you controvert my resolution?"

He raised his eyes and regarded her steadily when she ceased to speak. She looked taller for the regal pose challenging his dissent. Her eyes were large and luminous ; her lips scarlet ; the flush in her cheeks was fixed. All the woman was up in arms. Yesterday, she was as one who could die for her love. To-day, she would fight for him to the death, and scorn the grant of a life in which he had no part.

Obeying an impulse that proved him her peer, Fontaine held out his hand as to a comrade, she rising to take it. While he spoke he held it in a brotherly clasp.

"Yourself must know that I can render but one answer to your citation. At the tribunal of your conscience and of mine, in the hearing of the GOD whom we both serve, I say that your allegiance is due to the man you love, and who loves you!"

Before he could hinder her, Evelyn carried his hand, first, to her forehead, then to her lips. Both were burning, and the tear that fell with her kiss was hot. Solemnly he led her to her step-mother.

"She will need all the comfort your affection can bring!" he said to Madam Byrd. "She is in the right, and we must stand by her."

As the two women fell weeping into each other's arms, he walked to the window and looked forth with eyes between which and the landscape had fallen a black pall.

CHAPTER XVIII.

THE race-ball was on Monday night; the race and the race-dinner were on Tuesday; the *fête-champêtre* was on Wednesday afternoon.

At sunset on Thursday, all the Westover house-servants and field-hands were convened upon the lawn in obedience to the Master's summons. He made short work of the business in hand. Not one of them—man, woman, or child—was to quit the plantation until further notice upon any pretext whatsoever, unless by his express command or permission. He had given orders to the neighborhood patrol to arrest, tie up, and whip within an inch of his life any servant of his found out of bounds without a written pass signed by his own hand. Lest some might count upon cheating the patrol, he gave further warning that he meant to be his own constable for some time to come.

"You know what *that* means!" While he talked, he tapped the lid of his snuff-box with a shapely forefinger, the nail of which was in form like a filbert, and the color as delicate as the finest lady's in the land ; his smile was placid, his broad-lidded eyes were sleepy. "I can do with less sleep than anybody else on this plantation. For a fortnight to come, each one of you may depend upon finding me in the very last place in which he expected to see me, and at the exact minute in which he didn't care to set eyes upon me. Those who obey orders, stay at home, and mind their own business, have nothing to be afraid of. If one of you cross the Westover fence on either side, even to pick up a chinquapin that has fallen from a Westover bush upon Berkeley land, he will wish he had never been born, so sure as my name is Byrd. If I never was in earnest before, I am in earnest now. Now, be off, all of you !"

Colin Bass heard the imperial ukase from his writing-table, and smiled his pale, joyless smile to the vellum quarto. He had been closeted for two hours of the afternoon with his superior, and found an opportunity to confide to one who, he felt, ought to know whatever was going on upon the premises, certain ugly surmises forced upon his own unwilling mind by incidents connected with the visit of the Englishman, calling himself Francis. He—the respectful secretary—brought forward proofs in support of the theory that this same gentleman was better known elsewhere under another name. These proofs were mainly lapses in discretion on the part of Mistress Martha Jaqueline in speaking to and of Mr. Francis ; in the Englishman's inattention when accosted by the title he had given as his ; his familiarity with English high life ; his reserve as to his personal antecedents; lastly,—and here the ingenuous scribe made a pause that did honor to his heart and taste,—he had "chanced to overhear the stranger addressed in private conversation as 'Your Lordship' by—— one who never styled him thus in general conversation."

"Name him!" ordered the auditor, until now as impassive as ice, and as uninviting to the communicative.

The secretary hesitated, painfully.

"I beg you will not insist upon that demand, sir. Nothing but the certainty that your generous confidence was abused would have impelled me to the extremity of broaching a topic so disagreeable to myself, and, I doubt not, to you. The *lapsus linguæ* to which I refer occurred at the ball of Monday night, and was probably overheard by myself alone."

The Colonel smiled cynically.

"I should, then, have said, 'Name *her!*' Was the unwary fair one an unmarried lady?"

"If you will excuse me, sir——"

"Most certainly *not!*"

"Then, sir, the speaker was not a spinster."

"Was it Mrs. Harrison or Mrs. Carter?"

Another obviously reluctant pause.

"Neither, sir!"

"I have no further inquiries to make, Mr. Bass!" mildly courteous. "I thank you for your fidelity to my interests and commend your discretion. What you have said is safe with me. Heaven is my witness,"—a dreary smile wringing the healthful color out of the handsome face,—"I was never in bitterer need of faithful, incorruptible friendship. When a

man's foes are those of his own household, and he is
betrayed with kisses, he may well be ignorant where
to turn."

The unprecedented evidence of natural feeling moved
even the phlegmatic secretary. He cleared his throat,
and fumbled with his papers before replying.

"I am a blunt man, sir, and slow of speech, as you
are well aware. But whatsoever lies within the power
of one so humble as myself would be thankfully done,
if it could be of service to you. You have befriended
me, sir, when I most needed a helping and guiding
hand. Mine are not showy talents, but such as they
are, they are at your disposal. It is the old fable of
the lion and the mouse. I cannot protest, sir, but I
never forget a benefit, and your benefactions to me are
beyond number."

The Colonel pushed his chair away, and took a few
turns in the small room.

"I believe you, Bass!" he halted to say. "I am
warring single-handed, and against odds. Time was
when I could have fought the world with one arm
lashed behind my back. But I am nearing the age at
which one is afraid of that which is high, and things
deal deep wounds that would once have scratched the
surface alone. I know you for an honest fellow—and
a loyal. More than that, for a grateful. You cannot
eat my bread and drink of my cup, and yet watch for
opportunity to lift the heel against me. GOD help
me! I am not sure, just now, that I can lay my hand
upon another among the many whom I have befriended!"

It was in this hour of unprecedented weakness, when

his heart was smarting under what he esteemed as defection on the part of his closest of kin and nearest in interest, that he unfolded to the wily factotum all the latter had schemed to discover. The strongest and most self-reliant are not proof against paroxysms of self-distrust and morbid longing for sympathy. The sense of the awful loneliness of the human soul steals past the defences of pride, the guards of experience, the consciousness of native force, and compels the cry for succor. This is the solution of many an enigma involving the resort of the mighty to the weak, the unbosoming of the reticent, and the hold of the bad upon the good.

Bass hearkened with averted eyes and respectful humility. His whole mien was assuasive to the wounded spirit of one who faced failure as an unfamiliar enemy; with whom success was habit—not a happening. To a naturally arbitrary temper he joined belief in himself that was well-nigh sublime. Despotic in his principality; courted for wealth and personal accomplishments; admired for dauntless energy and infinite address,—his mental attitude of haughty surprise at the resistance opposed to his will by the young nobleman and the recalcitrant daughter who had so long meekly submitted to his decree,—was exchanged for wrath none the less deep because concealed, when he awoke to the humiliating truth of his own impotency. Both parties were of age. His authority as parent, magistrate, and freeholder could not, lawfully, hinder the marriage of these two, should they maintain their right and wish to be thus united. He had forbidden his daughter to hold any communication with her lover, with Martha Jaqueline, and with Berkeley, while the two remained there. He had threatened disinheritance, severance from home and kindred, the objurgation of neighbors and friends—and looked vainly for tokens of yielding.

She, who was erst the most amiable and docile of his offspring, had become obdurate and unfeeling. Had he struck her to the earth, he could fancy her rising to confront him with the steady formula,—

"My word is given. I must keep it!"

Dull red gathered under the thick skin of the secretary, and suffused his averted eyes in hearing of the girl's contumacy. The knuckles in the hand clinched upon his knee beneath the table stood up whitely, and the narrow line of his mouth thinned to a thread. Yet, under the knowledge of the fallacy of the audacious hope he had nursed; the stinging consciousness that to the high-bred woman he loved with passion amazing to himself, he was little above her groom in station by comparison with her titled lover,—there was ignoble triumph in the victory he had won over her father's prideful prejudice. Tyrant and tool had reversed positions. What he had listened to put the master into the servant's power—whether the master suspected it or not.

"Nothing, then, will move you from your purpose?" he asked, deferentially, when his chief seemed to expect him to speak.

. "Nothing in heaven, on earth, or in hell!"

Bass bent his head submissively, as one who has no opinion or volition apart from his superior's.

"Well! what have you to suggest?" said the Colonel, impatiently, when submission and silence had continued long enough to an angry man's apprehension.

"You may blockade the plantation,"—yet more deferentially,—"and for a season hinder correspondence. But 'tis manifest that the only sure preventive of an event you would deem disgraceful and deplorable, is to remove, at once and for all, the cause of the disturbance."

" What the devil——"

"Do not misunderstand my meaning, sir,"—undismayed by the flash of wrathful astonishment in the dark eyes. "I intimate naught that would offend the law. Nor am I prepared to designate by what means the offending party could be wrought upon to depart from a region into which he has brought such —inconvenience. But right sure am I that circumstance may be found that will bring about this end. With your permission, I will think the case over for a night. We must have time."

The Colonel eyed him with a mixture of new-born respect and vexed amusement. The calm assurance that a way would be found out of a complication that had baffled the older and wiser man, carried weight with it, little as the Master guessed of the subordinate's inchoate designs. Bass had a cool head and a long one. It was a prudent thing to call him into counsels the proud man would have sworn, three hours before, that he would share with none alive.

Least of all was he inclined to confer with him whom he had jestingly commended to his wife's confidence. Mr. Fontaine had not remained to dinner, nor had the

Colonel received any report of his visit. Madam Byrd and Evelyn had sat at table, apparently composed to quiet cheerfulness. Little was said by either, but that was without effort or constraint. Yet the change did not look to the cynic like Christian resignation induced by ghostly admonition. It lacked the limpness that goes after chastening. It was more likely that Pierre Fontaine, like the high-minded, sensible gentleman he was, had declined to take sides in the family squabble. If this were so, he, Colonel Byrd, would not drag him into it. He could rule his household without priestly interference.

Secretly, he cared not to tell to the rector a story he had had no difficulty in relating to the secretary. With all his gentleness, Fontaine was as fearless as his patron's self, and no respecter of persons. He let pass the raillery directed at his profession by his powerful parishioner; the enumeration of the hundreds of Christians the chaplain made by baptizing the children of heathen Indians and Gentile whites in the expeditions led by Colonel Byrd into North Carolina and Virginia. He smiled silently when held up to general notice as the stubbornest of water-bibbers, and did not rebuke verbally coarser jokes, some of which the maker thereof thought worthy of perpetuation in his diary. But where the Right was imperilled by sophistry or by dissolute living, Elijah was not braver, or John the Baptist more outspoken, than the mild-mannered descendant of a persecuted race. The Colonel had doubts as to his own ability, clever reasoner though he was, to persuade his reverend neighbor to regard Evelyn's recusancy as heinous, or the parental opposition to the projected union as entirely righteous. He had no doubts, moreover, as to how Fontaine would receive the declaration of the autocrat's resolution to prevent the marriage by stringent measures, should pacific fail.

Bass was the safer ally of the two for the enterprise in hand.

Bass's own opinion was emphatically to this effect. He could have assigned a hundred cogent reasons for it, as he lounged down the rose-alley leading to the church-yard that evening. He usually took his after-supper smoke among the tombs, a privilege nobody disputed.

" Wonder ef *he* got er parss !" sneered Caliban to the colored cabal, seeing him pass the kitchen-window.

The secretary's acute hearing caught the gibe and the shrilly-derisive " *ki-yi !*" applauding it. He could let the dogs yelp. He owned their master. He put it broadly to himself, with all that it conveyed. He had been careful not to suffer the potentate to feel that he had stooped lower than ever before in his honorable life. To humble him would be to alarm arrogance and prick pride into fury. The tongue the owner thereof was pleased to stigmatize as "slow," had glozed over the truth of debasement on one side, and vulgar victory upon the other. He was never more obsequiously the Master's instrument than when he sat down upon the tomb of the first William Byrd of Westover, and struck a light with flint and steel, holding the well-filled pipe in his left hand.

The tobacco did not ignite at once. Three times the blue spark snapped viciously at and caught the tinder, revealing every sunken letter in the Latin inscription registering provincial offices filled by the sleeper under brick and marble, and his demise—"*4th Die Decembris 1704 post quam vicessit. 52 Annos.*"

Each time he waited until one might count thirty before making another attempt. The third essay was successful, and he smoked tranquilly, his face riverward, his legs, disproportionately short for the trunk they supported, swinging idly against the brick wall of the ugly parallelogram.

It was a safe place for meditation. The negroes feared to cross the church-yard after sunset, and the whites were not nocturnal prowlers. There were bats in the conical bell-tower set upon the chapel-roof, and, annoyed by the light, one flapped Colin's hat with his loathsome wings, in a downward swoop. He made a futile pass at the thing with his hand, never withdrawing his gaze from the river. The ruddy flicker of the pipe-bowl showed his heavily-moulded features, stolid, but for the gleam of the deep-set eyes. The rest of the figure was in obscurity. The moonless night was the blackness of darkness under the trees. While he stared at the water, something like a falling spark illumined the filmy surface and was gone. Another followed presently, and after an interval, a third. The secretary smoked on placidly to the bottom of the pipe, pocketed it, and lounged aimlessly down the declivity to the beach.

The shadows stirred uneasily twenty yards behind him. Something only distinguishable as a darker shade skulked over the supple, uncut grasses, lurking now behind a tree, then wriggling, serpent-like, in the open spaces,—always in the lounger's track. When he stopped at the water's edge, the shadows were still; but Caliban, barefoot, and stripped to his shirt and breeches, lay flat among the willows within ten feet of him.

The muffled stroke of oars was already audible. Before the keel could touch ground, the secretary landed, with a spring, in the bows, and the craft, a dark oblong among the mists, swept into the stream.

Caliban stood upright, gaping after it, foiled and furious, for one despairing instant. The next, he had cast off his garments twain, and slipped into the shallows like a water-snake. There was no time for thinking, yet a glint of fun went through his mind with the first stroke in deep water.

"Marster ain' neber say northin' 'bout takin' ter de *water!* He say, ' Don' sot you' fut on nobody else's *lan'.*' Reckon I done been got ahade o' de partrollers, dis time!"

He could swim as fast and as soundlessly as an eel, and float by the hour on his back, the water on a level with his mouth. If his enemy thought to elude him by quitting *terra firma*, he reckoned without account of a riverside and "quarters" education. Some rays the sun had forgotten to recall lingered in mid-stream, but the kindly fog would soon blot them out. Should he be perceived by the inmates of the boat, he had only to dive and swim away under water. Rash as the expedient appeared, he was safer than on a land-hunt. The oars were plied slowly; he swam fast, almost too swiftly, for he was brought up alongside of the boat by the sudden slackening of the rower's stroke.

"Hold up!" said Bass, so close to the lad that he ducked, dived under the keel and came up on the other side, a little farther away. "'Twas well you were on

the look-out. I was afraid you mightn't be, and I
wanted particularly to see you to-night."

"Thar was two on us, then! I was a-layin' by
on a-purpus to see could I git sight or word o' you,"
chuckled the captain of the smuggling-vessel.

"What's the matter? Anything wrong?"

"Maybe you kin tell bettern me. I've got the chance
of a passenger."

"To Norfolk?"

"To Norfolk—and clean across?"

"Who is it? and what'll he pay?"

"I didn't ask his name, but he's a English gent by
the cut on him. Overhauled us this arternoon 'bout
a hour o' sundown. A-rowin' of hisself in a tight little
canoe. Had the pull o' the devil's race-horse. Said 's
how he was out on a breathin' spell, jes' to stretch his
arms. He was a-stretchin' on 'em proper, too. He
slacked up an' hove 'longside on seein' me a-leanin' over
the guards. We'd dropped anchor for th' night 'bout
a mile below Wyanoake, an' the men was all ashore."

"After chicken-roosts, I'll be bound. If you don't
have a care, my man, one of your rascals will bring
back a spare bullet to you, one of these fine nights, or
you'll have to look up another hand."

"The niggers goes bail fur 'em gin'rally. It's few
fat pullets gits jerked off the roosts by Jack. A string
o' beads to a wench, and a taste o' liquor to a buck, pays
honest for all the poultry. Let my lads alone for keep-
in' whole skins! But, 'bout my passenger! We falls
inter talk, me bein' lonesome an' sociabel-inclined, an'
pres'ny I axes him aboard. He sez he don' keer ef he
does, an' I draps him a line to make fast his skiff, an'

when 'tis done, he comes up on a rope, han' over fist, like a reg'lar seaman, an' sots down for a chat. An' sez he, pres'ny, 'What's your cargo?' So I sez, 'Ginseng an' pelts an' potatoes an' a little tobaccy, when I ken git hold on it honest an' reasonable,' sez I. 'For bein' as how I'm marster o' my schooner,' sez I, 'I can't take no heavy risks,' sez I.

"So I mixed two horns o' grog, stiff an' sweet, an' he tossed off his like a man, an' praised it too, an' pretty soon I was a-showin' on him how I'd things tolerable ship-shape fur a sea-farin' man, in cabin, an' fo'kiskle an' all. 'An' when do you sail?' sez he, when he'd sworn he'd never see a cleaner hole, an' that he wouldn' min' eatin' off the decks. 'A-Monday night,' sez I.

"'Aha!' sez he, sort o' struck-like, an' goes off inter a brown study.

"By 'n' by he speaks up in a' off-han', free-n-easy way,—'Be hanged!' sez he, 'ef I'm not in half a min' ter take passage with you, myself, ef you ken make room fur me. Have you any other passengers engaged?' he sez. 'I don' hanker arter passengers in a gin'ral way,' sez I.

"'But 'sposin' you're well paid for it?' sez he, kind o' jolly. "Thar's that tidy cabin o' yourn,' sez he. 'Would you think a hundred poun' a fair price fur it, all the way to Liverpool, for one—maybe two passengers, who'd lay in their own vittels in Norfolk?' sez he. 'I'm dog-tired o' knockin' roun' the world!' sez he. 'You look like a man as ken hole his tongue,' sez he. 'I'm a-stayin' with frien's on the river, an' ken bring my mails aboard Sunday night, to be all stored away snug, an' come aboard myself, Monday midnight, with a frien' or two whar will see me down the river,' sez he.

"Well! I played off a little for the sake o' business, an' knowin' I dassent clinch the bargin' 'thout askin' you, seein' you're the biggest owner o' the schooner. 'T las'—to belay this d——d long tongue o' mine, I promised he should have a' answer ter-morrer evenin', 'bout sunset, an' the men ter know nothin' 'bout it, for fear thar mought be fuss with frien's whar's expectin' to have him pay *'em* a visit——What the devil's the matter with you? You'll capsize her, if you thrash 'roun' that ar way!"

"A d——d mosquito!" Bass slapped his hand smartly. "Keep her moving a little, won't you? so they won't settle so thickly. If I'm not mistaken, Providence, or luck, or the devil, have helped you to the very business I wanted to see you about. What was your Englishman like?"

"A d——d personable chap! Blue eyes, with a laugh in 'em all the time. White teeth, an' lightish, a'most sandy hair. He'd a ring on his little finger with a big stone in it that was jes' the color o' deep-sea-water. Hands like a lady's, but they had the grip in 'em when he laid holt on them oars o' hisn!"

The information was received in silence so profound that Caliban dared not strike out with hand or foot. Turning slowly over, he floated like drift-wood in the languid wake of the boat, his toes almost touching the stern, the water displaced by the oars closing over his face in alternate waves, so that he had to watch his opportunity to take breath.

"Tell him you'll take him!" said Bass, finally, in tones hoarsened by the fog, or other cause. "Don't seem over-willing, you understand? but don't let him

slip for a thousand pounds! The job may be worth
all of that to you——What the deuce is that?"

Caliban's nostrils had shipped a sea, and a sneeze,
uncontrollable and stertorous, was the consequence.
The two men listened with suspended oars and breath.

The mists unfolded like rolls of cotton-wool upon
the surface of the water; from the land came the hoarse
bay of a hound upon a night-chase over the low
grounds; the wash of the river against the sides of the
boat was a dying whisper. All else was as still as
death.

"Sturgeon, or a porpus!" the seaman said, carelessly.
"They're the d——dest creturs for outlandish noises at
night. A-chasin' an' a-nosin' one another, an' sometimes a'-squealin' 'n' a-gruntin' like horgs. They call
sturgeons 'Charles City bacon,' you know."

Caliban heard every word, still floating like a becalmed log, returning unuttered thanks to the hoary
curtain settling between him and the speakers.

"Maybe so!" There was a dubious inflection in the
tardy accent. "But even so, there's no wit in talking
business so loudly that the fishes can hear."

They whispered after that so cautiously that only an
occasional word reached the half-breed. His limbs
were numbing with inaction in water colder than on
summer nights. Should the secretary take a notion to
go directly home and institute inquiry for him, trouble
might ensue. He would better get to land silently and
speedily. The conspirators did not hear the cautious
sweep with which he struck out straight for the haven.
His lithe, naked body slid through the water as an
arrow parts the air. Not until he shook himself,

spaniel-fashion, on the beach, did he indulge in an audible inspiration.

He got into his few clothes slowly and ruminatively. The adventure had been unsatisfactory. Mistress Martha Jaqueline's sweetheart was, of course, the Englishman who wanted to go home. But unless— which the boy could not believe—he meant to run away from her, there was no reason why he—Caliban— should concern himself with his proceedings. The Harrisons—and maybe the Carters—were teasing him to stay longer in America, and he was homesick,—that was the upshot of the matter. Bass would probably pocket two-thirds of the passage-money, and Caliban would rather that he should not; but that was nothing when weighed against the delight of leading Colonel Byrd to the cave on the very night set for removing the smuggled goods, and seeing the entire party bagged. Then, his master would be compelled to believe his tale of how the plot was discovered. For a few minutes, he meditated conference with Mr. Francis, but the attempt would involve personal peril, and that gentleman would laugh at the story. If the cargo were seized and the captain arrested, no harm could befall the passenger except a delay in the time of embarking, and Mistress Martha would not object to that. On the whole, there seemed to be no reason for changing the well-concerted policy of silence and vigilance.

He lay in the flags on the river-bank until Bass returned, an hour later; dogged him up the bank as he had dogged him down; saw him into the house; peeped in at the window to behold him settle himself with three long candles on the table, to writing in the ponderous book Caliban knew as well by sight as the scribe did himself,—then, the spy betook himself to his pallet, assured that he might conscientiously dismiss the guard for the remainder of the night.

CHAPTER XIX.

THROUGH the windows of the Berkeley manor-house, lances of light fought with the fogs rolling up to the house walls. The master's recent illness made him suspicious of night damps, and a fire of "lightwood-knots" and cedar logs crackled behind the brass fender. Wax-candles in silver candelabra were upon a table that had been rolled back from the middle of the floor to make room for the circle of chairs about the hearth.

Genuine fire-worshippers then, as now, the Virginians seized upon every excuse for adding this element of comfort to living-rooms where cheer and *home-iness* were the desiderata. They wished to see, rather than to feel, the flame. The family-party, enlarged by unexpected arrivals at supper-time, fell into form, naturally, with the red hearth as centre and motive. Girls in flowing muslins, and matrons in brocade, sheltered their eyes from glare and heat behind screens that were fashionable *bric-a-brac* in the drawing-rooms of that time. Attendant beaux stood or sat behind them, glad to be a degree further removed from the fiery heart of the chimney. Yet all felt the scene to be the fairer, and the spirit of the hour more glad, for the leaping, writhing, dancing blaze.

Martha Jaqueline—her dark, piquant beauty well set off by her favorite yellow taffeta, a cluster of golden-rod in belt and hair—was directly opposite the windows of the inland front of the house. Her cheeks were like the sun-kissed side of a Georgian peach ; her eyes glowed with what most of the spectators read as tenderness that disdained concealment, in meeting the upward regards of him who sat upon a cushion at her feet, tuning a guitar, while he talked with her.

The picture was perfect—as a picture,—but certain lately-arrived spectators marvelled inly at the complacency with which Lieutenant Maynard, albeit only a former suitor, surveyed it as an episode in the love-making of these two. The Englishman's profile, clean-cut as a Grecian god's, was cast up strongly against the oaken wainscot beyond him. The graceful abandon of his attitude, the debonair archness with which he looked up and replied to his mistress while his white hands toyed with string and screw, and slipped along the frets of the instrument,—every detail of the gracious whole was noted at its fullest worth by a man who, having left his horse at the gate, loitered upon the porch, unseen and unheard.

While he looked and tarried, the drawing-room troubadour began to sing,—still looking into the warm duskiness of the eyes above him, as if drawing melodious passion from their depths,—

> " When the willow-sap was flooding,
>   All the tender boughs a-budding,—
>   When hoar-frost and sun were gilding
>   Twisted nests of thrushes' building,—
>   It was then I saw my Norma,
>   Through the bare hedge o'er the lea.

" When the murmuring leaves are sighing
O'er the silent brook low-lying,—
When the thrush's brood are sleeping
'Mid the darkening shadows creeping,—
There I wait and watch for Norma
By the thick hedge o'er the lea.

" When the willow droops the greenest,—
Sweeps the streamlet's rim the cleanest;
When the young bird flies the strongest,
When the sky-glow shines the longest,—
It is then I'll take my Norma
From the green hedge,—o'er the lea." *

As dreamy yearning arose into the full, rapid tide of rapturous anticipation and the sighing of flute-like tones was exchanged for the ringing peal of a clarion, the unseen spectator wheeled abruptly away and walked to the edge of the porch. His strong, slender hands beat upon one another to bruising; he looked up at the heavens, inky beyond the shimmering bands of radiance outlined by the window-frames,—and a cry broke from him :

" Ah, Lord ! he has everything, and I—since this morning—naught !"

The rich man with his exceeding many riches of flocks and herds; the abundance engaged by express blessing of the Christ to him who hath,—he would not have been human had not thoughts of these racked him into arraignment of Divine justice and mercy. This darling of fortune—princely in beauty and in wealth; rich in all enslaving arts; audacious, yet generous, in the buoyancy of youth, health, and happiness—

---

* By Jesse Lynch Williams.

was a *robber!* For one black, blinding minute, he hated him! For a longer minute, he stood, balancing the inclination to abandon the purpose that had brought him hither, against the remembrance of what he had decided, before leaving home, to be duty, based upon the best thing a mortal creature can know as faith and practice,—self-sacrifice for another's weal. With head bared to the dank darkness of the dumb night, he prayed briefly and wordlessly,—a cry out of the depths beneath to the depths above,—and walked quickly to the door.

His knock was unheeded by the gay company within. Francis was singing again—a rollicking roundelay, with an accompaniment all run and sparkle. Three or four servants had stolen to the closed door of the drawing-room to listen to the music, and one answered Mr. Fontaine's summons.

"Show me into Mr. Harrison's office!" he said. "I see that they are getting cake and wine ready in the dining-room. When you take it into the drawing-room, manage to let Mr. Francis know that some one wishes to see him. Say 'some one,' and let nobody hear you excepting himself. Do not give my name."

The fellow was quick-witted. Mr. Fontaine had not to wait many minutes in the host's " study" or " office," environed by law-books, tobacco-boxes, pipes and stoppers, guns, stirrups, walking-sticks, a fox's head, a deer's antlers, pistols and holsters, a cavalry-sword and spurs,—when a light step rang upon the floor of the passage, and the Englishman entered.

He brought in with him a breath of the presence he had left. The faint incense of balsamic woods, the smell

of flowers, the bouquet of the rare old wine he had
quaffed,—hung in his garments and bright hair. The
smile had not passed from his mouth, or the flush from
his face.

"Mr. Fontaine!" he cried, hurrying forward with
extended hand. "I did not look for this pleasure!
The servant's speech of 'some one who would see me,'
misled me."

"He but discharged himself faithfully of the message
committed to him, my lord."

Fontaine had bowed respectfully, not seeming to
observe the offered hand. Still standing, one arm
cast behind his back, the hand of the other in his
breast, his soldierly figure erect, he sustained calmly
the piercing inquiry of the startled eyes, as the title
met the ears of the peer.

"You come from Westover, then!" the debonair air
giving way to serious anxiety.

"Not directly, my lord. But, as you have divined,
my errand has to do with that which nearly concerns
my friends there—and yourself."

The young nobleman put his arm about the rector's
shoulders, with a frank and most engaging smile.

"Come, Mr. Fontaine! let us sit down and talk
together as befits the good friends we have grown to
be in these last four weeks of daily companionship.
No 'my lording,' and no diplomatic beating about the
bush. Until I leave this, I am Charles Francis, and
the nature of my business in this country is known to
none but the few who can be intrusted with the secret.
You will take my word for it that I am right glad to
reckon you in the number—and second to none. I

confess that my impulse upon perceiving you here"— with a light-hearted laugh—" was to ask, ' Come you in peace or in war?' But the second glance assured me on that score. You were at Westover to-day noon. Was word of any sort sent to me from thence?"

" None there knew of my purpose of coming hither. Nor was it a purpose until an hour ago. How knew you of my visit to Westover?"

Francis laughed again. The excitement—even the suspense of this critical period of his life—quickened his blood pleasantly. Lord Orrery had written truly that the fondness for adventure was transmitted with his grandfather's blood and title. He would have headed a hopeless charge with a cheer, ridden gallantly, his blue eyes unclouded, upon a belching battery.

" As one of us, you should know that the incomparable Mistress Lotsie walked boldly into the lion's mouth—or at least his den—this morning; by a *coup d'état* gained the heart of the citadel. Caliban was here at sunrise with despatches apprising us that war had been declared and that there was menace of a blockade. Whereupon, that admirable friend of her species departed straightway for the enemy's country. She went by way of church-yard and river-road across the lawn, right in at the front door, and hearing the rattle of cups and sound of voices in the breakfast-room, took her way up to Miss Byrd's chamber, where she tarried, closeted with the occupant thereof for four hours. For fear of implicating Mrs. Byrd, and thereby causing trouble with her husband, that dear and worthy lady was not taken into confidence. Our valiant emissary escaped from the premises while you were in the library with Madam. The puzzle is simple enough, you see.

"I wish to heaven"—a shade falling upon his animated countenance—"that all others pertaining to this affair were as easily solved. Or, that the brunt of the battle fell upon me. I swear to you, Mr. Fontaine, that when I think what is laid upon the delicate, sensitive being I would fain shield from every breeze of adversity, I am driven past my patience and well-nigh out of my wits. It is small matter for marvel that I should gird at the needless delay of so much as a day in releasing her from tyranny and captivity fitter for the Middle Ages than this most Christian century. I had a few lines from her by the hand of our faithful Mistress Lotsie."

His hand moved toward his bosom never so slightly, but Fontaine felt sure that the billet lay over his heart. As himself had but yesternight borne home the flower that had fallen from her hair!

"She is unconquered—and unconquerable!" continued the lover's softening tones, a beautiful light flooding his eyes. "She does not even say to me that she suffers, lest I should have the more to bear for the knowledge. Mistress Lotsie tells me that she is as pale as a lily, though heroic as Joan of Arc. I likened her Monday night to a lily among thorns. If only I might gather the thorns into one sheaf, as Arnold von Winkelried the foemen's spears, and sheathe the barbs in my bosom, that she might go unscathed! Show me a way by which to do this, my dear friend,"—letting his hand fall to his companion's knee,—"and I am forever your grateful debtor!"

"I would that I could!" in sincerity that was almost vehement. "I fear me there lie yet severer trials before her—even a siege that would chafe to breaking a spirit less finely tempered. Her father is inexorable."

"Therefore, we shall not adventure his displeasure needlessly. He will be forced to hearken to no more prayers from his child, to no further arguments from me. Unless he bind her, hand and foot, she will come to me before another week goes by, and, hand-in-hand, we will voyage toward the rising sun."

In a few sentences he narrated the incident of the afternoon, and how like the finger of fate had seemed the rencounter with the captain of the schooner.

"A trig little craft, and not incommodious. I half-suspect that my burly sea-dog would not rise superior to the temptation of contraband tobacco and spirits, were the chance offered him of running them safely into an English port. I trust to make him accept other freight better worth risk and trouble."

The end was then, so near! Something hammered fast at the base of Fontaine's brain; the hand he passed across his mouth was chill, and strange prickles were creeping over the back of it.

"I fancy that I know vessel and man," he said, choosing his words with precision. "Is she not *The Mocking-Bird*, and is not her master a thick-set man of forty years, with a decided cast in the left eye?"

"The very man—and the name of the schooner! Is he, then, respectable, and not blackguard?"

"Respectable enough, to the best of my knowledge. He ran away to sea when a lad, and led a roving life until he was past thirty, sometimes not revisiting his home in Williamsburg for years at a time. Latterly, he has settled down into the owner and master of a trading-vessel. This is the story I have from his mother, who is my parishioner it is now three years, and a decent body, but stone-blind. *The Mocking-Bird* was bought from Colonel Byrd two years ago, and, having been built to his order, is stanch and sea-worthy."

"I could wish, of course," resumed the other, the tender light lingering in his eyes, "that my bonny bird had a daintier cage; but, the voyage over, I can make amends for discomfort and privation. We shall put in at Norfolk for such matters as that small seaport can supply toward softening prison-fare. *The Mocking-Bird* weighs anchor Monday at midnight, the tide serving then. Mr. Harrison will, on that afternoon, privately procure a marriage license.——The law requires this, does it not?" he interrupted himself to ask at something he saw in the other's face.

"Before you say further, let me explain what brought me hither."

Fontaine drew away, involuntarily, and the caressing hand slipped from his knee. Powerful as was the Englishman's personal magnetism,—admit, though the unavowed lover must and did, the sincerity of his devotion to his intended bride, and the ingenuous manliness of every utterance,—the bruised heart flinched, under the increasing pressure. It was not easy for the self-contained master of himself to lend patient heed to the details of that which would beggar him forever. The effort to hide his hurt constrained his manner to coldness.

"Among the arguments adduced by Colonel Byrd why this union should not take place was the positive assertion that, in your eyes, the solemnization of the marriage by a Protestant clergyman would have no binding force whatsoever. If I add, in what may seem but bald parlance, that which her mother furthermore confided to me, you will comprehend that sincerest regard for her whom you seek to marry moves me to plainness of speech. There is no clergyman of your communion within one hundred miles of this. The endeavor to procure one would be attended with inconvenience and loss of time that would be warning and gain of time to Colonel Byrd. As a minister of GOD's word, I must remind you, my lord, that should you esteem the Church of England form of marriage maimed rites, and the obligation thus imposed null and void in conscience and in law, you have no right to desecrate what is to you a sacrament, by an empty form of words. To wed a woman here and thus for the satisfaction of her conscience, and to voyage with her to England, even with the intention of having the marriage solemnized there in such fashion as accords with your faith, would sully her fame in the eyes of your compatriots and fellow-religionists. Miss Byrd has no elder brother. I am here in the stead of one to institute inquiry into what nearly affects her honor and happiness."

Lord Peterborough was upon his feet, his face darkening haughtily.

"I am glad to know that the inquiry is of your and Mrs. Byrd's institution. Had you intimated that her daughter had part or lot in it, I should have flung a

denial into your teeth. *She* knows—and"—reproach-
fully—"I had hoped you, also, that I would go back
to England as I came—alone—sooner than have my
wife's fair fame overcast by the shadow of a shade.
Colonel Byrd is a citizen of the world and a man of
honor. That he has put forward this damnable insinuation is but one proof the more of the inveterate hatred
he bears my father's son. Miss Jaqueline may surely
be trusted to be jealous for her friend's reputation.
Before we left Jamestown, in hopeful anticipation of
this contingency, she had opened correspondence with a
venerable French abbé resident in Norfolk. She will,
herself, company down the river with us, and with her
duenna witness the second ceremony legalized by a
license taken out in that town. We shall, then, be
beyond Colonel Byrd's jurisdiction and such violent
measures as he might set on foot in a neighborhood
where his will is law."

"If this be your design, why risk discovery by the
license in this county and the Protestant ceremony?
To the conscience of a Church of England communi-
cant, the service uttered in GOD's name by the lips of
an ordained clergyman, of whatever creed, would be
sacredly binding."

The young peer came nearer, a smile of extreme
sweetness on his lips, his eyes soft and bright. Laying
one hand on the rector's shoulder, he brought him face-
to-face by grasping the hand hanging, cold and passive,
by Fontaine's side.

"Cannot you guess, dear friend? Would I bear
away my bride and leave unsatisfied one desire that I
could fulfil? She loves her church as I love mine.

Shall I cast dishonor upon that church by seeming to scorn her ordinances? Have you known me so imperfectly as not to divine that the first ceremony would suffice for me,—heart, soul, and mind? The second is for the world of carping scandal-mongers. The first gives me *my wife!* for richer, for poorer, for better, for worse, so long as we both shall live. And these words I know, dear Mr. Fontaine, Evelyn would have you utter above her head. Your benediction will best atone to her for the loss of her father's blessing, the lack of a mother's kiss. Are you satisfied?"

Pallor such as overspread the face he gazed upon he had never seen except upon the cheek of the dead. The form almost within his embrace swayed slightly; the eyes closed for a second under knotted brows. When they opened, their misty agony was alarm and mystery to him. The mouth moved twice before words would come :

"You ask much! But I will do it !"

"Am I selfish, then?" queried the other, perplexedly. "Would your action, were it discovered, bring about a rupture with Colonel Byrd? I would not injure you with him——"

A gesture, haughty to disdain, replied before Fontaine spoke :

"I care naught for what he—for what any man may say or do! Since this is *her* wish, what else should avail ?"

"I thank you in her name and in my own. I ought, perhaps, to grieve somewhat"—the moved smile again touching lips and eyes—"to rob Virginia of her rarest jewel. And *she* has told me once and again of the love and reverence she bears yourself. How your brotherly sympathy and advice have been balm and strength to her in the hours of need—and they, pure soul! have been but too many! Of the sweet counsel you have held together——"

"For God's sake, no more!"

The ejaculation tore like a bullet into the hearer's brain as it had torn from the anguished soul—and he was alone!

When the rushing shock of amazement and compassion suffered him to pursue Fontaine in the swift retreat to the outer entrance, he was just in time to hear the thud of a horse's hoofs down the avenue leading to the highway.

CHAPTER XX.

"Looky hyur, Ann' Isy! I don' wan' ter be cross long-a you, an' I don' keer fur to cuar' no tales inter de house, so you better lemme off er holpin' seed dem 'ar grapes ter night!"

Caliban said it judicially, leaning half his length upon one end of the kitchen-table, his face golden-bronze in the flare of lightwood torches stuck into iron sockets at the mouth of the chimney. At the other end of the table loomed up the white turban of the Egyptian deity, her fat arms bared to the shoulders. Before her were bowls and pans; beyond them was a mountain of fox-grapes, filling the room with true Falernian fragrance. Along each side of the board were ranged five sad-eyed assistants, boy and girls, furnished with small, keen knives, with which each grape was to be halved, then seeded, with as little waste of juice as might be. Caliban had, at the petition of Isis, been excused from house-duties directly after supper that he might bear a distinguished part in the task. His deft fingers made him invaluable in the finer offices of kitchen and pantry; his saucy chatter kept the young laborers awake and enlivened the spirits of the elder. He lied as fast as he could talk, as everybody knew; but the tales of which he was invariably the hero, were none the less entertaining for that, while his prankish humors were an increasing source of excitement to the mates who envied, while they had not the hardihood to imitate the tricks that earned him many a "lick" from clothes-stick or rolling-pin.

"An' *you* looky hyur, you imp o' Satan!" retorted the mistress of ceremonies; "I aint got no time fur to steddy 'bout no sort o' sassiness you got in you' hade. Mistis done been give me *my* orders fur ter git all dese yer grapes stone' by bade-time so's she ken see de sugar put wid 'em fo' she go to sleep, an' set 'bout her marmerled early in de mawnin'. An' I ain' got more 'n haff han's 'nuff fur ter git de wuk done—not ef ebery one o' dese yer lazy niggers was to wuk ten thousan' time mo' harder 'n' dey eber did in all dey born libes. Soon's Mistis done tole me what she wan' done, I jes' step out dar in the grabe-yard 'n' cut dis nice little slip offen a honey-locus' tree whar growed 'pon a grabe. Dar ain' nothin' like a stick whar's growed outen a dade pusson fur to make folks wuk."

She exhibited a long wand, pleasingly adorned with bark and stubs.

"I knowed who 'ould be de fus' one ter ketch it, too! Take you' lazy copper-colored karcuss off er dat 'ar table, 'n' set 'bout you' wuk, or I'll limber it outer you' hide, you Ingin puppy, you!"

Caliban dragged himself up without indecent haste.

"*Now*, Ann' Isy, you know I'm better at dodgin' 'n you is at hittin', an' you don' wan' ter w'ar you'self out a-chasin' roun' arter grease' lightnin'. Ef you do, good-by to de grapes!"

Infuriated by the snicker running down the table, Isis started up, shillalah in hand, Caliban sidling toward the door as she advanced upon him. He eluded a well-directed blow by leaping backward down the steps, and, keeping at a prudent distance, began a low-toned parley with his foster-mother.

"I couldn' say it in dar whar *dey* is, Mam' Isy," wheedling and important; "but I 'clar fo' gracious dat I is jis' *obleege'* fur ter look arter sompin' petickler ter night. Dar's de debbil ter pay, an' dis yer nigger is wanted fur ter keep de pitch hot. Dat's a fac'! I'll tell you all 'bout it Chuesday mornin'. Ef I don' git off ter night, dar won' be nothin' ter tell."

The swart Eve loved scandal better than her own ease. She raised her voice, backing toward the kitchen steps,—

"Well, go 'long! Ef *Mis' Evelyn* wan' you, I ain' got nothin' fur ter say. I been hyur somebody callin' f'om de up-sta'rs winder, but you tell Mis' Evelyn I hadn' no notion 'twas *her*, or I'd a sont you right straight off. Tell her I mighty sorry I been keep you so long, an' *ef* she please, ma'am, fur ter sen' you back soon's she done wid you!"

Caliban heard but four words of the sentence of release, a matter of no consequence, since it was concocted and delivered for the sole benefit of the disappointed crew within doors.

Bass had gone out this evening, unperceived by him, but he counted upon the time lounged away by the secretary over his pipe in the church-yard, and was not uneasy until, stealing down to the lower gate, he missed the red spark under the trees, and creeping nearer, saw that the tombstone whereupon Colin usually enjoyed the "bewitching vegetable" was empty. Caliban made a cautious circuit of the little chapel, keeping close against the wall, peered, in the starlight, behind every tree, and was returning, baffled, upon his track, when his name was called softly.

"Sh! sh! I thought it was you!" whispered Martha Jaqueline, emerging from the denser shades of the grove. She was attended by a lanker and taller shape Caliban knew for Miss Lotsie.

"I can trust you to the world's end!" pursued Martha. "Here is something for you!" pressing a coin into his hand. "Run to the house as fast as you can race, and tell your Mis' Evelyn (let nobody hear you!) that *the course is clear.* You understand?"

"Ya'as, ma'am! but Mis' Marthy, ef you please, ma'am, Mr. Bass he smoke he pipe hyur mos' ebery night!"

She laughed.

"Good boy! I saw him not ten minutes ago. He's off on patrol-duty in another direction. Now, run!"

He was off like a kill-deer, and half-way up the main alley of the garden almost ran against his young mistress, hastening in the direction of the church-yard. She said nothing in response to his breathless message, but he ran ahead to open the gate at the end of the walk for her, saw her pass through into the gloom that swallowed up the cloaked and hooded form, and recollected how much time he had lost by the little adventure.

Bass had gone on patrol-duty, Miss Jaqueline had said. Caliban knew better, and took a bee-line for the spot where the boat was beached last night. The evening was fine and dry, and the water would be chilly, but he would track the thieving traitor at the risk of cold and cramp. As he ran down the bank, regardless of the precautions he had observed when Bass was certainly but a few feet before him, he grinned to think how "Mis' Marthy had fooled Marster." That something had marred the cordial relations existing heretofore between the Berkeley and Westover households was an open secret in the kitchen council. That it had to do with Miss Jaqueline, and, incidentally, with her sweetheart, was almost certain. Miss Evelyn was greatly afflicted by the separation from her dearest friend, and the servants' sympathy was entirely with her. Every one of the house-servants was cognizant of Miss Lotsie's stolen visits, and nobody would have betrayed it, under the lash, to Colonel or Mrs. Byrd. It was natural, to Caliban's understanding, that the young ladies should meet by stealth, and simple loyalty on his part to afford them every facility in his power.

Otherwise, he could have cursed the encounter that had cost him the chagrin of finding the landing-place deserted. He strained his ears for the beat of oars.

The lap of water running inshore before the fresh breeze would have drowned the sound had the muffled rowlocks been within a rod of land. Far down the river he saw a spark like a star,—a lantern hung to the yard-arm of a vessel riding at anchor. This might be the smuggling-craft awaiting laden boats from plantations on both sides of the stream. It would round off his plot handsomely if he could have certain proof that Bass was tampering with overseers and negroes from other places as well as robbing his own employer.

Anyhow, he would have a nearer look at that schooner. A tough river-rat like himself need not be afraid of a cold bath, however strongly his predilections might set in favor of water with the chill taken off. He stripped, and stepped into the lapping stream.

"What are you about, you rascal?"

The speaker was Colonel Byrd. He sat at ease upon a fallen tree, his figure undistinguishable in the darkness from the fringe of bushes at his back.

The lad leaped back to shore, shaking, as in a tertian ague, but ready with a lie.

"I wor goin' fur ter take a wash, suh. Dat's all!"

"Since when have you been so fond of cleanliness? I have a great mind to make you scrub with soap-and-sand, and then dry you off with a hickory-towel. Don't you know better than to lie to *me?*"

"Ya'as, Marster!" miserably penitent, rooted as motionless in the sand as Cleopatra's Needle in the desert.

"Speak the truth, then, if you can! Why are you here? and whither were you going?"

The obelisk had an impulse that turned it as upon a pivot.

"I won' tell you no lie, suh! I wor a-goin' fur ter swim out ober yarnder"—pointing up the stream—"fur ter look arter a net I see one o' de fiel' han's a-settin' ter-day fur ter catch catfish an' eels."

He knew by his master's tone that he smiled.

" In other words, you were about to steal another man's fish! Don't you get enough to eat in my kitchen ?"

" Ya'as, Marster !" shamefacedly.

" So you steal for the love of stealing ? Come hither, you young villain ! Take that ! and that ! and *that !* You are the fellow I heard boasting under my window, last Sunday, that he knew the Ten Commandments by heart !"

Whack ! whack ! whack ! whack ! *whack !* WHACK ! WHACK ! WHACK !

"That is to teach you that ' Thou shalt not steal' is Number Eight. You'll get thirty-one more the next time you are caught in such a mean piece of deviltry as thieving from a *field-hand !* I thought you had too much pride for such a low trick !"

The cane was of lance-wood and well seasoned, and the boy cried out sharply, but not loudly, at each cut upon his naked body. He sobbed ostentatiously when accorded permission to " get himself into his clothes, and begone to the house."

" Hold that snivelling !" ordered the Master, whose tone throughout the episode had not evinced the least heat or discomposure. Indeed, Caliban suspected that he was not sorry to kill some minutes of waste time in what fell so opportunely in his way.

" Ya'as, suh !" with a strangled sob.

He gulped up another, and a third, mingled with an artistic whimper, in climbing by the shortest route to the upper grounds. Then—perhaps because the grass was cool and his back was hot—he lay flat down at a convenient distance from the path by which his master must mount, and waited to see why the latter was keeping watch on the river's brink, alone and by night.

He was as fast asleep as an "Indian puppy" ever sleeps, when the jar of feet vibrated upon his sensitive tympanum.

Colonel Byrd spoke when opposite the prostrate listener.

"He can answer for his crew?"

"To a man, sir. He has a tight hold upon every one of them," replied Bass. "Most of them are never quite easy when on shore—for reasons best known to themselves and the captain."

"It is settled that the mails are to be brought—not sent—aboard?"

"It was the passenger's own proposal. He will, at the same time, make certain final arrangements of which he could not talk this afternoon. 'If a friend—or two—were to accompany him to Norfolk, he supposed there would be no objection. And if he should take aboard another passenger at Norfolk for the whole voyage?' The Captain said, 'There would be no objection so long as the passenger was quiet and peaceable, and willing to pay well for good accommodations.' The answer was that the respondent would be responsible for all that. The Captain reports that the respondent was mightily amused by the questions as to peaceable disposition and so on."

"—— him!" muttered the Colonel, angrily.

" Yes, sir ! The matter would seem to have arranged itself with little interference from us——"

Caliban could wriggle through supple grasses like a snake, but bushes would rustle, and these lined the footpath from the top of the bank to the river-wall. The safer course was to cut diagonally across the intervening ground, scale the wall and reach the house before the Master and his secretary entered.

The pair, thus left behind, became taciturn when the level was gained, perhaps from thought, perhaps from prudence. Their route skirted the church-yard, and in the brilliant starlight reflected from the river, they could have threaded their way among trees and tombs but for the forgotten circumstance that a grave had been filled that day in the lower section of the cemetery devoted to family servants. A superannuated seamstress had died yesterday, and been buried this afternoon. Beside the mound stood a wheelbarrow, with pick and spades laid within it, and all were veiled by the shade of a honey-locust. Colonel Byrd had passed them safely by a step or two, when his companion's shins collided violently with the front of the barrow, and he pitched forward into it, upsetting it and the contents. In attempting to regain his balance, he fell over the pile of moist red clay, floundering there, head downward, until the Colonel, hastening to extricate him, discovered that the trestled bier on which the body had been transported to its last home, was on the other side of the grave, and oddly entangled with the legs of the struggling figure.

Colonel Byrd was courteous and humane to a proverb,

but his sense of the humorous was too finely developed to permit the maintenance of gravity in the situation. His mellow, irresistibly-contagious laugh, first a ripple, then a surge, lastly a billow of merriment—swept over the humbler graves to the marble-topped constructions above the dead Byrds, and was heard by two people sitting on the chancel-steps, their feet upon the slab covering the remains of Theodorick Bland, the builder of the family chapel.

There was enough light from the stars to show the windows as glimmering oblongs set high in the walls, not enough to reveal the movement with which Evelyn Byrd cast herself into her lover's arms, and the defiant air with which, holding her fast, he looked toward the door.

"Hush!" whispered Martha Jaqueline from her seat in the pew nearest the porch. "The door is locked on the inside! We have but to remain perfectly quiet!"

The Colonel's shout to the neighboring quarters followed his laugh:

"Halloo! some of you fellows there! fetch hither a light!"

The flicker of lightwood flambeaux ruddied the glass on the lower side of the church, illuminating dimly the tableau in front of the altar: a woman whose face was as pale as her gown, with her arms about the neck of a man who had involuntarily clapped his hand upon his sword-hip. They moved not during the brief while in which the hubbub of voices went on outside; then the torch-light moved along the opposite wall, and the Master was heard, right under the windows, ordering the bearers back.

"Let the fellow who left that wheelbarrow and bier there report himself to Mr. Booker to-morrow! I wish he had tumbled over them, instead of Mr. Bass, and broken his own neck to boot!"

The danger over, Evelyn trembled like a leaf in a storm.

"The peril is too great!" she faltered, when her betrothed would have rallied her in playful soothing. " Indeed, Charles, we must not linger a moment longer. We are never safe, whether he be in the house or out of it!"

"Blessed be wheelbarrows!" called Martha, cautiously, in accents broken by laughter. "I owe half a crown to the fellow who left it in the path! I shall leave it with you, Evelyn."

"And I a sovereign!" added Lord Peterborough, in the same key.

In subdued tones, he went on to Evelyn:

"It shall be as you will, dear heart! You need to husband strength and nerve for three days longer,— thank heaven, for no more! The continual strain draws cruelly upon you. This little hand is slighter than when I last kissed it. In a week's time you would be resolved into thin air—clear spirit! If you love me, sweet, have a care of what is most precious to me. Keep yourself in health and spirits and hope. You were ever wont to be despondent, and I to look at the bright side of destiny. Until we meet again—a meeting that will, please GOD! have no parting this side of the grave—take a leaf out of my book, and believe that

Fortune must favor those who obstinately refuse to distrust her; that right makes might, and that naught but death can separate you and me!"

In the eloquent pause that ensued, they could hear the boisterous laughter about the doors of the quarters, evidently at the expense of the luckless nightly prowler.

"Now, love!" resumed the tones fraught with fondest feeling,—"always and everywhere my love, and mine alone! on Monday night at ten o'clock, Mr. Fontaine will meet us here, and the hopes of years of weary waiting be fulfilled. Until then, have a brave heart. Trust our friends here and at Berkeley to attend to the lesser concerns pertaining to our voyage. Bring me but yourself at the appointed hour.—What is it, dear?" feeling her slip something into his hand.

"I have a desire—a foolish fancy, you may think it," whispered the girl. "I should like to have you take the ring I have worn with your picture about my neck, except after the door of my room was bolted at night, and put it upon my finger now. Wish it on— if you will! It may be superstition—the belief that it will make me the stronger to endure and to hope. Am I silly?"

"With a sweet and holy folly, my darling!" He kissed the ring when it was fitted upon the tremulous hand, holding it to his lips, passionately and long. "It is 'wished on,' my lily, until I withdraw it to make room for another that will mean liberty and love!

"Mother Mary and all the blessed angels have you in their gentlest keeping until we meet again, my pearl of price!"

CHAPTER XXI.

OF the Berkeley Harrisons, there were in church on Sunday morning but the father and two children. Miss Lotsie Johnson, gaunt and smileless, sat bolt upright in the family pew, found the places for Charles and Nat in Prayer-Book and Bible, and never turned her eyes in the direction of the Westover seat until service was over.

The clear face of the rector, olive-pale above his surplice, was thin as from recent illness; his black eyes were deep and solemn, as he arose from his knees and faced the congregation:

"*I will arise and go to my father, and will say unto him, Father, I have sinned against heaven, and before thee, and am no more worthy to be called thy son!*"

"*Enter not into judgment with thy servant, O Lord, for in thy sight shall no flesh living be justified!*"

His voice, ever full and sweet, had, to-day, an undertone almost plaintive, yet manly.

Evelyn Byrd, kneeling in the end of the pew next the wall, was choked by tears as she would have followed him in the General Confession. When the rest arose, she remained kneeling, battling bravely with the tide of softness unsealed by the opening words of the service.

Some one, presently, reached past her step-mother and the two little girls, to lay a vinaigrette upon the wet leaves of her Prayer-Book. A thrill went through her as she recognized the hand, which the various labors and exposures in which he sustained the pioneer's full part, could never make coarse, or other than elegant. The wave of filial tenderness that responded to the act, nearly broke down what poor remains of self-command were left to her after four days of torturing anxiety and struggle. He had spoken kindly to her at breakfast-time, drawing her into talk such as he had not held with her since his return from his journey, and, in other ways, had testified a disposition to renew their former affectionate relations. She thanked GOD for the gentler memories thus given her of this, the last Sabbath she would ever spend in the home of her infancy and childhood. It was such mournful gratification as swells the heart when the dear face, soon to be hidden by the coffin-lid, wears its loveliest look.

She had no hope of recall in the years to come. The strain of steadfastness that informed her fidelity to her lover was drawn from her father's soul. In becoming a wife, she would cease to be a daughter. The world might be before her. The door of her father's house, once closed behind her, would never be reopened while he lived.

And he was so dear and noble in all else than his opposition to her marriage with the man she loved! so indulgent to, and proud of her, his favorite child! Mr. Fontaine had said that she did well in keeping her troth,—yet why had he selected that passage for this day of all others? Why had he not been near her since the forenoon on which he had learned what was the resolution, he might, for aught she knew to the contrary, consider, upon calmer reflection, unmaidenly and undutiful? Lord Peterborough had told her of his interview with the rector, but with true delicacy, withheld the description of the manner of their parting, and the revelation it conveyed to him of the nobility of the man who stood their friend at such terrible cost to himself. He had promised to bind her in wedlock to him for whom she would forswear parents and native land. Was the text that sank into her soul the priestly probe of a conscience he could not coerce, but must warn?

She heard not a word of litany, or gospel, and of the sermon but one sentence :

"God is not like Jacob, who had only one blessing in store. He hath millions of millions to bestow upon those who love and fear Him."

Had she limited Divine grace in all the years in the which, refusing to be comforted by other mercies, she had cried, night and day, "Give me this desire of my heart, or I die!" Had she submitted patiently to the will of earthly and heavenly parent, would not comfort and compensation from the exhaustless storehouse of blessing have been added unto her?

Rising, wan and weary, from her knees after the benediction, and mingling with the retiring congregation, she was jostled by Miss Lotsie, and descried the swift motion that slipped a letter into the reticule that hung at Evelyn's side. The ring she had worn, boldly and unquestioned, since Friday night, seemed to tighten upon her finger ; the sick heart lifted itself in a quick throb.

"Right or wrong, I cannot and will not give him

up!" she said, inly. "The consequences be upon my head, and mine alone!"

But she must have her word with Mr. Fontaine. He stood just without the church-porch, exchanging greetings with such parishioners as had come from a distance, and whom he seldom met, except on Sunday. A little apart, sweet-faced Mrs. Carter talked with Madam Byrd. Lady Bess left her mother's hand to scamper up to Evelyn the moment she saw her.

"I doin' to dinner at 'ou house!" she proclaimed. "Mamma says so; an' 'ou an' Misser Fonten 'ill show me 'ee pitters in 'ee bid boot—'ont 'ou?"

"O, what a crooked tongue!" cried Evelyn, taking her up in her arms, and hiding her face in the plump white neck. "If you like, my pet! I shall be very happy to have you. Go, ask Mr. Fontaine about the pictures!"

She watched the little witch fly up to him, saw him bow his ear to what the embryo coquette preferred as a confidential petition, and the grave-eyes light in a smile, in glancing inquiringly at herself. At her slight nod he came toward her, Bess swinging upon his hand.

"You would have me dine at Westover to-day? Will it be a relief—a help to you in any way? You know how earnest is my will to serve you."

"I _need_ you!" was the low reply. "I never needed you more!"

They walked around by the lower slope of the lawn, instead of following Colonel and Mrs. Byrd and their guests by way of the garden. Lady Bess made a third in the little party, and did so much of the talking that they were half-way to the house before Evelyn could put the question trembling upon her tongue.

"Did your selection of the opening sentence of the service have to do with *me!*"

"With you? How?"

His unfeigned surprise lightened her heart.

"I fancied—I feared—I wondered if you had changed your mind since Thursday," she stammered, vexed to find herself blushing painfully. "The thought has given me a wretched morning!"

"Lady Bess!" said Mr. Fontaine, "run and see what that is shining in the grass over there! It looks like a diamond! You must believe me," he continued, rapidly, to Evelyn, "when I declare that my own heart dictated the selection to which you refer, and that the application was to myself. Believe me, too, that I can never cease to honor your constancy to your betrothed, or to believe that, with respect to your father, patience has had its perfect work. There is a love that outranks filial duty. 'For this cause shall a man leave father and mother and cleave unto his wife.' You asked me on Thursday what I would say to my sister were she in your strait. I have said it!

"Only a dew-drop, Bess!" as she held up two rueful wet fingers. "That happens, ofttimes, little one, and to older people than you!"

He allowed himself not another syllable that might be construed into complaint of his lot. At the table, full of chance guests, he was ready and adroit in keeping the talk away from Evelyn and Madam Byrd without seeming to shield them from notice.

Madam's sanguine complexion was lowered beyond

its wont; her bright eyes were languid. By common and tacit consent, she was not taken into the secret of the projected elopement. In the hour of discovery and investigation, she would be able to look her lord in the face and say with truth, " I knew no more than you !"

Evelyn would see to it that suspicion should not light upon the woman whose warm heart had opened to her step-child in the hour of need, and dealt out love and sympathy in unstinted measure. The letter to be left for her father lay in a locked drawer upstairs. She would leave nothing for the last day that could be done beforehand. Under cover of the darkness, the faithful Caliban had obeyed without question the direction to carry and leave in the church-porch, the night before, a hamper containing all that she would take away from her father's house. She would go to her lover poor in all but the treasure of love that had gathered and kept, according to the rule of divine usury, the interest of seven years.

"Husband your strength," her betrothed had enjoined. She strove to obey him to the letter. The winds that had swayed resolution and hope during the morning service, were a surprise of which she was ashamed.

She appreciated, and gratefully, Mr. Fontaine's tact in diverting attention from her, but felt strong enough to meet whatever the occasion might demand. In the seclusion of her room, she had read the missive dexterously delivered by Miss Lotsie. It rustled softly in her bosom now, as if trying to whisper to her the love-words, sweet, pure, and solemn, penned by the beloved hand.

"*J attends!*" was set below the signature. And after it—" Heaven be praised! I write it for the last time!"

Had Colonel Byrd divined the suspenseful perturbation of his spouse, the longing to know everything, and the dread lest she should, accidentally, learn anything; the certainty that something eventful was in near store, and crass ignorance as to time, place, and circumstance of the event,—and divining all, had he pitied her from his heart for what she was undergoing and must not show—his deportment toward the harassed matron could not have been more chivalric. Without embarrassing her by downright compliment, he contrived to show her and her doings in the most favorable light; quoted her and consulted her, and left no possible wish ungranted.

At her right sat Mr. Randolph from Tuckahoe, and between him and the host the ball of badinage bounded gayly back and forth to the contemptuous bewilderment of Lieutenant Maynard, who was Evelyn's *vis-a-vis.* The naval officer made a strenuous effort, at length, to introduce topics which would be, he fancied, more interesting to the company at large.

"I was at Wakefield, Friday, Colonel, and had a talk with Nat Harrison upon something that concerns you nearly," he began, raising his voice to address Colonel Carter, who sat at Evelyn's elbow. "He says, unless measures be set on foot to suppress it, that smuggling upon the James and York and Pamunkey will subvert all honest trade. He is of opinion, likewise, that the skippers of many of the so-called trading vessels, licensed to convey our exports to the other side, are not averse to doing a tidy bit of 'running' on the sly. As river-admiral, he is mightily exercised by these suspicions, and would fain have the planters on the James strengthen his hands in respect to patrols by water and by land."

"One moment, if you please, Lieutenant!" said Colonel Byrd, in suave apology. "Before organizing our patrol, taste that liqueur! It is my Lady's latest composition and her best. Which conveys a volume of praise to those acquainted with her skill as a vintner. She put up, last spring, birch wine that has the very spiciness and life-giving breath of the forest. The receipt was obtained—I forget from whom, my dear?"

Madam supplied the name, and certain particulars respecting the manufacture that excited lively interest on the part of the housewives present, and silenced ignorant men.

Her lord lent an indulgent ear, and when the discussion flagged, applied another spur:

"My Lady's achievements throw Mrs. Rundle and Mrs. Glasse so far into the shade that I am unwilling to have her light smoulder under a bushel, albeit her modesty inclines her to invert the measure over the candle. You are confessedly an epicure, Mr. Randolph, and must coax from her a small box of the caviare which is like to hand down her reputation to remote generations. She is exceeding stingy with it, and jealous of adventuring it upon untutored palates."

"'It is caviare to the general!'" quoted Mr. Randolph. "I thank you for crediting me with taste capable of valuing it aright."

"Harrison is, moreover, firmly convinced," resumed

the Lieutenant, "that smuggling is the high-road to piracy. He has grievous suspicions touching a certain ill-favored skipper——"

"Pardon me again, my dear Maynard, but I chanced to hear Mrs. Carter name the 'Beggar's Opera' just now, and would ask her, lest I forget it later, if she have ever read it?"

As the lady accosted had never so much as heard the name of the play before, her command of feature and presence of mind were praiseworthy.

"I have never had that pleasure," she replied.

"Then, Madam, if you would enjoy a rare intellectual treat, allow me to lend the book to you. Then capture Mr. Randolph, there, holding him in ward until that he read it aloud to you. You have not forgotten, Randolph, the time when I was storm-bound at your house, and Mrs. Fleming and yourself triumphed over the bad weather by reading this same work?"

"I recollect how admirably Colonel Byrd read it," corrected Mr. Randolph.

"Nay! but you two finished it. Evelyn, daughter! you will kindly look up the book after dinner and have it put into Mrs. Carter's carriage. 'Twas a droll history this comedy had in London!" The servants were removing the cloth preparatory to bringing in the dessert, and he addressed his discourse to the whole party. "Not altogether in consequence of the wit and humor that sparkled in it, but owing to some political reflections that seemed to hit the ministry, it ran for forty nights successively and gained four thousand pounds to the author. The Duchess of Queensbury was his patroness, and no man with half an eye in his head or half a guinea in his pocket could resist her. Her Grace, like death, spared nobody, but even took my Lord Selkirk—the stingiest peer in England —in for two guineas, to repair which extravagance he lived upon Scotch herrings and water for two months afterward. But the best story was that she made a very smart officer in His Majesty's Guards give her a guinea. She plied him for five, but he swore one was all he had in the world. When her Grace came to consider the matter, she was so touched with compassion that she sent the young liar fifty guineas out of her own pocket the next day to reward his obedience. I think this anecdote was my contribution to the entertainment on that soaking day—a bagatelle by comparison with the excellent reading with which Mr. Randolph and accomplished Mistress Fleming favored me."

The vein of court and literary gossip being opened, smugglers and buccaneers had not a show of a hearing before the ladies quitted the table.

"Lieutenant Maynard is positively absurd with his sea-stories!" Mrs. Carter remarked to Madam Byrd, seated in the wide front of the hall. "But for Colonel Byrd's skill in parrying them, we should have had naught else all dinner-time. His smugglers and pirates exist nowhere save in his imagination, or Nat Harrison's. One is as bad as the other."

When the hour of parting came, Lady Bess was seized with the notion that she would stay all night with her "Eva,"—passing from coaxing to storming, from storming to such piteousness of weeping and brokenness of heart, that even the august host interceded with her mother to grant her prayer.

"But the child's stubbornness must be conquered, some time!" reasoned the parent, one of the many whose theory as to the training of their young is perfect, and whose intentions are above reproach.

"Grant her one day's grace!" pleaded the Colonel. "My girl here will be the happier for one more night with her pet bed-fellow before the breaking-in begins,"—passing his arm about Evelyn, fondly. "She misses our sprightly Mistress Martha, whom she will, I trust, have back again ere long. The house is dolefully quiet for the withdrawal of her winsome presence."

Mrs. Carter did not note the slow mist of unshed tears in the daughter's eyes, or the amazement in her step-mother's at what sounded natural and characteristic to herself. Colonel Byrd's faultless manner to other women was perfected by domestic practice. The neighbor did not credit one of the whispers that would make him out a despot when thwarted. She had been heard to wish that *her* Colonel would go to school to him.

Evelyn was not averse to the companionship thrust upon her. She loved Bess, in spite of the minx's waywardness, and was glad to purcha-e distraction from haunting thoughts by showing her the " pitters" in the big Dutch Bible, Mr. Fontaine turning the leaves with her, and telling Scripture stories that kept away pertinacious question from his ally. He was passing gentle, this afternoon, and his seriousness had in it nothing forbidding to the child. She sat in his lap, her head upon his shoulder, her eyes riveted upon the quaint cuts. Once in a while she sighed in excess of content. Twice she lifted her hand to pat the olive-pale cheek touching her curly pate. The second time, she cooed :

" I yove 'ou dee'ly, Misser Fonten !"

" Who does not ?' responded Evelyn, lowly.

" Thank you !"

That was all. Neither by look nor accent did he betray suffering past or present. She should have nothing painful to remember in these last fleeting hours.

At the picture of the Scourging, he looked across the book to Evelyn. She answered as if he had spoken :

"So much has happened since ! So much that has proved you the truest friend woman ever had. If in the years to come we can ever show our gratitude in other ways than in words, you may be sure——"

"Say 'e hard words !" said Bess, imperiously.

He repeated the Latin text. The harder words were said afterward :

" I have done my duty—nothing more. There can be no question of gratitude."

The " we" and " our" were poisoned points that brought the blood. So long as the surface visible to her was unstained—what matter ?

The study-door had swung ajar, although there was no wind. Through the crack, a pair of heavy gray eyes surveyed the group, and the thin mouth that went with them widened tigerishly. The spy feared this rival no longer, but he gloated over the thought of what impended above one he believed to be ignorant of nearing events. The unruffled mien and the flawless courtesy of the thoroughbred deceived the student of human frailties; the lower nature expressed some assuasive ooze for its own hurt from anticipation of a better man's sorrow.

The afternoon was as sultry as mid-August. All day the river had lain like a sheet of pewter under a sun that wilted the grass and curled the fallen leaves. The sun-setting had the lurid glower of pit-fires. Behind them, the sky showed coppery and sullen; the water was dusky crimson, shot with dull yellow; the land had caught a baleful glow under which it seemed to shrink and hold its breath.

Mr. Fontaine had said "Good-by" in the presence of a dozen people, and gone home, and Evelyn, struck with a sort of uneasy awe by the unearthly light and breathless atmosphere, walked down the front steps with Lady Bess, and so on to the eastern gate,—partly to seek coolness, partly to have a more extensive view of the phenomenon. On the other side of the fence, screened from the house-windows by a clump of calycanthus-bushes, was Lieutenant Maynard, steadying a field-glass upon the top-rail, and gazing so intently at some object up the river as not to see her until she spoke.

"Are you on the lookout for your buccaneer, Mr. Maynard?"

He started violently, recovered himself upon seeing who were the intruders, and answered with a half-laugh:

"It may be nothing worse than a smuggler, but I dare be sworn there's something wrong about that tight little craft over there. I passed her on Friday, some miles below, and had a sight of her skipper, and if he's an honest seaman, I'll eat my cutlass. I'd wager the same that I've set eyes on him before, and in none too respectable a place. I hailed him, and held a parley over the side to see if I could fix the recollection, but he was shy of showing too much of himself, and, after all, I may be a fool to distrust a man because one eye looks nor'east and the other sou'west."

"The evidence would hardly carry weight with a jury," said Evelyn, demurely. "What is the name of his vessel?"

"*The Mocking-Bird.* I talked to that sober-sides of a Bass about it, awhile ago, and he says she was bought of your father, and is run by reputable parties. If I liked Bass better, I'd, maybe, be less distrustful of his schooner."

"His schooner!" catching at the word with terrified eagerness.

"Of course not! I meant that he spoke well of her, and her owners—whoever they may be."

Bess, who was amusing herself by swinging on the gate, her toes wedged perilously between the pickets, projected her quota into the conversation.

"Misser Bass is a velly wittet man! He too*t* mine p'itty bo*t*s. I wiss 'ou 'ould *t*ill him *dead!*"

"Fie! fie! is this the little lady who was listening to Bible stories just now?" chided Evelyn. "She has a long memory for one of her years," smiling aside to Maynard. "Poor Mr. Bass affronted her mortally and mysteriously, it is now five weeks ago. She will none of him since."

"She may not be far wrong. The fellow has a shifty

eye, and children's instincts are oftener right than we believe. I wish your schooner had another voucher."

Evelyn turned her head to hide a smile. Mrs. Carter's epithet, "positively absurd," recurred to her. The gallant pirate-hunter was a man of one idea, and worked it hard.

"You would hardly board her, cutlass in hand, on that account, I suppose, any more than you would put her skipper in irons for having a cast in his eye."

Maynard's eye was again glued to his spy-glass.

"They are confoundedly busy on board for a Sunday afternoon, when Jack Tar likes to be drunk on shore in his best toggery. She's built for speed, too, and could show a pair of clean heels did she choose. I wonder where I have seen that skipper before! And he skulked as if he knew me. I'll ask your father to whom he sold the vessel, and if she's likely to have changed hands since. To-morrow, I'll run down to Wakefield, and stir up Harrison to send out a revenue-cutter to demand her papers—bill of lading included, and see if her cargo corresponds with them.—Bless my soul!"

Lady Bess, in swinging the gate shut, had thrown such weight and energy into the emprise as to jar her hands from their grip upon the pales, and, her feet remaining between them, she had fallen backward and head foremost into the pit of the officer's stomach.

CHAPTER XXII.

When Lady Bess's shoes were removed that night, a bruise, about the size of a sixpence, was perceptible upon one instep,—a novelty that lashed her imagination into a gallop. The wounded member must be rubbed with opodeldoc, then chafed by Evelyn's velvet palm; lastly, done up in linen cambric and laid upon a pillow after she was put to bed, as she had seen " Mamma *fits* Sharley's foot when it was b'*oken*."

The injured part of her frame disposed to her satisfaction, she informed her patient slave that she would like to hear over again *all* the stories Mr. Fontaine had told her in the afternoon. She never drooped an eyelid until Cain and Abel, Noah and the Dove, Joseph and his Brethren, Little Samuel, and the list of intermediate biographies up to the New Jerusalem, were given in detail.

It was half-past eight, and, at this season, pitchy dark without, when Evelyn sat down to write a note, the subject and wording of which had engaged her thoughts throughout the automatic rehearsal of the histories aforesaid. Bess had rebuked her, judicially, for inaccuracies, and justly. No well-instructed damsel of four years, less three months, would in that generation, swallow, unconvulsed, the statement that the chief butler saw in his dream a ladder upon which angels were going up and down.

Bess had doubts as to the ladder, even when it was relegated to the right dreamer.

"What for did 'ey *tate* a yadder when 'ey had wings? *I*'ould have f'ewed up and down. *So!*" flapping her night-gowned arms.

"We must ask Mr. Fontaine about that, some day," said poor Evelyn, and was suffered to proceed.

She had treated Maynard's talk of smugglers and river-patrol lightly in the hearing. Later, it returned upon her memory, and begot solicitude. *The Mocking-Bird* would drop down the river to-morrow midnight, and while, with wind and tide in her favor, she would pass Wakefield before dawn, it would be awkward should the admiral's zeal for the integrity of revenue laws incite him to challenge the outgoing schooner. Moreover, and contrary to reason, the insinuations touching the captain wrought upon her imagination. She wrote frankly to her lover all she had heard, and begged him to push, through Mr. Harrison of Berkeley, inquiries into the skipper's character. They could not, in the circumstances, afford to be over-nice in the selection of instruments for furthering their flight, but might it not be prudent to shift quarters at Norfolk, should he be dissatisfied with what he learned of this man's antecedents?

She implored the forgiveness of her almost-bridegroom if her over-wrought nerves made her foolishly timid. Whatever might be his decision, she would acquiesce in it cheerfully. Nothing and nobody could work them serious harm when once they were together.

The letter written, she summoned her maid and sent her privately for Caliban.

The boy appeared promptly, but Evelyn remarked immediately a certain disorder of mien unusual in the spruce lackey. His fingers puckered plaits in the sides of his breeches; his lips were loose, and twitched oddly, his eyes roved from right to left, up and down—anywhere rather than to rest upon her face.

"I sent for you, Caliban——" she began. "What ails you? are you ill?"

"Naw'm! Dar ain' nothin' ail me, ma'am!"

"You behave so strangely!" pursued the young lady. "I was fearful that you had gotten into trouble, and thought I might help you. If you have, come to me when you get back, and tell me the whole story. Just now I am in great haste. Come close to me and listen heedfully.

"About half-way between this and Berkeley a schooner is anchored to-night. At ten o'clock, Mr. Francis will be on board of her for a little while. I wish him to have this letter before he gets to the vessel, if possible. If he is already on board, wait until he leaves the schooner before you give it to him. My skiff is chained to the Westover pier. Here is the key of the padlock. Get into her, and pull toward the vessel, and keep near her until you see Mr. Francis going or returning from her. His boat will be rowed by Roger from Berkeley. Follow this boat and give the letter into Mr. Francis's own hands. Repeat to me now what I have told you, that I may be sure you understand."

The grave simplicity of her address steadied the messenger's head, as her kindness nerved his sinking heart. He recited the orders he had received without a blunder.

Besides the honor of serving her, he had the stimulus of the promised hearing when his mission should be done. His eyes, wistful and honest, did not leave hers while she subjoined :

"That is well done, Caliban ! I am putting a great trust into your hands. It is very important that Mr. Francis should have that to-night. I would send you to Berkeley, but I will not tempt you to disobey your master's orders. I know that I can depend upon you to tell nobody where you are going. Be as swift as you can, and when you get back, come at once to me. Viney will be on the watch for you and bring you up-stairs."

There was not a touch of the saucy rascal in the sober face the page carried down-stairs, and the resolute pace —the long lope he might have copied from his father— that took him down to the pier.

He had had a trying—a disastrous day. While the "white folks" were in church he had betaken himself, leisurely, up the river's edge. Stopping here, to shy a stone at a snipe or bull-frog, halting there, to stare at a passing boat, scraping his bare toes in the wet sand, and kicking the pebbles idly—he reached the wooded mouth of a ravine half a mile from the Westover dock. Into this thicket, first looking up and down the stream, to make sure he was not observed, he plunged, creeping under the mat of vines and putting aside boughs, without breaking a twig. Before he got to the stone masking the mouth of the tunnel he discerned tokens of recent visitors. The shingle bore the prints of foot-steps, imperfectly covered ; withering leaves bestrewed the ground, and bruised vines drooped in the sun. Making no more noise in the undergrowth than a rabbit, Caliban, armed with a hickory-stick, cut in the uplands, crawled to the cave-door, pried out the stone with a few skilful thrusts, and the green light filtered through the foliage into the paved interior.

The tunnel was empty as far as the eye could penetrate the obscure depths! With a low howl of rage, the half-breed dashed in, and groped along until stopped by a mass of fallen masonry and earth. There, he struck a light. Not one bale or keg remained to corroborate the tale of his midnight adventure! Without them, he had no tale to tell. As the truth burst upon him he flung himself upon the flags and cried piteously. His schemes of revenge, renown, reward, were like the " devil's snuff-box" into which he had dug his heel wantonly on his way hither. There was nothing left but choking black dust.

A thought drifted to him, by-and-by, that dried his tears with sudden fire.

" I gwine ter see Granny, now, *shore!* Mis' Evelyn, she ken git me er parss. I'll git even wid dat po'-white-folks-Satan, shore's I born! He ain' fitten ter libe, an' he ain' fitten ter die. De Lord, He don' wan' him, an' de debble, he won' habe him, ef he ken holp it. But he *got* fur ter start 'pon he trabbels fo' long. Ef I kent pay him out one way, I will in anodder!"

He turned over, preparatory to rising, and his hand struck something that rolled and rattled. It was a silver pencil-case, and one that he knew. Colonel Byrd had given it to his secretary last Christmas. The initials " *C. R. B.*" were engraved upon one side.

Here was a scrap of proof! The plunder had, undoubtedly, been removed on Saturday night. Bass had gone early to his room, complaining of indisposition, and Caliban, like a fool, believing in the excuse, had treated himself to a long night's sleep. After the house was still, the villain must have stolen out to the rendez-vous. Caliban recollected seeing him make numerous memoranda in his note-book at supper-time from Colonel Byrd's dictation, and that he used this pencil-case. The lad gnashed his pointed, glittering teeth in figuring to himself how securely the wretch had sat here, perhaps upon a keg of stolen spirits, and made inventory of the contraband cargo as it was taken out and to the boats.

A grin checked the gnashing.

"Don' I wisht I may see him when he misses *dis?* He *got* ter arsk for it, some time. Den, I gwine ter cuar' it ter Marster, an' tell whar I done fin' it."

He pushed the stone into place, crawled through the undergrowth, and went home, a sadder and a wickeder boy for the disappointment. His spiritless performance of the onerous duties of the Sunday waiting elicited sundry reproofs from his mistress, whose own temper was somewhat the worse for wear just now, and entailed upon him the unforeseen result of detention in the dining-room when the other servants were dismissed for the night, while he set in order under Madam's eyes a sideboard, into which she had detected him hurrying plates and dishes, helter-skelter, without regard to age, value, or pattern.

The work was just completed when Miss Evelyn sent for him. Colonel Byrd, Lieutenant Maynard, Mr. Randolph, and two or three others, had taken their chairs to the broad stone landing of the front steps, and sat there smoking. Bass had gone away on horseback that afternoon and not returned. It never occurred to the lad that he might be upon his enemy's trail until, when he got to the pier, he found the skiff gone. The padlock had been opened with another key than the one Miss Evelyn had given him, and the boat loosened, after which the lock was again made fast upon the chain and laid carefully beyond the reach of the waves. It was a clean job, and with lightning instinct the boy felt that but one man belonging to the plantation would have dared commit the trespass.

His heart pumped boiling blood into his temples while he stood, trying to bring together the various threads of the plot he began to feel was weaving about him.

That his courtly master could be interested in securing or preventing Mr. Francis's passage in a vessel of which Bass was chief owner; that Miss Evelyn corresponded secretly with the pleasant, generous English gentleman whom Miss Martha was to marry; that so nice a gentleman was in such haste to get away from people who thought the world and all of him that he could not wait for a larger and genteeler vessel,—a merchantman instead of a schooner, and a smuggler at that,—were, considered separately, incontrovertible facts. They defied his cunning to dovetail them.

In the confusion, he got hold of two ideas:

1. Miss Evelyn's errand must be done. If not in one way, then in another.

2. Bass must be followed. It was remotely possible that he would be on the schooner to receive the passen-

ger. The two had never seemed fond of one another, but there might be business ties,—a realm in which Caliban knew himself to be all at sea.

When he got home, he would make a clean breast to Miss Evelyn—sweet saint that she was!—of everything he had discovered and suspected. She had promised to listen, and she might be able to help him out of the muddle.

The schooner was over a mile away, at the most. He had swum three times as far on a warm night, and this was almost as hot as the day had been. While taking off his Sunday clothes, folding and hiding them under a bush, he devised a scheme for carrying the letter in safety. He wrapped it tightly in lily-leaves, picked from the bank; bound oak-leaves about them, and tied up all with a bit of twine. This he laid in the centre of a silk bandanna handkerchief, his choicest piece of finery, folded the latter in close bands, and, passing it over the top of his head, tied the ends under his chin. Tickled at the ingenious conceit, he walked out until the water reached his neck, and swam leisurely up-stream, pausing, every hundred yards or so, to listen for paddles or voices.

A shimmering veil had shorn the sun of rays during the day, without mitigating the heat. It now hid the stars, but a strange glow, like that of red-hot metal, lay upon the river. The west was inky, and the play of heat-lightning showed the cause of this depth of gloom to be a horizon-line of jagged cloud. Whispers and puffs of sultry air crisped the breast of the water. The swimmer soon made out the outline of the schooner, not at anchor, but lying becalmed in mid-stream. Beside the feeble rays of the binnacle-light, the deck was dark, but two of the port-holes were faintly illumined. Upon the weird glimmer of the water near the black hulk was something like a blot with edges blurred by the encompassing dusks. Caliban had floated and swum at a safe distance from it for, perhaps, fifteen minutes, when some one who appeared to lean over the guards in the fore-part of the deck, just above the moveless blot, called, rather cautiously than loudly,—

"Halloo, there, Roger!"

"Ya'as, suh!" responded a negro's drowsy voice.

"Cast off your rope there, and go home. The captain has to send a boat up the river in an hour or so, and Mr. Francis says he will wait and go back in her."

"Ya'as, suh!"

The oars rattled in the rowlocks, and the blot spread into the blackness beyond.

Caliban *flattened* himself into the water. He could not dive without wetting the top of his head. The Berkeley boatman, a dull-witted and indolent giant, only recognized the voice, disguised by falsetto inflections, as that of one in authority, and obeyed, unquestioningly. The unseen listener's senses, naturally acute and whetted by hatred, could not mistake it. Bass was on the schooner, and with power. For the first time in the bold expedition, an eerie dread crept over the lad. If he waited the hour or so, and swam after the schooner's boat, the chances were that his enemy would be in it, and how could he deliver Miss Evelyn's despatch with the secrecy she had enjoined?

A blaze of lightning split the horizon-cloud in two, and showed the toothed edges rising into peaks. A flaw of wind rocked the vessel uneasily, and brought the angry mutter of thunder. By the flash, Caliban saw, nestled close under the hull of the schooner and fastened to it by a rope, the stolen skiff! To swim up to it, cast off the line, clamber into the seat, and grasp the oars, was the work of a minute, and he felt himself master of the field, whether flight or strategy were to be the order of the night. While uncertain on this point, he would lie by and be vigilant.

The cloud, rocking before winds that as yet drove but shallow furrows across the water, was seen by the next flash, towering to the zenith. The river-rat looked anxiously at it:

"I'd make a run fur lan' ef I could git red o' dat 'ar letter!" he said, half-aloud. "Dar's gwine ter be a harrykin, ef I'm any jedge o' signs. An' dis boat ain' much better 'n' er aigshell fur dat kin' o' wuk!"

He pulled the skiff entirely around the schooner, from the deck of which he now heard the tramp of hurrying feet and the hoarse call of the captain's voice. The men were making ready for the gale. The boat would not be lowered until it was over. He had just made up his mind to turn his skiff shoreward, and to revisit the schooner when the danger should have passed, when the port-hole nearest him was dashed open, and a voice like a trumpet-call pierced the darkness,—

"Ho, there! Roger! where are you?"

"*I'se* hyur, Mr. Francis, suh!" cried the boy, in shrill excitement. "What mus' I do, suh?"

"Go to Berkeley, and tell——"

Caliban—standing erect in the skiff, holding her away from the hull of the schooner with an oar—never heard the rest.

At the sound of his voice, a head was thrust over the taffrail,—a face was seen distinctly by the blinding pour of blue flame over heavens and earth; there was a flash of redder fire, a report was lost in the bursting thunder, and the skiff was flying down the river before the scud and roar of the gale.

<hr>

CHAPTER XXIII.

Colonel Byrd and his guests watched the tornado from the windows of the drawing-room after the violence of the wind drove them in-doors. At the zenith, the black cloud took the form of a huge funnel, the conical end descending rapidly until it touched the river. There it tore along, an awful besom of devastation, a bellowing monster with outswooping arms, lustful for prey. The play of the lightning was incessant and vivid, and from their outlook the gentlemen saw, so near the Westover pier it seemed impossible that she should not dash against it, a schooner racing before the wind under bare poles. The livid glare showed every taut rope and that her deck was empty.

A shuddering groan broke from the group; then, they waited in breathless silence for the next flash. The flying craft was already almost out of sight.

"That was *The Mocking-Bird!*" said Lieutenant

Maynard. "The gale has broken her loose from her moorings. Her skipper keeps her nose well before the wind, but unless he knows the channel better than he knows his prayers, and she obeys the rudder uncommonly well, I wouldn't give a pinch of rappee for the chances of schooner or crew."

"The Lord have mercy upon their souls!" said Mr. Randolph, fervently.

"Amen! and upon those of honester men!" responded Colonel Byrd. "'Tis an ugly outlook, gentlemen! We will have in lights and bar it out."

A footman, upon whose complexion yellow-gray ashes had settled, answered the bell, and brought in candles. About the flame of each hovered a sallow halo which the negro regarded, awe-stricken, when he had set them on the table.

"What are you about, blockhead?" demanded the Master. "Light the chandelier!"

The shaking hands did the work awkwardly, and, as a terrific stream of blue fire filled the room, the flambeau upheld to the wax candles dropped to the floor, and the fellow to his knees.

His master laughed, good-humoredly.

"It is lucky that the fall extinguished the torch, or we might have been roasted—a worse fate, I judge, than being frightened to death. 'The devil damn thee black, thou cream-faced loon!' Get you gone and send Caliban hither. He has brains in his skull, and keeps his head in the right place."

The negro picked himself up, and, knock-kneed and with chattering teeth, tried to articulate.

"Please, suh, I was skeered! Beg your pardon,

suh! An' Caliban, he—O Lord!" crouching behind a chair at another flood of flame and bursting report.

"Speak louder, my good fellow!" The Master was amiably amused. "The thunder outbellows you. 'Caliban, he'—what?"

"He ain' hyur, marster, ef you please, suh!"

"We can see that for ourselves, and it does *not* please me! Shall I kick you out before you will go to look for him?"

"Please, suh, he ain' nowhar!"

The Colonel took snuff patiently.

"My man! you must know that, dead or alive, one is always somewhere! Go, fetch Caliban—or his corpse! He would be livelier dead than you at your living best!"

"Ya'as, suh!" cowering before the almond-shaped eyes more abjectly than at the lightning. "Caliban, he ain' been 'bout hyur nowhar fur right smart time now, suh! One de chillun say he reckon he been gone to de riber fur er swim. He seed him go dat ar way 'bout a hour ago, an' he ain' been sawed sence."

"Go, light your torch, and come back to finish what you were doing. Tell Osiris to bring in pipes and tobacco," said the Master, coolly.

"I hope no harm has come to the boy!" observed Maynard, when the footman had departed. "He is a likely young rascal."

"A good scare would be wholesome for one of his kidney," returned the Colonel, in unruffled serenity. "He has more brain than any other negro I have, but he is too bumptious. A more daring, venturesome young devil never danced upon bare toes. He will fare better than likely if he do not dangle from a hempen noose at the length."

"American hemp, I suppose?" said Mr. Randolph, dryly.

"Nay—that is one of Spotswood's hobbies, not mine. He would insist that I should sow the seed of our native hemp upon a fat acre of my low grounds, and make fair essay of it. He has tried the experiment, and it came up very thick. He sent about five hundred pounds of it to England, and the Commissioners of the Navy, after a full trial of it, reported to the Lords of the Admiralty that it was equal in goodness to the best that comes from Riga. Set that tray here, Osiris. What is it?" seeing the butler fall into an attitude of respectful waiting.

"Please, suh, my mistis would like to know if you think there is any danger?"

The chief butler, having stood for a score of years behind the Colonel's chair at home and abroad, had taken on by natural accretion a veneer of speech and demeanor that suggested a ludicrous resemblance to his model. In the thickest of meteorological phenomena that had driven his compeers in service to their prayers in the darkest corners they could find, he bore himself like a man, and that man, Colonel Byrd.

"My compliments to your mistress, and say that, in Lieutenant Maynard's opinion, the gale is expending itself as rapidly as could be desired or expected, and, therefore, is more nearly exhausted than it was a while ago. Say, moreover, that Lieutenant Maynard is an authority upon gales and that his word is of value."

"Yes, suh!"

Without the twitch of a muscle, Osiris bowed and backed himself out. In equal gravity, the Colonel proceeded with the dissertation upon American hemp:

"I told the Governor if our hemp were never so good, it would not be worth the making here, even though they should continue the bounty. And my reason was because labor is not more than twopence a day in the East where they produce hemp, and here we can't compute it at less than tenpence, and considering besides, that our freight is three times as dear as theirs, the price that will make them rich will ruin us, as I have found by woful experience."

"You have the air and appurtenances of a pauper," put in Mr. Randolph, glancing from the stately figure in the tall-backed chair to the silver and cut-glass flashing back the fitful play of wax-lights and lightning.

"Moreover," went on the imperturbable lecturer, "if the King, who must have the refusal, buys our hemp, the Navy is so long in paying both the price and the bounty that we, who live from hand to mouth, can't afford to wait so long for it. Ah! Maynard is put upon his mettle by the responsibility cast upon him by my message to my Lady."

The Lieutenant was at the window, shielding his eyes with his arched hands to obtain a better view of the tempestuous outer world. He deigned no reply, and the Colonel gave another pull at his hempen thread:

"And then, our good friends, the merchants, load it with so many charges that they run away with great part of the profit themselves. Just like the bald eagle which, after the fishing-hawk has been at great pains to catch a fish, pounces upon and takes it from him."

"I would give all the hemp in both hemispheres," Maynard wheeled about to interject, "to be assured that naught human is abroad to-night!"

"Unless it be smuggler or buccaneer," subjoined the Colonel. "Tush, man! take a stiff glass of brandy-and-water, gird up the loins of your spirit, and forget the hurt you cannot help!"

"Brandy—even such as your poetical English guest likened to topaz, honey, and oil—cannot stupefy a brave man into forgetting that, while he has a tight roof above his head, better and braver men than he may be perishing beyond the reach of mortal aid."

The delicate curves of the host's mouth straightened; the cleft in the chin was shallow; the broad lids drooped over the eyes. He chose his words deliberately and critically.

"I have ever discouraged in myself and others, my dear Lieutenant, the disposition to sentimentalize over seeming evils which are of our own deliberate brewing, or the dispensation of an all-wise Creator. I have somewhat that I wot of at stake in this storm,—which I would remember is none of my work,—and perchance more than I have knowledge of. GOD knows" —reverently—"that the thought of the loss of human life is unspeakably dreadful to me. Whatever of suffering, merited or undeserved, I may impose upon my fellows, my skirts are clear of so much as the desire of bloodshed. These things being so, is it not the Christian's part, when Providence has put a snug roof over his head and stanch walls about him, and good brandy that maketh strong the heart of man before him, to say for himself and for those exposed, by ordinance of the same wise Providence, to the horrors of wreck by land and sea,—'The will of the Lord be done!'"

The fury of the tempest was spent by midnight. Up to that time the party in the drawing-room sat over pipes and glasses, spell-bound by the rare personal magnetism which was the pre-eminent gift of their philosophical entertainer.

He bade them a cheery "Good-night, and only such dreams as they would pray to have visit them!" a smile upon lip and in eyes, and when all had gone drew back the ponderous bolt of the front door, and stepped out upon the stone platform. The moon was not up, but a diffused brightness along the eastern horizon betokened her approach. The rain had ceased; the lower currents of air were sobbing penitently in the wet trees, more scantily clothed than at sunset; the higher were tearing crevices in the clouds through which tremulous stars peeped down. The world was sweet with the smell of the rain and the fallen leaves. They were a sodden carpet under the watcher's feet as he walked down the rose-alley toward the calycanthus gate, bareheaded, his hands clasped behind him. At the gate he halted to gaze toward the quarter in which the madly-scudding vessel had disappeared.

As the winds died down, the wash and roll of the river, the wrath into which the gale had lashed it, still unappeased, were audible; the odor of bruised and soaked roses was joined to the stronger breath from the dying leaves; in the clear fields of heaven a thousand stars shone limpid; a slim crest of silver showed itself above the eastern line of forest. Nature was mar-

shalling all gracious and soothing forces to atone for
the paroxysm of rage that had spared not her best-
beloved.

The Colonel looked and listened for long. Exquisitely susceptible to the influence of beauty and music,
he threw open the windows of his soul to admit the
white peace these inspired.

"I had no hand in *this!*" he said, aloud, at last.
"Whatever I may have willed, the doing and the end
are GOD's !"

In passing along the upper hall to his own room, he
saw a line of light under his daughter's door. It
burned all night, and the woman who watched beside
it never slept. Walking, kneeling, sometimes prostrate
upon the floor in abandonment of anguished suspense,
she dragged out the terrible, *endless* hours to the dawn
of what should be her marriage-day.

By sunrise she was on the road to Berkeley. Wan,
wild-eyed,—her feet, drenched with wet, seeming to her
frenzied self to lag like lead,—she sped down the garden-
path, past the church-yard that was to have echoed her
bridal vows, across the fields as the crow flies, with
never a glance at the river wallowing tawnily to her
left, yet seeing naught with the mind's eye but the
hungry torrent. A lorn, bedraggled ghost, she thus
burst into a group collected upon the lawn, all looking
at the river, all pallid with unsaid fears.

Martha Jaqueline was first to see her, and ran toward
her with a great cry of horror and surprise.

"My darling ! my darling ! how came you here?"

The women—there were none but women there—
gathered about her, tears contending with the deceitful

cheer they would have brought. Evelyn caught hold of Miss Lotsie.

"*Where is he?*" whispered the parched lips—demanded the wide eyes.

The spinster lifted her in her powerful arms and carried her with loving violence into the hall. As she went, she said : "We haven't given up hope, yet. Compose yourself. He may come!"

She got dry shoes and stockings for her; wrapped her in a blanket, and fed her with hot negus and toast. Martha, seated upon the floor, Evelyn's hands in hers, told her, as was merciful, all that was known as yet. The gale had caught the Berkeley boat on its way back from the schooner, as Evelyn's fears had divined. When neither of the occupants returned, Mr. Harrison had got ready a gang of men as soon as the storm abated, and with boats had spent the remainder of the night on the river. Five miles below the Berkeley landing they came upon the missing boat, floating bottom upward. Upon the opposite shore, three miles higher up, lodged against a tree, was the body of the negro boatman. He had apparently clung to the lowest boughs when exhausted by swimming, and been beaten to death by the waves that had drifted his corpse inland. His fists still clutched leaves and grasses. His companion had not been found, but the boats were still out.

Evelyn heard it without tear or sound, and then lay motionless, gazing at the ceiling with eyes set in awfulness of despair. Mrs. Harrison's caresses and Martha's fondest exhortations to hope, did not win a look or sign. Miss Lotsie sent, privately, a note to Mrs. Byrd, telling what had happened, and sat down with the other women to wait, with folded hands and sinking heart, for the worst, if there were a worse woe to come.

Two hours went by, and there was no news from the water.

"Ben will not come home until he has something to tell," Mrs. Harrison said, once. "He blames himself bitterly for allowing the boat to go without him. But it was thought best that he should not appear openly in the affair, lest it might breed trouble at Westover, or some of the crew, recognizing him, might bruit the news of his visit abroad. He regrets, now, that he yielded to what was most thoughtful and generous in —our friend."

The colorless mouth stirred ever so little, but without voice. Even praise of him she had lost could not galvanize the palsied nerves. Tears flowed silently down Martha's cheeks, dropped upon her friend's hands, and lay there until Martha wiped them off.

As she did it, she felt a thrill like an electric shock run through Evelyn's frame; her head was raised; into the dull despair of the fixed eyes shot a ray. Before Martha could hinder her, she sprang from the sofa, was at the door and upon the lawn, and was running down to the pier like a mad thing. The others followed, hurrying the faster as they caught sight of a boat approaching with a smaller one in tow.

Mr. Harrison shouted to them from the foremost:

"Go back! go back! and send some men to me!"

Only his wife hesitated, and she but an instant. Evelyn was at the landing before the larger boat touched it. With a look he never forgot, she leaped into it, passed Mr. Harrison and the oarsmen ere one could raise a finger to stay her, seized the tow-line and pulled the skiff within reach of her hand. Something in the bottom was covered by a cloak.

"For God's sake!" ejaculated Mr. Harrison, darting forward.

He was too late. Her swifter movement had torn aside the cloak and revealed the ghastly features of poor Caliban! A bloody bandage was about his head; his eyes were closed; the displaced covering exposed his naked shoulders and chest.

The girl staggered back into Mr. Harrison's arms; threw up her hands with a piercing shriek, and fainted. They bore her to the house, and close after her the senseless figure they had thought breathless when found. The skiff had been driven into a small inlet, and, wedged among the bulrushes, like the ark of the Hebrew infant, had outlived the tempest that foundered the larger craft. There, exposed to the rain and gale, the insensible lad had lain for twelve hours, the flags, beaten flat by wind and rain, masking the creek and deluding the eyes of the search-party. His condition was a dense mystery. The puzzle of his presence, naked, in Evelyn's skiff, and how he received his wound, was complicated by the surgeon's announcement that he had been shot, the bullet fracturing the skull. But for the banded handkerchief about his head, it must have entered the brain and caused instant death.

"He may live a few hours," the surgeon was saying as Mrs. Harrison, too anxious to wait longer without the chamber, appeared to inquire if she could be of service. "But the end is certain, and not distant."

Mrs. Harrison's eyes filled.

"Poor child!" she murmured. "Who could have had the heart to hurt him? I should have said he had not an enemy in the world!"

"I fear me much that his own misdoing led to this end, my dear lady!" said familiar tones, and Colonel Byrd, of whose presence in the house she was not aware, stepped from behind the bed-curtains. "I caught him, three nights ago, in the act of stripping to swim out to a net set by one of the field-hands. He is a born poacher—thanks to both of his parents. He was pert with his fellows, too, and tricksome. But I could better have spared a dozen better servants!"

The handkerchief taken from the wounded head, soaked with blood and water, had been tossed into a corner, and the folds falling apart showed green leaves, pressed oddly together. Mrs. Harrison took it up, gingerly, while the Colonel talked with the surgeon, and there fell out a parcel bound flat with twine. Taking it over to the window, she undid it and took out a sealed letter stained and wet. The blurred address was "*To Mr. Francis,*" and the billet was secured by strands of dark hair caught under the seal Evelyn Byrd always used.

Mrs. Harrison escaped, unnoticed, from the chamber, and ran with the fresh mystery to Martha Jaqueline.

Neither of the loyal friends would break the wax while there was a probability that Evelyn might revive sufficiently to explain this turn in the enigma. Nor was a hint given to Colonel Byrd that the supposed poacher was the messenger, leal and ingenious, between his daughter and her lover.

But the discovery added tenderest assiduity to the nursing bestowed upon the hapless boy whose days were numbered.

CHAPTER XXIV.

MADAM BYRD and Miss Lotsie divided the duties of chief nurse in the temporary hospital set up at Berkeley. Evelyn rallied from her swoon only to relapse into a stupor that lasted all day and far into the night. Her step-mother and Martha Jacqueline, watching beside her at midnight, saw the beautiful eyes unclose suddenly in the glare of delirium. She plucked at her ring, muttering rapidly under her breath :

"To make room for another that will mean liberty and love ! liberty and love ! Mother Mary and the holy angels ! Mother Mary ! Moth-er—Ma-ry !"

The mutter became a drowsy whisper.

Madam Byrd's eyes dilated with horror.

"He has proselyted her !" she whispered to her companion. "Oh ! if this be so, it is better she should die ! Her father would sooner see her in her coffin !"

"When she *is* there, it will be religious bigotry and wicked hatred that have murdered her !" retorted Martha, in righteous asperity. Then, melting into tears, "O, my lamb ! my pretty ! that I should live to see you thus ! He called you his ' lily among thorns !' Thorns that have let your sweet life out !"

At the warm rain upon the restless hands the loving hold could not confine, Evelyn opened her eyes again.

Holy, chastened light flowed over her face; her voice was unearthly in musical speech, with a tender undertone of solemnity. It was like a martyr's death-chant.

"*I, Evelyn, take thee, Charles, to my wedded husband, to have and to hold from this day forward, for better, for worse, for richer, for poorer, in sickness and in health, to love, cherish, and to obey,—till—death do——us—part!*"

Martha Jaqueline looked upward, as the accents trembled into an awful stillness.

"In the name of GOD, Amen!" she cried. "This was to have been their bridal hour, and the wrath of man cannot put them asunder. In the sight of heaven and the holy angels, they are wedded, and you and I are the earthly witnesses!"

Colonel Byrd carried a heavy heart homeward from his visit on Tuesday morning. Caliban lay in a deathly lethargy, only showing that he was alive by breathing. Evelyn was raving with brain-fever.

"Talking herself to death!" was her step-mother's report to the father. "She will have none near her but Martha, and Lotsie Johnson, and Anne Harrison. Me, she will not abide. She mistakes me for Sycorax, the mother of Caliban in Shakespeare's 'Tempest.' I have always protested, Colonel, that no good could come of your giving servants such heathenish names. The poor child fainted at sight of the hole in Caliban's head; and she and Mr. Francis—I would say, 'Lord Peterborough!'—and Martha Jaqueline and Mr. Fontaine made a play of reading 'The Tempest' aloud the day before the races, and all has got mixed up together in her brain.

" And no mortal will ever know what the poor dear went through on Sunday night, knowing as she did—although I had no idea of it—that *he* was on the water just at that hour, and in that terrific storm.   Do you suppose, Colonel, there is the shadow of a hope that he is alive ?"

" How the devil should *I* know, Madam ?" growled her irate consort.

He said it over to himself many times, with many variations, riding slowly along the road, head depressed and eyes dreary.

It was uppermost in his mind when, entering his study, he beheld his secretary bent over the vellum MSS., his pen moving as sedately as if he had not taken it from the page, except to dip it into the standish, since he had sat in the same place last Saturday afternoon. He had, as has been stated, left Westover on horseback Sunday, after dinner, with the expressed intention of spending that night and Monday—perhaps Monday night—with friends in Williamsburg. On horseback he had returned while the Colonel was at Berkeley ; heard, without comment or visible emotion, the tragic story of Roger's death, Caliban's wound, and Evelyn's illness, and, after calling for a biscuit and a glass of cool milk, settled into the oiled groove of his every-day life.

The kitchen-cabinet, convened at an irregular hour, and with safety, in the absence of master and mistress, declared, with no ado of discussion, that " he hadn't no mo' heart 'n thar is in a bull tadpole."

Himself was better pleased with himself than usual. Napoleon proclaimed Providence to be on the side that had the heaviest artillery. Mr. Colin Bass, after inspection of his muniments, greeted Providence as a redoubtable and indubitable ally.

He arose to salute his superior in ceremonious deference—thrown away upon the anxious parent.

"Ah! Good-morrow, Bass!" he said, laying off his hat and pushing back the hair from a forehead creased by a faint line that was not there at their parting. "When did you get back?"

"About an hour ago, sir."

"You had a prosperous visit, I hope?"

"Reasonably pleasant, I thank you, sir. My friend's wife was quite ill all of yesterday in consequence of fright at the tornado of Sunday night. Otherwise, all went well."

The Colonel had dropped heavily into his chair, and sat, drumming upon the desk with his elegant finger-nails, staring at the opposite wall.

"You have heard, I suppose, what has happened hereabouts since you went?"

"Of Miss Byrd's illness; the drowning of one of the Berkeley boatmen, and that Caliban was shot, by accident, or of design, upon the river yesternight? Yes, sir. I regret that I should have been absent at a time when I might have been of service to you."

The drumming went on, and the Colonel had not removed his gaze from a fixed point.

"*The Mocking-Bird* was driven out to sea by the gale, and has not been heard from since."

"That is news, sir. Is it certainly known that she did not weigh anchor and sail of her own accord, with crew and passenger on board?"

The Colonel darted a look of fierce impatience at the impassive visage.

"Not 'certainly known'! —— it, man! How could anything be certainly known in such a —— of a gale? We saw her drive past at the rate of a knot a minute. Whether or not anybody save the crew were on board; whether the Berkeley boat capsized before it reached her, or after leaving her; whether the schooner went down out of soundings, and every soul on board found a watery grave, or if she outrode the gale, and is now on the high seas—HE, alone, who sent the storm can tell."

The secretary reflected a minute before replying:

"In any event, sir, the result to yourself will be the same—for awhile, at least. If the schooner were wrecked and if her passenger have perished, you have thrown away fifteen hundred pounds which, had you been endued with the spirit of divination, might have been saved."

"—— the money!" ejaculated the Colonel, with an irritable motion of the foot, indicative of a frantic inclination to kick somebody.

"Yes, sir. I was about to add, that, supposing the vessel to be safe, the fifteen hundred pounds were well expended in insuring for her a twelvemonth cruise, with the guarantee that your name is never to be mixed up in the affair. The involuntary voyager will be well treated, and allowed the liberty of the schooner excepting at such times as his confinement between-decks will be a matter of necessity during the vessel's stay in foreign ports. These periods being few and far between, it can easily be seen that no hardship need befall the noble passenger. He left England for an uncertain period, in quest of adventure. He has gotten what he sought,"—a sardonic smile, pale and inclement, flitting over his face. " It will be long before inquiry is made for him. When he is allowed to escape from the vessel, it will be in China. Before the story of his kidnapping can be told in England, *The Mocking-Bird*—thanks to your liberality—will have a new coat of paint, a new name, new colors, a new skipper, and a new career, or should you prefer, she will be deserted and scuttled. The hardy skipper can retire upon his gains—or, what is the more likely, can turn pirate in dead earnest. You will have gained a year and more of time, with the choice between the belief that the noble peer is seeking his pleasure in other lands, or that he is feeding the fishes at the bottom of the sea. He took his mails on board on the very night on which the schooner was to sail; he went with her, and has since made no sign, although alive and well. Or—he went on board, intending to revisit his friends at Berkeley—and West-over! She was broken from her moorings, and foundered, carrying him down with her. Or—still again, he was drowned in plebeian association with negro Roger. Any one of these beliefs will suit your turn, as I look at it."

" Oh! it is a devilish fine plot, I grant you, and you appear to be devilish proud of it, to judge from the zest with which you rehearse the particulars, and weigh the pros and cons of a living death, and bodily decease. Should you and I, between us, have killed that poor girl——"

He compressed his lips to stop their quivering.

Almost unknown to himself, he was more irked by something unnatural and unexpected in the secretary's manner of stating the case with needless circumstantiality, than in the presentation of the particulars themselves. Without trenching upon disrespect, the man's tone was of conscious power; of prideful assurance that to him his patron was indebted for relief from an intolerable weight, and that he meant to have credit for the deed. While pretending to confer with his chief at every step of the audacious undertaking, his policy of partial confidences had been pursued throughout. His own hoard was the richer by five hundred pounds for the care of the Colonel's reputation that led the emissary to conduct all negotiations in his own name. He had prime reasons for believing that the skipper would never give him up as a confederate, and should he turn king's evidence, the Williamsburg visit was in support of an *alibi.*

Roger, who might have known his voice under the falsetto disguise, was dead; Caliban, who had called Francis by name, and looked straight at Bass as the latter shot him, would soon be out of the way. Francis had not seen him on the vessel, and she had touched at Norfolk just long enough to put Bass ashore in the early morning. Had not the diplomatist cause to be content with the work of his own brain and the connivance of Him Who holds the waters in the hollow of His hand, and the winds in His fist?

His intention not to mar the fair emprise by letting the Colonel know now, or ever, that he had been on *The Mocking-Bird* on Sunday night, and run a common risk with the victim of the plot, in the headlong race of the gallant little bark to the mouth of the river—was as firm as his design of making the imperious magnate feel, from time to time, the bit his hireling had clamped upon him. The scribe was guilty of no accidental displays of feeling or temper. The, for him, long speech to his employer was the first pull upon the rein, and it had *told!*

"To say that I admire the scheme I have rehearsed to relieve your apprehensions would describe my feelings more fitly than to say that I am 'devilish proud' of it," he returned, provokingly cool. "If strategy that quails not at possible consequences be novel business for you, allow me to utter my admiration in yet fuller measure. If I, the humblest of Miss Byrd's admirers, may express my regret at her illness, I owe the privilege to her father's condescension."

His smirk pointed and aimed the sentence. The Colonel started up and grasped his riding-whip.

"*You hound!*"

The scribe had arisen also, his lips thinner for their sneer.

"A hound, if you will, Colonel Byrd! and never more entirely at his master's service than when noble game is to be hunted down—*to the death!*"

With not another word, the unhappy father—debased for the first time in his own eyes—sank into his chair and let his proud head fall upon the arms crossed on the desk-lid.

Bass sat down and took up his pen:

"Two People were as indifferent company as a man and his Wife, without a little Inspiration from the Bottle, and then, we were forced to go as far as the

Kingdom of Ireland to help out our Conversation. There, it seems, the Colo. had an Elder Brother, a Physician, who threatens him with an Estate some time or other. Tho' possibly it might come to him sooner, if the Succession depended on the death of one of his Patients."

The pen was wiped and laid by, and the page sanded. The secretary turned his chair about to face his nominal master.

"I grieve, Colonel Byrd, that you take a plain truth so heavily to heart. You desired a certain end, and applied to me for means. A danger was imminent. You appealed to me, by *my loyalty* to you, to avert it. I laid hold of the only instrument available in the urgency of the circumstances,—the nearness of the danger. You made but one stipulation. In scriptural meaning, if not in phrase, you said, 'Touch not his life!' I sent your enemy away in safety and in comfort, you supplying the expenses of his voyage. If he be alive when the schooner arrives at the West Indies, word will be sent to you through me, and the same from other ports. It rests with you whether or not the young gentleman's well-wishers in this neighborhood are left in ignorance of his condition and whereabouts, after this information is placed in your hands—should it come. Should inquiry from the other side be instituted, Mr. Harrison, and not yourself, will be the one to satisfy it. This is the frank statement of a condition of affairs that should be solace—not sorrow. Nevertheless, I am prepared, should you desire it, to explain the precise circumstances to your family, and the community in general. I have naught to fear for myself.

I am—borrowing again from your Scriptures—but clay in the hands of the potter."

There was no response from the bowed figure at the desk.

The secretary surveyed it in mute contempt. That a man who had gained that for which he had sinned, should have twinges of conscience as to the means by which it was obtained, was beyond his comprehension. *His* self-respect hinged upon other things than the preservation of a pure heart and clean hands. Failure was crime; success,—by whatsoever road,—virtue. From this stand-point he made his next address:

"My respectful mention of Miss Byrd wrought so unhappily upon you but just now, that I scarce dare repeat the assurance of my sympathy in your natural uneasiness at her present state. If I might, I would fain couple with it the hope that her sickness is but a passing attack—such nervous disorder as is common with her sex under like afflicting conditions. You said, not a week ago, that you would the sooner bury her than see her wed to him who, by the ordinance of Divine Providence, and by reason of his felonious intent to rob you of your fairest treasure, was placed in peril of his life yesternight. I would, likewise, venture to remind you that had you with violence seized him and hurried him into the vessel wherein he met his fate, there might be cause for repentance which does not now exist."

The Colonel raised himself, a tolerable assumption of the old haughty grace clothing features and form.

"Enough of this for this once!" he said, waving his hand. "What is done is done, and I am no craven to shirk the consequences of mine own deed. I have acted, with the lights vouchsafed me, for the best good of one whose happiness is as a sacred trust in my keeping. She may live to thank me for that which the Searcher of hearts knows has cost me dear enough in many ways. If not, I must look for justice to a Future beyond the tomb!"

CHAPTER XXV.

THE hurricane that cut a broad swath through acres of forest as the scythe through grain, swept down the river in mid-October. Christmas-snows had melted from off the winter wheat, and the budding catalpas, horse-chestnuts and maples were shaking off brown water-proofs to show spring clothing, when Evelyn Byrd was lifted into the Westover chariot, and driven carefully over the soft road to the gate of her home.

The same day, Caliban alighted from a spring-cart at the kitchen-door; stared stupidly about him, and slouched along into the familiar precincts without acknowledging the storm of tearful welcomes poured upon him.

Isis had set her own rocking-chair, lined with feather cushions, in the hottest heart of the chimney-corner, and, upon a table close by, were smothered chicken, waffles and honey, and coffee. When she had ensconced him in the midst of the puffiness, set a stool for his feet and urged him to eat, she threw her apron over her head and wailed aloud :

" He ain' no mo' de chile whar went 'way f'om hyur,

dat turrible Sunday night, dan er serup is like er coal-
black Et'op!" she bemoaned him in a fine flight of
fancy and feeling. "What dey been do ter you, boy?
Tell Mam' Isy, honey! Who been strip you' good
cloes off, an' den shoot you *dade*, an' *den* drownded
you?"

He looked at her with lack-lustre eyes, his jaw hanging in a foolish grin. He had grown fleshy, yet flabby;
the golden brown of his skin was a dirty yellow. When
left to himself, he crossed his hands at the wrists, where
they dangled loosely, as if jointless. He shambled in
his walk, and stammered in his silly prattle. Many
words and people were altogether forgotten. Doctors
from near and from far agreed in pronouncing him
hopelessly idiotic, and his restoration to physical health
miraculous. The flattened bullet had been extracted
from under his scalp, but no attempt made to raise the
depressed skull from the brain. Since the inevitable
consequence of the accident must be death, the torture
of subjecting him to an operation was needless. To
the surprise of the local practitioner, the bone knitted
healthfully, and the scalp closed above it in a firm
cicatrice. His appetite was abnormally hearty; he
could walk after a fashion, and regained strength
rapidly. Memory was so nearly gone that he recalled
nothing that had happened at or near the time of his
hurt, and every effort to stimulate his recollection, or
suggest incidents, was as futile as Mam' Isis's exhorta-
tion.

On Christmas evening, Mrs. Harrison, with tenderest
tact, told Evelyn how and where her last note to her
lover had been concealed. The boy's clothing, found

under the bushes on the river-bank, made it certain that
he had undressed with the intention of swimming to
the schooner; yet the discovery of the bolted padlock
showed that he, or some one else, had unloosed the skiff.
Perhaps it had drifted away before he could get in, and
he had swum out to it.　But why the ingenious disposition of the billet in leaves and bandanna, when he
could have pulled the boat back to shore for the letter
and his clothing?

Mrs. Harrison related all to her guest—conjecture
and baffling difficulties, and the total failure to piece
together a plausible theory of the casualty.　Finally,
she produced the pacquet, discolored and creased, yet
unopened.

Until that day, not a tear had softened Evelyn's eyes;
her lover's name had never passed her lips since the
return of the unsuccessful search-party.　Except that
she would lie, hour after hour, slipping the ring he had
" wished on," up and down her wasted finger, and that
she always slept with his miniature clasped in her hand
—memory of the tragedy might have been as extinct in
her as in Caliban.

She hearkened dumbly to the tale,—truly a gruesome
one for Christmas-tide ;—held out her hand as dumbly
for the letter ; turned it over, half-bewildered, then
broke the seal.　With the reading of the first line, the
spell was dissolved.

" O, my love ! my love ! my love !"

The cry reached Mr. Harrison in the room below.
He hurried up to find Evelyn weeping wildly in his
wife's arms,—ever and anon ejaculating that the poor,
faithful boy had lost reason, and, perhaps, life for her.

"Don't you see how it was?" she reasoned, when calm enough to speak connectedly. "Somebody had stolen the skiff. I gave him the key, and told him to take the boat and lose no time. When he found it gone, he recollected that I had charged him to deliver the letter at, or near the schooner. He swam to the vessel,—I am sure of it,—and the thief was there, too, with the skiff,—perhaps on board of the schooner. Caliban got into the boat—was discovered by that other, and in the quarrel my poor lad was shot. O, I hope"—lifting her almost transparent hands to heaven—"that the murderer did not die in the same moment with my darling! that his spirit did not take flight in such companionship!"

After that, she spoke—not freely, but without reserve—of her lover as beyond doubt dead. *The Mocking-Bird* had been spoken by an incoming merchantman off Cape Henry. A stiff breeze was blowing, and the two skippers could make out little that was hallooed through their trumpets; but there was no doubt as to the vessel, and that she was outward-bound. Mr. Harrison brought the story to her, he having seen and catechised the captain of the merchantman. She thanked him, and said she had not hoped for better news. Then a gentle melancholy settled upon her in place of the apathetic despair that had excited fears for her reason.

On New-Year's Day, she expressed a willingness to see her father, whom, up to then, she would not admit to her presence. There was no scene of formal reconciliation, but a calm, kindly meeting as of friends who had been parted for a season. His visits after that were daily, never prevented by weather, or delayed by other engagements. There was a deprecatory shade in his demeanor, an anxiety to please, and an effort to amuse the invalid, that chance observers considered exquisite, and at which the Harrisons chafed in secret. Evelyn accepted it all without comment, or apparent emotion of any kind. The spring of active feeling seemed to be crushed.

When her step-mother could not speak for tears, in receiving her upon the threshold of her home, she smiled faintly.

"The journey has not tired me as you feared it would," she said. "Belus drove with great care, never touching a stone. Am I to go to my room, or do you think it better for me to lie down down-stairs for a while?"

Between her father and Mr. Fontaine, she was supported to the drawing-room, but it was Colin Bass who wheeled the sofa toward the fire, and when she was laid upon it, took the tray containing wine and biscuits from Osiris, and on one knee before her, offered it.

The action would formerly have surprised, perhaps offended her. As it was, she accepted the attention with the same languid smile, tasted the wine, set the glass back with a murmur of acknowledgment, and closed her eyes in utter weariness. Bass passed the tray to the waiting Osiris, whose inaudible sniff and toss of the head were infinitely eloquent. Then, instead of withdrawing from the room, as he would have done a half-year ago, the secretary stood at the back of the sofa as one whose right to minister to the invalid was not to be questioned.

Mr. Fontaine was at the foot of the lounge, and glanced inquiringly from the trespasser to Colonel Byrd, a flush of indignant amazement mantling his forehead. The Colonel seemed ignorant that aught unconventional had been done, and Madam Byrd had followed Osiris to the door for a whispered consultation. The eyes of the two men met in the mirror over the mantel. Fontaine's were full of haughty surprise: Bass smiled, quietly confident in the strength of his position. Between them, as they stood, was reflected the recumbent figure, the lily-pale wraith of the beautiful being they had seen framed by the marble vine-leaves and fruit five months before. Both thought of that other scene,—one with a gush of generous sympathy that softened every lineament, the other with arrogant hope and vulgar triumph.

This was the first overt assumption of the secretary's new station in the household. He never lost the vantage-ground it gave him. Men had commended Colonel Byrd's selection of a factotum so clever, yet who knew his place so well; praised his modesty almost as much as his ability and honesty. Before the summer had passed, gossip was busy with rumors of the evident mastery of the plebeian over the patrician. There was a change in the matchless autocrat of the Westover principality. His forehead was beginning to show wrinkles, and a fine net-work of care-lines was drawn about eyes, always brilliant, often restless now. His grand air was a part of his personality as were the rolling periods of his speech, but the rich resonance of his voice was fitful, and he was subject to seasons of reverie approximating moodiness.

Bass, by degrees alternately insidious and audacious, possessed himself of the reins slipping from the master's fingers. The servants hated him more than ever, but they had learned to dread him as well. It was significant of their deep devotion to their young mistress that they endured without murmur the sight of their master's neglect of their interests because of the evident absorption of his every thought in his daughter's condition. She did not rally in strength or in heart with the spring weather that allowed her to spend many hours of each day in the summer-house on the outer verge of the lawn, to drive to Shirley, and sail down the river to Brandon and Wakefield. Her father was her escort everywhere; his loving solicitude more and more apparent as the leading motive of his daily action. She turned to him, insensibly to herself, more fondly and continually as her weakness made her dependent upon the tender offices of those about her, and never had suffering woman a stancher support. All the resources of his magnificent intellect were taxed to afford her entertainment; his versatile fancy devised diversion and light occupations for her stronger days, comforts for the hours of pain and weakness, which, he fondly persuaded himself, were fewer as the summer advanced to gorgeous prime.

In August, he fitted up a schooner we would now call a yacht, and took the whole family upon a cruise as far north as Boston, spending some weeks in Massachusetts, and stopping at most of the chief towns in the New England Colonies. Voyaging southward, they visited the Bermudas, and sailed leisurely in summer seas until early October.

Evelyn had forgiven, long ago, and striven to forget that, but for her father's refusal to sanction her betrothal, her lover would not have been abroad on that fatal night. She was very grateful that none interfered with her mourning for the beautiful young life quenched in the cruel river. She almost believed that, were the last year to be lived over again, her father would have learned to like and respect one all-worthy of esteem. There was balm in the thought that wrought more potently than sea-breezes and invigorating changes of scene to coax back elasticity to her frame, color to her cheek, and hopeful light to her eyes.

Still it was a faded image of herself that trod the gangway laid from the yacht to the Westover pier, on the afternoon of a golden autumnal day. Mr. Fontaine's heart sank with dismay he would not name as he grasped the hand he felt was smaller and thinner than when it last lay in his.

"I am better! much better!" she said, accepting his arm for the climb up the winding steps, seeming not to see that Bass pressed to her other side with offered assistance. "And I have a world of things to tell you when the time comes. That will not be until I have heard everything that has happened at home while we were gone. How lovely the dear old place is! Seven weeks is a long time to be away from it. But we have seen and done so much that the days flew by."

Fontaine was not deceived by her forced vivacity, but Bass, to whom it sounded like the gladsome overflow of a heart at peace with itself and full of delight in the reunion, could have torn his rival limb from limb as he saw him check her upon the first landing,

v

and compel her to sit down upon the wall to rest. To the apprehension of the slighted lover, it was a subterfuge to gain a *tête-à-tête* interview, Madam Byrd and the children, with their retinue of servants, having hastened up the hill.

The manager let the Master of Westover speak to him twice before he appeared to hear him. The two men were upon the wharf with no one else within earshot.

"I asked you if there were news of *The Mocking-Bird?*" said Colonel Byrd, more peremptorily than Bass was in the habit of hearing himself addressed of late.

He answered sententiously :

"None!"

"None since she was spoken off Cape Henry, more than eleven months ago! What make you of that?"

"Nothing—because nothing can be made of nothing. It is a matter of little moment to either of us, so far as I can see."

The bronzed visage of the Master gloomed while Bass feigned to be occupied in pulling about the boxes the crew were bringing ashore, but he waited until the factotum deigned to approach him again with a look that was more incisively interrogative than became their relative positions. The look he received in return staggered him. The king was upon his throne again; the man was master of himself, and resolved upon mastering others. His voice rang out in the remembered accents of command.

" Whatever may be your estimate of the importance of the matter you wot of, I rank it as so nearly supreme that I shall set all agencies on foot, forthwith, to discover the fate of the vessel, and to recall her passenger—if there were one. After conference with Mrs. Byrd, who is thoroughly advised through Mr. Harrison and his family of the hour at which the boat left Berkeley on that Sunday night, the probable time consumed in the row to the schooner, and in disposing the mails in her hold—I judge that the unfortunate gentleman may have been on board when the gale broke over her. Joining this to the fact that his remains were never found while those of the negro were, I deduce the likelihood that when *The Mocking-Bird* was driven out to sea, she carried him with her. The first step is to discover, through English and American ship-masters, what has become of the schooner. To these you will address letters to-night under my hand and seal, instructing them to spare no expense in obtaining the needed information."

The man was grand even in error. In the enunciation of the royal pleasure, he ignored the possibility that his amanuensis might presume to question his will. Serene and imperative he spoke, and looked to have it done.

"And now"—in a more colloquial tone—"what of plantation-affairs?"

"This, first of all, sir." In emulating his chief's tone, he achieved doggedness. "You will be so kind as to suit yourself with another manager at your convenience. I shall not retain the post more than a month longer."

"Very well, Bass. The yield of corn was good this year, or promised to be, when we left home. And the tobacco?"

"My books are ready for your inspection, sir. At the risk of angering you, Colonel Byrd, may I ask if you are prepared to accept the consequences of this remarkable reversal of sentiment and intention. They may be grave."

"They *must* be grave. I am prepared to accept them."

They were ascending the zigzag causeway; a turning made visible Evelyn and Mr. Fontaine, met at the top of the flight by an uncouth figure that grovelled, dog-like, upon the ground at his young mistress's feet. Bass looked at his companion with a disagreeable smile.

"They *will* be serious. It might be well to weigh them well before adopting measures that cannot be recalled."

"I have had time and opportunity for mature deliberation. We will not debate the business further. It is mine—and mine alone!"

Evelyn's hand closed convulsively upon her escort's arm as Caliban shambled toward them, his tongue lolling like a dog's in the breathlessness of his haste, his face broad with ecstasy—a sickening spectacle. In another second she stooped to pat his head, while he kissed her feet with disjointed exclamations of rapture.

"My poor fellow! are you so happy to see me again! Me who caused you such sorrow!"

Her eyes swam with tears, but she forced a smile. The home-coming was a crucial test of strength and courage, and this meeting not the least trying stage. Her father's daughter would not blench.

"I must tell you," she continued to Fontaine, walking slowly up the lawn, Caliban gambolling beside her, "of something Papa has promised me. We met an eminent English surgeon in Boston, and became well acquainted with him. I told him of this poor lad's misfortune, and since his intention is to see Virginia before his return, Papa invited him to visit us. While here, he is to examine Caliban, and perhaps perform an operation—trepanning, it is called. He says that such things have been—and wonderful cures effected.

"I must tell you, moreover,"—hurrying to say it before they reached the house,—"what he—Papa—has been to me while we were away. No woman—not mine own sweet mother whom I shall ever remember as an angel of love and mercy—could have been more tender, and Mamma was all goodness. When I remember these things, I know it would be ungrateful not to be glad to be at home again, and willing to take up what of life is left to me. Help me, dear friend!"

He pressed her hand in releasing it from his arm, at the door.

"Depend upon me to do my utmost!"

The latent heroism in the woman who had ceased to be a girl, was developing nobly in the furnace that tried her. The inner light shone white and clear,—and none, not even the parent who had grown to be the dearest of earthly things to her, or he who loved her so entirely that self had no part or lot in his hopes for her, suspected the fragility of the vase that held the lamp.

It was at Colonel Byrd's express and personal invitation that Martha Jaqueline and Miss Lotsie spent a week at Westover soon after the return of the family to the homestead. The visit included the anniversary of the day that had widowed the bride who was never to be a wife. No verbal notice was taken of the incident in the household, but Colonel Byrd rode away upon Pluto soon after breakfast, and was not seen again until nightfall, and Martha and Mrs. Harrison sat for a silent, sacred hour in the church-porch while Evelyn prayed within, kneeling in the chancel, living over each minute and hearkening in spirit to every love-word of that farewell interview until memory became a present and blessed reality.

The face she brought forth to the anxious waiters was transfigured by peaceful radiance; she moved with the grace of a wind-swayed flower; the beauty of her early youth was renewed and sublimed. Upon the hand clasped over her prayer-book gleamed the " wish-ring" she would wear to her grave.

The yellow sunshine lay level across the burial-mounds and burned like watch-fires in the windows; the river was crystal and flame ; the painted leaves of the maples drifted as soundlessly as the sunrays ; the tinkle of herd-bells was melodious in the distance. The three women lingered under the trees, the fallen leaves rustling and whispering after them as they walked.

"I am here every day," said Evelyn at the upper bend of the path. " For awhile, pain went before the comfort I was sure to find at the last. Latterly, it has been all rest and peace.   When I have gone quite away, I shall pray that I may be let to come back on such an evening as this, and meet one, or both of you, just here, where we three now stand. Charles and I parted on this spot. You will not forget ?"

There was no outcry against what must precede the tryst. The simple earnestness of the pledge was met

by like simplicity of spirit. As they passed through
the west gate and along the rose-lined alleys, Evelyn
talked hopefully of the operation to be performed upon
her *protégé* by the London surgeon, now at Brandon
and expected at Westover on the morrow.

"It is not wise to delay the attempt to save the boy
from what is worse than death," she said. "While
we were absent he was nearly uncontrollable at seasons.
Once he ran away and was gone three days. His
Indian grandmother brought him back. He had found
his way to her house alone. Occasionally he fell into
strange rages. In one of these he threw a hammer at
Mr. Bass. A fire was kindled under Mr. Bass's bed
one night, and my poor, witless Caliban was suspected
of the act. Papa is loath to put him under restraint.
What would I not give to have back my merry, gamesome imp! We were great friends—Caliban and I."

They were under the study-window, and the secretary
was within, surrounded by the plantation-books. His
short, thick fingers opened and shut spasmodically, as
he listened, and a muscle in the right side of his face
contracted suddenly, drawing down one corner of the
eye and mouth.

For a wonder he was idle. The vellum MSS. were
completed, and stored in a library-closet. There were
the weekly accounts to be gone over, and letters to write,
but he was disinclined to touch them. For a week he
had not been well. Doughty as was his tone in offering his resignation, the blow of his confederate's defection had fallen heavily. For six months he had lorded
it as virtual ruler of the plantation, saying in his pros-
perity, "I shall never be moved!" security founded

upon the belief that his clutch upon the Master was as inexorable as death.   In his presumption, his ambition meditated further humiliation for his dupe and triumphs for himself,—a final *coup* that was to make the daughter's hand the price of his continued discretion.   In his opinion, the submission of the chastened spirit to the inevitable, and the affectionate duty rendered her parent, were abundant proof of the supremacy of the latter, and his ability to coerce her into whatsoever course he might decree.   Bass had heard twice from the skipper of *The Mocking-Bird.*   In curt, rough fashion he had been told that " him you wot of keeps well, but aint so mighty easy in his mind."   And again, " Somebody makes friens with the men, moren I could like.   I'm glad time's 'most up."

Bass had intended to use this last intimation as a lever in the execution of his daring scheme.   Gauging his employer by his own standard, he reckoned confidently upon the effect that would be produced upon Colonel Byrd by the suggested prospect of Lord Peterborough's escape and return, and the accompanying threat upon his—Bass's—part, that, in such an event, it might be obligatory upon him to save himself by giving up the real criminal.   The obvious expediency of guarding against the worst consequences of the Englishman's reappearance by giving his daughter in marriage to an honest man whose influence in her father's behalf would thus be secured, would finally be brought forward to calm the fears of the principal party in the outrage perpetrated upon a peer of England.   Safety was to be found alone in unity of sentiment and interests.

That the well-digested plan could be foiled by a single act of moral courage would have seemed preposterous, yet through this short, straight avenue had ruin entered. The lion had rent the net with one stroke of his paw. Intimidation and cajolery would be alike ineffectual in dealing with one who faced the consequences of an evil deed as brave men face an honorable death.

Defeat and discomfiture are not synonyms to steadfast souls, and such Bass held his to be. He could still have wrestled with destiny and escaped a stunning fall had not physical force failed him. He, who had boasted himself to be made up without nerves, and his phlegm to be invulnerable; to whom sleep came at call, yet could be dispensed with when need arose for vigil continued for nights together,—was a prey to nocturnal horrors, sleeplessness that was anguish, childish dreads of formless ills. His appetite was capricious; he started like a woman, if a door were slammed, or one spoke abruptly at his ear, and involuntary facial twitchings threatened to make his pitiable state known to others. His habits had always been temperate. He smoked with others because it was the custom of gentlemen, and the act symbolized his equality with such, and drank for no better, and no worse reason. In his solitary occupation of the great house, he had kept a demijohn of the finest Westover brandy in a closet opening out of the study, and compounded a mint-julep or a glass of brandy-and-water for his private delectation when work pressed him hard. Lately, the potation cleared a brain that never used to be foggy, and braced up spirits that fluctuated irrationally.

28*

This afternoon, as I have said, he was not working. Dull pain behind the eyes, slight nausea, and what felt like a sinking of the material heart, robbed him of the disposition to be industrious. He had sat for nearly an hour in his chair, elbow on table and head on hand, thinking of nothing in particular, yet oppressed with a sense of general misery of body and soul. Evelyn's voice aroused him to steal on tiptoe to the window and peer out. The trio of friends had paused where, by leaning forward, he could touch Evelyn's head. In the flush of her glorious early womanhood she was never lovelier than now when bloom and contour were refined by time and suffering. He contemplated with devouring eyes the blue tracery of the veins on temples and hands, the shell-shaped ears, dainty, fine, and clear; the arch of the dark hair at the back of the neck, the classic profile; the scarlet of lips that was vivid by contrast with the waxen skin. His passion was as fierce as it was useless. He could have beaten his eyes blind because he could not withdraw them from her; he stretched out his arms to empty air and drew them in closely upon his breast as one might crush a human form against his heart.

And, in accents that would have wooed him back to earth were his foot over the threshold of heaven, she lamented the lost wits of the chattering ape who got only a modicum of his deserts in the bullet that cracked his skull !

He got out the demijohn when the ladies moved away, and mixed a potent draught. It made up to other men for thwarted ambition and unrequited passion, and, after all, he and other men were of one common clay.

CHAPTER XXVI.

THE hush of intense excitement pervaded house, kitchen, and quarters upon the day in which the great London surgeon was—to quote Isis—"ter breck inter dat po' boy's hade an' let in his senses."

By ten o'clock in the forenoon all knew what was in progress, and hundreds of hearts beat in one suspenseful throb while the hours lagged on. At noon, Osiris, the only servant who had been retained in the closed chamber, next to Miss Evelyn's own, appeared in the kitchen. His face was of a curious dun-color, his lips were a faded purple,—otherwise, his deportment was, if possible, more consequential than in ordinary. Sinking into a seat, he waved back the inquisitive crowd, and said, sepulchrally—"*Cider!*"

Isis's own hands brought it in a lordly beaker. He swallowed it to the last drop and wiped his mouth:

"In all my travels, the 'xperience of this day is the most wonderfullest 'xperience I've *ever* 'xperienced. Thank GOD it is over an' done with! I could not have borne myself up with credit ten minutes longer. An' the subjee' is alive an' probable to do well. Stop!" as a hum of pious rejoicing threatened to swell into the wordless surge of thanksgiving peculiar to the negro fanatic. "I wish it understood—*distinct*—that the battle is not *one*—but, as I might say, *two!*" Pleased with the daring epigram, he elaborated it. "Yes, *two!*—that is, two chances. This han', life,"—

sprawling a flat palm, dirty-pink in hue,—"this han',
death!"—jerking out the left. "Moreover, when a
nisher" (issue) "is not certain, it is more than ap'
to be *uncertain*, even when a famous Lunnon chirog-
rapher weaves what may be called the axe of fate."

The room was full by now, the outermost and latest
comers crowding to get sight of the oracle. A buzz
ran swift from the circumference to the oratorical hub.
He got himself to his feet with alacrity incompatible
with the exhaustion under which he had collapsed, a
minute ago, and tugged at his pepper-and-salt forelock
to his young mistress just entering the kitchen. She
stopped near the door, looking around upon the dusky
sea of faces, her own colorless, her eyes like stars for
prayerful gladness.

"I came, forthwith, to tell you what I knew you
would be most thankful to hear," she said. "We may
hope that Caliban will soon be well again. I ask in
my own name that you keep the house and grounds
very quiet for a day or two, until the danger of fever
has passed. You shall be told, every few hours, how
he is getting on. I ask you, too, to join your prayers
with mine that our dear Heavenly Father will carry
on the good work begun in the poor lad."

Isis pressed nearer:

"Please, my Miss Evelyn, ma'am,—is he got *all* his
sense back? He done been los' a heap!"

Evelyn smiled.

"That will not be known until he awakens. They
had to give him large quantities of opium to dull the
pain of the operation, and he is sleeping from the effects
of it."

The head-cook was still revolving with brain and tongue the possibilities formulated by her query, when a shadow fell athwart the bowl in which she was shredding vegetables for soup, sitting in the noon-sun on the kitchen steps.

Bass was sauntering by, tracing listless patterns in the fine gravel with his stick, his eyes fixed on the ground.

"Mr. Bass! suh!" challenged Isis.

Usually she would have scorned to apply to him for information upon any subject, but her heart was full and soft.

He stopped and eyed her sullenly.

"Ef so be dat po' boy up yarnder"—nodding her turban sideways at the house—"gits back his senses whar was spilt out in de riber dat night, ken he tell, right, straight, smack, smoove off, who been hu't him, an' how it all happen'?"

Bass's eyes were bloodshot and stupid while he seemed to ponder the query. His face twitched so fast and violently that he put up his hand to hide the tremor or to keep it still.

"I—don't—know!" he said, at last.

His tongue was clumsy; his lips hardly moved. He made as though he would say more, but moved on, leaving it unspoken.

Isis shook her head many times and portentously.

"Dat 'ar gittin' silly, or he drinkin' mighty hard!" she said to her corps of helpers. "Thank de Lord 't don' make much diff"ence to we-all, now Marster done got on de box agin an' tuk up de lines, an' bless 'n' praise His holy Name fur dese 'n' all udder marcies!"

Bass sauntered on, trailing his cane behind him, to the church-yard and his accustomed seat upon the tomb of William Byrd the First. It was not easy to rally and mass his mental forces nowadays, but Isis's question had shocked them into temporary activity. The horror of the idea broached by the illiterate woman grew apace upon him. He tried to recollect an old story he had heard of the return of memory to a man who lay for six weeks, senseless, after a fall that produced concussion of the brain. He had caught a sentence spoken by the surgeon last night to Evelyn, as she parted from him near the study-door.

"I will not flatter you with false hopes, my dear Miss Byrd, but surgery has before now given speech to the dumb, eyes to the blind, and wisdom to the fool."

Icy, viscid drops oozed out upon the thinker's forehead; a horrible sickness possessed every square inch of his body. The persuasion that paralyzes the boldest energies,—let it be superstition or deduction from undeniable circumstance,—that the wheel of fate has begun to turn backward for him, changed his heart to water. Things had gone wrong until neither he, nor the Providence that had so lately seemed all on his side, could stem the current. A month ago he would have defied a thousand negroes, all telling the same tale, word for word, to win Colonel Byrd's credence in opposition to his unsupported statement. In that unfortunate cruise, when father and daughter were thrown into closest intimacy, and long voyaging over trackless seas and between the stars and the deep had brought season for honest introspection and just weight of men and measures, his work of years had been undone. His whilom dupe had arisen in pristine strength, clothed with native integrity and in his right mind—the more resolute for good for shame that he had listened for a while to evil counsel.

Caliban was Evelyn's *protégé.* She would lend eager heed to every incoherent phrase that embalmed her lover's name. Her woman's wit would knit stitch to stitch, and the clue once given to his own presence upon the schooner when Francis was trapped, like a partridge, in the cabin, would be followed, until——

He could not frame it, even in thought. Shaking, as in palsy, he struck a spark into his pipe, and smoked by fits and starts; his limbs aching, yet numb. He might go away—to England, for instance. He had a tidy sum in foreign securities of which his employer did not dream. Or—there was the river—or the holster hanging in his room with a pair of pistols he always kept clean and loaded. An odor of burning arose to his nostrils, and he looked down to see a thread of red flame creeping along the earth. A spark had fallen from his tinder, or a fiery ash from his pipe, upon the carpet of dead leaves. Being a thread, although flame, it was extinguished by one stamp of his foot. Action and occasion awoke a thought that warmed his languid veins, infused courage into his heart. A touch would strike out the life wavering in the breath of fate, in the stilled chamber over there. If the touch were dealt before reason awoke in the drugged brain, all was safe.

From that moment of hopeful inspiration, opposing forces kept watch,—the one without, the other within the darkened chamber wherein the injured boy was

swimming for his life. If the watchers beside his
pillow counted every respiration and hung above the
immobile visage with hope that strengthened every
hour, the prowler skulking up the stairs, lying in wait
in dark corners of the upper corridor, listening with
ear laid to the panel for sound or silence that might
indicate whether the helpless boy were guarded or alone,
was on the fiercer alert.

"That secretary of yours is in danger of delirium
tremens or something worse," remarked the surgeon to
Colonel Byrd, as they smoked together in the drawing-
room the third night after the operation.

"O, I think you mistake there. He is a temperate
fellow—steady as a clock, albeit somewhat upset just
now by the prospect of leaving my service. The question of drunkenness being disposed of,—in my mind,
at least,—what is the worse peril?"

"Paralysis—or some cognate seizure. His hand is
tremulous, uncontrollable muscles draw his face awry,
he drags the right leg slightly in walking. If he do
not look out, he will not, as the vulgar say, make old
bones."

While they talked, the doomed man was feeling his
way through the familiar gloom of the upper hall. He
had peeped into the still-room window, and seen Madam
Byrd, with two colored women, busy scraping opium
from poppy-pods that had been scarified in their green
prime that it might exude. The milky sap turned dark
in stiffening, and when hard was taken off and treasured
as a valuable addition to the domestic pharmacopœia.
Madam had an acre of poppies sowed yearly, and herself visited them in the season, daily, armed with a

needle for scoring the seed-vessels, and shears for clipping the ripe ones. Removal of the precious deposit was a nice process, and she deputed the superintendence of it to no one. The pile upon the table insured her occupation for an hour to come.

Colonel Byrd, the surgeon, and Mr. Fontaine were in the library, and Miss Byrd's maid had come downstairs a half-hour ago, announcing to Osiris in the hall that " Mis' Evelyn had a mighty bad headache, an' was goin' ter bade right off."

The patient was undoubtedly left in the care of a negro woman renowned for her skill in nursing. It would be an easy matter to offer to take her place for a couple of hours. A thumb and finger upon the thorax, a displacement of the bandages, would suffice after that,—and nobody would tell tales. He had but to aver that the patient was as he had found him. Negro evidence went for nothing. Such a conjunction of circumstances might not occur again. It came none too soon. The evening bulletin from the sick-room reported the continued absence of febrile symptoms, also that the patient had spoken rationally—only to ask for a drink, but in a natural tone. Then, he had dropped off into what the surgeon said was healthful sleep, not stupor. The morrow, it was believed, would see yet more decided improvement.

The door of the hospital-chamber was ajar a few inches, and by the glimmer of the night-taper Bass beheld, with a shock that left him weak and quivering, Evelyn Byrd seated by the lad's pillow. Perfectly motionless, her head laid against the back of her chair, she looked, with her waxen-white face, closed lids, and folded hands, more deathlike in the low light than the form upon the bed. As if disturbed by the viewless proximity of his enemy, Caliban stirred with an inarticulate murmur. His young mistress bent toward him, took in her slender fingers the tawny hand tossed out upon the coverlet, and spoke soothingly:

"What is it, Caliban?"

He opened his black eyes to their fullest width, his teeth showed in a pleased smile:

"Mis' Evelyn, ma'am—is that you?"

"Yes, my boy. You must be very quiet. You have been ill, but you will be well soon—very soon!"

The rush of blood to her heart almost suffocated her, but she compelled herself to outward composure.

"Ya'as, ma'am. De skiff war gone, Mis' Evelyn, when I got to de landin'. I was jes' 'bleeged fur ter swim, you know, ma'am."

Agonizing as she was with anxiety to hear his story, the listener tried to check him. One hand went up to her throat; her words were divided by short, broken breaths.

"Yes, my good, faithful lad! We know that you did your best. But you must sleep now. To-morrow you shall tell me all."

"Ya'as, ma'am!" his features working piteously. "I jes' wan' ter say 's how de letter is wropped up, safe 'n' soun', up *hyur!*" raising his hand to his bandaged head. "I ain' los' it! I can't 'member what come nex'! Who fotch' me in dis room?"

Heroically, Evelyn endeavored to calm him, drawing down the wandering hand and patting it playfully.

"Now, Caliban! you always mind me, you know.

Don't try to think, to-night. Shut your eyes and sleep, or I must go away. You have been ill, as I told you. And because we all like you so much, we brought you up here that we might take care of you. Won't you obey me, and talk no more?"

He lay still so long with closed eyes that the secretary began to breathe freely again. A gentle rain was falling outside; through closed doors he heard Colonel Byrd laugh—guardedly, lest even at that distance he might disturb the copper-colored devil laid in state among linen and down.

The boy started convulsively; his eyes flew open; his accents were strained and piercing; his words poured forth in a torrent that could not be forced back.

"I 'member it all now, Mis' Evelyn, ma'am! You better sen' right straight off' ter dat ar' schooner! Mr. Frarncis—*he* dar! Mr. Bass, he been call ter Roger— kinder high-up like, but he couldn' fool *me*—an' he say, 'Go home, Roger! we gwine ter sen' boat up de riber pres'n'y, an' Mr. Frarncis, he'll go in her.' An' Roger, he pull up de riber. 'Twas arter dat, right smart while, an' de storm was comin' up fas', dat I see de skiff. Close by de schooner, she war, an' I jomp into her, an' bymby Mr. Frarncis, he knock open de pote-hole, an' halloo out loud an' fierce-like,—' Roger! whar are you?' An' I say, 'Here me, Mr. Frarncis, suh! What mus' I do?' An' he call out, 'Go ter Berkeley, an' tell——' Den, Mis' Evelyn!" his voice rising into a scream, "he tuk an' *shoot me!*"

"*Who!*" cried the horrified woman, throwing her arms about the form that struggled to sit up. "Not *he!* Never! never!"

"Dat low-live' Bass look ober de side o' de schooner, Mis' Evelyn! Den, he shoot me!"

"You lie!" thundered a terrible voice.

A frantic figure with livid face and starting eyes dashed at the bed. More quickly, Mr. Fontaine, just entering by another door, threw himself in the madman's way. They were locked together, one swaying, wrestling shape, the resolute purpose of the taller and slighter man bearing the other toward the doorway and further from the woman whose utmost strength was required to hold the lad upon the pillow—when Colonel Byrd and the surgeon rushed up.

Before a separating hand could be laid upon the combatants, there was a gurgle and a lurch,—the thud of a lifeless body upon the floor.

The three men took up the secretary and bore him to his own chamber. His face was distorted grotesquely when he revived and tried to speak. But half of his body was alive and sentient.

The "worse peril" was upon him.

- - - - - -

CHAPTER XXVII.

Had Caliban lied in a tale so graphic that the least important feature of it haunted Evelyn's imagination as if the experience detailed had been her very own?

The question was not to be settled for days, each of which was a draught upon the reserves of her life. A slow fever consumed her by night, and the dregs were the daily lassitude it was no longer practicable to conceal. She had no pain,—so she protested,—and, therefore, must rally with time. Instead, she wasted like an untimely snow-fall, hidden fires licked up her strength as the sun the dew. In after-days those who were continually about her soothed remorseful regrets by recollection of distracting interests that inclined notice and solicitude from her unmurmuring self. Caliban's relapse, incident upon the frightful scene in his room, brought him nearer the edge of the grave than had the original wound. Even the London surgeon gave up hope after twenty-four hours of delirium. Then, the marvellous vitality inherited from a savage ancestry reasserted itself; the fevered brain cooled, and reason reentered, as it were, a house swept and garnished. Conversation was strictly prohibited, and he throve apace, enjoying with childlike glee the delicacies sent up by Isis, and content to pass most of his time in sleep.

He was in the second week of his convalescence when a startling discovery was made. In the bottom of the demijohn of brandy kept by the secretary in the study-cupboard, and from which no one else was ever known to drink, was a deposit of pounded roots which Colonel Byrd identified as the most deadly poison known to the gatherer of simples in Virginian forests. The specific action of it was upon brain and nerve, and it was but too probable that the luckless man's frequent potations of the noxious decoction had undermined an iron constitution, and indicated the direction in which the arrow of incurable disease should be sped.

Cross-examination of every negro who could have had access to the room and closet failed to elicit any

testimony bearing upon the mystery. If Isis recollected, shudderingly, the visit of the Indian doctress,
she held her tongue, and when the incident was referred
to by a younger and less discreet witness, she was ready
to risk her soul's safety upon the asseveration that the
squaw stayed but three hours on the plantation, and did
not set foot in the mansion. Caliban's rooted hatred of
Bass was likewise descanted upon, but the preparation
of the poison, and the introduction of it into the demijohn usually kept under lock-and-key, argued a degree
of intelligence the quarter-witted boy had displayed in
nothing else since he received his hurt.

To save the family credit, Osiris set on foot the story
that the secretary had malignantly contrived his own
poisoning by slow degrees and ingenious processes of
torture. It was, in the chief butler's opinion, " a low-
down trick, but only what might be expected from a
man o' no fam'ly and no bringing-up to speak of.
'Twas pity he hadn't done the thing in genteeler style,
and made a respectable corp' of himself, instead of a
half-rotten lorg like that stretched out up-sta'rs."

And so October—St. John the golden-mouthed
among the twelve fathers of the year—went, and in
the second week of November, on a day when dis-
heartened drizzle, gray as lead and chill as snow, alter-
nated with angry showers that pitted the river with the
force of bullets—a sloop was lashed up the stream by
east winds, and moored at the Westover dock.

Two well-known figures came ashore, and mounted
the winding flight of stone steps that were as slippery
as glass. They were Martha Jaqueline and Miss Lotsie
Johnson.

"Does Evelyn know that I am here?" queried the former of Madam Byrd, who met her in the hall.

"No. She has not been down-stairs to-day. She is not so well for a week past, and her father counselled her to remain in her chamber until the weather changes."

"Let nobody bear the news to her until I have seen Colonel Byrd. My first errand is with him. He is in the library—do you say?"

Madam watched her to the library-door and ventured not to follow her. The serious directness of the visitor's address, the grave dignity of her bearing, rebuked curiosity. Something had happened, or was to happen, and the experiences of the past year made the good woman timorous of getting herself "mixed up" with new adventures.

The sun, whose existence was that day received as a fact by faith alone, was an hour nearer his setting when Colonel Byrd handed Miss Jaqueline up the stairs and to his daughter's chamber. His wife, meeting them on the way, after one glance at him, passed on without speaking. His face was haggard, the down-drawn lines cut deeply as if never to be erased. It was the first look of age she had ever seen there, and it terrified her to tears.

He pushed back Evelyn's door softly. A faint voice, like a tuneful whisper, was singing:

> "When the willow droops the greenest,
>   Sweeps the streamlet's rim the cleanest;
>   When the young bird flies the strongest,
>   When the sky-glow shines the longest—
>   It is then I'll take my Norma
>   From the green hedge—o'er the lea!"

A long, trembling sigh followed.

Evelyn sat before the fire in an easy-chair, propped by pillows, her feet upon a cushioned stool. Upon the chill, neutral-tinted light—if that be light which can only be said not to be darkness—falling sluggishly through the windows, the flaming logs tossed rosy waves that ran up the still folds of the dim-blue gown enwrapping the invalid ; kissed and flecked and dallied with the folded hands ; struck prismatic sparkles from the " wish-ring," but kept back from the white face with its deep, shining eyes and nameless look of serene expectation which those who have once seen it upon a beloved visage, know ever afterward as the light that comes at eventide.

Martha brought her hands together in an impulsive gesture, and laid her brow upon them for an instant ; her features worked as she signed to her companion to precede her.

"It is I, my daughter !" There was a palpable and successful effort to bear himself as she was used to see him. "And I have brought a visitor whom you will be more glad to see—Mistress Martha Jaqueline !"

Evelyn settled her eyes searchingly upon her friend's face, as the latter arose from her embrace :

" You bring me news !" she said, confidently. " Sit you there, and tell me all."

" You are right, dear !" Martha sat down upon the foot-cushion, leaned her arms upon the elbows of the chair, and returned the gaze by one full of love and meaning. " I have tidings. I came hither for no other purpose than to bring them to you. It is your father's wish that all shall be said in his presence."

Evelyn reached up her hand to touch his cheek, and motioned to him to sit beside her.

"Papa and I have no secrets from one another. Say what you will!"

"Dear heart!" While Martha talked, she never withdrew her meaningful eyes from the lily-face drooped toward her; her fingers were interlaced to torture, but her tone did not falter. "All that Caliban said was true. The hearing of it should have prepared you for what is coming. When the gale drove the schooner out to sea, she carried Charles Mordaunt with her. She was heard from, you know, within a few weeks afterward. We did not dream then how closely the news concerned us. We have heard again of her— and of him. He is living, and well!"

For reply there were the closer clasping of one wasted hand upon the other, the upraising of eyes glorious in devout gladness, the fluttering breath between the parted lips. The spirit, like a captive dove, strained at the cord withholding it from the sun-bright fields of ether.

Martha's intent gaze stirred not from the rapt face.

"He is well and faithful, dearest!"

A beautiful smile, proud and sweet, prefaced the response:

"Living or dying, he would be *that!*"

"Yes—living or dying, every beat of that true heart is yours. He was at the other side of the world when he wrote to me—on his way to England whither imperative business called him. He will be here ere long. Are you hearkening, my darling? He did not go so far away of his own will. Nor did the

storm beat the vessel out of her course. It was intended that he should be borne off, and you were to
suppose that he had deserted you——"

A motion of fine disdain checked her.

"But I should have *known* better! He did not fear
that! Go on!"

"He boarded the schooner of his own motion, and
went below to see his boxes disposed in cabin and hold.
Poor Roger was sent home without his knowledge.
When he would have quitted the cabin, the door was
fast. He struck open a port-hole and shouted to
Roger. Caliban answered. Then the hurricane came
upon them.

"Sweetheart! my part of the tale is told. The
residue you will have from other lips. Before I quit
you for a little space, I pray you hold to your heart
the honey and wine I have brought. Say, while you
listen to the rest, 'He lives! he loves me! He is
coming! coming! coming!' and put from you what
would else be as bitter as gall. My snow-drop! mine
bonnie, bonnie bird! kiss me once, and let me be gone,
that what is to follow be done quickly!"

Evelyn looked after her in bewilderment, then inquiringly at her father. He had arisen to open the
door for Martha to pass out. He now came around
before his daughter, and bent one knee to the floor. At
the sunken cheeks, the dreary eyes raised to her, Evelyn
cried out, dismayed,—

"Papa! oh, what is it?"

"You have heard that your lover was spirited
away—and why. Against his will, he was a wanderer
upon the face of the deep for six months. It was

meant that a full year should pass before you could hear from him. That he whose sentence this was, was himself kept in ignorance by the interposition of a providential agency, of the fate of this most unfortunate gentleman, is no excuse for the crime that cost him his liberty and happiness—that has broken your heart! Can you forgive him?"

She stroked his hair; stooped over to kiss him between the eyes; the serenity of countenance and attitude told that she was feeding upon the honey and wine left to her in such bounteous measure.

"It was that unhappy man that lies speechless and nigh unto death, I suppose. Martha warned me, once and again, to beware of him, and I believed her not. Poor wretch!"

"Child! child! no! He was the tool—*mine* was the hand! It is your father who, on bended knee, confesses that he has sinned against heaven and against you, and begs you to forgive *him!*"

She recoiled sharply,—made as though she would spurn him as he clung to her knees,—a horror of loathing, a terror of him as of something base and noxious and abhorrent, was instinct in every feature. She tore her gown from his hold, struggling to her feet as if to escape from his touch and presence.

"My GOD!" she cried, frantically. "And this man is *my father!* Why was I not let to die before hearing it?"

In another second, she had fallen upon his neck.

"Papa! Papa! May the Saviour of sinners forgive me as I forgive you!"

When Martha Jaqueline again looked into the room,

the father sat with his child in his arms, her head
cradled on his shoulder, her wasted hands clasped behind his neck. The fire-waves had washed the gray
light so little removed from shadow, back to the windows and out into the stormy gloaming. Upon the
daughter's uplifted face was the radiance of an infinite
blessedness,—but the friend beheld, with a failing heart,
in eye and upon cheek, the shadow of a mightier
Coming,—even that of the Guest that knocks but once
at the door of every human heart, and will not be turned
away.

CHAPTER XXVIII.

It all was so long ago, dear reader, that many echoes
of that eventful Past dispersed into naught before you
and I or our parents were born.

Hence we have no further word, traditional or doc-
umentary, of the stricken secretary after we leave him
lying, a bit of worthless drift-wood, in his upper chamber dependent for daily tendance upon menials who
despised him, the scheming brain benumbed, the facile
tongue and fingers alike palsied. From obscurity he
came, into obscurity he returned.

Caliban, we are told, lived to a dignified old age, not
scrupling to derive a liberal percentage of the respect
awarded him by old and young, from the ever-growing
narrative of the deed done upon his cranium. In
time, when those who could have established or refuted
the tale had passed away, it came to be believed that a

silver plate had been inserted in place of bits of bone shattered by the bullet. The scalp, taking kindly to the substitute, had healed over it, leaving a ridge about the metal edges. Capillary growth was more scrupulous, and the bare space upon the butler's pate was regarded with reverential curiosity by his juniors.

A story that does him more honor is that, in dying, he asked and obtained the promise from his "young master,"—then a middle-aged man and Colonel of a Colonial regiment of Virginia troops,—that he might be buried at "Mis' Evelyn's" feet. Whether or not this be authentic, no trace of the grave remains.

The little chapel was, by order of the second wife and widow of William, the Third Byrd of Westover, removed, brick by brick, and reconstructed at Evelynton, about three miles farther inland, and is still used as a house of worship. The flat stone covering the mortal relics of Theodorick Bland marks the place once enclosed as a chancel.

This is Christmas-week, and wassail, like unto the times that are no more, and can never be again, prevails at Westover. A cold rain set in at nightfall, but "curtained, and closed, and warm," I sit before the glowing grate in the drawing-room, in converse with the sunny-faced, sound-hearted châtelaine of the ancient homestead, and let the storm drive and the hours fleet by. From the billiard-room, in the third story, ripples of merry talk and leaping rills of laughter fall down the stairs that once echoed the firm tread of the courtly Master of the realm; the curiously-twisted balustrades of which were swept by Madam's brocades and Evelyn's muslins and taffetas.

It was at supper-time, and in gay chat with her young guests, that our hostess introduced the topic that has engaged her tongue and mine since the boys and girls went off to their balls and cues.

"You must go on a rainy midnight, such as this will be, each of you alone,"—she said, in mock solemnity,—"to Colonel Byrd's tomb out there in the middle of the garden, and, putting your lips close to the ground, say, 'Colonel Byrd! do you know any reason why you should lie here, in unconsecrated ground and alone, while the rest of your family are buried together over yonder in the grave-yard?' Say it distinctly and respectfully—each by himself or herself, out there in the rainy midnight—and he will answer, '*Nothing— nothing!*'"

The tall monument, defaced by the storms of one hundred and fifty years, says enough to justify his silence. He was the *élève* of Sir Robert Southwell, "the bosom-friend of the learned and illustrious Charles Boyle, Earl of Orrery. . . . To all this were added a great elegancy of taste and life, the well-bred gentleman and polite companion, the splendid economist, the constant enemy of exorbitant power, and hearty friend to the liberties of his country."

In his diary he sets down, with no flourish of self-glorification :

"We laid the Foundation of Two large Cities, one at Shoccoe's, to be called Richmond, and the other at the Point of Appomattox, to be called Petersburg."

The ambitious structure in the middle of the garden, and Westover, lifting high in air the peak of its windowed roof, are but two of his many monuments.

The Colony owed him much; the State owes him no less.

Our hostess is the direct descendant of sweet Anne Harrison, and while in the four-feet-on-a-fender intimacy of the wintry night, our thoughts mingle spontaneously in one deepening channel, she tells me how her ancestress and Evelyn Byrd loved and sought one another; of the promise made, a month before the death of the younger woman, to show herself to her friend even after she should have "gone quite away."

"The story runs,"—says my companion,—"that, on the anniversary of that mid-October day, Mrs. Harrison visited the church-yard, and, while sitting there and thinking sadly of her lost friend, she saw Evelyn glide toward her from the church-porch, between the graves. She was robed all in white; she moved lightly and swiftly; her face was bright with ecstasy, and more beautiful, with an elevated, ethereal beauty, than ever in life. She paused beside her own grave-stone. You know she is buried on the spot where her last parting with her lover took place? There she stopped, threw a kiss to her friend, with a smile of unutterable love and happiness—and vanished!"

A less pleasing legend, and less credible, is that the pale shade of "The Fair Evelyn"—as she is named in family tradition—walks by night in the corridors of Westover and along the rose-alleys, wan and woful, forever plucking at the ring placed upon her finger by her titled lover.

We have seen, to-day, her portrait, transferred from Westover to Brandon, when her grand-niece married a Harrison of Martin's Brandon. Near it hangs that of her father in court-dress. The resemblance between them is marvellous, especially in the brows, the brilliant, broad-lidded eyes, and the delicately-symmetrical hands. Evelyn's gown is blue, faint and dim in shade, and modestly *décolleté* in cut. Her abundant hair is rich brown ; her perfect hands are binding flowers about a shepherdess-hat ; a rose is over her left temple. By a conceit characteristic of the artist of the period, said in this instance to have been Sir Godfrey Kneller,—a red *bird* is perched in the tree at her right ; over her left shoulder is a lane with sheep.

There is nothing in the picture, with its conventional affectation of pastoral life mocked by court-costume, to hint at the constancy that made her life romantic, or the sorrow that lent it tragedy, unless a certain pensiveness of the dark eyes be premonition of coming shadows. It was painted in England, before the shadows gathered.

"She was beloved by and betrothed to Lord Peterborough, a Roman Catholic nobleman, but her father prevented the marriage on account of the noble suitor's religion. Refusing all offers from other gentlemen, she died of a broken heart."

I have copied the few, pregnant, pathetic lines from a time-spotted family MS., as an abstract of what parent and child chose to have the world know.

"Of Mr. Fontaine, who spent his whole ministry of about forty years in the county of Charles City" (in which Westover is situated), "with the exception of a short time at Jamestown and Wallingford parish, it becomes us to add something more," is the preamble penned by a distinguished Bishop of his Church to a glowing recital of the virtues and works of this one of the Church's servants.

The same pen copies a letter which includes affectionate mention of " my highly-respected aunt, Martha Jaqueline, who died at the age of *ninety-three*. . . . Our dear aunt, Martha Jaqueline, chose to take upon her the title of ' Mrs.' at the age of fifty, this being the custom with spinsters in that day."

We saw at Shirley yesterday the portrait of Lady Bess, the "good-humored little Fairy" of Colonel Byrd's diary. The picture was painted when she was seventeen, just prior to her marriage to William the Third of Westover,—the match agreed upon between the parents of the contracting parties. The midnight hour strikes while I listen to the tale of a union made unhappy by strifes of temper between two spoiled children, of her mother-in-law's intolerance with " Betty's" frivolous tastes and extravagances ; lastly, of her death by the fall upon her of a heavy oaken press, or *armoire*.

Hapless little Fairy ! We give her more than one sigh in returning to her whose petted darling she was.

"And Evelyn died without seeing Lord Peterborough again ?" I lament.

The door uncloses to admit a man who catches the name. He repeats it, in drawing a chair up to the fire.

"Lord Peterborough won the cup at the International Steeple Chase at Baden-Baden in 187–," says the President of the Gentleman's Riding Club, whose own prizes for similar victories are notable.

x   30*

We look at him in amazed interest that moves him to add particulars.

"The Major and I were abroad together that year, and went to Baden-Baden to attend the races. The young English lord rode magnificently!" warming with his theme. "A noble-looking fellow he was, too, with fair hair, blue eyes, and as fine a pair of shoulders as you ever saw!"

This true "happening" is but one of many proofs we term idly "coincidences," that the world is round, and generations are but so many circles intersecting each other, most often at the most unlikely points.

In at the opening door, like the bound of a brook in June, all sparkle and laughter, troop the young people. A girl flutters to the piano and begins to sing. A sad ballad, of course, such as only happy women dare to sing. As with full heart and eyes I steal away up the stairs, I hear the burden :

> " My eyes are filled with tears
>   And my heart is numb with woe—
> It seems as if 'twere yesterday,
>   And it all was Long Ago!"

In my chamber—once Evelyn Byrd's—the little incident of the Baden-Baden steeple-chase banishes sleep from my eyelids. With only the soft coal fire for confidante, as I hearken to the heavy east wind, the plash and drip of the rain against my panes, I paint to myself the picture of the Berkeley race-day, and the hero of the course, the knightly youth with the broidered scarf crossing a heart bounding high with love, and hope, and courage,—and the grand stand, with that other superb figure in the front rank of spectators.

With the scene before me, "as if 'twere yesterday," I marvel anew at the chance word that, a century-and-a-half later, has dashed upon the canvas the sketch of the fair-haired, blue-eyed "crack" rider of that other course across the sea, winning the cup under the eyes of the present Master of Westover.

THE END.